Praise for J. M. Hochstetler

"J. M. Hochstetler is able to bring history to life with her exceptional prose and attention to detail. If you want a *Last of the Mohicans*-type adventure with a hearty dose of romance and realism, buy these books! My only regret is that she doesn't write fast enough and there aren't enough books like hers! Wonderful, inspiring, educational reading!"

—LAURA FRANTZ, AUTHOR OF *The Colonel's Lady*

"*Native Son* picks up where *Daughter of Liberty* left off and doesn't let go of the reader even beyond the last word on the last page. Ms. Hochstetler has crafted a story full of intrigue, romance, and heart-racing action, all woven around the most accurately portrayed historical events and settings this reader has ever seen. Her characters—main and secondary— come alive on the page and stay with the reader long after the book is over. The spiritual conflict is both touching and challenging. Hochstetler is a skilled author whose style engages and allows the reader to get lost in 1775 . . . I can't wait to read the next installment."

—KAYE DACUS, AUTHOR OF THE RANSOME TRILOGY

"Hochstetler introduced me to a fascinating aspect of the revolution here and I'd say more except I don't want to give away too much of the first book. I highly recommend you read the series in order. I loved the glimpse into the lives of George Washington as he built his guerrilla forces into a fighting army, and the names and actions of the factual British generals, intermixed with the fictionalized daring of our heroes. Fiction like this is a great, fun way to teach history."

—MARY CONNEALY, AUTHOR OF *Out of Control*

"While I was swept away by the first book in the American Patriot series by J.M. Hochstetler, I was thoroughly grabbed emotionally as well by this second in the series, *Native Son*. The newfound romance between American spy Elizabeth Howard and patriot Jonathan Carleton suffers an abrupt interruption: While they are planning their wedding, General Washington is sending them on dangerous missions that will separate them by hundreds of miles. Their intense love is put to a test. Can they put the needs of their new country struggling for freedom over their personal desires? It is a heartbreaking, thrilling, and gut-wrenching journey on these pages filled with rich historical detail that will be visualized with clarity in readers' minds. I am so anxious to pick up Book Three in this series, as my own heart wants resolution for this couple. A definite "Must-Read" for lovers of American History—as well as for lovers."

— ELAINE MARIE COOPER, AUTHOR OF *The Promise of Dear Run*

"*Native Son* is an intensely moving story, impeccably researched and excellently written. It is an intricate look into some aspects of the birth of our nation, and the struggles and temptations faced by two unforgettable characters. J. M. Hochstetler expertly weaves a tale of historical fiction with a romance that must survive the trials and dangers of the times. Outstanding!"

— ERIKA OSBORN, *Christian Book Previews*

"I found it refreshingly honest and devoid of religious platitudes and cliche. . . . Heartbreaking and brutal at times, Carleton's journey in particular resonated with me. His battle to retain faith in the midst of personal, political, physical, and total upheaval left an impression as few other stories have—challenging my own conventions, foundations, and moral bedrock. As the first in the series, *Daughter of Liberty*, was, this is a wealth of research and regional history. From the southwestern New York border where much of the book was set, I recognized and appreciated the veracity and intimacy of her details in native custom, flora, fauna, and people. Almost Michener-esque in scope, this is a historical fiction piece worthy of note."

— KATHLEEN L. MAHER, REVIEWER

Native Son

THE AMERICAN
PATRIOT SERIES
~BOOK 2~

J. M. HOCHSTETLER

Charlotte, Tennessee
37036 USA

Published by Sheaf House®, a registered trademark of Sheaf House Publishers, LLC. Requests for information should be addressed to:

Editorial Director
Sheaf House Publishers, LLC
3641 Hwy 47 N
Charlotte, TN 37036
jmshoup@gmail.com
www.sheafhouse.com

Library of Congress Control Number: 2011945413

ISBN: 978-0-9824832-9-9 (softcover)

All scripture quotations are from the King James Version of the Bible.

"Thou Hidden Source of Calm Repose," pp. 197-198, by Charles Wesley, 1749.

Painting on front cover, Battle of Oriskany (The Oneidas 1777), by Don Troiani, www.historicalimagebank.com

Cover design and interior template by Marisa Jackson.

Maps by Jim Brown of Jim Brown Illustration.

12 13 14 15 16 17 18 19 20 21— 10 9 8 7 6 5 4 3 2 1

MANUFACTURED IN THE UNITED STATES OF AMERICA

To Jay

O Lord God of my salvation,
I have cried day and night before Thee:
Let my prayer come before Thee:
Incline Thine ear unto my cry. . .
Thou has laid me in the lowest pit,
In darkness, in the deeps.
Thy wrath lieth hard upon me,
And Thou hast afflicted me with all Thy waves.
Selah.
Thou has put away mine acquaintance far from me;
Thou has made me an abomination unto them:
I am shut up, and I cannot come forth.
Psalm 88:1-2, 6-8

Now faith is the substance of things hoped for,
the evidence of things not seen.
Hebrews 11:1

An award-winning author and editor, J. M. Hochstetler is the daughter of Mennonite farmers, a graduate of Indiana University, and a lifelong student of history. Her contemporary novel One Holy Night was the Christian Small Publishers 2009 Book of the Year and finalist for the American Christian Fiction Writers 2009 Carol Award.

The Indian Territories

OTHER BOOKS BY
J. M. HOCHSTETLER

DAUGHTER OF LIBERTY
The American Patriot Series, Book 1

WIND OF THE SPIRIT
The American Patriot Series, Book 3

ONE HOLY NIGHT
(2009 Christian Small Publishers Book of the Year)

FORTHCOMING BOOKS IN THE AMERICAN PATRIOT SERIES

CRUCIBLE OF WAR, Book 4 (September 2012)
VALLEY OF THE SHADOW, Book 5
REFINER'S FIRE, Book 6
FORGE OF FREEDOM, Book 7

In the previous volume . . .

BOOK 1, DAUGHTER OF LIBERTY

EASTERTIDE, APRIL 1775. In the blockaded port of Boston the conflict between the British Regulars and the Sons of Liberty is rapidly escalating toward a fateful confrontation. Caught in the deepening rift that divides Whig and Tory, Elizabeth Howard is torn between her love for her prominent parents, who have strong ties to the British establishment, and her secret adherence to the cause of liberty. By night she plays a dangerous game as the infamous courier Oriole, hunted by the British for smuggling intelligence and munitions to the patriot leaders. And by day she treads increasingly perilous ground as she flirts ever more boldly with British officers close to her parents to gain access to information the rebels so desperately need.

Elizabeth's assignment is to pin down when the Redcoats will march to capture the patriots' hoarded munitions. But she hasn't counted on the arrival of Jonathan Carleton, an officer in the Seventeenth Light Dragoons. To her dismay, the attraction between them is immediate, powerful—and fought on both sides in a war of wits and words. When Carleton wins the assignment to ferret out Oriole, Elizabeth can no longer deny that he is her most dangerous foe—and the possessor of her heart.

As the first blood is spilled at Lexington and Concord, Carleton fights his own private battle of faith. And headstrong Elizabeth learns the bitter consequences of following her impulsive heart when her dangerous role thrusts her into the carnage of Bunker Hill.

Chapter One

"**N**O CHANCE TO GET AWAY to see Beth tonight either, I take it," Major Charles Andrews ventured.

Brigadier General Jonathan Carleton threw his aide a brooding look as he urged his bay stallion forward, farther out of earshot of the riders trailing down the road behind them. It was nearing two o'clock, Sunday, July 2, 1775. Pulling off his wide-brimmed slouch hat, he wiped his brow with the back of his gloved hand before settling it back on his head with a jerk.

"We'll undoubtedly be tied up with the generals until late."

Andrews pulled his mount alongside Carleton's. "I thought you'd break away yesterday when we stopped at Watertown to meet with the Provincial Congress."

Carleton shook his head in frustration. "The General insisted I attend him. But I mean to see Beth tonight, even if it's past midnight before we get there."

"Washington has kept you on a short rein ever since we met him in New York."

"All to your credit, Charles. If you hadn't felt obliged to share every minute detail of my arrest and imminent hanging, we'd have been in Roxbury days ago."

"It's a good thing the General is being cautious," Andrews countered. "If Isaiah hadn't been on the alert on the road to New York,

Gage's agents would have us aboard ship to England by now, trussed up like a pair of Christmas geese."

"And thank you for contributing a report on that little incident too," Carleton returned sourly. "You managed to persuade Washington that the price Gage has put on my head—and on yours—will prove too tempting for someone whose need for cold coin is greater than his allegiance to the cause of liberty."

Andrews returned a grin. "I'm a small fish. It's you Gage wants. Considering the reward he's offering, he obviously means to exact revenge for his humiliation at your hands. After all, you did pluck him clean of all the intelligence the Committee of Safety could have hoped for—while nestled sweetly in the general's bosom."

Carleton's face clouded. "That's what I despise about this. I should never have allowed myself to be persuaded to take on such a dishonorable role."

"But spying in time of war is an ancient and necessary profession—even a biblical one. Don't forget the twelve Hebrews who spied out the land of Canaan for Moses."

"Yes, and because they listened to the ten who had no faith instead of the two who trusted God, the children of Israel wandered in the desert for the next forty years," Carleton responded with a short laugh. "May our country not be so unfortunate."

With each step, the horses' hooves plopped deep into the muddy road. The day was hot and humid following an early morning rain, and thunderclouds were again building overhead. At ground level, the rising wind stirred the trees that shouldered each other along the road's edge and drove patches of shadow and sun across the low, wooded hills four miles from Boston Harbor.

"I hate to admit it, but in this beastly heat and humidity these buckskins are not as comfortable as our new uniforms would have been. And it occurs to me—too late, as usual—that we'd make a better impression on Ward and his staff in full regalia than in Indian dress."

Andrews surveyed Carleton's leather hunting shirt, leggings, and moccasins that matched his own. "I'm surprised to hear you say it," he retorted with a smile. "I've not observed that you're often overly concerned about making an impression, favorable or not."

Carleton struggled to adopt a wounded expression. "Now, Charles, you hardly know me at all if you can say such a thing. Besides, the New Englanders are already suspicious enough of us Southerners being foisted on them without their having any say in the matter. And you know full well how reluctant I always am to add fuel to a fire."

Andrews snorted. "I can imagine what they'll think if your former connection to the Shawnee comes out. But, at any rate, it's a tad late to transform ourselves into proper officers now. We'll have to bear their disapprobation with fortitude."

"I'd as soon arrive in war paint with my head shaved," Carleton growled, turning serious. "Let them think we're true savages, and maybe they'll mend their ways. But then, I've never been renowned for being exceptionally politic."

"That's an understatement, my friend. And speaking of diplomacy, how much have you told the General about you and Beth?"

Carleton grimaced. "Too deuced much, I fear. He seemed extraordinarily interested in Beth's role as spy and smuggler for the Sons of Liberty. But when I mentioned our intent to marry, he changed the subject rather abruptly."

Andrews raised an eyebrow. "You think he opposes your plans?"

His mouth tightening, Carleton turned in the saddle to measure the distance to the officers who rode at a leisurely pace behind them. All except their commander appeared too involved in conversation to pay him and Andrews much attention. As Carleton's glance met his, however, Washington spurred his white stallion forward.

"I suspect I'll soon find out," Carleton said in an undertone as Washington closed the distance between them.

Both officers saluted when the newly elected commander of the Continental Army drew up beside them. Forty-three years old, with auburn hair and grey-blue eyes that smoldered with an inner fire, General George Washington exuded an immense physical energy that was both intimidating and highly attractive. A born horseman, powerful in build despite narrow, sloping shoulders, he possessed a natural charm that equally drew men and women to him.

On occasion, however, Carleton had witnessed the prodigious temper that lay beneath that charm. Most of the time it was clamped under iron control, but it was a force Washington had learned how to unleash to the greatest effect when other means failed to motivate those under his authority.

Studying his commander, Carleton harbored no doubt that the Continental Congress had chosen the right man for the difficult and delicate responsibility of molding into an effective fighting force the undisciplined and often contentious militia units besieging Boston. Considering the conflicts between the various factions in the Congress, he was confident the choice had resulted from much more than a merely human decision born of political considerations.

"I expect you are impatient to call on that young lady of yours," Washington observed.

Carleton forced a smile. "Indeed, I am. Miss Howard and I—"

"Unfortunately, I am going to need you at Cambridge until late," Washington cut him off. "We have urgent business to settle with Ward and his staff before any of us will be free to attend to personal interests."

Carleton felt Washington's penetrating gaze on him, but deliberately did not meet it. Keeping his expression and tone carefully neutral, he said, "I wait upon your convenience, sir."

Frowning, he stared along the curve of the road that stretched before them to the small town of Cambridge, currently the center of the rebel army besieging Boston and its garrison of British troops commanded by Lieutenant General Thomas Gage, commander in chief of His Majesty's armies in North America. To their right, the land sloped to the banks of the Charles River, where the knee-deep grasses had been mown and raked into windrows to provide fodder for the army's horses.

He drew in a deep breath of the wet hay's heavy, sweet fragrance but could take no pleasure in it. Once more the subject of most interest to him had been abruptly turned aside. And the feeling that this boded no good to his hopes sank to the bottom of his gut like a leaden weight. The low growl of thunder in the distance did nothing to assuage his spirits.

Three-quarters of a mile ahead, past the handsome mansions dubbed Tory Row for the politics of their wealthy owners, the road terminated in a wide, grassy field at the town's center. Formerly a pasture for the townspeople's animals, the Common had been entrenched and turned into a campsite for soldiers, as had every available field in and around Cambridge—around every town surrounding Boston, in fact, from Dorchester to Winisimmit.

Along the Common's farthest boundary Carleton could make out the three-story red brick buildings of Harvard College. With the beginning of the siege, they, as well as many other buildings in the town, had been commandeered to house rebel troops.

As they drew steadily nearer, Carleton noted idly that on this quiet Sabbath large groups of soldiers lounged at ease among the weathered tents and ramshackle huts dotting the Common. Here and there the smoke of campfires swirled upward in the light wind, adding another pungent scent to the sea tang blowing off the bay. At the field's far side a group played a game of rounders, hitting a ball with a stick, then running from one base to another.

Washington followed his gaze. "What is your estimation of the troops' discipline and abilities?"

Carleton wrenched his thoughts back from the subject that had occupied very nearly every waking moment since he had left Roxbury a fortnight earlier. "Judging by their performance on Charlestown peninsula, their abilities are excellent. As far as discipline is concerned, there's much work to do, not only among the rank and file but among the officers as well."

"New lords, new laws," Andrews put in, his tone dry. "What's needed is some extensive housecleaning."

Washington shot him a keen glance. "Which will not be welcomed by anyone. We need to tread carefully if we hope to gain the army's cooperation."

Each occupied by private concerns, they rode without speaking until they reached the street that curved around the northern boundary of Cambridge Common. This terminated at an intersecting thoroughfare that ran southwest through the town and on into the country, a road with which Carleton was well familiar. After crossing the Charles River, it curved back to the southeast toward Brooklyne. Four miles farther along it, the village of Roxbury nestled on the bluffs above the bay, overlooking the narrow neck of land that connected Boston to the mainland.

As it crossed Stony Brook on the edge of this village, the thoroughfare passed the mansion of Tess Howard, who with her niece Elizabeth played the part of loyalists to the crown. From the beginning of the conflict between Britain and her colonies, however, both had secretly used every wile and resource to aid the Sons of Liberty.

It had been two weeks since he and Andrews had left Tess's home for New York following Carleton's rescue from a British scaffold, two weeks since he had held Elizabeth Howard in his arms and tasted the heady wine of her kisses. But although the longing to see her, to receive reassurance of her love, had intensified into an almost unbearable ache deep in his breast, he took care to reveal nothing of his thoughts.

Also to the right along this intersecting road and directly opposite Cambridge Common stood an imposing gambrel-roofed mansion formerly owned by Harvard's steward, Jonathan Hastings. Currently the house served as headquarters to General Artemis Ward, commander of the left wing of the rebel army encamped around the perimeter of Boston since the skirmishes at Lexington and Concord two and a half months earlier.

There another road branched off, one Carleton could not keep from mentally tracing as well. It angled northeast, leading inexorably to Charlestown peninsula, where the charred ruins of that town bore mute testimony to the savage battle fought on the heights above it while he had suffered the agonies of the damned in a British gaol.

Fighting the dread certainty that Elizabeth was in the midst of the battle. Terrified that she would be killed. Wrestling with physical extremity brought on by brutal beatings, deprivation of food and water, fearful anticipation of the hangman's rope that awaited him.

How could he not have known that she would find a way to save him? She had led him back to the Lord, after all, had been the instrument God had used to impart forgiveness and reconciliation to his prodigal son.

All Carleton wanted now was to spend the rest his life loving this remarkable woman. But relentlessly the fear tightened around his heart that even as the physical distance between them grew shorter, the sweet hopes he cherished were slipping ever farther out of his reach.

He would not allow that to happen, he assured himself. No matter what the consequences, he would never again allow any obstacle to part him from Elizabeth.

"PLEASE! DON'T TAKE MY LEG! Dear God, don't let 'em take my leg!"

With the assistance of the two surgeon's mates, Elizabeth Howard wrestled the screaming soldier onto the makeshift surgery table. Satisfied that the mates had their patient under control, she cautiously relinquished her hold.

While they held him down, she deftly buckled leather straps across his chest and arms, his pelvis, and his healthy leg. Finished, she covered him with blankets and slipped a small pillow under his head.

"Whatever happens, hold the leg steady until I finish the cut," ordered Dr. Benjamin Church, directing a frown at his assistants. "I don't want to splinter this limb."

"God, help me! I cain't tend my farm if I'm a cripple!"

Elizabeth dabbed the perspiration from her forehead with the edge of her apron and impatiently pushed out of her eyes the dark auburn curls that had escaped from her chignon in the struggle. Wringing out a cloth in the basin of water, she leaned over the anguished soldier to sponge his face, fighting not to gag at the stench of rotting flesh, blood, and sweat that pervaded the room.

"Other men have managed quite well," she soothed him. "You will too. You still have one good leg, and before we release you, you'll be fitted with a peg leg that will allow you to do most of your farm work as you always have."

He stared up at her, his eyes boring into hers, pleading. "My wife don't need no useless cripple to take care of with three young 'uns."

"I suspect she'd rather have you alive and by her side than in a grave. We've done all we can. If we don't amputate, you'll die."

"I'd be better off dead than alive and half a man!"

As gently as possible Elizabeth forced a twisted length of cloth between his clenched teeth. "I assure you, Sergeant Wilkerson, your manhood will remain fully intact."

Both mates guffawed as the sergeant's face mottled to a dull red. Grinning meaningfully at each other, they positioned themselves on either side of Church.

Elizabeth shot them a severe look. "Faith, but this is hardly a laughing matter. You wouldn't be quite so brave, I think, if it were you on this table."

The two mates studiously applied themselves to holding their writhing comrade still while Elizabeth cut away the bandage that wrapped the sergeant's right leg from thigh to ankle. Checking the tension of the tourniquet's heavy, worsted tape that was wrapped around the man's upper thigh, she adjusted the screw slightly.

Church tapped the curved amputation knife against his other hand. "You gave him plenty of rum?"

With a practiced motion she wound several lengths of tape around Wilkerson's bare leg just below the site of the cut. "All we could spare. Our stock is so depleted we've been forced to water it down. I'm afraid it won't do him much good."

The doctor sighed in resignation. "With luck, he'll pass out quickly. Most do."

He bent over the swollen, blackening leg veined with malignant crimson streaks that radiated from the site of the festering bullet wound just above the knee. Elizabeth motioned to the mates to hold the leg still. Wasting no more time, Church began to cut through the healthy flesh above the diseased area, ignoring the soldier's muffled screams as he exposed the bone.

Closely following the movement of the knife with the curved point of a tenaculum, Elizabeth drew out the end of each severed artery and tied it neatly off with a ligature of waxed shoemaker's thread. As soon as the cut was complete and all arteries were tied off, the mate nearest the tourniquet released and removed it.

At the same time Elizabeth wrapped a narrow leather strip around the bone, using it to draw the muscles above the cut out of the way of the saw. Holding the leather strip steady in her right hand, with her left she sponged seeping blood away from the bone. Church exchanged the knife for the saw one of the mates extended. The thick thighbone took greater effort to cleave. By the time he finished and handed the detached limb to the mate, the doctor was sweating profusely in the July heat.

Both his coat and Elizabeth's apron were splattered with gore. The sergeant's head lolled to one side, and his irregular breaths rasped in the silence. Mercifully he had lapsed into unconsciousness.

CARLETON, ANDREWS, AND WASHINGTON had tethered their mounts to the hitching post before the rest of their party drew to a halt in front of the Hastings mansion. In the lead rode Major General Charles Lee, a British officer of some reputation who had immigrated to the colonies from England to embrace the cause of rebellion. As usual, he was trailed by his pack of dogs, and when he dismounted they crowded closely around him, whining for his attention.

Lee stroked their heads with one hand and with the other indicated the mansion with a lofty gesture, his angular face contorting into a grimace that Carleton took for a smile. "So much for your ragtag rank and file. At least our officers have the sense to accommodate themselves in appropriately elegant style."

Carleton surveyed the general with a distrust he found difficult to dissemble. Short and thin to the point of emaciation, Lee by habit dressed negligently. With his big head, whose main feature was a comically large nose, he reminded Carleton of nothing so much as a scarecrow. Although their association had thus far been a short one, Carleton was rapidly developing a keen suspicion that Lee's eccentricity cloaked an ambition bound to collide with Washington's.

Washington's handsome young aide-de-camp, Thomas Mifflin, gave a sanctimonious sniff. "What better use for the Tories' ill-gotten property than to house the instruments of their most deserved destruction." Dismounting, he threw his horse's reins over the hitching post.

The General's military secretary, Colonel Joseph Reed, directed a characteristically dour frown toward Mifflin. "From the looks of this army—if you can call it that—the Tories' destruction isn't assured quite yet. You'd best not count your chickens a'fore they're hatched."

Carleton gave Andrews a wry glance. He was learning to expect nothing but platitudes from Mifflin and gloom from Reed. Andrews suppressed a snicker.

"It is not the army's appearance, but their resolve, that will determine the outcome of the contest. In view of what they have accomplished thus far, it would appear that, at least, is not in question."

There was reproof in Washington's tone as he straightened to his full height. At six feet, three inches, he towered over the other officers, surpassing even Carleton by an inch.

Carleton had left his servant, Private James Stowe, behind in New York to take care of a business matter for him, but Private Henry Briggs, Andrews's servant, rode with those bringing up the party's rear. These included Sergeant Isaiah Moghrab, a free black man who had been employed by Elizabeth's father until the skirmishes at Lexington and Concord.

When the colonists had laid siege to Boston, Isaiah had joined the Lincoln regiment commanded by Elizabeth's uncle and had quickly been promoted to lead a platoon of black soldiers. With him was his seventeen-year-old son, Sammy, a private in the army whose well-muscled form and proud stature gave promise of the powerful man he was destined to become.

Washington's valet and companion, Will Lee, a youthful, round-faced mulatto clad in formal livery with his head wrapped in an exotic turban, completed the entourage. A horseman by every measure Washington's equal, wherever his master went, Will followed.

The previous day Reed had sent a message from Watertown advising Ward of the approximate time of their arrival, and it was quickly evident they had been anticipated, though not with exceptional delight. Before they could mount the steps to the front door, it was thrown open and Ward's aide sauntered down them as the strengthening wind spattered the first drops of rain on their hats and shoulders. Greeting them with admirable restraint, he ushered Washington and his officers inside, his mouth drawn up as though he had just bitten into an unripe persimmon.

Washington led the way into an expansive room at the front of the house. They found Ward waiting to receive them along with several members of his staff.

A few years older than Washington, the newly promoted major general disguised his average height and portly figure beneath an impressive powdered wig and long, silver-buttoned coat. With him were Major General Israel Putnam and brigadier generals John Thomas; tough, seventy-year-old Indian fighter, Seth Pomeroy; William Heath, who had led the rebels during the British retreat from Concord back to Boston; handsome, impetuous John Sullivan of New Hampshire; and tall, slender Richard Montgomery, veteran of the French and Indian War.

Ward's bluff countenance remained sober, his bow stiffly formal, echoed by the other generals as Carleton introduced each in turn. There was no mistaking the tension that charged the air. Remembering their private discussions about how likely these Yankees were to accept orders from a Virginian, Carleton threw Washington a veiled look, to which the General responded with a faint smile.

As Washington exchanged pleasantries with the man he was to supersede, his subordinates openly took the measure of their new commander through narrowed eyes before transferring their attention to the rest of Washington's party. From their raised eyebrows, it was obvious that Carleton's and Andrews's choice of dress was not making a favorable impression.

"Looks like we're commissionin' savages as officers now," Pomeroy rasped.

"The next time we face down the might of the British army, we may find it useful to have a savage or two on our side," Carleton returned. "If it would help, I'd be glad to supply the war paint—but then, I seem to recall that you all do have some expertise in that area."

He studiously ignored Washington's displeased frown. The scene reminded Carleton of his first meeting with Ward and several of the other generals the afternoon following his rescue from a British noose.

Even the explanations offered by Colonel Joshua Stern, Elizabeth's uncle, that Carleton was a close friend of Washington and Patrick Henry, that Joseph Warren, the handsome, personable leader of the rebels in Massachusetts, had worked with and trusted him, and that Carleton had just narrowly escaped hanging for his efforts on their behalf hadn't diminished the officers' reserve. They had made abundantly clear that, as far as they were concerned, the fact that Carleton was a Virginian and a British officer effectively negated all the rest.

With his wealth and social connections, to say nothing of his training and experience in the Light Dragoons, Carleton knew he was considered a threat to the colonial officers' ambitions. They had regarded him then, as now, with varying degrees of suspicion, jealousy, and dislike.

The trouble was that among the officers of the Northern colonies only Warren had known the full extent of the service Carleton, as the spy Patriot, had rendered in service of his country. But Warren was dead, killed during the final British assault on Breed's Hill a fortnight ago.

Church rinsed his bloody hands in the basin of water. "I'll let you finish, Miss Howard."

A muted flash of light and the rumble of thunder brought Elizabeth round to glance toward the window. Hissing in the rising wind, the bushes outside beat softly against the glass. Frowning, she perched on a tall stool beside the table and concentrated on carefully cleaning fragments of bone from the exposed end of the sergeant's now truncated thigh. Church pulled up a chair and sat beside her to watch.

In his early forties, the doctor was handsome, stylishly dressed beneath his surgeon's smock. Elizabeth had heard the shocking rumors of his recent separation from his wife and that he kept a young mistress whom he entertained lavishly and who was now pregnant with his child.

Deftly she drew the exposed muscles over the end of the stump, holding them in place two round pledgets of lint, then covered it with fine linen. Over this she methodically wrapped lint sprinkled with flour and additional pledgets of tow and lint, which she held in place with two long strips of linen crossed over each other.

"Your father taught you well. You do fine work."

Elizabeth regarded her handiwork with a critical eye. "Thank you. I only wish we had anaesthetics on hand for these cases so the men wouldn't have to suffer so."

Church snorted. "We're lucky to have enough ligatures and bandages—for today, at least. But I suppose we shouldn't complain. Powder and cartridges are in dangerously short supply throughout the camp—which does provide the benefit of making it highly unlikely that we'll undertake another attack anytime soon. However, should Gage and Howe decide to take the initiative, I'm afraid they'll overrun our lines with little effort."

Occupied in wrapping the sergeant's stump neatly in bandages, Elizabeth threw a furtive glance at the doctor, amazed at his talkativeness. From her uncle Joshua Stern, colonel of the Lincoln regiment, she knew that the shortage of ammunition was not something the rebel leaders wanted to broadcast, particularly not to someone like her who was believed to be a Tory. The confidante of men on the highest levels of the rebel leadership, Church should have been well aware of that fact.

And why had he implied that the rebel army had attacked the British when it was the other way around? Had it been merely a slip of the tongue? Or was he testing her?

Church glanced at the soldier, who had begun to moan and roll his head back and forth. "I was confident we could save the sergeant's leg," he noted with a sigh.

"I'm so sorry we couldn't."

At the sincere regret in her tone, Church gave her a probing look. "It's hard to believe you're a Tory, as kindly as you care for our wounded. I've heard claims the British suffered many more casualties at Breed's Hill than we did and are in desperate want of surgeons. I'm sure they could use your expertise in Boston."

She kept her head bent, her eyes on her work. "Unfortunately my aunt and I are stranded here, for the time being, at least. At any rate, I've never connected politics to the practice of medicine."

Leaning back in his chair, the doctor conceded lazily, "I agree with you there. If I were in Boston, I'd certainly offer my services."

He remained silent for several moments before adding, "I've been privy to some idle talk linking your name with that officer who escaped hanging by the British and joined our side right after the battle. Evidently our new commander has made him a general. Carleton is his name, I believe. Any truth to the rumors?"

She felt her cheeks warming. "He was a mere major when I knew him. It appears his treachery has resulted in a considerable elevation of his fortunes—though a temporary one, I devoutly hope. Believe me, he is nothing to me."

Church laughed, then sobered. "You'd be advised to dissemble your venom in public. General Carleton has done the cause of liberty an exceptionally good turn if the reports I've heard are accurate— which they undoubtedly are, considering the reward Gage is offering for his capture, dead or alive. It's so generous I fear it might tempt even one of our staunch Sons of Liberty to betray him."

"Let's hope he receives his just deserts then."

Elizabeth prayed her frosty tone would quash the doctor's interest in the subject. Struggling to keep any trace of concern out of her face, she finished the dressing and covered the bandaged stump neatly with a knitted woolen cap made for the purpose.

She couldn't help inwardly breathing a plea for Carleton's safety. It was almost two weeks since he had left for New York hoping to intercept General Washington, and he should have returned by now.

The two men had long been friends, she knew. Along with Patrick Henry, Washington had persuaded Carleton to obey Gage's summons to Boston after his return to Virginia at the death of Sir Harrison Carleton, the wealthy uncle who had reared him. As the spy Patriot, Carleton had provided the rebel leaders in Massachusetts with a wealth of military intelligence while serving as Gage's aide-de-camp. But for Elizabeth, who in the guise of the rebel courier Oriole had rescued Carleton in a daring raid on the British gaol, his body would now be rotting at the end of a gibbet on Boston Common.

Suppressing a shudder, Elizabeth left her perch to wash her hands, then removed her stained apron and replaced it with a fresh one. Rain drummed down outside as the half-conscious soldier was carried from the surgery.

No sooner had the stretcher disappeared through the doorway than her cousin Captain Levi Stern stepped into the room. Outfitted in the new uniform of the Lincoln regiment and carrying a musket, he feigned a scowl as he blocked Church's path.

"Is Miss Howard ready to go? My orders were to have her back at her aunt's house a'fore noon, and it's already past two."

"I'm afraid we had an emergency, captain."

Turning back to Elizabeth, Church took her lightweight cloak from the hook by the door and held it for her, then offered her parasol. Bowing, he motioned her to precede him through the door.

"You will be on duty again tomorrow morning?"

"Certainly, Doctor Church. It means a great deal to me to have useful work to do while we're unavoidably detained here. I thank you for your kindness in vouching for me in spite of your colleagues' opposition to employing a woman—and a Tory at that."

"As much as we need qualified surgeons, I can hardly turn away one who has the ability and experience you do, regardless of your sex or your politics. Good day, Miss Howard." Bowing again, he strode off down the passage and disappeared into another ward.

The hospital had been set up in a once-luxurious house on the south edge of Cambridge that had been abandoned by its Tory owner at the start of the siege. Bereft of most of its fine furnishings, it now accommodated an assortment of beds, cots, and pallets for the use of the army's wounded and ill.

Pretending not to notice the disapproving stares of the hospital matron and the two nurses they passed, Elizabeth opened her parasol and hurried outside to run through the downpour after her rawboned, tow-headed cousin. Wasting no time, they crossed the expansive lawn of the estate to where her phaeton waited, its black top raised over its gleaming, moss-green body against the rain. She settled herself on the oilcloth that covered the padded, velvet-covered seats, while Levi, his uniform drenched through, climbed up beside her. After stowing his dripping musket beside his feet, he slapped the reins across the chestnut gelding's rump.

When they had navigated the puddled road to a safe distance outside Cambridge, he gave her a sidewise glance. "How much longer you aimin' to keep up this charade?"

"I don't know. Jonathan fears that if I reveal my true loyalties, someone might suspect that I've been on the side of the patriots all along and connect me to Oriole. And if that were to happen, I'd be in the same situation Jonathan is since there's a price on Oriole's head too."

By the time they reached the outskirts of Brooklyne, the rain had let up. Although the wind still gusted, lancets of sunlight broke through from scattered patches of cerulean sky.

As Levi eased the phaeton through a wide stream flooding across the road, Elizabeth caught hold of the side of the carriage to steady herself. "Dr. Church said the reward for Jonathan's capture is so high it might tempt someone on our side to betray him. He said it almost as if he were tempted himself."

Levi slowed the horses as they passed a company of Mahican volunteers clad in linen hunting shirts, leggings, and breechcloths, who were marching purposefully in the direction of Cambridge. "I can't imagine anyone with Church's reputation and connections in the Sons of Liberty turnin' his coat for money. But it's a good bet someone'll take the bait sooner or later if Gage's agents don't capture Jon first."

"I haven't received a letter from him for several days. They should be back by now, shouldn't they? You don't suppose something has happened?"

He glanced over at her, quickly placed his hand over hers, and squeezed it in apology. "If it had, we'd have heard about it, Cuz. I'm talkin' out of turn. Everything's all right, I'm sure."

They passed through the village without speaking, weaving around ox-drawn wagons full of supplies and additional militia units marching in formation along the road. Crossing the bridge over Muddy River, Levi clucked to the gelding. The phaeton gathered speed and rolled smoothly down the road toward Roxbury.

"Trouble is, feelings are runnin' so high against Tories now that you're in danger from our own side as long as you stay here," he said at length. "And if you and Jon are plannin' to marry—"

Staring down the road ahead of them, Elizabeth pressed her fingertips against her temples. "I don't know what to do, especially since I hope to be of some service to General Washington. But that would mean Jonathan and I would have to keep our marriage secret. I wish we'd had more time to discuss it before he had to leave."

"You're not lettin' him talk you into something you're doubtful of?" Levi questioned gently.

"No!" she protested, her voice softening. "I love Jonathan with all my heart, Cuz, truly. I can conceive no greater happiness than to be his wife."

❋ ❋ ❋

WHILE ON THE WAY from Philadelphia to New York, Washington had received preliminary reports of the recent battle that had greatly concerned him. He was eager for a firsthand report. Under British arrest throughout the battle, Carleton and Andrews were equally anxious to hear the officers' assessment and for the next hour, as outside the rain drummed down, they listened intently while Ward and his staff outlined the details.

Initially the engagement had been considered a defeat for the rebel forces because they had been driven from Charlestown peninsula. In the battle's aftermath, however, information filtered into the rebel camp that considerably altered that perception.

In fact, the British had suffered staggering losses, which included many of their most experienced officers, while the rebel army's casualties had been comparatively light. The rebel force had stood its ground in the face of three brutal frontal assaults by a force that far outnumbered and outgunned them and had been driven from the peninsula only when their ammunition failed. Even then, units had covered the retreat with exemplary skill and resolve, avoiding capture while allowing most of the dead and wounded to be carried from the field. By the time they finished, the rain had blown out to sea.

Encouraged by what they heard, Washington and his officers spent another hour settling into temporary accommodations. The new commander in chief, his aide, secretary, and servant took over the three-story, hip-roofed mansion that had been the residence of Samuel Langdon, the president of Harvard College. Carleton and Andrews were soon comfortably established in the Lechmere mansion a short distance down Tory Row. As a concession to propriety, before joining the others to survey the nearby fortifications, they exchanged their buckskins for the handsome blue and buff uniforms they had acquired in New York.

Late in the afternoon they rode a mile north to Prospect Hill, called Mount Pisgah by the army. From the fort at its summit they could see the arrow-shaped peninsula of Boston lying in deceptive peace in the harbor to the southeast. Directly to the east, on the other side of a small prominence called Cobble Hill, loomed Charlestown peninsula and the double bulk of Bunker's and Breed's hills, guarded now by British soldiers. Even at that distance Carleton could make out the glimmer of red coats in the glow of the lowering sun.

Refusing to allow his thoughts to stray to more appealing subjects, he noted with approval that the colonial force had entrenched a number of naturally strong defensive positions. As he, Lee, and Washington consulted, they concluded that by making a few adjustments in the placement and design of several of the forts, it should be possible to contain the British while building up the army.

Later, when they gathered for dinner with Ward and the other generals back in Cambridge, Washington drew Carleton and Andrews aside. "I think it advisable that we review the disposition of our right wing this evening as well. As soon as we can get away after dinner, we will ride to Roxbury and—as a courtesy, of course—drop in on Colonel Stern. That will give me opportunity to speak privately with you and Miss Howard without compromising her guise as a Tory."

The knot in Carleton's stomach tightened. "There's something in particular you wish to discuss with us?"

"It will wait until later." Washington's expression revealed nothing. Turning to Andrews, he said, "Major, I want you to ride to Roxbury and advise Colonel Stern and the Misses Howard that we will call on them this evening. We will meet you there."

Andrews responded with a brisk salute. "Your Excellency." Giving Carleton a quick, sympathetic glance, he left.

The hours that followed were pure torture for Carleton. It took every effort of his will to pretend an interest in the officers' conversation. Dinner stretched on interminably with no apparent end in sight, fueled by an abundance of toast—which considerably improved the camaraderie of the colonial officers with their new commander in chief, but left Carleton in an extremity of frustration.

In spite of himself, at odd moments his last meeting with Elizabeth replayed itself in his mind. She had clung to him, not wanting him to go, but knowing he had no choice.

"Return as quickly as you can," she had pleaded, her large, expressive eyes filling with tears. "I shall long for you every second of every day you are gone."

The image of her beautiful face filled with sorrow at their parting and the exquisite memory of her nestled in his arms came close to driving him mad. How many times on the journey to New York had he fought to keep from turning his mount around and going back to take her away with him to Thornlea, his estate in Virginia, there to make her his wife and stay where they would be safe.

But could they ever be safe anywhere now? Or was that entirely a vain hope?

He also had to ask himself if his allegiance to the cause of his country's liberty and to the path God had called him to tread was so fickle that it could be undermined by a woman's love. Yet he knew as well that God had given him and Elizabeth to each other.

It was a dilemma that seemed to have no solution. And so, with stubborn determination, he forced his mind to overrule the tender yearnings of his heart.

Chapter Two

"CHARLES!"

With a squeal of delight, Elizabeth threw herself into Andrews's arms, all but knocking him back against the front door through which he had just entered. Regaining his balance, he lifted her off her feet and swung her around, laughing down at her.

"I swear you're more beautiful each time I see you."

A blush climbed into her cheeks. His fervent words and glance brought back in a flood the memory of his avowal of love several weeks earlier, before she and Carleton had at last acknowledged their deep feelings for each other. At the same time she became uncomfortably aware of her aunt and uncle's unspoken disapproval of her usual impulsive behavior.

Standing directly behind Elizabeth, Tess Howard characteristically held herself as erect as a soldier, lending an imposing majesty to a figure that had begun to tend to stoutness. In her early fifties, she possessed classically handsome features that at the moment were drawn into an imperious expression. Had Elizabeth not known so well the tenderness of her aunt's heart, she would have been intimidated. Instead, she giggled.

Tess could not have provided more contrast to Elizabeth's maternal uncle, Joshua Stern, the colonel of the Lincoln regiment, who stood off to one side, slouching, his hands shoved into his breeches' pockets. As usual, his blue uniform coat was rumpled, and his curly, steel-grey hair stood on end as though discharging electricity. For all his casual, untidy appearance, however, Stern maintained tight discipline over the men who served under him, and brooked no nonsense when it came to business. Unlike the majority of the rebel camps that sprawled along Boston's perimeter, the Lincoln regiment's was precisely laid out, with sanitation, clothing, and equipment properly supplied, and the soldiers were rigorously drilled.

Elizabeth gave Andrews a quick hug, then extricated herself from his arms and took a step back. Her gaze traveled from his knee-length black riding boots to his blue and buff uniform and wide, white sword belt, ending at the red, white, and blue cockade that pinned back the brim of his hat.

"And how much more dashing you look in colonial blue than in British red!"

It was his turn to blush, the color rising to the roots of his dark blond hair. Doffing his hat, he swept her a deep bow.

"My plan was to impress you. I'm glad I've succeeded."

Giggling, she glanced over his shoulder to where Isaiah and Sammy waited in the doorway. "Jonathan didn't come with you?"

It was impossible to keep the disappointment out of her voice. She dropped her eyes from Andrews's, feeling clearly the pain it caused him each time he was reminded it was Carleton she desired and not him. But his gallant smile revealed no hint of his feelings.

"I was sent to advise you that he and Washington will call on you sometime after dinner." He included Tess and Stern in his apologetic glance before adding, "It may be quite late."

"We'll be pleased to receive them whenever they arrive," Stern returned gruffly.

Elizabeth breathed a sigh of relief that the first thing she had attended to on arriving home from the hospital had been a bath and fresh clothing. Wavering between delight and alarm, she mentally scanned her wardrobe for appropriate attire to greet not only Carleton, but also the army's new commander.

Andrews took in the two women, his eyes narrowing. "Now what mischief have you been hatching? You have a mighty guilty look."

Tess chuckled as she brushed cobwebs out of her black, silver-streaked hair with one hand and waved the white gloves she clutched in the other. "I spent most of the afternoon digging through boxes in the attic."

"She found Mama's wedding gown," Elizabeth confided. "I tried it on and it fits perfectly."

"Or will, once the hem be lengthened a bit," Sarah corrected her.

Employed as cook at Stony Hill until Elizabeth's parents had left the colonies for England a month earlier, the statuesque, coffee-colored woman had assumed the same duties at Tess's home in Roxbury. Now she and Isaiah exchanged a look of deep affection that Elizabeth noted whenever they were together.

Their fourteen-year-old daughter, Jemma, clung happily to her father's waist while seventeen-year-old Sammy, looking as much a woodsman in his buckskins as Isaiah, and fifteen-year-old Pete, who had taken on a variety of duties in the household, waited for their parents' notice. But Elizabeth had the impression that for the moment nothing existed for Isaiah and Sarah except each other.

No one could be more attentive parents, yet it was equally clear that their relationship took priority. And humbly, remembering the love between her own parents, Elizabeth breathed a quick prayer that God would bless her and Carleton with that same bond of devotion.

Feeling Andrews's sober gaze on her, she playfully took his arm and led the way into the parlor. Sarah and Jemma disappeared in the direction of the kitchen to begin preparations for their visitors, while Pete and Sammy returned outside. Isaiah lingered just inside the parlor door, however, leaning his back against the jamb while the others found seats.

Elizabeth patted the cushion of the couch beside her. "We expected you days ago," she chided as Andrews obediently joined her. "But it appears that while we were pining away for you here, you and Jonathan were ravishing the fine ladies of New York with your martial splendor."

Andrews laughed in spite of himself, but his smile quickly faded. "Whether the ladies were ravished or not, our delay was due to other reasons. If Isaiah had not been on his guard, Jon and I would be languishing in the hold of a British ship on our way to London."

Exclaiming in horror, Elizabeth and Tess turned expectantly to Isaiah. He dismissed the major's words with a shrug.

"Sammy and me was in the right place at the right time, that's all."

"You're too modest." When the two women returned their attention to him, Andrews explained, "The night before we reached New York, we stopped for dinner at an inn we thought suitably remote. Whether due to our carelessness or to the workings of Providence, unknown to us, several agents sent out by Gage were staying there too. Isaiah thought them suspicious, and he and Sammy secretly followed them to the stables and overheard their conversation.

"Evidently someone alerted Gage to our plans to meet the General in New York. Gage sent a detachment in civilian dress to lie in wait, and if Isaiah hadn't followed his instincts, we'd have been snared in their trap. Instead we got away before they saw us."

Tess directed a warm look toward Isaiah. "That was no coincidence."

"Indeed, it was not," Elizabeth echoed. "My mind was at ease knowing you were with them, Isaiah. I can't thank you enough for your care."

A smile creased Isaiah's ebony countenance. Embarrassed, he gave her a quick nod before ducking out of the room.

"Gage didn't learn of your destination or route by chance," Stern noted, his tone and expression grim. "The few who had any knowledge of your leaving Cambridge were told you were bound for Virginia by way of Providence."

"Oh, there's no doubt Gage still has at least one contact in our highest councils," Andrews agreed. "The question is, how do we smoke him—or them—out?"

Stern shook his head, frustration lining his features. "He's been operating for a long time, and we're no closer to finding him now than we were at the beginning."

"Lest we forget," Tess reminded them, "the traitor could easily be a woman."

They all acknowledged her point.

After a brief silence, Andrews said, "We heard there were several skirmishes while we were away."

"Our gunners traded fire with the British a few times," Stern responded. "They caused minor damage, that's all."

Elizabeth twined her necklace around her fingers. "Stony Hill was hit by several stray shots last week, and I went down after dark that night. The house is too unsafe for anyone to live in now, and the stables are destroyed."

Andrews took her other hand and squeezed it. "I'm sorry. It's a shame your home had to end up in the crossfire between two armies."

"We're about to sit down to dinner, Charles," Tess intervened. "You'll join us?"

Andrews accepted the offer gladly. After calling Jemma, Elizabeth followed Tess upstairs to dress. Jemma scampered through her chamber door and to the bed, which was awash in a drift of silvery satin and lace.

Although she did not give in to the young girl's eager pleas that she try the gown on again, Elizabeth couldn't resist gathering the shimmering fabric against her. The petticoat was very full with a wide flounce at the hem, while the low-cut bodice and long sleeves were snugly fitted and trimmed with a tracery of delicate beadwork. Whirling around, she laughed at her reflection in the full-length mirror.

Jemma danced excitedly around her, as graceful as a young gazelle. "Oh, you'll be the most beautiful bride in the whole world!"

Laughing, Elizabeth carefully laid the gown back on the bed and turned to take the young woman's chin in her hand. "And you shall attend me since Abby can't be here to do it."

Jemma clapped her hands in delight. But Elizabeth sobered, reminded of her sorrowful parting from her ten-year-old sister a month earlier. A hard lump choked her throat.

Deeming it unsafe for his family to remain in Boston amid escalating warfare, her father, Dr. Samuel Howard, had insisted they return to England. A close friend of General Gage and many of the high-ranking officers in the British garrison, he had made it clear that if the colonies won their freedom, he would never return.

Only the intervention of his older sister, Tess, had persuaded him to give in to Elizabeth's adamant refusal to leave her home and native country. But the tearful separation from her father, mother, and sister had come close to overpowering Elizabeth's resolve.

Had she lost them forever? Her heart ached at the thought. If her involvement with the Sons of Liberty should come to light, it would be far too dangerous for her ever to set foot on Britain's soil. And with at least one spy operating at a high level among the rebel leaders, until the patriots won their freedom she remained at risk of exposure and arrest.

With an effort, she banished her gloomy thoughts. After some consideration she settled on a gown of moss-green silk whose classic lines provided the perfect accent for her natural beauty.

Appraising her reflection in the mirror, she loosened several curls from her upswept hair, allowing the glossy auburn strands to trail onto her shoulder. A fragrant trio of cream-colored rosebuds that

Jemma fetched from the garden and pinned inside the lace at her neckline to nestle against her skin completed her ensemble.

When Jemma had gone, Elizabeth went to the escritoire and took a letter from the drawer. Arriving several days earlier tucked inside a packet addressed to Stern, it was the only one Carleton had been able to send her since leaving for New York. She unfolded the page and studied the words, though she had memorized them within minutes of the letter's arrival.

New York
June 26, 1775

Dearest,

Forgive me for not writing sooner. I've finally found a courier I'm assured will deliver this safely. We are delayed here as Washington did not arrive until yesterday. I cannot tell when we shall be on our way back, but I will come to you as quickly as I can.

Every day that passes impresses on me how dearly I love you and long for the day when we shall never again be parted. Sweet love, do all you can to have everything ready for our wedding when I return. I cannot bear to wait an hour more.

With all my love,
Jonathan

A film of tears blurred the graceful script. The hurriedly scribbled note held an urgency that troubled her, as though there was something behind his words that he did not want her to know. The separation of the past two weeks had been even more painful than she had expected, and now that he was only a few miles away, the hours until his coming were all the harder to endure.

On impulse she pressed his signature to her lips, then at last refolded the letter and returned it reluctantly to the drawer.

❂ ❂ ❂

"So this young lady is the infamous Oriole."

As she rose from a deep curtsy, Elizabeth raised her eyes to meet Washington's approving gaze. Feeling the warmth rising to her cheeks, she placed her hand into the one he extended.

He bent to kiss it. Straightening, he placed his other hand over hers and directed a pointed glance at Carleton.

"Now I understand why you were so anxious to call on Colonel Stern."

His comment drew a laugh from the others. Smiling despite herself, Elizabeth hazarded a tentative glance at Carleton. He met it with one that deepened her blush, before making a graceful bow.

The pace of her heart quickening, she hastily transferred her gaze back to Washington. "You are most kind, Your Excellency. We are greatly honored by your visit."

For a moment longer Washington held her, his glance so piercing that she dropped her eyes, wondering what he had gleaned from his scrutiny. She was relieved when Tess stepped forward to shepherd their visitors into the parlor, leaving Elizabeth and Carleton to follow them.

He bent his head over hers, so close that he could easily have kissed her, and for that moment consciousness of anything but the depth of emotion in his eyes faded. Could she have forgotten in the space of only two weeks how handsome he was, how the sight of him had an amazing effect on the beat of her heart?

The soft candlelight burnished his blond hair to gold, while the deep hue of his uniform coat intensified the warm blue-grey of his eyes. The light in them, and his smile, enfolded her like a loving embrace more intimate than a physical touch.

There was no need for either to speak. As that first time they had met, when she had tumbled by accident into his arms, he studied her with frank admiration.

And with something deeper: an emotion that ignited liquid fire in her veins and made her hungry to taste the fullness of all the future surely held for them.

Feeling that she moved in a sweet haze of happiness, she took the arm he offered and allowed him to lead her into the parlor, though she doubted that her feet touched the floor. Certainly she did not dare to meet his eyes again if she was to maintain any degree of self-possession.

Much safer to focus on the new commander in chief. That, thankfully, did not prove difficult.

Clad in a striking deep blue uniform coat with gold epaulets and buff facings and cuffs, a buff waistcoat and breeches, and knee-length boots, Washington would have captured the center of attention in whatever circle he found himself due to his height alone. Yet it was quickly apparent that he possessed as well an irresistible personal force part raw physical power, part a winning grace born of genuine interest in and concern for those around him.

Watching him interact with her aunt and uncle, Elizabeth noted with amusement that they were already wholeheartedly charmed. In anticipation of the visit, Tess had put on her finest gown, a soft grey taffeta that flattered her still-trim figure. Stern's appearance was also impressive for a change. His uniform coat and white breeches had been brushed and pressed. He was freshly shaved, and his hair had been tamed, for the moment at least. All that was needed to restore it to its customary unruly state, Elizabeth reflected with a smile, was a moment of excitement or frustration, when he was likely to tug at the mass absentmindedly.

To Elizabeth's disappointment she was left no choice but to join Tess on the sofa. Washington, Stern, and Andrews had claimed the wing chairs closest to it, leaving the one on the General's other side and farthest from the ladies for Carleton. He slouched into it and stretched his long, booted legs out in front of him. Leaning his head against the chair's high back, he let his eyes drift lazily shut, to all appearances wholly indifferent to the conversation.

Although she pretended profound interest in Stern's description of the American right wing's dispositions, Elizabeth found it impossible to concentrate on what he was saying. From time to time she threw a quick glance at Carleton, and each time she did so, unexpected anxiety tightened across her breast like an iron band.

The fatigue that shadowed his features worried her. She couldn't help thinking how close he had come to being captured and taken from her forever.

They will never give up. Sooner or later they will find him. And then . . . ? Is there any longer a safe place for either of us?

As though sensing her thoughts, Carleton turned his head to meet her gaze. Her heart sank when she read the weary resignation in his eyes that reflected her own conclusions.

As long as the conflict between Britain and her colonies lasted, the two of them would find no haven. Their only choice was abject surrender—and death—or to fight with every weapon that came to hand.

Tess's voice brought her back from her troubling reflections. "How long have you and Jonathan known each other, Your Excellency?"

Washington glanced over at Carleton, smiling. "Our acquaintance began back in '55, when I dragged him out of the brush that night after Braddock's debacle outside Fort Duquesne."

With a grimace, Carleton levered himself up straighter in his chair. "I was convinced you were going to slit my throat."

"I came very near to doing so. It was black as Hades, and you were tall for your age. At first I thought you were one of those infernal Indians who'd attacked us, what with your breechcloth and leggings and that feather in your hair. When you cried out '*Mon Dieu!*' I decided you were a French soldier and surely deserved to die.

Thankfully, once I had the knife to your neck, I saw that you were a mere lad."

"You saved me from a tight spot," Carleton admitted. "It had been a fine adventure roaming through the woods with the Shawnee. Then they joined up with that French detachment and were persuaded to help set an ambush for Braddock. While I didn't relish joining in on the annihilation of my countrymen, my companions believed I was French, and I couldn't very well pipe up and say, 'Sorry, lads, but I'll have to pass on this one.'"

All of them laughed at the prim accent he feigned.

Carleton grinned. "At any rate, I was highly relieved to be rescued from my dilemma—even at the point of a knife."

"Another of your little adventures into Indian territory when Sir Harry thought you were off hunting, I take it," Elizabeth said, referring to Carleton's uncle, who had adopted and reared him.

Washington chuckled. "That time Sir Harry found out the truth. I was almost dead with the fever, but I managed to drag this young cub home on my way back to Mount Vernon. Believe me, I made sure Sir Harry heard the full story."

Carleton rolled his eyes and sighed. "As a consequence, it was some months before I was allowed out of Sir Harry's sight again, much less to go hunting with my friends. I tended to disappear too frequently."

Elizabeth couldn't help laughing at Carleton's rueful expression. "I've heard the Indians don't take kindly to their captives trying to escape. How did you manage to pass back and forth so easily?"

"I was never a captive. Most of the tribes speak French because of their long contact with the French trappers and traders, and—"

"And since your mother was French and you speak the language fluently, that was what they took you to be," Elizabeth guessed.

"It was a natural conclusion, and one I didn't dispute. Unlike the British, who try to steal the Indians' lands and drive them out, the

French live as a part of the native cultures. They pass back and forth between the tribes and the white settlements unhindered. I was given the same freedom."

Elizabeth became aware that Washington watched Carleton with a peculiar intensity. It was obvious the two men liked each other immensely, but tonight she also sensed a subtle undercurrent of tension between them that surfaced in an occasional comment or glance.

Again Tess interrupted her thoughts. "Elizabeth and I certainly are not free to come and go as we please. Jonathan insisted it would be too dangerous for my niece to reveal any sympathy with the rebellion right now," she explained to Washington. "He's undoubtedly right, but we're consequently forced to live as if we're under house arrest and to have a military escort whenever we leave the property."

She made a dismissive gesture. "Of course, considering how high feelings are running against anyone who professes loyalty to the crown, perhaps it's for the best. A number of our neighbors have been tarred and feathered, and I'm beginning to wonder when our turn will come."

Stern snorted. "Your concerns are premature, if some among us have their way. Evidently a number of the delegates to the Continental Congress are again calling for negotiations with England regardless of the fact that during the past ten years the king has contemptuously dismissed every petition for the redress of our grievances."

"I see no reason for us ever to beg any human government to accord us the natural rights God has given us," Washington said forcefully. "They are ours by birth."

"If the king and Ministry refused to hear our pleas for justice when they were proffered by our diplomats, they are not likely to do so now at the point of a sword," Carleton pointed out.

Washington leaned back in his chair, his arms crossed. "Quite right. Since both sides have already taken up arms, regardless of the belated efforts of the few who desire peace at any cost, the issue will be decided on the battlefield."

Stern tugged at his hair, setting it on end. "If we do not succeed there, and quickly, then we will lose even those who profess to support us. This rebellion is still in its infancy. What will happen when the novelty wears off and hard reality sets in, when harvest time comes and our soldiers face the choice of providing for their starving families or fighting for their liberty, when British reinforcements keep coming and more lives are lost and more property is destroyed, with no end in sight?"

His gaze fixed on Washington, he added, "Massachusetts is bearing the brunt of this conflict. How many of our countrymen will stand with us? How many of the colonies will support us with more than words?"

"Virginia will, for one. We are as deeply committed to this cause as you are. And so are the others, regardless of the opposition of the fainthearted."

Holding Washington's steely gaze, Stern relaxed. Before he could respond, Carleton intervened.

"The hard reality we face is that, in the end, this will be a war of attrition. As long as we can maintain a force on the field—and we must find a way to do so—then England must either fight or surrender. All the reinforcements and supplies they need will have to be transported three thousand miles across the ocean. Our task is to raise the cost so high and cast the king and ministry in such a villainous light at home that they will lose the support of both Parliament and the common people and finally find it impossible to continue the conflict."

"There is much to be done if we are to maintain a credible force in the field," Washington observed, rubbing his chin. "In spite of the fine face Ward attempted to put on our situation, it appears that all manner of supplies, beginning with powder and bullets, are wanting.

The troops are undisciplined and lacking shelter, and I am afraid it will take months of our most stringent efforts to correct the deficiencies."

"Then I pray you will at least give Jonathan leave long enough to attend our wedding, Your Excellency."

Elizabeth's teasing words did not have the effect she intended. Far from laughing, Washington looked away with a frown. Neither would Carleton meet her puzzled glance. Instead, he continued to regard his commander with a brooding look.

"Forgive me if I said something I shouldn't have," she ventured.

Abruptly Washington stood and bowed, while the others sprang to their feet. "There are matters I need to discuss with you and General Carleton, Miss Howard. I would prefer to do so privately. Is there somewhere we could speak alone?" He directed a questioning glance at his hostess.

"You're most welcome to sit in the library, if that would be suitable," Tess volunteered.

When Washington inclined his head, she led him across the passage to the library, with Elizabeth and Carleton following. The pounding of Elizabeth's heart sent the blood rushing into her cheeks, while an unwelcome feeling of foreboding settled over her.

The wavering light of candles softly illuminated the long room. On the opposite wall, tall, floor-length windows stood open to the rear terrace, admitting a lazy, cooling breeze that wafted the heady aroma of roses inside.

Washington thanked Tess before stepping across the threshold. As her aunt discreetly withdrew into the parlor to rejoin Stern and Andrews, Elizabeth hesitated just outside the door.

Carleton stood so close to her that her full petticoats brushed his boots. Feeling that an unseen chasm had opened between them, she searched the depths of his eyes.

"What is wrong? Your heart has not changed?"

"Have I done something to make you doubt me? I have not changed, nor shall I while I live. I am more certain now of my feelings than when I left you two weeks ago."

She gave him a tremulous smile. "It isn't you I doubt, but only my good fortune in possessing your love."

His hand closed over hers with gentle pressure. "I am the one who is most fortunate."

He directed his gaze to where Washington waited for them in the center of the room. "We'd better go in."

Chapter Three

"PLEASE SIT DOWN, MISS HOWARD."
Gathering her wide petticoats, she settled gracefully on the chair he indicated, scrutinizing the General's face and eyes for any clue as to what was coming. Carleton also gave his superior a keen look before drifting to the open windows that let onto the terrace. Half turned away from them, he stared out into the indistinct gloom of Tess's rose garden.

Glancing over at him, Elizabeth thought how often she had seen him standing just so, the taut line of his tall, lithe body reminding her of a powerful cat tensed to spring. The first time she had met him he had stood so at the window of the library in her parents' town house, and already she had sensed, however dimly, how dangerous a foe he could be.

She found herself wondering who this man was who had captured her heart with such unexpected ease in spite of every barricade she had erected to keep him out. Amid the bedlam at Lexington, and then again at Concord, she had watched him instinctively take charge of the men around him as though he had been born to command. And later, before either of them had known the other's clandestine role, he had gone in the space of a heartbeat from wooing her with sweet passion to interrogating her with an icy ruthlessness that had left her shaken and off balance.

In the three months she had known Carleton, in fact, she had barely begun to penetrate the depths he kept so carefully concealed. Would he ever open to her completely the hidden recesses of his soul? That easy charm, coupled with a wry, self-deprecating wit, guarded his mind and soul as effectively as a high stone wall.

Will had tried to warn her, but she had not believed him.

At the memory of her dearly loved cousin, Stern's elder son who had been killed by a British bayonet during the chaotic retreat from Breed's Hill, she was overwhelmed once more by the anguish of that instant when she had known that he was dead. Will. And Dr. Warren. Both loved and now gone into darkness. Her parents and Abby separated from her by thousands of miles of ocean. How many more of those she loved would be torn from her arms by this war?

Was Carleton to be taken from her too?

Sensing Washington's steady gaze, she transferred her attention back to the General, uncomfortably aware of how much of her heart must have shown in her eyes. The best defense, she concluded, was an unexpected and speedy offense.

"I assume you are aware that we plan to be married as soon as possible, Your Excellency. I most sincerely hope we have your blessing."

For a moment that stretched out too long, Washington hesitated. When he spoke, it was clear he chose his words with deliberation.

"I am delighted Jon has found such a charming and worthy companion for his life. I wish you both a future of the greatest happiness. However, I cannot consent for you to wed as long as this conflict with England remains unresolved."

After a moment of tense silence, Carleton said, "May I ask why?"

Though he spoke calmly, he could not quite keep the tightness out of his voice. Elizabeth could see the muscles tensing in his jaw.

Washington's fingers massaged his chin, only partially concealing his sly smile. "As I recall, Deuteronomy 24 states that when a man marries he shall not go out to war, but stay at home and give his new wife pleasure for one year. I am afraid I cannot spare you for that long."

Carleton made an impatient gesture. "You think I cannot be both a husband and a soldier?"

Washington sobered. "I need your full attention on the task that lies before us, Jon. Our country needs the talents and abilities you bring to this conflict, which promises to be a long one. Whether short or long, it will require great sacrifice and suffering if we are to reach the great goal to which we have pledged our lives."

"I'm fully aware of that, and—"

"If you marry, I fear you will be even more distracted than you are now. Can you tell me that in the week we have been together your mind and your heart have not been continually elsewhere?"

"Once Beth and I are married—"

"Once you are married, do you think that during long months of separation and privation you will not yearn all the more passionately for the comforts of your hearth and your wife's arms? And what if there were to be a child, as most likely there would be? Would you leave her to face childbirth without you, to manage an infant and your household alone while you are away at war? And if you die?"

Elizabeth flinched under the hammer blows of Washington's quietly spoken words. Carleton had gone white. He stared at Washington as though his commander had struck him.

"You would deny me the comfort you have in a wife and children." His harsh words trembled.

Washington stared into the air, and his hands flexed on the arms of his chair. "I know the reality of it. There are enough of us who bear the burden of separation from our dearest loves and the loneliness that follows. I am trying to spare the two of you that."

"By separating us." Carleton stopped, drew in a ragged breath, and tried another tack. "Beth and I are the only ones who can judge what is best for our lives. For you to deny us the right freely to wed is to make a travesty of the liberty we fight for."

As though he had anticipated this argument, Washington countered, "When you joined the army you gave up the rights that belong to the common man and submitted yourself to the command of your superiors."

"And if we marry in spite of your objection?"

"Then I will have no choice but to revoke your commission."

"Sir! You force me to choose between the love that alone makes life worth living and my honor!"

"There is no true love apart from honor."

Elizabeth felt as though the bottom had fallen out of her stomach. Disappointment flooded through her, so intense she felt physically ill.

Before her eyes danced the vision of herself in her mother's wedding gown descending the stairs on Stern's arm, the light in Carleton's eyes as his gaze followed her, the heady fragrance of flowers, and the laughter and love that would surround them on their wedding day. And dearer still, the tender, passionate caresses she longed to cherish for a lifetime.

All the beguiling, romantic dreams her fierce heart had refused to give way to until Carleton had walked into her life and demolished her defenses with a smile and a touch. Dreams that now faded and melted into a vapor before her eyes.

She was careful to keep her gaze fixed on Washington, yet even from across the room, Carleton's dismay was as palpable to her as her own. When she found courage to glance over at him, she saw that though he remained very pale, his expression was as effectively masked as though he played at hazard.

She reached out to him. "My love, we have committed ourselves to this cause. We cannot turn our backs on it now, no matter what it costs us."

He turned on her a glance that stabbed through her like a dagger. "So we are left no alternative but to walk away from each other."

Her eyes blinded by tears, she stared down at her hands clenched in her lap. When she again looked up, Washington was studying her, his expression reflecting emotions only partially disguised.

"Believe me when I tell you that this gives me no pleasure. I know what it is to long for a relationship that is impossible to have."

Before either of them could speak, he added painfully, "There will be time for the two of you when this war is over. But we are now at a critical juncture. The great cause we serve cannot be put off for a more convenient time. If you marry, you can be of no service to me."

Feeling numb, Elizabeth asked, "What service can I render you?"

Washington leaned forward in his chair. "More even than men or ammunition, I need intelligence. I have no doubt at all that even now Gage's spies are operating in our midst. If I do not know how much he knows, then we can easily be undone by persons we trust. And if I do not know what he plans, then I cannot prepare to counter him.

"I have great need of someone who is resourceful, daring, and courageous, someone whom Gage knows and trusts. Up to this point, you have held his complete confidence, thus access to a wide range of intelligence. But if you marry a man the British consider to be a traitor, one who is an officer in the army of rebellion, then your true sympathies will be undeniable. There will no longer be any possibility for you to help us."

"If we were to be married in secret—"

Washington shook his head. "How shall you be able to keep such a connection secret? And can you tell me that you have never used your feminine graces to charm information from a British officer? Could you force yourself to do what might become necessary, if you had just left your husband's arms?"

Elizabeth felt her cheeks growing hot. The accusing memory of how often she had flirted—at times shamelessly—with British officers in order to distract them into revealing intelligence made it impossible for her to meet Washington's probing gaze.

Carleton intervened, his tone edged with outrage. "What you imply, sir, is an insult."

Washington did not turn his gaze from Elizabeth. "You see what I mean. Jon would be eaten up by it, and so would you. He would end up questioning your fidelity. Eventually he would no longer trust you. It would tear your marriage apart."

She bowed her head, knowing he spoke the truth. "What do you propose?"

"Your parents own a town house in Boston. You already possess secret lines of communication between here and there. If you and your aunt were to—"

Carleton blanched. "You can't be serious! You'd send Beth back into Boston when there is a high price on her head—?"

"On Oriole's head. From what you told me, there are only a few trusted men among us who know Oriole's identity, and no one in the British camp suspects her."

"How can we be sure of that? Even if it is true, you pointed out yourself that there are traitors among us. If Beth is discovered while she is in Gage's very hands, we will not even learn of her fate until her body lies in a British grave."

Silence hung heavy in the room. Feeling Carleton's intense gaze on her, Elizabeth looked up to meet his eyes.

"Beth, after all that's happened, surely even you can't consider acting so rashly as to take on this assignment."

His tone was flat as though the matter was settled. Nettled, she drew herself stiffly up.

"Faith, but you're a fine one to talk! It would seem I'm better able to take care of myself than you are. If it weren't for me and Isaiah, your head would be decorating a British pike by now."

Washington began to smile, then to chuckle. Carleton struggled to maintain his frown, but at last he also threw back his head, laughing in spite of himself.

"She's right, Jon." Sobering, Washington pointed out, "The truth is we don't have anyone who has the access to the British high command or enjoys the trust she does.

"I can't command you, Miss Howard," he continued, turning to Elizabeth. "But I am confident that your allegiance is as unwavering to our cause as mine and Jon's. I need you in Boston, but I will not ask you to go if doing so would be to send you to your death. If we can devise a way for you to return with a reasonable guarantee of safety, are you willing to take this assignment?"

"Yes, of cour—" She stopped, battling with herself.

For some moments she hesitated, finally amended, "I must pray about this. I confess, I am impulsive by nature. I cannot easily refuse a challenge or turn my back on what I passionately believe in. Too often I have run ahead of God's will, and as a direct result, Jonathan was captured, almost hanged."

She shuddered at the remembrance of her folly. "Mercifully, I was given grace to be the instrument of his rescue, but only after I had learned a hard lesson in obedience. So I have made up my mind that I will no longer act unless I am persuaded God's hand is in it."

"If it is not the will of Providence for you to do this, then it will not succeed. I also will pray—most fervently, I assure you," Washington added with a chuckle. "Will you be able to give me an answer in the next few days? I cannot afford to delay long."

"I will earnestly seek God's will."

Carleton slumped into a side chair by the fireplace. "How am I to sit idle and at ease behind our lines while you place your life at risk?"

"That is not exactly what I have in mind."

His fingers digging into the carved wooden arms of the chair, Carleton gave his commander a bitter look, but said nothing.

"There are reports that Sir Guy Carleton plans to bring a force down from Canada to retake the forts at Ticonderoga and Crown Point." Washington gave a faint smile. "As you know, most of the Indian tribes are loyal to the British, and we have heard that your distant cousin is already negotiating with the Iroquois League to join forces with him. If only you were more closely related, you might be able to wield some influence with Sir Guy."

"Even were we brothers, it's unlikely he'd credit anything I might say."

"Likely not," Washington conceded with regret. "Well, the Mahicans have joined with us, but they are a small tribe. It would be greatly to our advantage if some of the others could be induced to support our cause or at least to remain neutral. I know no one else who has had as much contact with the Indians as you have or who knows their language—"

"The last contact I had with the Shawnee was more than ten years ago, before I returned to England at Lord Carleton's death," Carleton protested, referring to his natural father, an intimate of King George II. "I doubt I can even speak their tongue any longer."

"Translators and guides are easily engaged, and doubtless everything will come back to you once you are among them again. You have the advantage of being familiar with the tribes."

"I know the Shawnee well, the Cherokee and the Delaware passingly. I have little familiarity with the Iroquois tribes and none at all with the Abenaki and Caughnawaga on our northern frontier."

"You have a general acquaintance with the natives' cultures and customs. And you were a blood brother to the son of Black Hawk, one of the Shawnee chieftains. Surely that gives you some creditability and authority among them."

Carleton ran his fingers through his hair in a gesture of frustration. "Even back then I had enemies whose designs against me were held in check only by Black Hawk's strong medicine. I have now been gone for ten years without explanation since I had no opportunity to contact them before I sailed for London. I do not even know if Black Hawk or Pathfinder are still alive, and without them I can count on no protection from those who will not welcome me back."

Elizabeth stared at him, openmouthed. His words gave her for the first time a glimpse of an impenetrable past of which she knew the barest of outlines.

Now Washington meant to send Carleton back to the native peoples among whom he had lived all those years ago in the distant forests beyond the far frontiers. Not only was the General refusing to allow them to marry, he meant to separate them by long miles and grave danger.

"I have no one else but you, Jon," Washington was saying. "Our ability to defeat Britain may depend substantially on whether the majority of the tribes stand with us or at least do not fight against us. I am not commanding you to accept this mission against your better judgment—you know the danger you will face and your chances of success better than I can. But if you do not go, then we lose our best opportunity to neutralize the threat the tribes pose to us."

Carleton snorted and folded his arms across his chest. "But you are not commanding me."

Washington's challenging gaze struck sparks with Carleton's defiant one. Finally Carleton drew a shaky breath and looked away. For some moments silence weighed heavily on the room.

"If you do go into Boston," he said to Elizabeth at length, his voice hoarse, "I cannot sit idle here and stare across this bay wondering if you are well, or suffering—or dead. It will drive me mad."

Elizabeth clenched her fists until the nails bit into her palms. The anguished glance Carleton directed toward her revealed how deeply he was torn.

Despite his protests, she sensed that much in him urged him to go, longed to vanish once more into the deep forests as he had so often as a youth. The mountains and the rivers, the woods and the native peoples who lived in them ever stretched out before his mind's eye, she suspected, luring him westward, holding sway over his blood as powerfully as the life of the soldier or the country gentleman. Perhaps even more.

Premonition warned her that even his love for her might not hold him completely. That if she allowed him to go from her now, she might lose him forever.

Yet if she truly loved him, she realized suddenly, she had to release him.

He shrugged, misery shadowing his features. "I might as well face my own demons. The truth is, I've known since I set foot on this soil again that I must return to the Shawnee."

"You will never live at peace if you do not," she agreed, trembling.

The tautness of his body relaxed a little, though despair still haunted his eyes. "How can we do this, Beth? There has been so little time for us—and now there will be none."

She bent her head, unable to meet his gaze. "I will carry your love with me. And mine will go with you, no matter how many miles lie between us or how long until you come to me again."

Washington rose from his chair. "I know how difficult this decision must be for you both. You sacrifice much, and I am greatly in your debt—nay, our country is in your debt."

He bowed. "It grows late, and I must return to Cambridge. If you decide to take this assignment, Miss Howard, we will meet to discuss the necessary arrangements. You will not forget our meeting tomorrow morning, Jon?"

"I'll be there."

Washington bowed once more before striding from the room, leaving them alone.

Chapter Four

"**H**E ASSUMES YOU WILL DO IT."

Elizabeth tried to swallow the lump in her throat. Without success.

"It's likely that you would be arrested as soon as you reached the gate."

She stared bleakly at him, her mouth gone dry. "Yes."

He leaned forward, his elbows on his knees, his face buried in his hands so she could not read his expression. But she knew well enough what he was feeling. They were the same emotions that pierced her heart.

At last he lifted his head, met her gaze with a tortured one. "They may not believe your story. They may suspect that you are Oriole. Or know it. You may hang."

"I am a woman," she replied, keeping her voice steady and level. "My sex is my advantage."

"Women have been hanged for petty theft in Boston."

She closed her eyes, fighting vainly to still her trembling, opened them again. "All I can do is to seek God's will and entrust my fate into his hands."

"Is this God's will? You consider walking into the lion's den as if it were nothing."

"God shut the mouths of the lions—"

"You are not Daniel!"

She bit her lip, almost dissuaded by the vehemence of his response, finally tried another tack. "Esther, then. God blessed her when she faced death in order to protect her people."

"Beth, if you love me, don't do this! Don't put yourself in harm's way again!"

She pressed her clenched hand against her mouth, finally said shakily, "If it becomes clear that I am called to this, then I cannot refuse it. I cannot place you above obedience to my Lord."

He let out his breath as if she had struck him, stared at her, his face gone blank. "If I lose you, how am I to go on?"

The broken, anguished words hung in the air between them, twisting a lancet of pain under her ribs. With an effort she said, "You go into greater uncertainty and danger than I. If I lose you, how am I to bear it?"

He sprang from his chair, paced across the room and back again. "And even should we survive, who knows how long this conflict will last? It may be years before we finally can be together."

"Perhaps it will not be so long now that Washington is in command. Once we force the British out of Boston, then—"

"What will that accomplish? Can you seriously believe Britain will simply turn her back on all the commerce, taxes, and power these colonies represent? Unless we cravenly give up the fight, this will be a long war, and the outcome is highly doubtful."

The angry sarcasm in his voice caused her to flinch and turn away. Instantly contrite, he said, "Please forgive me. I am too concerned for your safety to be rational."

She blinked back tears. "Regardless of what happens, we must be obedient to God's calling. He'll help us to endure as long as we must."

His shoulders slumped, he turned away. "Well, at least you won't have to worry about explaining to your parents why you've chosen to marry a notorious traitor to the crown."

"Jonathan, don't," she pleaded, stricken.

"That's how they'll see it." He swung to face her. "You haven't written them about all this?"

"I began a letter several times. I couldn't finish it."

He nodded, relief softening his features. "The fewer people who know of your role, the safer you'll be."

"I wanted to explain to them why you did what you did. I can imagine the reports they'll hear, and they'll believe the worst about you."

"That doesn't matter."

"It does! It matters to me."

"Perhaps someday the record will be set straight. But for some, the reasons will never matter, only the actions. And in your parents' eyes, my actions must be reprehensible."

He dismissed his own words with an angry gesture. "Curse the day I allowed myself to be persuaded to become a spy, to betray men I respect—though I despise their allegiance to a corrupt Ministry and to a king who is a madman."

"I bless that day." Her voice choked on a sob.

In the passage outside they could hear Washington taking his leave, the others' answering voices. His movements jerky, Carleton strode across the room to softly shut the door the General had left open.

Turning, he leaned back against the solid wood as though to block anyone who might attempt to enter, reached out his hand to her. She flew to him, and he pulled her hungrily into his embrace.

She felt his chest rise and fall in a deep sigh. He was trembling as much as she was.

"How I've longed to hold you and never let you go," he whispered into the fine tendrils that curled at her temple. "Is this all we are to have—this moment, and nothing more?"

Bending over her, he cupped her face in his strong fingers and tilted her chin up, his other arm around her slender waist, drawing her hard against him. Her knees weak, she clung to him, lifted her mouth to his, and for heart-stopping moments gave herself up to the kisses that trailed fire across her lips, her eyes, her throat, the fragrant, silken valley between her breasts.

By degrees she became conscious of footfalls approaching outside the door. Pulling back, Carleton leaned his head against the polished panels behind him, his eyes closed.

Someone rapped lightly. "Elizabeth?"

She rested her forehead against Carleton's chest. "In a minute. We'll join you in a minute, Uncle Josh."

For several seconds there was no reply. "In a minute, then," Stern said finally in a hard voice. "No longer, please. We'll be in the parlor."

"Yes, Uncle Josh." The words were almost impossible to speak.

The footfalls receded across the passage.

Carleton spoke urgently. "One of my ships is due to reach New York from France within days. I left Stowe behind with orders for the captain to return to sea immediately and intercept the rest of my fleet so they can return to France before the British can commandeer my ships. We could easily be in New York in five days. My mother's brother has an estate outside Nice. We'd be more than welcome . . . "

His voice trailed off. She raised her eyes to his, wanting to agree, wanting to turn her back on what she feared must lie before them if they stayed.

The tears at last prevailed. She shook her head.

"We could not do it. In the end, it would tear us apart."

He looked away. "I know."

Softer footfalls crossed the passage and again a hollow tap echoed in the room. This time Carleton released her, tore open the door.

Tess stepped hastily out of his path. "Forgive me—it's just that it's growing terribly late. The General told us about . . . about refusing

consent to your marriage . . . and that he's asked you to take an assignment of some sort. He said you would tell us the rest. Are you all
right?" she added, looking anxiously from one to the other.

Carleton's laugh was short and harsh. Placing his arm around
Elizabeth's shoulders in a protective gesture, he escorted her into the
parlor, where Stern awaited them. When she was seated on the
loveseat beside Tess, he lowered himself into the chair next to it, his
expression mingling defiance and despair.

It was equally impossible for Elizabeth to conceal the depth of
her distress, pointless even to make the attempt. Overcome by misery, she stared into space, unable to meet the others' eyes.

"What happened?" Stern demanded at last.

Carleton explained the situation in blunt words. Stern swore.

Her face gone white, Tess demanded of Elizabeth, "Did you
agree to go back into Boston?"

"I told the General I'd pray about it. I do have some sense that it
is God's leading," she added reluctantly.

"Well, you're certainly not attempting this unless I go with you."

"That's the condition, Aunt Tess," Elizabeth responded meekly.
"If you will not go, I cannot consider it."

Stern rounded on Carleton. "He's sending you off to the Indians
so you won't be here to interfere with his using Elizabeth as a spy."

Carleton gritted his teeth. "That's one way of looking at it."

"What are the chances you'll come back?"

Carleton studied the older man. "About the same as Beth's, I'd
say."

Stern swore again, with profound vehemence. "I must strongly
counsel you both against taking on these fools' errands."

While he was still speaking, the mantel clock began to chime
eleven o'clock. Getting stiffly to his feet, Carleton looked around him
as though he had lost his bearings.

"We're all exhausted. We'll be better able to sort all this out in the morning. Where's Charles?"

Tess rose, as did Stern. "He went back to Cambridge with the General," she said. "You'll stay the night?"

"I must be in Cambridge by eight, but I'm too weary to ride so far this late."

Shaking his head with frustration, Stern went outside to check with the sentries, while Carleton and Elizabeth followed Tess upstairs. Bidding them goodnight, she discreetly retired, leaving them alone in the passage outside the door of Elizabeth's bedroom.

He glanced down the passage to the open door of the guest chamber at its end, then back to her. "I want to make love to you," he murmured, his voice breaking. "This night may be all we ever have. I want to hold you until the morning."

"I want you to," she answered tremulously, blinking back the tears that stung her eyes. "Dearest, I cannot refuse you anything."

Lightly he brushed his hand across her cheek, his thumb tracing the contour of her lower lip. "And if we did, I would have to leave you to face the regret and the consequences alone. I would sacrifice my honor and yours and no longer be worthy of you." He stopped, drew in a painful breath. "I love you too much for that."

She put her hand over his, pressed it to her cheek. "I love you, Jonathan. I don't want you to go. Not tonight. Not ever."

Agony and longing in his gaze, he pulled his hand away. "Sleep well, little Oriole, if you can. Pray for us."

Turning abruptly, he strode to the end of the passage. She watched him walk away, wanting to cry out to him to come back to her. But she could not make a sound.

Nor did he turn again. Without a backward glance, he walked through the open door as though pursued by demons and closed it behind him like a shield.

Chapter Five

"If I may enquire—what are you doing here, Miss Howard?"
Taken aback, Elizabeth met Carleton's arrogant gaze. The icy
sarcasm of his tone instantly quenched the surge of delighted welcome that had come close to betraying her.

The night had been long and she had slept little. Exhaustion,
added to preoccupation with her patients, slowed her mind. She struggled to collect her wits, finally responded with equal hauteur.

"That would seem to be obvious, sir." To her relief, her voice
remained steady, and her tone dripped appropriate contempt.

His unexpected appearance at the hospital had taken her completely off guard. She had straightened from her examination of a
patient to see him striding purposefully between the beds where the
most badly wounded from the recent battle jostled each other across
the makeshift ward. Her hand shaking, she placed the roll of bandages she held onto the small table at her side, waiting for some cue as
to what he expected of her.

For the moment, he ignored her. As though looking for someone
else, he surveyed the high-ceilinged, sun-dappled room.

Suddenly his gaze fixed on a point behind her shoulder, and a
shock passed through him. At once his jaw hardened, and his eyes
turned a wintry grey. Wavering between concern, amusement, and
vexation, she turned to see Dr. Church hurrying in their direction.

"Good day, General," the doctor began officiously, offering a deep bow. "How may I be of—?"

"Pardon me, Dr. Church, if I find it astonishing that you would employ a confirmed Tory to care for soldiers who were wounded defending themselves against the minions of that tyrant king the lady supports."

It seemed to Elizabeth that Carleton deliberately spoke loudly enough for everyone in the room to hear. Church appeared to be as nonplussed as she felt.

"We . . . ah . . . we have not so many competent surgeons that I have the luxury of turning any away for the sake of politics—"

"Politics, sir? I am speaking of what this woman must surely see and overhear in the course of her duties. Who knows what use she may make of what she learns. You must know that she and her family are close friends of General Gage and his top officers."

Elizabeth's jaw dropped. "Do *you* accuse *me* of spying, *Major* Carle—No, I will not further defame the rank you have disgraced beyond redeeming by connecting your name to it."

He glared at her. "Silence, woman! I accuse you of nothing more than opportunity, which I intend to deprive you of herewith."

By now it was obvious that everyone in the ward was following their confrontation with an interest that was rapidly turning into hostility. Several of the nurses and other doctors had gathered just inside the doorway, and the looks they and the wounded men directed toward her were becoming, by degrees, threatening. Angry voices became audible in the low murmur that rose from the knots of onlookers.

"Did ye hear that? Why, she ain't nothin' but a dirty traitor!"

"What's the likes o' her doin' here anyways? No woman ought to fancy herself a doctor."

"Send 'er back where she come from. Let the bloody-backs deal with 'er if she likes 'em so much."

She was shaken by the animosity Carleton's charge had elicited from their audience, even though the reasons for his coldness were beginning to sink into her consciousness. Fighting to keep the consternation out of her face, she rounded on Church, only to discover that the doctor's previous support had wilted in the face of this unexpected assault.

"You asked me to work with you, Dr. Church, and I have done so to the best of my ability, asking no recompense," she reminded him with all the dignity she could summon. "Do you wish me now to leave?"

He shifted from one foot to the other. "Ah . . . well . . . I believe we will be able to carry on quite well without your help from now on. I'm grateful for all you've done, of course."

Carleton cut off the doctor's hasty profusions with curt insolence. "General Washington will wish to speak with you as soon as he has reviewed the troops and taken over command, Miss Howard. I've taken the liberty of ordering a guard to escort you to his headquarters, where you will wait upon his convenience."

Refusing to face him again, Elizabeth bit her lip hard and blinked back the tears that stung her eyes. The contrast between his behavior now and his tender caresses the previous night could not have been more stark.

Never had he spoken to her so harshly, even during the past two months when he had been most suspicious of her true loyalties. And although she was certain by now that his scorn was feigned and that the scene had been fabricated for the benefit of those who watched, his manner toward her still stung like the lash of a whip.

If he noticed her distress, he gave no outward sign, but snapped his fingers in the direction of the soldier who stood just outside the door. The man, a hollow-chested young ensign whose oversized coat hung loose on his spare frame, hustled over to them, musket in hand.

"Take the lady to General Washington's headquarters and wait there with her. Do not let her out of your sight until His Excellency arrives." With that Carleton stalked out of the room, leaving her to trail after her guard.

Head held high, she followed the young officer past the cluster of doctors and nurses at the doorway and on outside, every step of the way feeling the resentful, slit-eyed stares of her countrymen searing into her back.

STANDING AT ATTENTION on Cambridge Common, Carleton threw an appraising glance at the ramrod-straight figure of his commander. Shaded by a tall elm tree whose leafy branches fanned them lazily in the mild sea breeze, Washington stood in front of his officers, reviewing the troops who marched across the muddy parade ground in the blazing sunshine, their faces beaded with sweat.

An occasional unit moved in smart cadence, the members' fingers touching hats or caps in brisk salute as they passed the group of officers. These soldiers shouldered gleaming muskets, and their uniforms or smocks and breeches appeared clean and in good repair. The majority, however, gave a decidedly contrasting impression.

It was all too evident that most of the units suffered from a serious neglect of discipline. They shuffled past sloppily, shoulders drooping, steps out of rhythm, looking to the front or to the side, anywhere but in the direction of their new commander. The condition of their clothing and weapons testified to the indifference or inexperience of officers elected to their positions by the very men they were expected to command.

More intimate inspection of the threadbare tents and dilapidated huts strewn haphazardly across the Common had not instilled a greater confidence than they had the previous day from afar. Ignoring the half-amused, half-exasperated glance Andrews directed toward him, Carleton gritted his teeth and struggled to keep his dismay from showing on his features. As for Washington's two aides, Reed's morose countenance was becoming progressively longer as the morning wore on, and Mifflin made no attempt to conceal his distaste for soldiers he clearly considered beneath him.

Among the officers present, only Lee observed this transfer of command from Ward to Washington with apparent glee. Carleton decided that Lee's pleasure undoubtedly stemmed from the conviction that the army's disarray would soon cause Washington to appear a failure, opening the way for Lee to take over command. If Washington noted any deficiencies in the command he had inherited, however, he showed no evidence of it. An imposing figure in his blue and buff uniform, he received the salute of men who raked him with variously guarded, suspicious, openly hostile, or skeptical stares, appearing entirely at ease and unconscious that anything might be amiss. From their private conversations, Carleton knew this to be a calculated pose.

As the review stumbled interminably on, Carleton's thoughts wandered into even more troubling channels: from the unpleasant, but necessary, confrontation with Elizabeth an hour earlier to the miseries of the sleepless night he had spent agonizing over the impossible choices the two of them faced, back to the strained breakfast they had shared early that morning.

HE HAD BEEN AT TABLE with Tess in the dining room when Elizabeth joined them, subdued and as heavy-eyed as he was. The cheerful sunlight streaming through the tall windows had done nothing to lighten their mood. The same hopeless thoughts that had revolved on an endless circuit through his mind during the dark hours, he suspected, had also kept her from slumber.

She had a hard time meeting his eyes and murmured only a brief reply to his greeting. All three of them were painfully conscious of the question that hung over the table, though none of them wanted to broach it. Their conversation was correspondingly strained, and it was a relief when Sarah and Jemma served breakfast.

Trying to maintain a pleasant exchange with Tess, Carleton found it difficult to concentrate with Elizabeth seated so alluringly opposite him. Even though her face was drained of color, her pallor, heightened by the dark shadows beneath her eyes, only emphasized the sweetness of her beauty and made it difficult for him to focus on anything else. In his distraction it took several minutes before the simple blue linen gown she wore, covered from neck to hem by a long, white apron, arrested his attention.

Evidently Tess noted the direction of his gaze and his sudden questioning frown. As she refilled his cup with steaming coffee, she explained, "Elizabeth has volunteered at the hospital in Cambridge the past couple of weeks. I suppose you'll be over there most of the day again, dear?"

Elizabeth directed an apprehensive glance at Carleton. "I'll stay as long as I'm needed."

"I thought we'd agreed that you would avoid exposure as much as possible until I returned and we sorted all this out." With heroic effort Carleton managed to keep his tone neutral.

Elizabeth self-consciously tucked a stray curl back into the white chignon that could not quite confine her uncooperative tresses. "I intended to, Jonathan, truly, but after the battle they were desperate for surgeons. Uncle Josh thought it would be safe enough. It's been difficult sitting here with nothing to do, and this way I can be useful."

Her smile held both apology and appeal. He concentrated on laying his napkin on the table beside his plate.

"You know how dangerous it is for you to show any hint of sympathy toward the patriots."

"A trained doctor is expected to give humanitarian aid. And Levi accompanies me to and from the hospital every day to keep up the appearance that I'm an untrustworthy Tory. No one shows any doubt concerning my loyalty to the crown or even questions it. In fact, they make it quite clear they're not jumping for joy to have me around."

His mouth tightened, but he resisted the temptation to demand how she could possibly know, until it was too late, whether she had compromised her masquerade. Determined to avoid her eyes, he stared with distaste at the untouched food in front of him while she pretended to eat by pushing hers around her plate with her fork.

Exasperation finally got the better of him. Reaching for his cup, he shook his head and growled, "I might as well try to grasp quicksilver with my fingers as attempt to keep you out of harm's way."

"Even Dr. Church is completely convinced that I—"

"Dr. Church?" Carleton stared at her, his coffee cup halfway to his mouth. Transferring his gaze to the saucer, he carefully set the cup back down, then looked from Tess back to Elizabeth, one eyebrow raised. "You've been working with Church?"

"Of course. He's in charge of the hospital. In fact, he's begun to ask for me to assist him in surgery."

Carleton leaned back in his chair, considering her thoughtfully, his fingers stroking his chin. "You've had no personal conversations with him?"

"No. Of course not. Well . . . not until yesterday." She pushed her plate back. "He said he'd heard that you and I were romantically involved and asked if there is any truth to the rumor. Naturally I assured him that I hold you in utter contempt."

"Naturally," he said, his tone dry.

She tilted her head to study him with puzzled concern. "Is something the matter?"

"No, no. Nothing at all."

He was reasonably certain that she did not believe him, but she did not pursue the subject further. His foremost concern was elsewhere, and for the time being he let the issue drop, though he remained troubled. After Tess excused herself, he sent Pete to bring his stallion, Devil, around to the front door, then escorted Elizabeth into the foyer.

"You're going back into Boston." It wasn't a question. He already knew the answer, though he dreaded her confirmation.

Looking down at his hands, which clasped hers, she absently traced the veins that stood out on the back of his wrist. "I spent most of the night praying. I keep coming back to the conviction that there's a reason why God has placed me in the position he has. And you."

When she looked up again, moisture shimmered on her long lashes. "I'm trying to trust that there is a reason for this separation as well and that if we give each other up to God's will, he'll bring us safely together again."

"And if he does not?"

The tears brimmed over. "Then what he has in store for each of us will be the very best we could ever have."

"Do you believe that?"

She clung to his hands as though to a lifeline, shook her head. "No," she admitted, her voice ragged. "Not yet. All I believe now is that if I lose you, I shall die. I keep asking myself why God would bring us together and cause us to love each other, only to separate us in the end.

"Last night, I was so afraid that if we didn't take what little comfort and joy we could have in that moment, we would be left with nothing. But you were right. And later as I prayed, I realized that even more than I want you, I want to learn to receive with gratitude and joy, in perfect trust, whatever God's will is for both of us."

For a long moment he stared into space, frowning, finally returned his sober gaze to her. "Well, little Oriole, both of us have too often followed our own imperfect understanding and failed to heed the Lord's leading in our lives—with predictably disastrous consequences.

I won't counsel you against obedience, if you are confident this is what God is calling you to do. Neither can I pretend that the prospect of your going into such danger makes me happy.

"I love you. And I fear for you."

She lifted her shoulders in an expressive shrug, her dark eyes filled with pain. "As long as we follow God's leading, then both of us will remain under his protection. We have to cling to that."

He considered this for several moments before nodding unhappily. "The irony is it's the very love God has given me for you that makes me want to hold you close where I can watch over you and keep you safe. Instead, he asks me to let you go. My mind tells me that he will protect you better than I ever could, yet this is the hardest thing he could ask of my heart."

Raising her hands to his lips, he kissed them, then released her. "Will either of us ever learn to trust completely, Beth?"

"Perhaps that is why we are being sent away from each other now," she ventured, the words tremulous, "to test God's love and care and learn that it is unfailing. As mine is for you."

CARLETON RELEASED an unconscious sigh. The last unit had passed, its colors snapping as the brisk tap of the drums and the high-pitched shrill of the fifes wafted away on the breeze.

He caught Washington's eye before Ward had a chance to step between them, raised an eyebrow in question. Receiving his commander's nod, he returned a quick salute, then turned on his heel and motioned to Andrews to follow him.

SURELY IT MUST BE PAST NOON BY NOW.

Casting an apprehensive glance at the mantel clock, Elizabeth registered disbelief that it was only a quarter past eleven. Not quite an hour and a half had passed since she had been ushered into the library at Langdon House.

She stifled an impatient exclamation and forced herself to maintain her primly upright posture on the edge of the chair. Outside she could hear the muffled pipe of fifes and rattle of drums still moving back and forth across the Common.

Washington was taking over command, she surmised. Ordinarily she would have been in a fever of impatience to view the exercises that were taking place. At the moment, however, as for the past tedious interval, her senses remained tensely alert for any sound of footfalls in the passage outside the uncompromisingly closed door.

In spite of every effort to relax, her stomach felt as tight as a clenched fist. Standing at attention where he blocked the path to the door, the young ensign showed no sign of relinquishing his post. Although she pretended he was invisible, she was keenly aware of his tight-lipped scrutiny and determined to give him no material for gossip.

Abruptly she became aware that the noise from the Common had ceased. For some moments longer only the monotonous ticking of the clock disturbed the room's silence.

It was not until her nerves had frayed to the breaking point that someone at last approached down the length of the passage. She sprang to her feet, ignoring the young ensign, who stepped forward to block her way. A nervous laugh escaped her when he made a quick jig to the side to avoid being struck as the door swung open.

She had expected Washington, but it was Carleton who strode inside. He gave her only a cursory glance before dismissing the ensign. The moment the younger officer had withdrawn, however, he crossed the room to take her in his arms.

"Remind me to never incur your displeasure in reality, sir," she grumbled in relief, eagerly turning her face up to his kiss.

He smiled deeply into her eyes. "I apologize that I didn't have time to warn you. But you reacted so believably to my accusations that no one could question your loyalty to the crown now."

"You certainly stirred up a hornets' nest. Did you have to be quite so horrible?"

He laughed. "You gave as good as you got, my love. The news that you and I despise each other will be broadcast throughout the camp by this evening, if not sooner, thanks to our charming friend Dr. Church."

Frowning, she disengaged herself from his arms. "It's curious, but yesterday morning when he asked me about our relationship, it didn't occur to me to question how he knew that we'd been romantically linked. To know anything about our association, he would have to have been in Boston after the beginning of the siege. But that's impossible."

"Don't be too sure of that. Church is one of Gage's spies and has been for quite some time. Whether he has actually been in Boston or not, he has contacts who are."

Elizabeth's mouth dropped open. "Dr. Church? You must be mistaken."

"Gage told me so himself. What with my arrest, the battle, and everything that's happened since then, that minor detail entirely escaped me until you mentioned this morning that you've been working with him at the hospital. So I staged our little scene mainly for the good doctor's benefit."

"But Dr. Warren trusted him completely," she protested in horror. "Everyone has! He's a member of the Sons of Liberty and the Committee of Safety. His reputation is unassailable."

"That's why he's been such an effective spy. Like you. He's been beyond suspicion. All the while, he and Hutchins were the source of much of our intelligence breach, placing you in considerably more danger than any of us knew."

At mention of her former fiancé, David Hutchins, a spasm of pain crossed Elizabeth's face. Seeing her flinch, Carleton captured her hands and pressed them to his lips.

"I'm sorry I ended up killing Hutchins. I had no choice. He was aiming at you."

"I'm almost certain he knew I was Oriole."

"Why else would he have come to you that night and told you Smith was waiting to arrest me?" he agreed. "He knew you'd try to warn me. He wanted you to."

"David knew I loved you, and he meant to destroy both of us because of it. I suspected it at the time, but I could not simply leave my dear Patriot to the Fates."

"Both of us knew we walked into a trap, and neither of us could avoid it."

When she began to speak, he laid his finger on her lips. "Right now, it's Church we must be concerned about. If reports implying that we are still involved in a romance—or even worse, are planning to marry—were to reach Gage, you would be irretrievably compromised. But now we'll see how long the report of that little altercation takes to reach our British friends."

"Then perhaps I'll be able to determine how and through whom Church is passing his intelligence," she said.

"Exactly. We're going to allow him to operate for the time being. But from now on he will learn only what we want him to know."

"But why would he choose to betray us and not just simply join with the Loyalists?"

"According to Gage, the good doctor is in need of regular infusions of ready cash," Carleton explained.

She caught her breath and pressed her hands over her mouth in horror. "Oh, no! He mentioned yesterday that the reward on your head would tempt even a loyal Son of Liberty. I thought at the time how odd it was for him to say such a thing, but he was undoubtedly speaking of what is in his own heart. Dearest, you will be careful? It's you they want more than anyone else."

He pulled her back into his arms. "Don't worry about me, but about yourself. I'll be far out of their reach for some time. It's you who are walking into the fiery furnace."

"You've done all this to protect me. How can I ever thank you enough?"

His arms tightened around her. "By staying safe. By waiting for me until all this is over and I can come home and claim you openly as my wife."

She twined her arms around his neck. "Dearest love, I will count the minutes until you are safely with me again. And if you delay your return, I swear I shall move heaven and earth to find you and bring you home."

"I believe you," he teased, his smile crooked. "You've more than proven your abilities in that regard."

Hearing steps and voices outside, they hastily moved apart from each other. There was a brisk rap at the door, then Washington strode inside and shut the door behind him.

He bowed to Elizabeth before moving to the chair behind the library table. "I heard Jon all but turned the hounds on you at the hospital this morning. I'm glad to see you survived unscathed."

"A minute longer and I swear they would have tarred and feathered me and ridden me out of town on a rail," she conceded with a droll expression.

Washington's smile warmed. "So you received the assurances you sought for undertaking this assignment?" At her confirmation, he continued, "When Jon and I met with Colonel Stern this morning, he assured me great care was taken to make certain that neither the soldiers actually involved in Jon's escape nor those who saw your party cross back through our lines would witness anything that could compromise you."

Elizabeth nodded. "Jonathan's servant, Stowe, rode in my phaeton disguised as me, along with Aunt Tess and my cousin Levi, who was made up to look as if he had the pox. They crossed our lines just moments ahead of our party. The only thing that could be questioned is whether Aunt Tess and I played a knowing part in the escape."

Motioning them to be seated, Washington lowered himself into his chair. For a long moment he studied Elizabeth through narrowed eyes.

"Then as long as the British believe the story about the pox, they could also believe you to be merely unwitting dupes who were used as a convenient diversion."

"General Gage would not willingly believe that the daughter and sister of his good friend are allied with the Sons of Liberty."

"You'll have to persuade not only Gage, but Howe, Clinton, and Burgoyne as well," Carleton pointed out.

"If Gage believes me, they will have no reason not to."

"Howe and his compatriots have not had the same associations with you that Gage has. They have no reason to trust you," Carleton reminded her.

"I will find a way to persuade them, if it becomes necessary—"

"That is easier said than done, Beth."

Washington intervened, his tone stern. "You and Jon were linked romantically—at least it's obvious there was much talk of your relationship," he amended as Elizabeth made a gesture of protest. "Your family had close ties with him and with Major Andrews. Therefore all of you must now be suspect."

Elizabeth leveled her chin, a determined glint coming into her eyes. "None of us knew anything about that traitor's involvement with the rebels or that he was a contemptible spy. Since he fooled Gage and everyone else, just as he fooled us, he is obviously a consummate actor. I despise him for his treachery."

Washington relaxed back in his chair. "My confidence in you is clearly well founded, Miss Howard."

"Aunt Tess and I should have no difficulty in justifying a move back into Boston. Every day more loyalists are being allowed in. All they have to do is to prove they're being harassed and threatened by the rebels. In our case that has certainly been taken care of."

She flashed a teasing smile at Carleton, but he returned a level, moody gaze that penetrated too deeply and left her uncomfortable. When she turned back to Washington, he was considering her with a troubled frown.

"Gage's spies concern me, even though we have just discovered one of them. Dr. Church is most assuredly not the only one. I would feel much easier if there was some way to ensure that no one will ever draw the connection between you and Oriole."

"There is. Oriole will die."

Both of them stared at Carleton.

"If Oriole is dead and buried, then all suspicions on that score will be allayed. Oriole died on Breed's Hill. James Freeman—isn't that the name Warren gave you, Beth?—was shot in the final assault. The British buried him with others in an unmarked grave."

"But Oriole carried out your escape two days later, Jon."

Elizabeth leaned eagerly forward in her chair. "Only a few people who were directly involved know that, Your Excellency, and I would trust each of them with my life. There is no evidence that directly links Oriole to the escape. If the British learn that Oriole was already dead, they will reason that someone else was the agent of Jonathan's rescue."

Absently Washington drummed his fingers on the table. "The information will have to be leaked in such a way that it will not be questioned."

"Our esteemed Dr. Church will be the perfect conduit."

"He will, indeed," Washington agreed with a chuckle. "Then I will trust you to supply the bait in such a way that he will not hesitate to swallow it, Jon."

Carleton inclined his head, his expression reflecting glum resignation.

Suddenly Washington stiffened. "It occurs to me, however—where was Church during your little rescue operation?"

"On his way back from Philadelphia. He arrived the day after Jonathan and Charles left to meet you in New York. All he knows is the story Uncle Josh circulated in the camp—that he brought out two officers who were defecting. The fact that Tess and I came through the lines just ahead of them was never mentioned. To all appearances it was a mere coincidence, one that was quickly forgotten in the sensation caused by the escape. By now I doubt anyone even remembers it."

"Then I will issue an order that, under suspicion of spying for the British, you and your aunt are to be removed from our lines," Washington decided. "Can the two of you be ready to leave by the end of the week?"

It was all moving too fast. Suddenly the terrible reality of the unknown dangers that she and Carleton faced seemed poised like a gleaming blade above their heads.

For a moment she could only regard Washington, speechless. "I . . . I believe so."

Washington rubbed his hands together. "Excellent. I will put in the order that you must leave the camp before sundown on Friday. Once you are established in Boston, for the sake of your safety report back to me only when you have urgent intelligence, such as a British move. Find a way by which you could leave at once should you come into any danger."

She and Carleton rose as Washington pushed back his chair and stood up. "I assume you will leave at the same time, Jon."

"I'd prefer to wait until Beth can send assurances that she and Tess are safe and all is well."

Washington nodded. "Then I want you first to go to Fort Ticonderoga. We need their cannon if we are ever to dislodge Gage from Boston. Take inventory and send me a report on how the guns can best be transported so we can make the necessary arrangements.

"From there you can travel south and west by water swiftly enough that by early autumn you should easily be able to meet with all the Iroquois tribes and possibly continue into Ohio Territory. After you returned to England many of the Shawnee moved back there to their ancestral lands."

"They were considering such a move before I left. If all goes well, I'll likely reach them before the first snowfall."

Coming out from behind the table, Washington escorted them to the door. "Hopefully this assignment will keep you from Gage's notice for a while. We will make it appear that I am sending you back to Virginia to raise that brigade of Rangers we talked about. It is most urgent that we foil any move from Canada, so stay out of sight and bend all your efforts toward securing the allegiance of enough of the tribes to help us oppose any movement by Governor Carleton. By winter the situation here may have changed enough for you to return safely."

"I doubt that's likely," Carleton objected. "While Gage may be on his way out, Howe has an equally long memory. Not to mention Burgoyne, who would love nothing better than to see me swing at the end of a rope."

Washington grimaced. "We will reassess the situation when you return. I do intend to send you to Virginia to recruit that brigade, and this winter is as good a time as any."

He turned to Elizabeth. "Are you ready?"

It took her a moment to absorb his meaning, then she nodded and drew herself stiffly to her full height. Pinching her cheeks to bring the color into them, she composed her features into an expression of indignant disdain.

Washington managed to produce a frown as foreboding as a thundercloud, though to Elizabeth it was clear he was having a hard time stifling a broad smile. At his nod, Carleton threw open the door. Giving a stiff bow, he waited for her to precede him.

Her chin tilted to a defiant angle, hands clenched at her sides, she marched past him and down the passage toward the front door while he followed at her heels. She made a show of ignoring the officers who hovered in the open doorways to each side, striving mightily to pretend they were occupied with their duties and had no interest in her presence or the meeting that had just taken place.

Outside, Levi and Andrews waited next to the phaeton, their expressions appropriately severe. Andrews handed Elizabeth up while keeping as much distance between them as possible, giving the impression that even touching her hand was repugnant to him. When she was seated, he and Levi climbed up on either side so that she was sandwiched between the two officers like a condemned criminal between his jailers.

"Be sure to take Miss Howard directly home," Carleton said with contempt, in a voice that cut like a razor. "She and her aunt are to be confined to their house. His Excellency will issue orders later today stating that they are to remove from the area of the encampment by the end of the day Friday. Until they do so, keep a careful watch on these Tory spies."

He spoke loudly enough for his words to carry to everyone in the vicinity. There was no need for Elizabeth to pinch her cheeks now. Her face flaming, she stared straight ahead as Levi slapped the reins across the gelding's rump and set the animal leaping forward.

AS IF HER HEART DID NOT ACHE ENOUGH, that night the British set fire to all the buildings between their lines and those of the rebels. The mansion at Stony Hill and all its outbuildings were among those put to the torch.

Watching from the spacious cupola on the roof of Tess's house, Elizabeth dabbed vainly at bitter tears as smoke and flame boiled upward into the night sky from the charred timbers of the home she had cherished as an invulnerable bastion against the turmoil raging on all sides. Tess wrapped her arm around Elizabeth's shoulders, while she watched until its brick walls were reduced to a hollow shell, aware of nothing beyond the grief that flooded over her like mighty storm-driven waves.

Why? Why are you tearing everything away from me, Lord?

Even as the anguished doubts assailed her, she knew there was no turning back. So much that was known and familiar and loved was lost to her now. She was being given no choice but to walk away from the past and into an uncertain and perilous future.

Alone. The word echoed fearfully in her mind.

By degrees she became conscious of her aunt's steadying arm. And with the warmth of that touch, a measure of reassurance returned.

No, not alone, she reminded herself, gratitude stealing through her veins, and renewed strength. For though Carleton was being taken away from her for the time, God had sent someone she loved and trusted to walk with her through the valley. Side by side she and Tess would face whatever the coming months held until he was given back to her again.

Chapter Six

"**C**AN YOU EXPLAIN why the deuce these Tories are still here?"
Stern stared at Carleton, his expression reflecting exasperation. "If you can remove them more quickly, General Carleton, I'm
pleased to allow you to do so," he growled. "It appears they've every
intention of taking the entire contents of the house with them."

Carleton allowed his gaze to drift to Elizabeth, who was stacking
one more box in the already packed wagon bed. She wore a gown of
blue silk with an under petticoat of narrow white, moss green, and
lemon yellow stripes. A saucy yellow and white cockade pinned back
the brim of her straw hat above her right temple.

His heart melted at sight of her, but he refused to allow her—or
anyone else—to see it. She was playing her part with skilled ease, radiating angry defiance in every line of her body, and he would do no less.

Behind her, Sarah, Jemma, Tess's maid Mariah, and Pete appeared
at the doorway of the house, each carrying an armload of boxes. As
Tess followed them outside to place her burdens next to the others in
the phaeton, she directed him a look of contempt he hoped was
feigned.

It was barely an hour and a half before sundown, Friday, July 7.
The small wagon, the only conveyance in the area besides Elizabeth's
phaeton that had not already been commandeered by the army, was
piled beyond the top of the side boards with two large chests and an

assortment of boxes until it groaned beneath the weight. Carleton eyed the swaybacked old draft horse Stern had found for them, wondering whether the animal would be able to pull the load.

He had arrived only moments earlier. All week he had avoided Roxbury as though it harbored the plague. He had no idea how he had managed to sleepwalk through his duties. Every minute of every hour had been shadowed by the specter of Elizabeth's imminent return behind the British lines into Boston.

As desperately as he had wanted to go to her, he could not face the prospect of that goodbye. It had been hard enough when he had taken his leave of her for only a few days to go to New York. This separation was inconceivable.

He had alternated between pleading with God for the two women's safety to railing at the Almighty. God had successively taken away from him everyone he loved, beginning when his parents had sent him to Sir Harry at the age of three and concluding with his adoptive father's death at the hands of the British. Now even Elizabeth, even the one he believed God had given him to be his life's companion, was to be torn from him.

As it had all week, sick dread twisted in his gut. Nothing about this was right. There was no possibility this insane scheme could succeed. But if it did not, then both Elizabeth and Tess would pay a hideous price.

Fearfully he glanced over at Andrews. Would this friend, closer to him than a brother, also be taken away from him in the end? Would he finally be left with no one?

Is my faith so fragile? he demanded in silent anger. He had witnessed such a short time ago the awesome power of God to protect and to save his children from the midst of dire circumstances. Yet once again he found himself fighting the onslaught of doubt, of even denial of God's goodness. Surely by now he had learned that the enemy's hand was in the attack.

He took a deep breath, steeled himself for what he must do. Gritting his teeth and throwing his head arrogantly back, he rounded on Stern.

"You have delayed long enough. They must leave at once. We will not harbor these vipers in our bosom a moment longer."

Turning on his heel, he stalked over to the wagon and jerked the traces free from the hitching rail. Tess hurried over to take them.

"I'll ride with Sarah and Mariah in the wagon," she said placatingly. "Elizabeth, Pete can drive, and Jemma will ride with you."

Elizabeth threw Carleton a stinging look he sincerely prayed was meant for the benefit of the soldiers who had gathered in random clutches to watch the fun, and not due to his cowardice in staying away that week. Ignoring the soldiers' rude, ribald comments, she tossed her head so that the dark auburn curls that trailed down her back danced in the sunlight, then made a deliberate detour around the far side of the wagon to avoid passing by him. Without waiting for any assistance she gathered her petticoats and climbed after Jemma into the phaeton behind Pete, while Stern helped Tess, Mariah, and Sarah into the wagon's seat.

Carleton wheeled away and went to confer with Stern. He had no idea what he said. He simply couldn't bear to watch the two women pull out onto the road to face the uncertainties of the next hours with nothing but courage and feminine guile.

It was obvious Stern read the agony in his eyes. Grabbing him by the upper arm, he led Carleton into the house gently, but insistently.

Once out of the soldiers' sight, Carleton slumped against the wall, shaking, his hand pressed over his eyes. He felt as though a cannonball had caught him in the chest, as though vicious fingers were choking his throat. He could hardly swallow or breathe.

He was only vaguely conscious that Stern stepped out of the foyer or that he returned a moment later. He pressed a smooth, metallic object into Carleton's hand.

Blankly Carleton looked down at it. It was a spyglass.

"You can see the town gates from the cupola."

The words were hoarse, thick. It dawned on Carleton that Stern was suffering as much as he was, but for the moment he couldn't force himself to care.

He nodded, walked woodenly to the stairs. It was an effort of will to climb the first few steps. He felt lightheaded, as though he had no strength left.

Then terror drove him upward, and he ran, taking two steps at a time.

HE HAD NOT COME.

All week she had waited for him. She had flown to the window at the sound of every hoofbeat approaching along the road outside, her heart contracting with hope and fear. But he had neither come nor sent any message, and as day after day had ebbed without word, the barbed claws of doubt had ripped deep into her breast.

She and Tess had become objects of derision and scorn in the rebel camp, and reason told her that it was too dangerous for him to come without an obvious pretext. For both their sakes, she and Carleton must maintain the appearance that they despised each other. During the day, attending to the details of preparing for her and Tess's abrupt departure, she could convince herself of that.

In the silence of the nights, however, fear whispered that he was angry with her. He was punishing her for having agreed to Washington's proposal, for not having gone away with him. And the doubts and the fears gave her no rest.

She had thought at least he would come early enough that they could take leave of each other in private. Time for the sweetness of one last embrace, one last, lingering kiss. Time to say: *I love you. I will pray for you. I will wait for you.*

She had alternated between hope and the terrible fear that he would not come at all. It had not occurred to her that he would come only to drive her and Tess coldly away.

As Pete turned the phaeton onto the road into Roxbury, Elizabeth could not stop herself from throwing one last look back in hope of seeing him standing there, watching them go with the same wrenching emotions etched on his face that twisted in her heart. Knowing that his cruelty was his greatest kindness, yet still it hurt to think that her last memory of him would be of anger between them, even though it was a pretense.

Seated in the wagon behind the phaeton, their faces also drawn and weary with the strain of the past days, Tess, Mariah, and Sarah waited for the carriage to move forward. Her heart contracting, Elizabeth searched anxiously beyond the crowd of jeering soldiers for that tall, graceful figure.

She found him at last at the head of the stairs into the house. Far from waiting until she and Tess disappeared from view, he had turned his back to them. As she watched, devastated, he walked with Stern through the doorway and out of her sight without a backward look.

FOLLOWED BY THE OVERLOADED WAGON, the phaeton slowly descended the dusty road toward the imposing walls of the fortifications that cut across the Neck some distance in front of the double brick arches of Boston's town gates. The red-coated guards on duty waved them to a halt outside the lines, muskets leveled to enforce their command.

The breath strangled in Carleton's throat as he anxiously watched the phaeton slow and come to a halt. The westering sun cast a deceptively mellow glow across its moss-green body and glimmered on the smooth waters of the bay that lapped almost to the road on either side of the Neck. For some minutes, guards swarmed around the carriage and wagon. Officers joined them from the blockhouse. One or another of the soldiers ran back into the building, after an agonizing interval returned. A detachment marched up from the gates.

He could make out Elizabeth's head bobbing, Tess gesturing as though explaining something. He wanted desperately to catapult down the stairs, leap into the saddle, and race to prevent them from following through with this ill-conceived madman's scheme.

The air in the cupola had become stifling. His fingers tightened over the spyglass until he was in danger of crushing it into a useless lump of twisted metal and broken glass. He did not want to watch anymore, yet could not tear his eyes away.

At last the guards stood aside and motioned the two conveyances to proceed. Before the phaeton could move, however, one of the officers took the reins from Pete, motioning him to sit with Elizabeth and Jemma, and climbed into the driver's seat.

They were too far away for Carleton to tell whether Elizabeth was frightened or calm. As the phaeton and wagon rolled forward, a contingent of guards closed in behind them and followed them through the town gates and out of his sight.

Chapter Seven

"HIS EXCELLENCY WILL BE JOINING US?"
Her lips tightening, Margaret Gage refilled Tess's teacup. "I have been dining alone of late."

Elizabeth directed an appraising glance at their hostess over the rim of her cup as she sipped the steaming liquid. The sad resignation that haunted the older woman's eyes gave jarring contrast to the serene grace of the wood-paneled drawing room where they were seated.

From the outer fortifications of Boston, Elizabeth and Tess had been brought directly to Province House, the residence of the royal governors of Massachusetts Bay colony, currently occupied by General Thomas Gage and his family. They had not expected to be welcomed with open arms, but the speculative stares of the soldiers who listened to their story without comment had been unnerving.

Even the officers, many of whom had vied for Elizabeth's favors in the months before the battle, had heard them out apparently unmoved. They volunteered no information and met the two women's questions with stony silence. Not even Elizabeth's sweetest smiles or most coquettish looks had drawn a response.

At length, after some deliberation out of their sight and hearing, the officer in command at the gates had sent a detachment to deliver them to the generals for questioning. Dismayed, Elizabeth asked herself whether Carleton had not been right after all and they had been sent on a fool's errand that was destined to end badly.

It was past six o'clock when they arrived, only to discover that the generals were meeting in the library and could not be disturbed. Instead, she and Tess were required to wait. Their discomfort had been temporarily relieved by Mrs. Gage, who welcomed them with genuine delight. If they were under any suspicion of taking part in Carleton's escape, Elizabeth concluded, Margaret Gage knew nothing of it.

Within minutes they were seated comfortably on the sofa in the drawing room and served tea. The heavy drapes were pushed back and the windows flung open to admit the freshening breeze that bore the hint of rain.

When Mrs. Gage insisted that they stay to dine with her that evening, Elizabeth hesitated, thinking anxiously of Sarah and her children standing guard over their possessions piled in the phaeton and the uncovered wagon in front of the mansion. If it stormed, much of what they had brought with them would be ruined. There seemed no diplomatic way to refuse, though she suspected that interrogation by the generals would provide the first course.

"You have been well?" Elizabeth asked, although the answer was unhappily obvious.

Mrs. Gage gave an elaborate shrug and directed a questioning look toward Tess. Reassured by Elizabeth's nod, she answered, "Why, as well as I may be, considering that I have lost my husband's love."

Elizabeth stared into the amber depths of her tea, at last set cup and saucer on the tea table in front of her. For the past two months she had been haunted by the memory of her last visit with Margaret Gage, and the muted anguish in her friend's voice brought a renewed pang of guilt.

Late on the afternoon of April 18, intelligence gleaned on the streets had indicated that later that night a substantial British detachment would march to Concord to arrest several of the rebel leaders and to confiscate the munitions the local militias had secreted in the town. Before alerting the Committee of Safety and setting a confrontation in motion, however, Dr. Joseph Warren insisted on confirmation and sent Elizabeth to verify that the preparations hastening forward in the British garrison were indeed the prelude to a move.

Elizabeth had called on her friend against her conscience. Torn between loyalty to her husband and concern for her countrymen, both of whom she dearly loved, Mrs. Gage had confirmed that the troops would move out at ten o'clock that night, headed for Concord.

Except for the detail's commanding officers, the only one to whom the general had confided this information was his American-born wife. She had become the immediate and only suspect in the betraying leak.

"I am so sorry," Elizabeth murmured, stricken. "It's all my fault."

"No!" Casting a guarded look toward the doorway behind Elizabeth, Mrs. Gage leaned forward and reached to squeeze her hand, her eyes burning with a fierce light. "I know you are as opposed to this rebellion as I and that you passed the information along only to safeguard the homes and families—nay, the very lives—of our brethren. I love my husband, but I despise what he has done in the king's name. I have no power to change his mind, but what little I could do, I did gladly, as you did."

Elizabeth blinked back tears, shame burning like bile in her mouth. "Yet it grieves me deeply to see you so unhappy and to know that I was the cause of it."

Tess concentrated on stirring a lump of sugar into her tea. "What will you do?"

Mrs. Gage forced a wan smile. "The children and I sail for England next month. I've already begun packing . . . " Her voice trailed off. "It's all so dreadful," she added into the silence that had followed her words. "You know that Major Pitcairn is gone?"

Elizabeth and Tess exchanged sorrowful glances. "We heard so," Tess acknowledged. "So many good men on both sides—" The words choked, and she stopped.

Just then the door creaked open. Instinctively Elizabeth touched her handkerchief to her eyes to dry her tears. Although the pounding of her heart brought the blood into her cheeks, the glance she threw over her shoulder was masked.

It was General Gage.

For a moment, his appearance shocked her. The past two months had not been kind to the man she had known and respected for his mild and self-controlled temperament. Now his militarily erect figure had begun to sag, and the lines of fatigue that marked his face had deepened even more. His hair had turned completely grey, and she detected a hardness in his features that had not been there before.

How much does he know? she wondered. *How much does he suspect?*

She noted unhappily that the glance he directed toward his wife was void of any hint of the affection that once had been so apparent. When he returned his attention to Elizabeth and Tess, his expression was not a welcoming one. He gave a perfunctory bow as both women rose and curtsied. When they resumed their seats, he came around to the center of the room to face them.

"My aide informed me that you are asking for refuge because of harassment by the rebels."

His tone was stiff, and Elizabeth answered with what she hoped was appropriate meekness. "Indeed, Your Excellency. Our situation has grown so intolerable since the battle that we've begun to fear for our lives. We hoped to move into my parents' town house. We've nowhere else to turn."

Gage's mouth tightened to a thin, hard line. "In the interests of security I cannot continue to allow this constant passage in and out. The decision has been made to close off all traffic across the Neck. You were brought here only for questioning."

Elizabeth stared at him, nonplussed. Of course, everything was different now that a state of war existed between England and her colonies. Following on the skirmishes at Lexington and Concord, then the full-scale battle for Breed's Hill, it was to be expected that harsh security measures would replace the former laxity that had made Boston a veritable treasure trove of intelligence as well as a reliable source of smuggled munitions.

She became aware that clouds had obscured the last of the evening's sunlight. A flicker of lightning shimmered outside the windows, reflected in the tall mirror over the mantel. It was followed within seconds by a sharp crack of thunder. The strengthening wind set the curtains fluttering in the room, and Mrs. Gage rang for the maid to come and draw the windows closed. At once stagnant, humid air pressed heavily over them.

When the maid had gone, Tess took a prim sip of tea. "General Washington issued orders requiring us to leave by sundown today, and—"

"I know," Gage cut her off, giving them a sour look. "I still have a spy or two left among the rebels."

Icy fingers of fear tightened over Elizabeth's stomach as she thought of her encounters with Dr. Church. But before she could follow up on the opening Gage had given her, Tess responded plaintively.

"The only possessions my niece and I have been able to salvage are in the conveyances outside. I don't know where we're to turn if you—"

"We hear horror stories every day of the harassment and insult those loyal to the crown are forced to bear and that their property has been confiscated or vandalized," Gage cut her off. "So it is when you trust in the mercies of these villains. My understanding is that you chose to return to Roxbury the very day that traitor, Carleton, escaped. Some, in fact, accuse the two of you of being involved in it."

"Thomas! How could you ever think that?"

Mrs. Gage looked startled. The wide-eyed glance she directed first toward Elizabeth, and then Tess, reflected a dawning apprehension. Elizabeth had expected this accusation, however, and felt on firmer ground.

"I'm sure the guards at the gate also reported that my cousin was terribly ill with the pox. We couldn't take the chance of spreading the contagion with the town under siege, and we were also afraid he might die apart from his family. The only reason we left early that morning was to take him home."

"I assure you, we knew nothing of . . . of Major Carleton's . . . " Tess stopped, her voice trembling, and dabbed at her eyes with her handkerchief. "To think we'd trusted the scoundrel completely! You can imagine our shock when we realized who was in the party that followed us out and what their purpose was.

"In fact, we weren't even aware they were behind us until the cannonade began, then we concluded they must be the vanguard of a new attack. Needless to say, we were terrified to find ourselves in the middle of it! Of course, once on the other side, we were made prisoners in our own home."

Elizabeth shook her head sadly. "My own uncle was involved in the escape. Oh, the shame and dishonor he has brought on our family!"

"I pray your cousin has recovered."

"He's much better now, Margaret," Tess assured her, patting Mrs. Gage's hand. "And happily he's been left with hardly a mark from the pox."

Elizabeth wavered between laughter at her aunt's inspired performance and a new wave of shame at the deceptions they were forced to practice. When she had first accepted the assignment as Warren's spy more than a year earlier, she'd had a general idea of the pretenses and outright lies that would be involved. She had not anticipated that the more deeply she was drawn into the web of deceit, the more her soul would revolt at it.

Yet if the cause of liberty was to triumph over the overwhelming power of its adversaries, they needed every weapon that came to hand. At the same time, she had to ask herself if, in the process, she was not becoming more like the very thing she hated.

Through their exchange, Gage continued to regard them with a coldly calculating look. But at last, to Elizabeth's relief, his expression softened.

She decided to play her trump card before he had time for second thoughts. "We have nowhere else to turn, Your Excellency. I know my father would be most grateful for any consideration you could give his daughter and sister."

"Yes, Thomas," Mrs. Gage intervened. "Surely you can't think of turning them away now. How could we ever explain to Samuel and Anne?"

His hand trembling as with a palsy, Gage rubbed his forehead. Thinking what intense strain he must be under, Elizabeth glanced at Mrs. Gage. She sat on the other side of the tea table, pale and immobile, her eyes fixed on her husband while he struggled to pretend she did not exist.

With a sigh and a reluctant nod, Gage finally conceded. "I suppose one or two more refugees won't make a difference."

Mrs. Gage gave Elizabeth a tight smile. "Your housekeeper has been looking after your town house, and I'm sure she will be delighted to continue in your employ."

Elizabeth couldn't help wondering whether Mrs. Gage's suspicions were, after all, allayed. She sensed a constraint between them, but felt confident that their friendship and the estrangement from her husband would keep Mrs. Gage from sharing any reservations she might harbor.

When another clap of thunder reverberated with a hollow boom across the harbor, Elizabeth rose, followed by Tess. "Thank you for your kind offer of dinner, but it grows quite late. We're exhausted, and as it appears it's going to storm, we'd better leave right away."

Before the two of them could move toward the door, the general blocked their path, his gaze fastened on Elizabeth. "I'm afraid I'll have to detain you a little longer. General Howe and the others wish to talk to you further, and so do I."

He transferred his gaze to Tess. "The detachment will accompany you and your servants and help you to get your things under shelter before it starts to rain. I'll send Elizabeth along in my carriage as soon as she has answered our questions."

His tone left no room for protest, and with an anxious glance at her niece, Tess took her leave. An uncomfortable tightness constricted Elizabeth's breast as she watched her aunt disappear out the door, but with it came the familiar surge of excitement. She prayed that this time her confidence came from dependence on God instead of from the impulsive nature she had since childhood more often given in to than held in check.

Breathing a prayer for guidance and protection, she allowed the general to usher her into the library. Just inside the threshold, hearing Gage shut the door behind her, she came to an abrupt halt, overwhelmed by an intense sensation of threat from forces she could not see or anticipate. For that moment courage deserted her utterly.

At her entrance with Gage, the room's occupants turned expectantly toward the door. She found herself the uncomfortable object of three sets of probing eyes.

Until that moment, she had not realized how much she benefited from the assumptions Gage made about her because she was the daughter of a man he liked and trusted. She had grown to know the British commander as a friend of her family. As a result, she had gained a good sense of what to expect from him and how far she could test him, all the while remaining under the protection of her parents' close relationship with the general and his wife.

Now, however, she faced interrogation at the hands of three men who were not only strangers to her, but also strangers to her parents—men whose power and experience in military affairs and in the ways of the world much exceeded her own. Dispatched by Parliament to prod Gage to action, they had set in motion the bitterly fought contest on Breed's Hill just three weeks earlier. And she could not help thinking of the events of that day, of all the men who had died or been horrendously wounded on both sides, and how narrowly Carleton had escaped hanging at their hands.

The latter was a fate the merest slip could make her own. And this time there would be no one to save her.

She tried to swallow, but her mouth felt as though it were filled with ashes. Had it indeed been God's will that had brought her there or her own foolish pride?

As she hesitated, the words of Joshua 1:9 echoed in her mind as they had the day she had finally surrendered her will to God's and had been sent back into Boston to rescue Carleton: *Be strong and of a good courage; be not afraid.*

A sudden flash of lightning illuminated the room through the drawn curtains, followed almost immediately by a deafening peal of thunder. The house trembled, shaken by a strong gust of wind, and as though the heavens had opened, the deluge struck.

Listening to the howl of the storm while Gage introduced her to each of the generals in turn, Elizabeth felt a small measure of confidence trickle back into her veins. Making a deep curtsy, she gave a playful laugh.

"I am honored, Your Excellencies. But I fear I have disturbed your deliberations." To her amazement, her voice sounded entirely natural, even mildly amused.

William Howe responded with a languid wave of his hand. "It's a welcome distraction, I assure you, Miss Howard."

The bored indifference of his lazy drawl bolstered her courage. When she was seated between Gage and Howe and across from the other two generals, she took the measure of her adversaries with every appearance of calmness.

Forty-six years old, tall, and black haired, Howe was reputed to be descended from George I through illegitimate channels. A swarthy complexion punctuated by thick lips, bushy eyebrows, and bulbous nose gave his face a perpetually glum expression. To all appearances, years of self-indulgence and indolence had conquered any military bearing his figure had once shown.

A sour smile briefly contorted Henry Clinton's round face as she transferred her attention to him. The youngest of the major generals at thirty-seven as well as the shortest, he was distinguished in appearance primarily by a jutting nose and an ample waistline.

"You honor us," he corrected punctiliously. "The fact is, we're quite eager to hear anything you can tell us about the rebels."

John Burgoyne merely inclined his head, but his hungry eyes raked over her slender figure with a bold, calculating appreciation that caused her skin to prickle. The oldest of Gage's three subordinates at fifty-three, although he ranked lower than his compatriots in seniority, Burgoyne cut a flamboyant figure perfectly complemented by his overbearing, pompous manner.

Briefly Gage relayed the reasons why she and Tess had returned to Roxbury and now solicited asylum. The generals listened to his recital, unimpressed. When he finished, Howe questioned Elizabeth about her relationship with Carleton. She repeated her avowal of contempt and disgust at his betrayal.

"I'm sure you know that he and the captain who deserted with him met this so-called 'General' Washington in New York and accompanied him back to Cambridge. Where are they staying?"

At Clinton's acerbic question, Elizabeth gave a regretful shrug. "In Cambridge, I assume."

Burgoyne waved his hand in a grandly dismissive gesture. "Considering that you volunteered at a rebel hospital in that town, Miss Howard, you must have heard or seen a great deal that could be useful to us. It is your duty to tell us everything you know."

The humid air in the room felt stifling. The stark evidence that one or more British spies operated within the patriot circles took her breath away.

Forcing a serene smile, Elizabeth pointed out, "I was compelled to volunteer at the hospital, sir. Because I am a trained doctor, I agreed to give what humanitarian aid I could. Everyone was aware of my sympathies, however, and both patients and staff were warned to limit their conversation in my presence. I'll gladly tell you what I can, but I fear that is very little."

"You lived in the same house with your uncle, who was instrumental in rescuing Carleton from the hanging he so justly deserves," Burgoyne insisted. "In addition, Carleton confronted you at the hospital earlier this week and sent you to be personally interrogated by Washington. Now surely at some point you overheard something that would point us to where that traitor is lodging or give some indication of where he might be intercepted."

Elizabeth studied the general for a moment before allowing her eyes to widen. "General Washington did make a comment about General Carleton's returning to Virginia to take care of some business or other."

The generals exchanged triumphant glances. "I'll send agents to Governor Dunmore at once," Gage noted.

"Just to make sure we don't lose him again, I'd advise that you have the roads between here and there closely monitored, but with more discretion this time so your agents are not discovered. And don't forget the ships scheduled to sail from all ports between here and New York." Thinly disguised insolence tinged Howe's languid tone.

Gage's eyes narrowed. "I intend to, sir."

Howe returned his heavy-lidded gaze to Elizabeth. "What is your impression of Washington?"

"He has a certain charm, to be sure, but the little contact I was forced to endure was far more than I would ever have voluntarily chosen."

Clinton smirked at the tartness of her tone. "If he is the best officer the Continental Congress can advance as a commander, then this contest should be quickly decided in our favor."

"I served with him during General Braddock's expedition to Fort Duquesne in the Seven Years' War, and we'd do well not to underestimate him," Gage broke in. "He was most instrumental in salvaging what little could be retrieved from that debacle."

Clinton dismissed his commander's observation without comment. "Forgive me for pointing out the obvious, but if my recommendations had been followed and the attack I planned had been undertaken on Dorchester within a week following Bunker's Hill, then we'd no longer be sitting in this cage with these rustics as our gaolers."

Gage made no pretense of smoothing over his rival's tactless comment. Glaring at Clinton, he growled, "Another attack would have met with the same success as the first. The ground on Charlestown peninsula is the strongest for the kind of defense the rebels made, and they defended it like demons. Considering the losses we sustained on that accursed hill, I doubt we could bear any more such victories, and Dorchester would certainly prove to be its equal.

"This garrison is still my responsibility, at least until Parliament sees fit to relieve me of it," he continued through gritted teeth. "In the meantime, our best course—indeed our only course—is to strengthen the defenses on our perimeter, as I am doing."

Far from appearing chastened, Clinton snapped, "Then we'll be locked up here forever. The only solution is an offensive."

"This place is not worth the casualties we've already suffered, much less—"

Howe frowned. "And having suffered them, we will not give it up. To do so would be to blacken our reputations beyond reclaiming."

Gage's face reddened. "I wish this cursed place was burned!"

"Tell us, how many casualties did the rebels suffer in the battle?" Clinton demanded of Elizabeth. "Serving at their hospital, you should have gained some idea of how their side fared."

"The casualties have not yet been completely taken account of. Preliminary reports placed the total of killed, wounded, and missing around 450."

She became aware that Howe was staring at her. "That can't be! We've lost over a thousand—"

He stopped and sat staring into space, a sick expression coming over his face. After a moment he slammed his clenched fist down on the arm of his chair. "Curse those rebels—that they would not flinch!"

Clinton also appeared nonplussed. "Are they planning a move anytime in the near future?"

"I was not privy to any discussions regarding their plans." She prayed her tone and expression were suitably self-effacing.

Clinton's mouth twisted. "We've received reports that the spy Oriole is dead. They appear to be reliable. Do you know that for a fact?"

"There was some talk at the hospital that he died in the battle."

"If that's true," Burgoyne put in, "then he can't have been involved in Carleton's rescue since that happened two days later. But there had to have been a contact inside Boston who set the affair up, undoubtedly a new leader who has taken over Oriole's band."

Elizabeth toyed idly with the ruched lace that edged the low-cut neckline of her bodice, keenly aware that Burgoyne's and Howe's eyes followed the movement of her fingers at her bosom. She struggled to suppress a smile at the reflection that, in the end, they were no different from the other officers she had so easily charmed—and distracted—over the past months.

There was no distracting Clinton, who returned to the attack like a bulldog. "It's obvious other rebel agents are operating here. We can't ascribe every exploit of these rebels to one insignificant courier."

"I'd hardly call him insignificant," Gage blustered. "He's done considerable damage to us, all the while eluding our best efforts to capture him."

"Then perhaps your methods aren't as effective as you seem to think," Burgoyne drawled.

A hot glance shot between him and Gage.

Howe's forceful reaction in curtailing the squabbling between Gage and the other two generals warned Elizabeth that Howe had begun to gather the reins of power into his hands. *How long will it be before Gage is relieved of his command?* she asked herself. *And what course will Howe pursue against us?*

Despite the bloodbath he had unleashed on Charlestown peninsula—or perhaps because of it—he was as yet an unknown quantity. Would his strategy be honed by the lessons learned on that fateful day? Or would his nerve ultimately fail because of that moment of horror she had witnessed when Howe, his white gaiters and breeches soaked with the blood of his own troops, had stood among his decimated forces staring blankly at the breastwork where the leveled muskets of the rebels had glittered like shafts of lightning beneath the hot June sun?

Chapter Eight

I T WAS PAST TEN O'CLOCK when she was finally delivered to her parents' town house at the terminus of Beacon Street at Charles. The storm had passed just before she left Province House in the Gages' carriage, and after the tense hours spent under interrogation in a shuttered room, the rainswept air felt cool and refreshing.

Past its zenith, the three-quarter moon peeped through the fleeting clouds in the western sky. Only one lantern glimmered through the darkness inside the house, casting a band of hazy light from the parlor across the foyer floor. Before she could move toward it, Tess ran out of the room. Tears in her eyes, she threw her arms around Elizabeth and held her fast.

"Praise God, you're finally here! All the others are asleep, but I've been praying ever since I left Province House."

For a moment Elizabeth clung to her, the tension of the past hours falling away. At last she drew back to look into her aunt's worried face.

"I most definitely needed your prayers tonight. And they were answered."

"Tell me what happened!"

Tess listened anxiously while Elizabeth recounted a brief summary of her meeting with the generals. "Then it appears Dr. Church passed everything along just as Jon intended him to."

Elizabeth nodded, her face drawn with weariness. "They were suspicious at first, but I'm confident that in the end they believed our story."

Tess gave a relieved sigh. "Sarah made a bite of dinner. It's not much, but—"

Elizabeth waved the offer away. Although her stomach complained of hunger, the stress of the past hours had left her feeling nauseated.

"I couldn't eat anything. A cup of tea would be wonderful, though."

While Tess was occupied in the kitchen, Elizabeth wandered into the parlor. The last time she had been there, on the day of Carleton's court-martial, the house had presented a scene of considerable disorder. Lord Percy, once Carleton's close friend, had made a thorough search earlier that day with a detail of his soldiers, overturning chairs, pulling out drawers, emptying closets, and leaving their contents scattered across the floor. They had gone so far as to slit open the mattresses on the beds and probe baseboards and floorboards for hidden evidence of Carleton's treason. By Carleton's foresight, they had found nothing.

Now a cursory glance told her that the housekeeper, Mrs. Dalton, had overseen repairs. The furniture had been uprighted and cleaned, and the floorboards had been nailed back into place, though they still bore the scars of the soldiers' wrath.

Within moments, Tess bustled in, carrying a tray on which were a teapot, two cups, and a small plate of sweet, crisp biscuits. Feeling greatly revived, Elizabeth asked her aunt with trepidation about the condition of the rest of the house.

Tess confessed she had not yet ventured upstairs. While the soldiers who accompanied her to the house had unloaded the phaeton and wagon amid the storm, piling all their possessions in the kitchen at the rear, she, Sarah, and Mariah had taken a quick tour of the first floor. But once the soldiers had secured the horses in the stable at the rear of the property and gone, Tess had spent the time until Elizabeth's arrival in passionate prayer for her safety.

Together, carrying the lantern and several boxes from the kitchen that held items needed for the night and the next morning, they climbed the stairs. The bedroom at its head that had been Carleton's had suffered the greatest destruction. On seeing it for the first time three weeks earlier, Elizabeth had wept.

The mattress still lay disemboweled on the floor, and the shattered pieces of one of the bed's tall posters lay beside it. But someone had set the mahogany highboy back on its legs and returned the drawers to their places, although numerous gouges and a broken finial marred its once-gleaming surface. The torn draperies had been taken down, the rest of the furniture pushed back into position. The crushed and torn papers and discarded books and clothing that had littered the floor had been removed.

By a miracle Carleton's violin escaped the carnage. Elizabeth had found it inside the hidden compartment inside the window seat and smuggled it back to Roxbury in her phaeton, along with as much of Carleton's clothing and personal possessions as she could salvage. She had meant to give it back to him on his return from New York, to ask him whether premonition had caused him to conceal it there, but there had been no opportunity. Knowing how he cherished the instrument that provided him so much solace, she had brought it back into Boston with her for safekeeping until he returned to her again. In truth, she could not bear to part with it, for its darkly polished wood and tautly wound strings bore his touch.

Although the other bedrooms were in better condition, much remained to do to make them livable again. Glancing at her aunt, Elizabeth saw that Tess felt as overwhelmed and exhausted as she did. All she wanted was to lie down in a clean bed. Thankfully, before retreating to the servants' bedrooms on the third floor with the others, Sarah had found fresh linens, pillows, and blankets for the beds that had been repaired.

Elizabeth took Tess's hand and squeezed it in reassurance. Forcing a cheerfulness she was far from feeling, she said, "Sarah, Mariah, and the children will be an enormous help, and I'm sure Mrs. Dalton will be willing to work for us again. We'll contact her tomorrow and see what can be done to repair or replace as needed, and to find a suitable butler. Before you know it, we'll preside over the most fashionable salon in Boston!"

Tess laughed without reserve, discouragement and anxiety smoothing from her features. Her own heart lighter, Elizabeth bade her aunt goodnight and retreated to the small bedroom at the back of the house that had been her own as a child.

In spite of her exhaustion, she found sleep elusive, however. By the time she finally slipped into a fitful, shallow slumber, the mantel clock downstairs in the parlor had marked the first quarter after midnight. The sound of it tolling four jerked her awake again.

There was no point in lying abed, she concluded. Rising, she pulled the shutters across the windows left open to admit the fresh breeze from the storm's aftermath. Finding the tinderbox, she struck a spark with the flint and steel onto a piece of tinder, and when the flame leaped to life, lighted a candle.

In its dim light she dug through the boxes she had brought upstairs until she found the items she sought. For Oriole's usual loose, tan farmer's smock, she substituted a dark green tradesman's blouse she kept in reserve along with a seaman's short jacket and slops.

Breeches, hose, and shoes were quickly donned. Her curly, dark auburn hair she pinned up, then wound a long silk scarf around her head and covered this with a brown tie wig and a wide-brimmed hat.

Satisfied with the transformation, she retrieved a green glass vial, a quill pen, an empty inkwell, and a small book of poems from another box. Carrying the items to the writing table, she carefully poured a small quantity of powder from the vial into the inkwell, then added a few drops of water from the china pitcher on the wash-stand.

She opened the book to page ninety-nine and scrutinized the lines of poetry on it before dipping the pen into the ink she had made. Between the last two lines she scrawled a brief message.

The ink dried quickly, fading until nothing at all was visible on the paper except the printed poem. Closing the book, she took a piece of heavy paper and a length of string from the desk drawer. When she had wrapped the small volume neatly, she dropped the package into the pocket of her blouse.

Her movements stealthy, she descended the stairs and slipped out the rear door of the house without making a sound. Invisible in the concealing shadows of backyards and alleyways, she made her way toward the wharves of the market district.

To avoid the guards who patrolled the wharves, she kept to the labyrinth of crooked lanes and narrow, refuse-littered alleys that honeycombed the area. Where Gallop's Alley intersected Fish Street across from Clark's Wharf, the secluded lee of a warehouse afforded concealment beneath the dense foliage of a massive chestnut tree.

Leaning her back against the rough brick wall, clammy with the night's dew, she stood for some minutes motionless, her arms folded across her breast, straining eyes and ears to catch movement or sound. To the east the cloudless, arched expanse of the night sky gradually began to show a lighter band of grey behind the indistinct, gently undulating charcoal horizon of the islands in the harbor and the jutting angle of the mainland beyond them.

The moon had set some hours earlier. Only the faint light that reached the harbor from the fading stars danced on the rising tide that slapped rhythmically against the pilings beneath the wharves. Shivering, she took a deep breath of the damp breeze that chilled her body through her light clothing. Its coolness felt refreshing, but the odor caused her to wrinkle her nose. Blowing out of the northeast, it was laden with brine and the less pleasant stench of tar, rotting fish, and refuse discharged from the town and the warships swinging at anchor in the harbor.

The scuff of footfalls approached along Fish Street off to her left. In a moment two guards materialized out of the darkness where the street crossed the base of North Square. Although they gazed out into the bay, she shrank back into deeper shadow as they passed. The two men exchanged gruff words but to all appearances neither saw nor sensed anything out of the ordinary.

After what she estimated to be a quarter of an hour and the passage of another patrol, a different sound caught her attention: the thrum of wind in sails, the creak of wood and rope, the swish of a hull slicing through water. Squinting into the darkness, she made out the indistinct shape of a fishing sloop heeling deftly around the black hulks of His Majesty's ships and closing quickly on the wharf. The night's catch had been a good one, for the boat rode low in the water.

A minute more, and she could make out the vessel's name in the bobbing light of a small lantern held just above the bow by one of the fishermen. Captain Dalton's *Prudence* was first in that morning.

Their housekeeper's brother-in-law, Dalton captained one of the fishing sloops that supplied Boston's tables in defiance of the dictates of a king and Parliament three thousand miles away. Over the past year Oriole had often passed in and out of Boston disguised as a member of his crew.

Whether Dalton surmised that his occasional deckhand was Oriole, Elizabeth did not know, nor did she wish to. That she transmitted intelligence to the rebels was enough knowledge for him and his crew to have. In the year she had worked with him, Dalton and his fishermen had always been trustworthy and discreet, eager to help in any way they could, and resolutely closemouthed about their passenger.

As the sloop neared the docks, the sails dropped, and the small boat maneuvered expertly to her berth. One of the fishermen leaped onto the wharf, and another threw him the rope, which the first wound fast around the nearest cleat.

In the strengthening light other figures, solitary or in clusters, walking or driving wagons or pushing carts, began to appear from the streets and buildings to each side. One by one other fishing boats bobbed into view and began to tie up at the wharves.

While she watched, the area came alive with color and motion in the steadily strengthening light. A hubbub of voices, the thump and scrape of heavily laden boxes, the clatter of wagon wheels across the cobblestones, and the screech of seagulls gliding above the swaying masts filled the air. Within minutes a brisk trade unfolded as the night's catch was brought up from the ships' holds and laid out for inspection and purchase.

Keeping a wary eye out for any redcoats, Elizabeth crept back along the lane behind her, detoured between the back lots of the nearby buildings, and came around onto Wood Lane. Hands in pockets, she shuffled back onto Fish Street, whistling, and eased into a group of shopkeepers intent on transacting business. When she stepped onto the wharf where the *Prudence* had docked, however, a rough hand grabbed the collar of her shirt from behind and almost jerked her off her feet.

"Where ye think yer goin'?" a gruff voice demanded.

Dragged backward, Elizabeth gasped and coughed as the fabric dug into her throat. For a moment she struggled futilely against the hand that held her fast, but finally gave up the attempt. She writhed around to confront her captor and found herself staring into the narrowed eyes of a short, burly soldier who carried a musket.

"Aye, sir, I've just come to fetch the fish for me master's market as usual, sir."

The guard did not relinquish his grip. "I ain't seen ye here a'fore," he growled. "Who be ye?"

"Eddie Martens, sir. My master is old John Luckett at the market over by Faneuil Hall. I comes 'ere most every day."

"I can vouch for him," a familiar voice put in. "He be one o' my regular customers, so if ye'll turn him loose, we'll finish our business and I'll send him on his way."

Both of them rounded on the tall, spare man who had come up behind them. A bolt of relief shot through Elizabeth at sight of Captain Dalton.

With obvious reluctance the soldier let go of her collar. Sneering, he admonished her to disappear before he returned and had her arrested.

As he swaggered off, the captain fixed her in a keen but kindly stare. "I been meanin' to ask ye. Be ye not one o' Oriole's band?" he asked in a murmur low enough that no one in the vicinity could hear.

Elizabeth straightened her shirt. "Mayhap. Mayhap not. Why ask ye?"

Dalton's face settled into grim lines. "We hear Oriole was killed in the battle."

"We heard the same. Don't make no difference. I got a package for Colonel Stern in Roxbury. Can ye get it to him today?"

The captain turned with a casual motion that allowed him to look around without appearing to do so. The guard was no longer in sight, and no one appeared to be paying them the least attention.

"I kin," he allowed, running a rough hand through his windblown mane of hair. "But ye best not be seen handin' me anythin'. Come along."

He led the way to the *Prudence,* Elizabeth at his heels. He had to bend almost double to duck through the hatch, and she followed him down the steep steps into the hold. The transfer was quickly made, and shortly they were back on deck, leaning on the side rail to watch the bustle of business along the waterfront. With a pang of sadness Elizabeth reflected that the number of fishermen and boats had declined markedly since the beginning of the siege.

"I take it ye have a new leader."

Elizabeth transferred her bland gaze to the masts of the British transport that gently rolled on the swell of the tide at her berth alongside the neighboring wharf. "I'll have a letter for ye from time to time. Mayhap I'll need passage to the mainland now and agin."

Suddenly Dalton looked down to scrutinize her more closely. How often during the past year he had slipped her aboard the *Prudence* in the early morning darkness, disguised as one of his fishermen, and provided her stealthy transport between town and mainland. In all that time, he had not appeared to take any special interest in her appearance.

Now, in the clear light of day, he did so. Her pounding heart sent the blood coursing into her cheeks, while she prayed he would come to no dangerous conclusions.

After a moment, a slow, twisted smile creased the captain's windscoured countenance, then he sobered. "Yer secret be safe with me. I lost a son up there." He jerked his head in the direction of Charlestown heights. "They kin cut me limb from limb, but they'll get nothin' from me."

"Thanks."

Without meeting his gaze, she walked to the gangplank, trying to keep her movements casual. Behind her she heard the soft, whistled notes of the oriole's call. At the sound, icy fingers of premonition squeezed the breath from her lungs.

Refusing to glance back, she jumped onto the wharf, slipped between the customers clustered around boxes overflowing with fish, clams, crabs, and lobsters, and disappeared back into the intricate maze of the market district's narrow lanes.

✸ ✸ ✸

STERN HELD OUT THE PACKAGE. Taking it eagerly, Carleton unwrapped it, for a moment stared at the book, puzzled. With a shock, he remembered where he had seen it before. It was the same small volume Elizabeth had snatched out of his hand and purchased at Knox's bookstore the day before the march to Concord.

At his surprised expression, Stern chuckled. "Open it to page ninety-nine and hold it close to the flame. Just be careful not to burn it."

When Stern handed him the candle, understanding dawned. He had heard of invisible ink, but had never seen it. Now, as he held the printed page near the candle flame, to his amazement a thin, spidery writing emerged between the last two lines as the page absorbed the flame's heat.

All is well here. You are in danger. Do not delay.

He looked up to meet Stern's alarmed gaze. "They must know exactly where you are, and there are undoubtedly new plans afoot to capture you."

Carleton set down the book. "Everything's prepared. We leave before dawn."

"You'll take Isaiah and Sammy with you again?"

Carleton nodded. "Isaiah has already acquired the trade goods we'll need. He and Sammy will ride directly to Albany to acquire a canoe, and on our return from Ticonderoga we'll meet them on the Hudson at the portage from Lake George. John Konkapot and Hendrick Aupaumut of the Mahicans will accompany Charles and me as translators and guides."

"Excellent. The Mahicans have long had dealings with the tribes of the Great Lakes and the Ohio, and they are trusted. Now you and Charles stay out of trouble. Knowing my niece, if anything happens to you, she'll have my hide."

"We should be safe enough among the outlaws of the New Hampshire Grants. Their leader, Ethan Allen, has proven they've no love for George the Third." When Stern opened his mouth to protest, Carleton added drolly, "To be on the safe side, however, we will endeavor to remain as invisible as the wind."

Chapter Nine

"**H**OW MANY GUNS did you say they can mount?"

"Around a hundred, or so I've heard." Carleton pulled off his hat and swatted at the gnats that swarmed thickly around their heads. "That's what we're here to find out."

Andrews arched a dubious eyebrow. A quarter of a mile in front of their small party, crowning a promontory one hundred feet above Lake Champlain's cold, crystal-clear waters, towered Ticonderoga's imposing, star-shaped, stone walls and red, peaked roofs.

He measured the distance to the top of the steep rise. "I wouldn't want the task of taking that hill. They'd blow you away before you ever reached the top."

Carleton snorted. "If the fort is properly manned, you'd never reach the foot of the bluff."

Andrews took in the deep waters that lapped against the base of the promontory before returning his gaze to Carleton. "How the deuce did Allen and Arnold take it then?"

Clamping his hat back on his head, Carleton took a tighter grip on the reins to curb his restive mount. "The fort's been left to rot over the years and was lightly defended. Allen and his Green Mountain Boys simply strolled in through an open wicket in the south gate in the middle of the night."

"If the British take it back, they divide the colonies north and south down the Hudson."

Carleton directed a sober glance at Hendrick Aupaumut, a lean, muscular eighteen-year-old. The more talkative and outgoing of the two Mahicans, Aupaumut stood a couple of inches taller than his older companion, John Konkapot.

"Undoubtedly that's their intention," Carleton returned dryly. "And that's what General Schuyler has been sent into Canada to prevent. From what I've heard about the condition of this fort, let us pray heartily that he succeeds."

Over the previous days, they had carefully avoided the string of forts along Lake George and the small settlement at Sabbath Day Point. That morning they had finally curved laboriously around the northern tip of Lake George through land as rugged and wild as it was beautiful. After following the portage that bypassed the winding creek's rapids and the waterfall that roared through a high gorge into Lake Champlain, they had forded the stream near an old sawmill to reach the rutted road to the heights.

Far beyond their sight, Carleton knew, this watery highway stretched northward through a narrow channel between the New Hampshire Grants and the colony of New York, emptied into the Richelieu River, and flowed at last into the Saint Lawrence River above Montreal. Lying at their backs, Lake George extended more than thirty miles to the south, linking to the Hudson River and the city of New York by way of a ten-mile portage. Whoever controlled this waterway controlled as well the movement of men and goods between the Northern colonies and the rest of the continent.

It was the twenty-first of July. Clad in the hunting smock and leggings common to the region's hunters, the four members of the party, leading pack horses laden with gifts for the northern tribes, had slipped out of Cambridge under cover of early morning darkness almost two weeks earlier. Leaving their own mounts behind at Roxbury, they rode the strong, fast saddle horses supplied by Stern.

Instead of taking the easier water route, Carleton had chosen to traverse the Grants in order to minimize contact with other humans, either white or native, until they had put Boston a considerable distance behind them. Their journey had been an arduous one through the Green Mountains' densely wooded and deeply carved terrain. Added to these obstacles, the numerous lakes and rivers that bisected the landscape had to be either forded or skirted, which at times added miles of hard riding. To make traveling even more uncomfortable, the weather had remained hot and humid, and evening and morning they were plagued with swarms of gnats, stinging flies, and mosquitoes.

By day they moved cautiously through the forest, guided by the two Mahicans, who had quickly proven to be invaluable companions. Avoiding settlements, they covered as many miles as possible until fatigue claimed man and horse alike, then set up camp in secluded sites beneath rocky overhangs near a stream or river where they could fish or hunt small game.

Now, for the first time since leaving Boston, Carleton allowed himself to relax. Breathing deeply of the crystal air, he drank in the intense blue of the cloudless sky, the silvery sound of the water rushing over the rapids and waterfall behind them, and the view of the imposing bastion named in the Mohawk tongue Ticonderoga or "between great waters" by its British conquerors.

After a brief conference, the two Mahicans rode off toward the north. Bound for the towns of the Abenaki and Caughnawaga, they took with them tomahawks and strings of wampum to present to the tribes' leaders as inducement to participate in a council at the fort.

Motioning to Andrews, Carleton spurred his mount onto the narrow, rocky road that wound up the precipitous rise to the outer curtain wall of the fortress. When they reached the top, they skirted the ruins of the village the French had destroyed on abandoning the fort to the British in 1759 near the end of the French and Indian War and at last drew to a halt in front of the outer wall's wicket gate.

They were admitted inside by a guard whose slovenly appearance and casual manner did not impress Carleton favorably. With Andrews at his heels, he followed the soldier through the dank tunnel that pierced the thick walls at the center of the south barracks. Reaching its far end, they emerged onto a broad parade ground, the Place d'Armes. On three sides, the steep, red, dormered roofs and tall chimneys of the barracks restricted their view of the sky and cast long shadows across the grass.

Colonel Timothy Hinman welcomed them and, with little persuasion, led them on a tour of the barracks, dungeons, storehouses, and ramparts, while Carleton made a mental note of the size and placement of the fort's armaments. At length they were escorted back to the parade ground, where the soldiers of the garrison waited in two wavering rows for their review.

With each passing moment, Carleton's unease grew. It was painfully obvious that without major repairs the fort would be impossible to defend against a well-equipped force. Worse, in spite of Hinman's obvious efforts, most of the troops under his command appeared poorly equipped and trained, grievously lacking in discipline.

He and Andrews shared a spartan dinner with the colonel, who rehearsed with admirable humor the difficulties he faced in commanding men who were lazy at best and openly insubordinate at worst. As twilight fell, Carleton pleaded weariness and excused the two of them for the night.

The afterglow of a brilliant sunset still stained the western horizon when they stepped outside, heading for their rooms in the west barracks. Beckoning Andrews to follow him, Carleton led the way up the ramp to the top of the wall.

They took a leisurely circuit around the ramparts. Carleton noted that from the vantage of the towering walls it was possible to detect at a great distance the movement of barges, canoes, and bateaux across the water as well as troops marching along the shore.

At each of the fort's four corners, an arrowhead-shaped bastion projected outward, giving the fort its star shape and allowing its defenders to pin in a lethal crossfire any force that attempted to breach the walls. On the northern and western sides of the fortress, two strongly built demilunes, crescent-shaped outer works connected to the fort by drawbridges, provided an additional shield.

When they reached the northeast bastion, Carleton paused. For some moments he stared moodily across the waters of lake and river glimmering in the fast-fading light.

Straight ahead to the east, on the shore of the New Hampshire Grants, loomed Mount Independence, with the Green Mountains rising like a wall behind them. In the west, near at hand, rose the shadowed outline of two hills dubbed Mount Defiance and Mount Hope. Beyond them the darkening peaks of the Adirondacks stretched from north to south, the misty blue of the lower hills giving way to the deep purple of the higher reaches.

Carleton pointed out the nearer peak, Mount Defiance. "If the British were to gain control of that hill, a few cannon would render this place untenable."

Andrews gave a short laugh. "Considering the condition of the garrison, not to mention the need for repairs to the walls, I doubt they'd put themselves to the trouble. It would be easier to take a page from Allen and Arnold's book and walk in under cover of night."

"You're right about that. Hinman was certainly singing a song of woe, and I can't help sympathizing. He hasn't enough men to service half the guns—if they even know how to use them, which I highly doubt. It looks as if we'll be spending the better part of the evening fleshing out our report to Washington with some warnings and recommendations. Unless Schuyler is far more successful against the Canadians than I fear he will be, we can't afford to lose this fort."

"How long do you think it will take to complete the inventory of the guns?"

Carleton shrugged. "Nor more than two or three days, if we get any cooperation. Hinman seems inclined to make sure we do."

"Did you mark the size of some of those guns? How in Hades can they be removed from here and dragged all the way back to Boston up hill and down dale?"

Carleton returned to his assessment of the waterways sparkling in the last rays of the dying sun. "Once the rivers freeze over this winter, they can be drawn by sledge."

He stopped, sighed. "Right now, I'm more concerned about getting us back and Beth out of that cursed town before she ends up on Gage's gibbet. If something happens to her, I'll never forgive myself."

Leaning on his crossed arms on the top of the wall, Andrews contemplated the forested landscape without speaking. After a moment Carleton touched his arm.

"I'm sorry. That was thoughtless. I know this can't be easy for you."

Andrews raised his hands in protest. "Jon, I love both of you. I want the best for you. And if that's for you and Beth to be together, then I rejoice in your happiness." He forced a wry smile. "It's just that I envy you a little."

When Carleton opened his mouth to speak, Andrews added in a steady voice, "I know that God has a plan for my life—and a love. I'm willing to wait for that. I want his best too."

Carleton studied his friend earnestly. "I value your friendship and your love more than I can say. In all the world, you and Beth are the dearest to me."

Wordlessly Andrews turned to clasp his hand.

DESPITE THE CONTINUAL NAGGING CONCERN for Elizabeth and Tess, one of Carleton's personal worries had been eased before they left

Cambridge. On the same evening that had brought Elizabeth's assurance of the two women's safety, he also had received a report that his ship *Destiny*, on reaching New York, had been sent immediately back to sea to intercept as many of the other vessels of his merchant fleet as possible on her way back to France. Meanwhile, Stowe, along with Andrews's servant, Briggs, was on his way down the coast to Philadelphia, thence to Baltimore, Norfolk, Charleston, and Savannah to warn away any of his ships that missed the *Destiny* en route.

The thriving import business he had inherited from his uncle would have to be confined to foreign markets for the duration of hostilities with Britain, he decided glumly as he considered his options late that night before retiring. Anticipating the difficulty of prying funds out of a Congress that had no power to levy taxes, he was personally funding this expedition, and he envisioned a long succession of similar circumstances before the war ended. If he was not exceedingly careful, he would quickly face financial ruin. For the sake of the cause he served and any future he hoped to have with Elizabeth, he would have to act with discernment.

At thought of Elizabeth, the constant ache to hold her safe in his arms deepened. A thousand desperate schemes stormed his mind: how on his return he would rescue her from Boston, carry her away with him to Virginia either to raise the brigade of Rangers he was commissioned to command, or if blocked by Washington, to sail to France, never to return. Finally he stopped himself with a disgusted shake of his head.

His responsibility was not to somehow save Elizabeth. It was to obey God's calling on his life, even as Elizabeth was striving to do the same. And pacing the narrow confines of the sparsely furnished barracks room in the wavering light of a battered lantern, he wrestled with desire and dread.

He had to admit that as he rode through the vast forests that blanketed this land, the wind in his face breathed an irresistible lure. A mysterious enticement lurked beneath the dense undergrowth, held sway over the ebb and flow of the blood in his veins.

It seemed almost that he could hear the whisper of ancient voices calling his name, and the promise of adventure drew him like a potent drug. It was more than simply the challenge of facing the unknown. Deep inside he harbored an elemental need to pit himself against that worthy opponent—and to win the contest.

In large part, the very danger of the assignment he had been given drew him to it, just as it had first drawn him to become a spy. That same daring spirit was the very thing he had chastised Elizabeth for, wanted to protect her from. Yet if he was honest, it was what had drawn him to her in the first place: that aversion to a calm and ordered existence, the need for adventure, for taking risks, to prove one's soul against adversity and peril.

At the realization, he gave a short, rueful laugh. How could he expect her to change when he could not? How well God had known them both in bringing them together!

He stopped at the window to stare out into the impenetrable night, the words from the last chapter of the Gospel of John resounding in his mind. When Peter had asked the Lord about the beloved disciple's calling, Jesus had admonished him, "If I will that he tarry till I come, what is that to thee? Follow *thou* me."

Unconsciously he sighed. Yes, he would follow, nor would he hinder her obedience. And if and when God chose to give Elizabeth back to him, she would be doubly precious in his sight.

By noon on the third day following their arrival they completed their inventory of the fort's armaments. They found seventy-eight cannon in good condition, in addition to mortars, howitzers, and a large supply of cannonballs, flints, and other supplies greatly needed by the Continental Army.

While Carleton was writing his report, Konkapot and Aupaumut returned, bringing with them representatives of the two northern tribes. After they had smoked the ceremonial pipe, Carleton assured the sachems that the colonists' quarrel was with the British army only, that the Americans respected the hunting lands, towns, and freedom of the tribes and were prepared to protect them. After giving each of the Indian leaders several gifts, he also presented them two long belts of wampum.

Denoting friendship and peace, the first belt was decorated with white shell beads with a row of purple beads running down the center to a human figure on each end. The second belt was made of deep purple beads and showed warlike figures on each end representing the conflict of the Americans and native peoples with the British.

In spite of the strong support of the two Mahicans, however, the Abenaki remained aloof, refusing the war belt and insisting that they would take no part in the conflict between the colonists and England other than to protect themselves. For their part, the leaders of the Caughnawagas reiterated their friendship for the Americans and in turn presented Carleton, Andrews, and Hinman with their own elaborately beaded belts of wampum and several exquisite pieces of hand-wrought jewelry.

The Continental Army did not appear to them to be strong enough to protect the tribes against retaliation by the British, they pointed out. Although they sympathized with the Americans' cause, they had no choice but to wait and see which side would gain the upper hand.

"It's what I expected, and I can't blame them," Carleton admitted to the others after the Abenakis and Caughnawagas had been generously fed and had gone. "They're outnumbered and outgunned. They can't afford to back the losing side or they'll be destroyed by the victors. If we expect to win the tribes' allegiance, we first have to prove our strength, both on the battlefield and by protecting and supplying their people."

"At this point, we're lucky if we can supply ourselves," Andrews pointed out, his expression glum.

Hinman stretched and rubbed the back of his neck. "I'll wager that after Bunker's Hill the redcoats won't be so inclined to underestimate us. We'll have more to do to beat them from now on."

"We Mahicans stay loyal to you to the death," Konkapot said. "But our peoples have all to lose and nothing to gain in the white man's quarrel."

Carleton put his hand on Konkapot's shoulder. "I will do everything in my power to protect your people, John. You know that."

Konkapot exchanged a sober glance with Aupaumut. "You are only one man," the youth returned. "There are too many who hunger for our lands. In the end, no one will stop them."

Chapter Ten

B Y THE AFTERNOON of July twenty-fourth, Carleton, Andrews, and the two Mahicans once more rode along the shore of Lake George, this time heading south. They were accompanied by a small detachment from the fort who would ride with them as far as the Hudson River. From there, the soldiers would return their horses to Cambridge and deliver Carleton's report directly to Washington.

On the second day of their journey, they reached the portage at the lake's southern end. No other traffic moved along the well-beaten path, and they pressed their mounts the ten remaining miles to the Hudson River. By twilight they reached the camp Isaiah and Sammy had set up along the riverbank.

A deep, wide-bodied, twenty-eight-foot canoe lay on the shore below the camp. In it Isaiah had stowed the bundles of fancy calicos, military jackets and medals, woolen blankets, beads, wampum belts, and tomahawks they would present to the leaders of the tribes they visited.

That night they lounged at ease around the campfire, comfortably full of the roasted trout and cornbread Isaiah skillfully cooked over the flames. Konkapot, Sammy, and one of the soldiers had taken the first watch, choosing posts at a short distance outside the camp. As the flames died down, one by one the others wrapped themselves in their blankets and, with loaded musket or pistol at their side, lay down to sleep. At length only Carleton and Isaiah were left on opposite sides of the fire's dying embers.

Carleton found himself studying the black man with curiosity. Reaching for the coffeepot, he filled his cup with the scalding brew.

"Dr. Howard once told me you lived among the Delaware as a youth."

His fingers curving over the bowl of his clay pipe, Isaiah lifted his gaze to Carleton's, his expression unreadable. "I be born a slave, but my mother be from Africa. She teach me my real name and tell me a strong man choose to be free. When I be eight years old, the master sell me to a man who beat me, but I get away. I make up my mind then that I never belong to no man."

Removing the stem of his pipe from between his teeth, he spat into the sizzling embers. "Especially to no white man."

Carleton did not drop his steady gaze. "How did you find your way to the Delaware?"

"They find me when I half dead of hunger, adopt me into their tribe. They call me Black Bear. I live with them until I be twenty-three, then I go to Boston to go to sea."

Carleton eased his back against the log behind him. "Instead you made the eminently wiser choice of taking employment with Dr. Howard."

"Dr. Sam going to marry Miz Anne, and he need someone to care for his horses and drive his carriage." Isaiah threw a stick into the embers. "It be because of Dr. Sam that Sarah and I marry."

Closing his mouth firmly as though he meant to say no more, he contemplated the thin thread of white smoke that twined upward from the bowl of his pipe to evaporate into the darkness above his head.

"What hand had Dr. Howard in your marriage?" Carleton prompted.

Isaiah slanted a glance in his direction, his face as inscrutable as carved, polished ebony. "Dr. Sam buy her at the slave auction in Philadelphia when he and Miz Anne be on their wedding trip."

Carleton raised an eyebrow. "I didn't think Dr. Howard held any slaves nor believed in owning human beings."

"He don't." Isaiah stared off into the mysterious shadows beneath the trees for some moments before adding, "I ask him to buy her. She be young and scared, and when I look at her, I think I look on an angel."

⊕ ⊕ ⊕

IT WAS HIS OWN AGONIZING MEMORIES of standing on the auction block as a frightened eight-year-old that had lured him on reluctant feet down to the auction house. The Negroes were kept in a large enclosure outside beneath the trees, like cattle, where the white buyers could size up the merchandise from a distance or have the man, woman, or child they were interested in brought out in chains for them to scrutinize.

Though fifteen years had passed since his own humiliation, the sensations he felt were as vivid to him now as they had been then. Rage had clenched his stomach and lungs with sickening pressure when the thick-necked white master had run his hands over Isaiah's young limbs and privates to make sure he had no defect, then forced open his mouth to evaluate his teeth as if he were a horse or a mule rather than a human.

He had wanted to curse him in the native tongue his mother had stealthily taught him against threat of reprisal. It had taken all his will not to claw at the groping hands that felt every part of his growing body without respect, nor to kick viciously the bulging calves that strained the white silk hose beneath the man's satin smallclothes.

Even at his young age, however, he knew well the penalty for resistance. He had forced himself to stand still and swallow the bile that rose in his mouth at the obscenity of that touch. Surely that must be what she felt now.

It was her defiance rather than her beauty that first captured his attention as she stood bound in ropes just outside the enclosure's gate, surrounded by the slave merchant and his assistants and the men who prodded and leered at her. But her beauty held him.

Could there be in the world a woman more desirable than the one across from where he knelt concealed behind a bank of bushes? Tall and graceful as a willow tree, she met her tormentors' stares with head held high and steady, defiant gaze.

When she was sold, she would fight the one who came to take her womanhood from her, to steal her dignity, to deny her right to choose the one to whom she would give herself. She would resist until they killed her, welcoming death rather than surrender to them. Every line of her tense body shouted it to the heavens, though the vultures who surrounded her remained oblivious.

Her skin was the warm, tawny brown of coffee mixed lightly with rich cream, touched with a faint blush of rose that defined the high contours of her cheekbones. Her features were fine and regular, her large, expressive eyes the deep, unfathomable umber of the earth of his native land as his mother had sung of it in secret lullabies that returned to him nightly in his dreams. Her head was wound in a colorful length of calico, and her neck described the long, graceful curve of a swan before molding into high, full breasts.

He could not bear to see such loveliness extinguished beneath the merciless paws of beasts. Such a woman must be treated tenderly, cherished for all her life.

Silent and unmoving, he waited until she was back behind the staves of the enclosure. Before long his patience was rewarded. The day was stifling hot, and she soon sought solitude and coolness in the deep shade just beyond where he crouched.

His low whisper startled her, and almost she darted away. But his reassuring words held her, and she crept closer. Until the red-orange sun set and the charcoal shadows gathered, they spoke in hushed tones, a cautious word at a time, exchanging the outlines of their individual histories.

Her name was Sarah, and she was only sixteen. Her master needed to pay gambling debts and had a wife who was jealous of Sarah's beauty and angry because of her husband's straying eye.

Sarah was terrified of what the future held for her. The offspring of a slave and the master's son, a fact that had gained her rejection by both Blacks and Whites, she had no intention of allowing her mother's history to repeat itself in her. If it became necessary, she would take her own life rather than suffer such ignominy.

When it became late, she begged him not to go. It was agony to tear himself from her. But he forced himself to walk away, leaving her clutching the bars of her prison with desperate hands as powerless as his to wrench them apart.

He went directly to Dr. Howard and his new bride. Not caring that he disturbed them at their dinner, he blurted out Sarah's story, the words tumbling out in an anguished plea. *Buy her,* he begged, casting aside his pride. *Buy her and I work for you without pay until I earn her freedom, no matter how many years it be.*

They heard him out in sympathetic silence. Still Dr. Howard hesitated, his repugnance for the buying and selling of human flesh almost overcoming him. But at last Anne drew him aside to talk in private. Waiting outside the door in feverish anxiety, Isaiah vainly strained to make out their words.

In the end, Dr. Howard agreed to go with him to the auction, though he made no promises. Yet the next day he bought Sarah, and the price to secure her from his competitor was a handsome one.

When the doctor handed over the purchase price, Isaiah swallowed hard. But one look at the dawning hope and astonished gratitude in Sarah's eyes dispelled all his doubts. He was even more astounded when Dr. Howard freed her immediately, asking only that she agree to work for him for seven years as a cook.

They had stayed and they had married. There had been no need to discuss it, for God's will had been abundantly clear. And neither one of them had ever regretted that decision.

⊕ ⊕ ⊕

AGAIN ISAIAH SPAT INTO THE FIRE. "White men don't think we be human beings too. We feel the same as you. We love the same as you."

"I know that," Carleton responded, his tone cold.

"You own slaves."

The black man's voice accused, gave no quarter. This time Carleton flinched, dropped his gaze from Isaiah's challenging one.

"Not many and not voluntarily, I assure you. I inherited the few I own from my uncle—"

Isaiah gave a dry laugh. "So you off the hook. But they still slaves 'spite all your fine talk of liberty."

For a taut moment, Carleton made no reply. Absently he picked up a stick and poked the shimmering embers.

"I am responsible for their lives. If I free them in the midst of a hostile society, where can they safely go? How long would they remain free?"

"You own ships. Send them home."

Carleton shifted, the log at his back growing increasingly uncomfortable. "All of them were born in this country."

"Then send them north."

"Slavery is legal in the North as well."

Isaiah smiled, but not with mirth. "If you free them, then who do your work for you? Who take care of your property?"

"I could hire help easily enough." Defensiveness edged Carleton's tone.

"Then your costs go up."

"I am considering what to do. I have no wish to own human beings. In the meantime, all of them are well treated."

"No man owned by another be treated well," Isaiah shot back. "But how would you know?"

Carleton stared into the glowing coals, his teeth clenched. Throwing the dregs of his coffee onto the fire with a jerky movement, he rose and stalked off toward where the horses were tethered.

He could walk away, he discovered, but the conversation continued to haunt him. How could the black man understand the issues or the difficult choices involved? Isaiah couldn't know how much or how long Carleton had agonized over the unwelcome situation he found himself in. It was not as simple a matter as Isaiah seemed to think.

Carleton meant to find a resolution when the time came. But at the moment, more pressing concerns demanded his attention.

AT FIRST LIGHT THE NEXT MORNING the soldiers left them, heading east toward Cambridge by the shortest route. As soon as they had disappeared from sight, Carleton's party broke camp and hastily stowed their gear in the canoe. Before the sun rose above the horizon, they pushed off from the shore.

On the breast of the swift current, they skimmed downriver, their paddles hardly disturbing the streamers of mist that rose from the surface of the rushing water. As they traced the twists and turns of the river's upper reaches, the translucent veils of fog that blurred the shore on either side parted briefly here and there to cast a misty ray of sunshine over the verdant trees and dense undergrowth that bent over the edge of the water.

In that ethereal landscape it was easy to believe they were entirely alone in a primeval world whose boundaries were the ever-widening river. Even the slap of water against the canoe's bow and the jewel tones of birdsong were muted by the dense forest and obscuring mists.

A deep unease filled Carleton despite the serene landscape through which they moved. He strained to detect any unusual sound and kept watch on all sides. The nagging consciousness of their vulnerability would not allow him to relax, and he noted that the others were equally on guard.

Riding the swift-flowing stream, they quickly reached the mouth of the Mohawk River. From there, progress was slower as they were forced to paddle upstream, traveling northwestward where every vista of mountain and forest offered breathtaking beauty. Even so, and in spite of taking extra care to attract no notice from the British forts along the way, by early on the third day they had come as far as the village of Oriskany.

There they exchanged their canoe for mounts and pack horses, then rode ever farther westward into a region cleft by wooded hills and mountains interspersed with gleaming lakes and streams. At each of the principal towns of the tribes that made up the Iroquois League they stopped to smoke the ceremonial pipe and present the sachems with belts of wampum, tomahawks, medals, military jackets, and lavish gifts of the other trade goods they brought with them. At each place Carleton offered the same message: a promise of uninterrupted, even improved, trade and protection from the British by their great father Washington.

Since leaving Cambridge, in conversing with Aupaumut and Konkapot, then negotiating with the sachems of the various tribes, the rituals of the native peoples and the cadences and idioms of their speech had come flooding back to Carleton. Washington had been right. Carleton found that he felt as comfortable among the Indians now as he had during his youth.

The differences in language presented considerably less of a problem than he had feared. Most of the sachems they encountered either spoke or understood enough English or French to communicate freely. Where any difficulties arose, the two Mahicans demonstrated an invaluable ability to provide fluent and perceptive translation. Fluent in the Delaware tongue, Isaiah also had enough acquaintance with the Iroquois languages to be helpful.

Carleton quickly discovered that he enjoyed the role of negotiator and that he had a natural ability to secure the Indian leaders' trust and respect, even when they opposed his message. Yet, harboring serious misgivings about whether the promises he made ultimately could, or would, be kept, he trod carefully.

Among the Iroquois, they found the Oneida and Tuscarora favorable to the Americans. The Onondaga, Mohawk, and Cayuga tribes remained aloof and suspicious, with some of their sachems flatly refusing to switch their allegiance from the British. At the urging of the two Mahicans, however, messengers went out to the major towns of the Iroquois to arrange a grand council at the town of Onondaga, the League's capital, to settle the matter.

Determined to first meet with the Seneca, the League's keepers of the western door, Carleton sent runners ahead of them to announce their coming. From Genesee they followed the river southwest, heading for Buck Tooth on the upper Allegheny.

Great Owl, one of the sachems of the Mohawks, insisted on accompanying them. The man had a sly, insistent manner and a way of staring at Carleton with a blank, unreadable expression that left him feeling uncomfortable. Concerned that refusing him would cause more problems than it would avoid, Carleton made him welcome in spite of misgivings that increased with every mile they traveled.

HIS BRAIN STILL WOUND in the mists of sleep, he jerked awake. Piercing blue eyes alive with love and kindly concern met his from that beloved, unforgettable face he had for so many years longed to see once more.

By some inexplicable means he must have returned to his childhood, for his uncle appeared to him as he had when Carleton had been a young boy. Meeting that gaze, a sensation of deep peace enfolded him like an embrace, leaving him weak with relief. With it came an upsurge of joy that choked the breath in his throat.

Sir Harry was not dead after all.

My son, don't grieve for me. Gently he touched Carleton's shoulder. *See—I am well.*

Carleton threw his arms around his uncle and clung to him, overcome with the rush of intense emotion. How could he ever let him go again?

God is watching over you. Though you suffer great affliction, he will bring you safely home.

That well-known voice was as clear as the rush and gurgle of the stream nearby and just as real. But already the image was fading from his arms into the black shades just beyond the bright circle of firelight.

Don't go, Sir Harry! I miss you so much. I need you.

All that remained was an indistinct, iridescent mist between the trees.

Jonathan . . . don't forget that I love you.

He became aware that he was sitting up, cross-legged, his face buried in his hands. Burning tears streamed down his cheeks and trickled between his fingers.

"I love you."

The words came in a husky whisper. Clearing his throat, he brushed his tears roughly away, drew in a shaky breath, and forced his blurred eyes to focus on the faint shimmer of the coals within the circle of stones.

The rosy glow beneath the ashes could not be the source of the light that had encircled him moments ago, nor of the intense warmth that suffused his body despite the cool air beneath the trees. The sense of Sir Harry's presence lingered like the stirring of a light breeze, but a greater presence still beat above the clearing on mighty, overshadowing wings, raising the hair on the back of Carleton's neck.

Shivering, he shook off his blanket and stumbled to his feet to look around him, still disoriented by the clarity of the dream. At last, careful to avoid the slumbering, blanket-wrapped forms scattered around the edge of the camp, he groped on unsteady legs across the clearing to the bank of the stream. There he stood motionless, staring off across the glimmering water into the shadows of the verdant forest beyond.

Out there somewhere lay grave danger. He could feel it like a palpable knife blade pressed against his flesh. They were riding toward it as a magnet draws steel.

Though you suffer great affliction, God will bring you safely home.

He turned to look back in the direction of the campfire. As he watched, one of the sleeping figures moved almost imperceptibly. In the fire's muted glow, Carleton could just make out that his eyes were open, and that he was staring back at him.

It was Great Owl. And as their eyes met, icy fingers closed over Carleton's heart.

Chapter Eleven

THE SUN HAD DIPPED below its zenith when they arrived on the outskirts of Buck Tooth, but even in the shade they found little succor from the humid heat. The town occupied a pleasant site, stretching for some distance along the banks of the Allegheny River where trees and underbrush had been cleared.

A palisade of sharpened logs surrounded a large area, inside which stood tidy elm-bark shingled longhouses with curved roofs, each elongated structure housing a number of families from a single clan. A couple of log houses were also visible, built according to the style of the white settlers. Outside the palisade, an extensive area of cleared ground belonging to the women had been divided between well-tended fields of ripening corn; plots of squash, beans, and other vegetables; and stands of fruit trees weighted with an abundant harvest.

The runners he had sent out had done their work, Carleton noted with satisfaction. His party was expected.

Close to the riverbank, between the cleared land surrounding the town and the edge of the forest with its dense undergrowth, a large fire sizzled and cracked, sending a pillar of pungent white smoke into the still air. At their arrival, the lookouts posted at the town's gates fired their guns into the air, and Carleton and the others with him returned an answering salute.

Amid the crack of rifle and pistol fire, the sachems, elders, and warriors of Buck Tooth and all of the nearby towns filed out of the palisade gates to meet them in a festive parade. From all sides women, children, and youths came at a run to crowd around the new arrivals, staring at them with bold curiosity.

As usual, most of the warriors had painted their faces and shaved or plucked their hair, except for a long scalp lock caught into an elaborately decorated roach at the top of the head, from which hung an eagle feather. A number of the men wore long braids instead, as did the women, with turkey or heron feathers stuck into their woven headbands. Many also wore fringed buckskin leggings, breechcloths, and moccasins, though Carleton noted that linen and calico shirts and leggings were more common than when he had been a youth.

He made a quick estimate: between thirty and forty chiefs and subchiefs were present. Among them were the Seneca's most important sachems, Cornplanter and Red Jacket, whom Carleton knew to favor close ties with the British.

Black Horse, the old, wizened sachem of the town, greeted Carleton and his companions with every show of courtesy and respect and escorted them to the fire. After several of the younger men led their mounts away, Black Horse motioned to them to take seats among the elders.

"You'd think they'd forgo the fire in this heat," Andrews complained to Carleton in an undertone as he mopped his brow with his handkerchief.

Carleton settled cross-legged beside him on the bearskin spread out for them. "Now, Charles, you know everything has to be done properly or none of them will be able to hear our words."

Andrews grimaced as Carleton accepted the feathered ceremonial pipe that was making its way around the circle. "Then I hope our discomfort ensures that this tribe hears us more clearly than those we've encountered so far."

Carleton took a long, thoughtful draught on the pipe. After releasing the smoke, he handed the pipe to Andrews. As he did so, he became aware that Great Owl sat on the opposite side of the fire next to one of the Seneca subchiefs from another town.

Both men were staring at him with an intensity that caused the hair on the back of Carleton's neck to prickle. Neither dropped his gaze when Carleton met theirs with a level one.

His attention was quickly diverted, however. As soon as Andrews had passed the ceremonial pipe to Isaiah, Black Horse rose with quiet dignity. He held out a string of wampum and nodded to each of his visitors.

"Brothers, you have come a long distance to bring us a message from your war chief, Washington," he began, speaking in halting, but understandable, French.

It was a ritual that had become familiar over the past weeks at each tribal town they had visited. Feeling drugged with fatigue and the midday heat, Carleton had to force himself to listen attentively as, pacing back and forth, his voice rising in a singsong cadence, Black Horse continued.

"On the way to our town you may have encountered many evils in the woods from the bad spirits who live there, who desire to hinder you from your business. The evil matter they have put in your way might have hurt your bodies, your eyes, your ears, your mouths, and your inward parts.

"Thus, my brothers, we give you this string of wampum to cleanse your eyes of tears and dust so you may look about you and see us clearly. I open your ears from any obstruction that may have settled there so you may hear our words. I free your mouths and minds of all grief and anxiety so you may speak without constraint of everything you have on your hearts. I brush the thorns from your legs and wipe from your bodies the sweat and dust of travel and bid you welcome among us."

He concluded by offering condolences to Carleton and the other members of his party to dry their tears and heal their hearts for any losses they might have suffered. Carleton and each of his companions responded to Black Horse's speech, and the ceremonial pipe passed once more around the circle. At last, at the sachem's signal, they all rose and followed Black Horse through the gates of the palisade.

The largest building in the town, the council house was seventy feet long, constructed, as were the longhouses, of a framework of sturdy poles shingled on the outside with wide strips of elm bark. A spacious common room where they now gathered took up the front half of the building. A passageway divided the rest down its center, with smaller compartments opening off to each side for the use of visitors.

A fire circle occupied the center of the common room as well as the center of the passageway in front of each of the compartments. No fires had been laid, however. Through each smoke hole in the building's roof, a shaft of misty light slanted to the floor, providing the only light except for the flame from a couple of torches. After the heat of day and the fire at the riverbank, the dim coolness inside was a welcome relief.

Shortly after they entered, a number of women brought in steaming cast-iron kettles of corn mush, cooked squash, and roasted venison. Once again they smoked the ceremonial pipe, and this time toasted each other with rum, though Carleton noted that both Cornplanter and Red Jacket remained noticeably aloof. Handsome and regal, Cornplanter, the son of a Seneca woman and a Dutch trader, listened intently to all that was said. Although he spoke little, it was clear his words carried great weight.

At the same time, Carleton became aware that Great Owl made a point of sitting close to him, along with the subchief Half Moon, who, Carleton was told, came from a town two day's journey farther west. Of medium height and lean, with hooded eyes and a hooked nose, Half Moon appeared to be about Andrews's age. Although he also spoke little, Carleton could not shake off an uneasy sense that Half Moon harbored ill will toward him, though Carleton could fathom no reason for it.

When everyone had eaten their fill, the women cleared the food away. Mulling over the possible reasons for the subtle malevolence in the two Indians' eyes, Carleton was relieved when Black Horse finally invited him to speak. His movements deliberate, he got to his feet and took the council bag from Konkapot. Making sure that each of the Seneca leaders followed his actions attentively, he took out the wampum belts for peace and war and laid them out on the low platform at the front of the common room.

Speaking in French with Konkapot translating his words, he first took up the peace belt and spoke at length on the desire of the Americans' war chief, General Washington, to ensure peace with the Iroquois, to maintain trade and close relations among their peoples, and to protect them from any harm the British might do to them. He had brought with him a letter signed by Washington stating the same, and this he read aloud word for word. Satisfied that he had the sachems' undivided attention, he laid the peace belt and the letter before them and took up the war belt.

Gravely, but with solemn emphasis, he outlined the grievances of the colonists against the British king and Ministry and reminded his audience of the injustices the Indian nations had also suffered at the hands of the British. Describing in detail the skirmishes at Lexington and Concord and the full-scale battle for Breed's Hill, he pointed out the ability of the Continental Army to win the conflict. It was in the best interest of the tribes to join forces with Washington against the British, he emphasized, or if they still hesitated to take up the tomahawk, to at least deny the British their support.

Finished, he laid the war belt ceremoniously before the assembly next to Washington's letter and the peace belt and sat down. A low murmur filled the room as each individual conferred with his neighbors.

It was obvious that Carleton's speech, coupled with the wampum and Washington's letter, had woven a powerful spell over the assembly. But although they passed the letter and the peace belt from hand to hand for close scrutiny, the war belt remained where Carleton had laid it.

At last Cornplanter got to his feet, his visage stern. Frowning, he said, "We have heard strong arguments for taking up the tomahawk against the British. Yet since the defeat of the French we Iroquois have benefited from our alliance with them, and to go to war against them now would be a serious matter, one that cannot be taken lightly. Our people have seen the power of the British, but we do not know the power of the Americans. It would be wise for us to sleep upon these words and take council in the morning to determine what course we will recommend to the Great Council of the League when the council fire is lighted once more at Onondaga."

His words were greeted with nods of agreement. With some reluctance, the council broke into small knots of two or three, each engaged in thoughtful or vehement discussion. It was some time before the assembly parted for the night.

Black Horse led Carleton and Andrews to a compartment at the building's far end. Isaiah and Sammy took the one directly across the passageway, while the two Mahicans shared the room next door.

As twilight faded into night, stillness settled over the council house. Sweating in the oppressive, humid air, Carleton and Andrews removed shirts and leggings and stretched out on the rush mats laid across the low sleeping platform built along the outer wall. Keeping their voices low, they compared impressions of the day's events.

Both concluded that, on the surface, the meeting had been favorable. Each of the tribal leaders had listened intently to Carleton's arguments, and so far none had shown any open opposition.

Regardless of the council's decision on the following day, however, the meeting of the full League would determine which side the tribes of the Iroquois would support. Even if the Seneca decided in their favor, Carleton pointed out, the League would be evenly split between those who supported the British and those who sided with the Americans.

At length Andrews rolled onto his side, and after a few minutes, his regular breaths told Carleton he had gone to sleep. Carleton tried to still his mind, to concentrate on praying for God's guidance, favor, and protection in the days to come, but it was some time before he could find a measure of peace.

His last conscious thought was the realization that in the commotion of the council's breaking up, Great Owl and Half Moon had disappeared. As he drifted off to sleep, Carleton wondered uneasily where they had gone—and why.

💮 💮 💮

THE BARELY PERCEPTIBLE AURA of pearl dawn softened the deep forest beyond the town's edge, bringing the vivid green-black of the pines and the brighter tones of the maples and oaks into tentative focus. None of the others in the council house had yet stirred, and no smoke rose above the longhouses visible near at hand.

The night had held little rest for Carleton. Disturbing visions had flickered in and out of his mind until he jerked awake to rise stealthily and slip outside.

The air was still heavy and motionless. Moving as silently as a shadow, he eased through the town gates and strode to the edge of the riverbank, intending to dive into the water for a cooling swim. As he stepped out of his moccasins, the fluid trill of a bird in the branches directly overhead arrested his movements.

It was the unmistakable song of an oriole.

Startled, he glanced up in time to see a flash of brilliant orange swoop from the limb above his head and flutter out of sight into the underbrush that crept to the edge of the town. With its passage, a deep sense of security and comfort flooded over him, sweeping away the unsettling dreams that had haunted the night. Relieved, he drew in a deep breath of the humid air, then parted the river's slow-moving waters with hardly a splash.

THE SENSE OF RELIEF AND SECURITY was short lived. By the time he returned from the river in the strengthening light of sunrise, clad only in breechcloth and moccasins, a number of the Seneca leaders had gathered outside the council house.

The members of Carleton's party stood slightly apart from them. Andrews looked troubled. Alarm etched Isaiah's usually inscrutable countenance, and young Sammy's brow was furrowed with unease. Even the faces of the two Mahicans reflected unmistakable concern.

Swiftly Carleton scanned the faces of the Seneca. Black Horse was nowhere in evidence, and none of the elders from Buck Tooth were present, only those who had come from a distance.

Those in Half Moon's party. And with them, Great Owl.

Raking his dripping hair back from his face, Carleton strode past them to Andrews. "What's going on?"

Andrews shrugged. "We don't know. Even Konkapot and Aupaumut haven't a clue. None of the fellows from Buck Tooth have shown up, and Cornplanter, Red Jacket, and many of the other sachems have gone. All I can make out is that they've already come to a decision, and they're not letting us in on it."

As on the previous day, Carleton felt hostile eyes boring into him. Glancing around, he met Great Owl's narrowed gaze. The Indian had stepped very close to him, and as their eyes met, the glint in Great Owl's brought the blood pounding into Carleton's ears.

Instinct told him he'd been a fool to leave the council house without rifle or pistol. But they were out of reach, along with his tomahawk and knife. He swung back with the sinking realization that none of his companions had their weapons either, in a suspended instant read the horrified warning in Andrews's eyes.

"Jon—!"

From behind him a vicious, glancing blow caught his head just above the right temple. Unbalanced, he reeled sideways and fell to his knees, one hand pressed to the sticky wetness oozing through his hair, the other outstretched to keep him from collapsing to the ground.

"No! Stop!"

"What be the meaning of this? Let us go!"

He was only vaguely aware of Andrews's shout, of Isaiah's angry demands. The Mahicans were calling out loudly, but all of them seemed to be far away and moving off into the distance.

He sucked burning air into his lungs. A black mist pricked by a thousand dancing, pulsating points of light obscured the periphery of his vision.

Before he could fight to his feet, they were on him. Rough hands shoved him back onto his haunches, another grabbed his hair, twisting it so tightly that he gave an involuntary cry. With a shock he realized it was Half Moon who held him.

"This is pure treachery! Let him go!"

"My brothers, how can you do this? We came to you in peace!"

The voices of Andrews and Aupaumut, along with the sounds of scuffling, diminished by degrees, drawing steadily farther away. Disoriented and faint, sick to his stomach from the viciousness of the blow, Carleton tried to twist around to see what was happening to the others. But his captors held him so that he could not.

"Charles!" His voice sounded so weak and hoarse in his ears that he doubted anyone heard him.

He felt the knife blade bite into the skin at his hairline, felt the trickle of blood along his brow. As his head was pulled viciously back, his eyes focused on Great Owl's face. The Mohawk glared at him, his face contorted with hate.

Before Carleton's eyes rose up a stark and horrifying image from one of his many sojourns in the forest during the French and Indian War: the bloated bodies of a family of seven slaughtered and methodically scalped by a band of Delaware, his Shawnee companions had told him, judging by the prints their moccasins had left in the dirt. It had been all he could do to keep from vomiting.

His blurred vision swam. As the last strength deserted his limbs, he cried out once more, his plea no more than a whisper.

"Jésus, m'aident!"

Chapter Twelve

ELIZABETH SQUINTED into the early morning light, her face turned to the fresh breeze and foaming salt spray thrown up by the sloop's raked prow. She glanced up to where foresail, mainsail, and jib billowed outward, heeling the boat well over to its port side. The creak of wood and rope, the thrum of wind in canvas, and the screech of seagulls banking sharply overhead filled her ears.

The sloop cut smoothly through the channel between Noddles Island and Charlestown peninsula. Straight ahead, the misty, wooded coastline for which she headed drew swiftly nearer. Illuminated here and there by shafts of sunlight slanting through the cottony clouds that floated above the eastern hills, details of the weathered houses and modest shops that made up the village of Winisimmit came into clearer focus with each passing second.

At the captain's barked order, Elizabeth sprang to the ropes with the crew to bring down the sails. Each expanse of canvas fluttered and dropped in turn, and the sloop lost speed, straightening until the deck rode level. As the crew scrambled to furl the jib, the pilot brought the small craft expertly alongside the single dock that jutted into the bay slightly more than a mile straight north of Boston's North End.

Tugging her fisherman's cap farther over her brow, Elizabeth caught up the small pack she had brought with her and slung it over her shoulder. It was a relief to finally escape from Boston's stifling confines. The six weeks that had passed since she and Tess had watched the gates of the beleaguered port close behind them felt like months—years.

In that time her intention to preside over the most fashionable salon in Boston had come to reality. Officers from the British garrison and leading Tories of the town flocked to the town house several evenings each week for dinner and card parties and musical performances. Still, the necessity to remain always on guard against any misstep, the inability to enter and leave the town at will, and the nagging anxiety for news about Carleton left her feeling like a prisoner in her own home.

At the moment, delight at her temporary release was tempered by the uncomfortable awareness of Dalton's covert scrutiny. She had the alarming sense that he suspected more than she wanted him to, more than was entirely safe. He had given her no reason to distrust him other than the overly familiar manner he had adopted since that early morning meeting six weeks earlier. But the subtle change in him awakened a strong sense of anxiety and danger.

It was as though he knew she was a woman. A man did not look at another man the way he had begun looking at her. At the memory of how he had scrutinized her face that morning after her return to Boston, a cold shiver prickled down her spine.

Dalton intercepted her before she left the boat. "Ye'll make it back a'fore we sail tonight?"

She nodded, quickly shifted her gaze away from the interest she read in his eyes. As she strode off in the direction of the village center, she found herself wishing mightily there were some plausible reason for the *Prudence* to stop at the Boston docks on the way out of the harbor so she could escape the necessity of spending the entire night at sea and under Dalton's control. But such a stop would draw immediate interest from the British sentries, interest she could not afford to arouse.

Another concern weighed heavily on her mind. She could not shake off an oppressive sense that somewhere far away Carleton's expedition had met disaster. Several times during the past few nights she had awakened from a dream that she could neither fully recall nor completely dismiss, one that left her shaken. If she admitted the truth, the main reason for her visit to the American camp was the hope that some news of Carleton and his party had reached it.

Resolutely pushing her unsettling thoughts to the back of her mind, she turned toward Cambridge, slightly more than three miles away. Before she reached the road to the ferry over the Mystic River, a supply wagon from one of the Continental Army's nearby camps overtook her, headed in the same direction. Gratefully she accepted the driver's invitation to join him.

By now the blazing August sun had burned off the mist, and its warmth, coupled with the motion of the horses plodding sluggishly along the dusty road, lulled her almost to sleep. She roused with a jerk when they rumbled over the Mystic River bridge, then again when the driver pulled his team to a halt on the outskirts of Cambridge, outside the lower fort overlooking the Back Bay. After thanking him for the ride, she walked the short distance into town.

Informed that Washington had moved his headquarters, she was directed to a gracious mansion that stood well back amid lush gardens along Tory Row, abandoned some time earlier by its owner, John Vassall. She took a post on the lawn, concealed in the shade of one of the stately chestnuts that surrounded the house.

For some time she watched the officers who passed in and out, at length decided there was no alternative except to beard the lion. Boldly she strode up to the front door, pretending more confidence than she felt and wondering how she was going to persuade the general's aides to give a lowly fisherman an audience with their commander.

She had just reached the steps when a rider galloped up the drive behind her and pulled his spirited white horse to a sliding halt at the far end of the walk. Washington sprang from the saddle and threw the reins over the hitching post. His brow furrowed in a disgusted frown, he strode up the walk toward her, every line of his body and countenance conveying bad humor.

He started to brush by her. Without thinking she reached out and caught him by the sleeve. "Please, sir, I must speak with you."

He halted and stared down at her, his face darkening even more. "I don't have the time right now, son," he returned, his tone gruff, though not unkind.

She threw a swift glance around her to make sure no one was in earshot, caught a fleeting glimpse of two officers approaching, one coming around the corner of the house, the other walking rapidly toward them from the carriageway. Both were glaring at her.

"But, sir, I have to return to Boston tonight. Lord Percy's ball is tomorrow, you see," she explained breathlessly, keeping her voice low enough that the rapidly closing officers would not make out her words.

Washington started and bent to scrutinize her face. Suppressing a smile, he grabbed her by the arm.

Just then the officers reached them. Recognizing the first, Elizabeth hastily averted her face from his annoyed gaze.

It was portly young Henry Knox, now an officer in the artillery corps. Before the skirmishes at Lexington and Concord, Elizabeth had spent many hours browsing in his bookshop and visiting with his young wife. The blood pulsed into her cheeks, and she bent her head so her hat shaded her face from his piercing grey eyes.

Washington raised his hand to arrest the two officers and directed a stern glance at the second officer, his aide, Colonel Reed. "I have pressing business with this young man. We are not to be disturbed unless the British begin an attack."

Without waiting for their response, he beckoned Elizabeth to follow and led the way into the house.

✹ ✹ ✹

WASHINGTON SAT BACK in his chair behind the writing table. "The truth is that if Gage does attack, we quickly will be reduced to fighting with rocks and clubs. Our stores of powder and ammunition are much smaller than I was led to believe."

"These constant bombardments can't help. We can hardly sleep at night for the shells flying overhead."

Washington gave an exasperated sigh. "I have given orders time and again that if Gage wants to waste his powder and shot, let him. His gunners are doing no execution at all, and our men are becoming exceptionally adept at dodging missiles. But no matter the orders, the men will return fire, even though I am sure they are having no more effect than our opponents."

Elizabeth grimaced. "We've taken an occasional hit, so their efforts haven't entirely been in vain."

For a moment Washington considered her without speaking, then, bitterness edging his tone, growled, "Every assurance I was given of the army's condition and situation has proven false. If I survive this assignment with a single shred of my reputation left intact, it will be a miracle."

On impulse, she leaned forward and grasped the edge of the table. "Your Excellency, there are many of us praying for you. You are not alone. Mighty forces will gather to your aid if you do not falter in your purpose."

She stopped, embarrassed, convinced she had gone too far. But instead of appearing annoyed, Washington relaxed perceptibly and conceded a faint smile.

"Thank you for that reminder. I do feel the prayers lifted up for me, and I am grateful for them. As long as the decision is mine to make, we shall stand firm. But I depend on the resolution of others, so you might include them in your prayers as well."

He changed the subject with a quick gesture. "The intelligence you have sent over has gone far in relieving my mind. I am afraid rounding up munitions and whipping the troops into some semblance of order will engage us for a longer time than I anticipated. I am not in any hurry for Gage to decide on a move—or has Howe taken over by now?"

"Nothing has been received from the Ministry, so Gage is still officially in command. But the officers I've talked to are convinced he will be replaced. They consider him highly ineffectual and believe the king must also."

Frowning, she pleated the hem of her short seaman's jacket between her fingers. "With the reinforcements that have landed recently, he has around six thousand effectives and sufficient ammunition for an attack. But all he does is extend his fortifications. Howe and the other generals are frustrated, to say the least."

She detailed the conflict and political maneuvering she had observed between Gage and his three subordinates. "If my impressions of Howe, Clinton, and Burgoyne are correct," she concluded, her tone dry, "then no doubt letters have been fairly flying between here and London—all to Gage's detriment."

"Which can only help us. Having been the target of a few such missives myself, however, I do sympathize with Gage's situation. By the way, how are you and your aunt getting along? We have heard many rumors about the unhappy conditions in the town."

Elizabeth shrugged. "I'm sure most of what you've heard is true. I've been volunteering in the hospital as much as I can, and conditions are still appalling after all these weeks. There've been so many funerals Gage ordered the churches to stop tolling their bells. There's almost no fresh produce, and even fish is scarce because so many of the fishermen have joined our army. The horses have hardly any fodder, and most of the cattle have been slaughtered to save them from starvation and to provide meat. We're seeing an alarming rise in all manner of illnesses."

"We have heard as much from the deserters who keep trickling in," Washington returned. "They are our only source of information these days except for what you have been able to send us."

"Gage has tightened security tremendously, so that is all the intelligence I have to offer. My real reason for coming is because we are dying for news—and because I'm hoping I can smuggle provisions back with me. Like everyone else, Aunt Tess and I have only what we can grow in our garden and what little is available at the markets, which is mainly fish, when we can get it." Laughing, she added, "In fact, I have strict orders not to return unless I bring fresh meat!"

Washington chuckled. "Colonel Stern has been anxious to see you. I am sure he can be persuaded to supply you with a hot meal and supplies to take along."

They talked for a short time longer. With Washington's stern caution to take care to attract no attention, Elizabeth slipped from the house through a back door. By good luck, she soon secured another ride, this time all the way to Roxbury.

She found her uncle at the edge of the camp conferring with his officers. Waving away the sentry who attempted to intercept her, Stern hastily finished his business, then accompanied her into the house.

"It's about time you showed up." Although his tone was gruff, his embrace assured her of his concern.

For several moments she clung to him, grateful beyond words to see him again. Almost as hard as Carleton's absence was the separation from this uncle she loved so dearly. At last she pulled back to look into his face, laughing.

"Now, Uncle Josh, you know I was under strict orders not to come over unless I had important business. And I do. Aunt Tess and I are fairly starving for fresh meat. We've eaten enough beans, salt pork, and fish to last several lifetimes."

Stern grinned. "So that's what it's come to. I've lost your affectionate regard to a pound of beef."

She giggled. "A pheasant or woodcock or two would do as well. In the end, I fear, the demands of the stomach outweigh even the most tender emotions."

He strode to the escritoire and returned carrying a small, sealed packet. "We shall see. Jon included this with his report to Washington from Ticonderoga."

"*Oh!*" Catching it from his hand, she pressed it to her bosom. "Fare thee well, then, poor stomach!"

With trembling fingers she tore it open and gasped with delight. Nestled inside were an Indian necklace hand wrought of silver, a matching brooch, and several rings, along with a letter.

Expectantly she unfolded the piece of paper that accompanied the items. Scanning it, she directed a questioning look at her uncle. Several lines of apparently random letters were scrawled across the page.

Stern handed her a small scrap of paper with a smug smile. "You'll need the key, of course. I don't suppose you'll want help translating his message."

The twinkle in his eyes caused her to laugh. "I don't suppose I will."

She hurried to the escritoire and sat down. Comparing the coded message to the key Stern had given her, she quickly translated the letter's contents.

My love,

We leave this morning. How far away you seem, and yet the next days will take me ever farther from your side. My only comfort is that every mile I travel from you now brings me closer to the day when we shall be together again—and, if God wills, remain so for all our lives.

Dearest, there is not a second when I do not yearn to hold you in my arms, to give you the kiss I dared not when we parted. Forgive me for my weakness that day. My heart was breaking, as I know yours was. Had I yielded then, I'd never have let you go.

Please accept these small tokens of my love. I pray that you are well and safe and that our great Guide will preserve and bless you until this separation is ended. I can write no more except

I love you.
Jonathan

She sat for some moments, motionless except for the heaving of her breast, her head bowed while tears fell upon the page. At length she became aware of Stern's hands gently massaging her shoulders. Rising swiftly, she turned to throw her arms around his neck and lay her head against his breast.

"I had not thought it possible to feel such grief and yet live."

"Ah, now, before you know it he'll be back, safe and sound, and this will all be over. You'll see."

She pulled away. Accepting the handkerchief he offered, with trembling fingers she dabbed at the tears that insisted on trickling down her cheeks.

"The last few nights I've had terrible dreams," she said, her voice ragged. "He is in some trouble or distress—I am certain of it."

"Dreams are nothing but the shadows of our fears," Stern scoffed.

"This is different. I'm so frightened, Uncle Josh. Something has gone horribly wrong—I feel it. The worst is that we may never know what happened."

He sobered. "If you're that convinced of it, then we need to pray. If Jon is under attack, his surest defense is the Almighty."

He took both her hands in his. Together they knelt and for some time pleaded for the lives of Carleton and his companions. Yet in spite of a clear sense of God's presence, no reassurance came to Elizabeth, and an ever deeper dread settled into her breast.

158 ❋ J. M. Hochstetler

❋ ❋ ❋

Rosy sunset melted into the violet shades of night, shadowing the wooded hills and the sprawling army camps that surrounded Winisimmit and casting a pale aura across the harbor. On the town's outskirts, Levi pulled the lumbering wagon to a halt beside a sandbank overgrown with sea grasses.

"I thought it would get easier with time. Instead, it seems like it gets worse."

Elizabeth leaned against him. "I miss Will too—more every day. But it's not your fault that you survived the battle and he didn't. If anyone is to blame, it's me."

Levi wrapped his arm around her and held her tightly. "Don't you go sayin' that, Cuz, for it isn't true. I keep askin' myself, if there is a God, why did he let Will die? But so many others died too, so why not Will, or me, or you? It's just that I'm feelin' right bitter. I'm workin' to get over it."

"I know how you feel. I tell myself it wasn't God who caused this war. He doesn't force anyone to obey him, though sometimes I wish he would."

Her voice trailed off, and she gave a short laugh.

Levi planted a quick kiss on her forehead. "Now you be careful goin' back. I sure wish you didn't have to go out fishin' with Dalton and his crew on your way back and forth. It's dangerous work. I couldn't take losin' you too."

She grabbed her bundle, now several pounds heavier, and jumped down from the seat. "It's the safest and least suspicious way in and out of Boston. And I can't sit idly by and watch the crew work, all the while wondering what I'm doing there. This way I'm just a boy Dalton occasionally employs for temporary work."

Levi returned her grin, then clucked to the horses and slapped the reins across their back. Turning them into the carriageway of the nearest house, he backed the wagon around and returned her cheerful wave as he passed by in the opposite direction.

Reluctantly she headed for the wharf, where the *Prudence* was docked. She had gone no farther than the tavern a short distance past the house, however, when the sound of a voice hailing her caused her to start.

It was Dalton. Standing on the tavern's porch in the shadows outside the bars of golden lantern light that slanted through the windows behind him, he leaned against the railing, smoking a pipe. The calculation in his narrowed glance brought all her worries flooding back.

He came down the steps to join her, and without speaking they strode together to the wharf. Aboard the *Prudence,* the crew already scrambled across the deck, making final preparations to sail.

Throughout the next hours, far out at sea beyond the coast, she threw herself into the night's work. As always, the sloop's crew accepted her comradeship as though she were fully one of them, with an occasional wink or encouraging smile. It was clear that, whatever suspicions they might harbor, none of them intended to delve into matters they did not conceive to be their business.

Unlike their captain.

Her thoughts ran on an endless circuit that went nowhere. *Did he see Levi and me embracing? He suspects that I am Oriole, and he almost certainly has concluded that I am a woman. If he saw me with Levi, must he not also suspect that I am related in some way to him and Uncle Josh?*

Her uncle and Dalton were casual acquaintances, she knew. It was Stern who had originally set up their contact, and all the correspondence she had passed through Dalton was addressed to her uncle. If Dalton knew that Levi was Stern's son—and more than likely he did—might the captain not conclude from seeing them together that her relationship with the Sterns was closer than that of mere acquaintances?

Certainly Elizabeth's identity would be easy enough to find out by means of a few discreet questions to the right people. Stern had no daughters. He had, however, two nieces, one of whom was a child three thousand miles away.

She felt sick with anxiety. The sense that far away in the wilderness Carleton fought for his life against an unknown enemy knotted her stomach until she feared it would give up its contents. And now this.

It was no coincidence, but a concerted attack. She knew it suddenly. Fighting to draw in the laden nets, shoulder to shoulder with her mates in the transparent, moonlit blackness of the night, tossed by the restless waves of the sea, she sensed demonic forces gathering around her.

Forces she could not see and against whom she held no power.

Chapter Thirteen

"**I** WOULD BE MOST DELIGHTED if you would favor me with the minuet, Miss Howard."

Elizabeth felt Tess stiffen beside her, but she pretended not to notice. The younger officers who clustered around them wasted no time stepping out of Burgoyne's way. Exchanging rueful glances, they drifted off in the direction of the punch bowl.

Forcing a smile, Elizabeth made a deep curtsy. "I am most honored, sir."

She allowed him to claim her hand despite a prickle of discomfort at the way his glance raked over her and irritation at his overbearing manner. The musicians had already begun to play the lilting strains of the minuet, and the general escorted her to the head of the gaily attired dancers.

An accomplished if flamboyant dancer, Burgoyne moved to the music with confident ease. The image that would not leave Elizabeth's thoughts, however, was of him sitting in the tribunal at Carleton's court-martial, smug satisfaction in his smile, while the bailiff read the charges of treason, desertion, and murder.

She intended to escape as soon as the minuet ended. But to her dismay Burgoyne refused to relinquish her hand and steered her to an out-of-the-way corner.

"I don't mind telling you how much you intrigue me," he drawled. "Ever since we met that day at Province House, I've been longing for an opportunity to speak with you privately."

He was far too close, and she earnestly wanted her hand back in her own possession. Favoring him with the sweetest smile she could muster, she searched for a diplomatic pretext to extricate herself from his company.

She had danced every dance without respite, and her head throbbed from the music, the babble of conversation, and the heat of the room. Given Burgoyne's reputation and his actions since arriving in Boston, he was very close to being the last person in whose company she ever wished to be, no matter how much intelligence he might let fall. Wishing she had heeded Tess's warning glance and pleaded a full dance card, she threw a surreptitious glance around the ballroom for rescue.

Her aunt was out of reach on the far side of the dancers, engaged in conversation with an animated group. Meanwhile, Elizabeth's usual circle of admirers appeared to be soothing their wounded pride with manly draughts of rum punch.

Just then Lord Percy stepped to her side, unwittingly saving her from an indiscretion. He swept her and Burgoyne a graceful bow.

"I do believe the gavotte will begin any minute. Would you favor me, my dear Miss Howard?"

Elizabeth transferred her hand to Percy's with more haste than she intended. Assuming an apologetic air, she said to Burgoyne, "You won't think ill of me, sir, if I give the next dance to our host?"

Burgoyne flushed, but after a barely perceptible hesitation, he bowed. "If you are free later, perhaps you will favor me with an audience."

Elizabeth gave a light laugh that implied consent, but promised nothing. Feeling as though she had been snatched back from the edge of a dangerous precipice, she allowed Percy to guide her through the crush of British officers and their ladies and the prominent citizens of the town.

Because of a shortage of candles, the expansive space was more dimly lighted than usual. The effect was to cast a romantic mood across an assembly that desperately needed cheer and distraction. In spite of an apparent gaiety, the ball was turning out to be a somewhat somber affair. The loss of so many officers in battle hung over the room like the shadows that moved restlessly across the walls. Everyone in attendance felt the void left behind by those who were missing.

As though in denial of more sober reflections, all across the room rustled the peacock hues of luxurious satin and silk, brocade, damask, and lace. In fashion and style, the embroidered waistcoats, elegant smallclothes, and powdered hair of the men gave no quarter to the elaborate petticoats stretched over wide panniers and the towering wigs of the ladies. Even the scarlet uniform coats of the officers hardly stood their ground against the brilliance of their rivals.

For the evening Elizabeth had chosen an elegant gown of gold brocade with a fitted bodice that showed her slender waist and full bosom to the best advantage. Already she had attracted the attentions of many of the higher-ranking officers as well as the younger ones. Even Howe and Clinton had briefly paid her court.

For the most part, however, Howe divided his time between his faro cards and Elizabeth Loring, the young, blonde wife of Joshua Loring. Her open flirtation with the general was drawing variously knowing looks or contemptuous sneers from Lord Percy's guests—though not from her husband. A coarse-featured wine and liquor merchant, Loring appeared more concerned with the potential advantages that might come to him from Howe's adulterous attentions than by the ruin of his or his wife's reputation.

Mrs. Loring was not beautiful so much as sensually alluring, Elizabeth decided. Her main interests seemed to be flirtation and gambling. There was a languid calculation in her manner that repelled Elizabeth, but Howe was clearly smitten with her.

Percy's voice jarred her from her reverie. "If I were you, I'd be very careful about accepting the attentions of a man like Burgoyne," he advised in an undertone as they reached the head of the line of dancers. "He looks at every woman as though he wants to devour her. I'm not so sure he'd take no for an answer if his advances were rejected."

She threw a glance in the direction of the general's retreating back, then looked up at Percy with a smile of genuine gratitude. "Thank you for rescuing me. Unlike some others, I do not enjoy or desire the attentions of a married man."

Percy bent to kiss her hand. "Then you are wise beyond your years. Promise me you'll never change."

The emotion in his eyes touched her, and she returned the gentle pressure of his fingers. "I will not, dear friend. I'll take your advice and gladly avoid Burgoyne from now on."

Since she had returned to Boston, she reflected, Percy had gone out of his way to be especially kind and thoughtful. She suspected he pitied her because of Carleton's defection and believed her heart to be broken. He must, of course, never guess the truth.

As they sought their places, and then waited for the dance to begin, he said gravely, "I had a letter the other day from Lady Anne. She wrote of meeting your parents at a ball and wished to convey their greetings as well as her own."

Pleased, Elizabeth said, "I do hope you will thank your dear wife for me for her kindness. I hope some day I'll have the opportunity to meet her."

"I hope you shall," Percy returned. "I miss both your parents a good deal. I can't imagine how painful their absence must be for you."

Tears sprang to her eyes, but before she could respond, the first strains of the music reached them. Struggling to concentrate on the intricate patterns of the gavotte, she felt herself torn between a genuine liking for Percy that made deceiving him especially painful, and the memory of his part in Carleton's court-martial.

After Gage, the earl was the one most responsible for Carleton's being condemned to hang. Yet she knew Percy had loved Carleton as a friend. It was that love that doubtless had made the revelation of Carleton's true loyalties and role as a spy all the more hateful to Percy and had left him feeling personally betrayed.

Returning that love freely, Carleton wrestled with his conscience over the part he had been persuaded to play, even as Elizabeth did. Was there any answer to their dilemma? Where were the boundaries in a time of war? Were there any?

She was relieved when the gavotte ended. Pleading a headache, she persuaded Percy to escort her downstairs to the quiet and relative coolness of the library. After promising to check on her within the half hour, he left, closing the door behind him.

With a sigh, she squeezed her petticoats with her arms to collapse the panniers and sank into a deep wing chair. Her elbow resting on the arm of the chair, her chin propped disconsolately in her hand, she tipped her face to the cooling breeze that wafted through the open terrace doors.

Outside, the lush lawns and extensive orchards that surrounded the palatial mansion glimmered faintly in the muted starlight. Built in the third decade of the century by Gardiner Greene, one of Boston's wealthiest citizens, the house occupied a portion of one of the three peaks that together made up Beacon Hill and provided a fine view across the city. Greenhouses on the grounds, the first in Boston, were the source of the lavish, fragrant arrangements of flowers that abundantly furnished the mansion.

Straightening, she pressed her fingertips hard against her temples, overcome by a tangle of emotions. She had not anticipated how difficult it would become to continue the charade she played. She had to humbly admit that Washington had been right. If she and Carleton had wed, her role would have become impossible. Yet it was vitally necessary if the lives and freedom of her countrymen were to be preserved.

She took a deep breath, fought to calm herself enough to consider with cold logic her best course in dealing with Dalton and now Burgoyne. Dalton knew far too much about her connection to Stern. And Burgoyne? Was he intrigued with her because of her connection to Carleton? Was his motive to gain revenge on a man he despised by ruining the woman he loved?

Again the uncomfortable memory returned of her encounter with Will shortly before he had been killed on Breed's Hill. *It's a pretty good bet you're flirting with them a lot to get the information you do, and maybe more than would be pleasing to God,* he had cautioned her. *No amount of intelligence is worth putting your reputation or your life in jeopardy. It may seem like a game to get what you want, but some men don't take no for an answer.*

As it did often at unguarded moments, a sharp lance-point of pain stabbed through her breast. How she missed Will! How she wished she could tell him now that he had been right and seek his wise counsel.

And Carleton's. A deep longing for the strength of his arms flooded over her. If only she could hear his lazy drawl, see that teasing smile that put everything into perspective and made anything possible, drink the fire and wine of his kisses.

He *had* to be safe. He *would* return. And then surely Washington would relent in his opposition to their marriage. But even if she and Carleton had to wait for a little while longer, the joy that lay before them would be worth any price.

It was only that the fulfillment of their hopes seemed so terribly far away, the road strewn with such daunting obstacles . . .

At the sound of the door creaking open and the scrape of a boot on the threshold, she started and sprang to her feet. Spinning around with guilty surprise, she faced Burgoyne.

"*Oh!*"

"There you are. I wondered where you'd run off to." Clicking the door firmly shut behind him, he crossed the room to her side in several long strides.

Pretending distraction, she imposed a short distance between them. "The music . . . I . . . my head is throbbing, and I—"

Again he closed the space between them, bent over her solicitously. "Is there anything I can do?"

"No! I mean . . . it's late and I'm quite exhausted. Lord Percy went to find my aunt to take me home."

Her bluff did not deter the general. "Then I'm afraid he's been waylaid. The last I saw him, he was dancing with Miss Inman."

Before she could step away, he captured her hand, his fingers tightening over hers so she could not snatch it away. Dismayed at her lack of composure, she struggled to persuade herself that chance had handed her an opportunity she could not afford to squander. Somehow she had to take control of this encounter and learn what the generals were planning. Instead, all she wanted was for him to go away.

"I'd like to talk to you for a moment, if I may."

At her questioning look, he continued, "I'd like to know more about your relationship with *General* Carleton." He twisted Carleton's rank into a sneer.

Her heart sank at the confirmation of her suspicions. She tipped her head haughtily to one side.

"Believe me, sir, as I have repeated many times, he was nothing to me before his defection, and he is even less to me now."

"I can't believe the feeling was mutual. To hear Percy tell it, Carleton was a man in love."

Elizabeth kept her lips curved into a smile, though she was very far from feeling merry. "If so, it was with someone else. Our custom when General Carleton and I were together was to dispute even the most trivial issues. As a consequence, we were generally at pains to avoid each other."

Burgoyne returned her smile with a fervent one, but she sensed that he was not convinced. "Please allow me the liberty of observing that if he was not head over heels, he was either blind or insensible. Your charms, my dear, would tempt the devil himself."

The message she read in Burgoyne's prominent, heavy-lidded eyes brought the blood into her cheeks. "And are you, sir . . . the devil?"

The words were out of her mouth before she could stop them. On second thought, she did not regret them, and she added a tinkling laugh.

Burgoyne flushed, then to her surprise laughed as well. Bending even more closely over her, he murmured, "I can assure you that the devil is a most delightful companion when it comes to the pleasures of the bed."

His gaze lingered at her lips, traveled deliberately to her bosom. Repulsed, she fought to suppress a shudder of disgust.

He slipped his other arm around her waist, drew her still closer in a grip that would not easily be broken. "What a woman like you needs is a real man."

She ached to slap him, to fight free of his grasp. Instead, she drawled, "And who would you have in mind, sir?"

"Oh, that I think you can guess."

She realized with dismay that he meant to kiss her. Hastily she averted her face, in the same movement wrenched her hand free of his clasp. His lips grazed her cheek, but before she could twist free from the arm that imprisoned her, he tightened his grasp.

"Please, sir!" she gasped, suddenly furious. "This is not seemly."

"I confess I have no resistance at all when it comes to a fiery wench," he murmured against her ear. "I know what a woman like you wants. Come away with me to my lodgings, and I'll show you what the devil can do."

"Sir, you are no gentleman!" Her voice shaking, she fought to break his hold, caring nothing now for what he might think.

This time his soft laugh held menace. "I never claimed to be one."

Behind them, the door abruptly flung open. Releasing her, Burgoyne straightened and swung to face Tess. Flushing at her cold look, he made a hasty bow.

Tess conceded the most perfunctory of curtsies in return, her glance traveling from him to Elizabeth's hot, tear-streaked face. Keeping her expression neutral, she said in a cool voice, "Please excuse my interruption, General Burgoyne. I was told my niece is unwell, and I thought it wise to take her home."

"She told me so herself," Burgoyne blustered. "I was on the point of coming to find you."

Tess's mouth curved into a smile that did not reach her eyes. "How kind." She turned to Elizabeth. "Are you ready to go, my dear?"

Elizabeth all but ran to her. "I believe I am." Without glancing back at Burgoyne, she added, "Good night, General."

Within seconds they waited on the front step while the footman brought the phaeton around. Blinking hard and biting her lip, Elizabeth frowned in an effort to focus on the shadowy trees on the other side of the carriageway. She wanted to run to their shelter and disappear.

"Percy related what happened with Burgoyne and told me he'd escorted you to the library. When I noticed the general had disappeared, I came at once."

"Thank you," Elizabeth whispered, her tearful voice shaking as much as her body. "You came not a moment too soon."

"You must never tempt a man like that. He has no scruples. Not all the intelligence in the world is worth your virtue, and I believe Washington would agree with me. I know Jon would."

Elizabeth nodded, her head bowed to hide her scarlet cheeks. Unbidden, the memory of Dalton's lingering gaze burned through her, intensifying her distress.

Almost she blurted out her fears to Tess, but she choked the impulse. Most likely she was overreacting. No need to alarm her aunt further at this point. The incident with Burgoyne was concern enough.

Still trembling, she waited for Tess to enter the phaeton, then allowed the footman to hand her up. Leaning her head against the seat back without meeting her aunt's sober gaze, she closed her eyes and tried to let the worries of the past days drift away with the carriage's soothing sway and the muted, rhythmic clop of the gelding's hooves.

Chapter Fourteen

D RIVEN BRUTALLY FOR TWO DAYS, during which he was repeatedly beaten and offered little food, drink, or rest, Carleton was already in physical extremity by the time his captors neared their destination. Late in the afternoon the party halted some distance outside the town and made camp while several messengers rode ahead to announce that a prisoner was being brought in the next morning.

He knew what lay ahead of him. As a youth he had seen the running of the gauntlet more than once on his forays among the Shawnee, and he tried to force his body to relax, his mind to focus on surviving the next day's ordeal.

But survive for what fate? he wondered, bleak despair flooding over him. *For torture designed to break me until I plead for death?*

He was grateful that he had never witnessed the Iroquois practice of killing a victim with excruciating slowness as a sacrifice to the spirit of war and hunting. He wished he had never heard the gruesome descriptions of it. Ingenious efforts were exercised to extend the ordeal for a minimum of twenty-four hours before the victim was allowed to die and his captors devoured his flesh so that they might absorb his courage and strength. For a warrior, this form of death was considered a high honor.

Carleton quailed at thought of facing such a test. At the same time, he knew absolutely that to show any hint of terror would be immediately fatal. Teeth gritted, eyes fixed straight ahead, he summoned his last reserves of determination to maintain a stony, defiant expression and not shrink when blows were directed at him. He resolved to die before he would beg for mercy.

Hunger, thirst, and exhaustion tormented him. The chill of the forest nights had been as miserable as the heat of the days and had allowed him no rest. A thunderstorm the previous evening had not improved matters. By now he was so weak he could no longer still the tremor of his limbs.

His bare feet were raw, torn and bruised from the punishing run through the forest, and his head throbbed without ceasing from the blow Great Owl had delivered. Itching welts from the bites of ants, mosquitoes, and bees increased his misery. When he was staked spread-eagled to the ground as on the previous nights, his suffering reached an intensity that made him doubt he would be able to endure the next few hours, much less run the gauntlet on entrance into the town.

Unable to sleep, he found himself wondering about Great Owl's part in the ambush. What had been the Mohawk sachem's motive? Was it possible he had learned about the reward Gage was offering for him?

The more Carleton thought about it, the more sense it made. If it was so and they meant not to torture him to death, but to turn him over to the British, then opportunities opened up for escape on the journey—if he could endure through the next few days.

A burst of elation was short-lived, however, replaced by equally deep sense of hoplessness at the stark reality that faced him. In the past two punishing days he had never been left alone or unbound, and the pace set by his captors had kept him too exhausted even to attempt escape, much less to succeed. That was likely to be the case no matter where they took him. And once back in the hands of the British, he would be summarily executed.

The worst agony that possessed his mind, however, was the nagging anxiety for Andrews and the others. What had become of them? Had they been slaughtered outright? Were they even now being tortured? Did they curse him in their torment?

It had been his decision to bring them on a quest he had known to be fraught with peril and likely to fail. The blame for their fate was utterly his.

And Elizabeth? Would he ever see her again? Would she ever learn his fate—or he, hers? What grief would she be forced to endure? Would she think he had abandoned her?

God is watching over you. Though you suffer great affliction, he will bring you safely home.

The memory of the vision in the forest on the way to Buck Tooth mocked him without ceasing. Had it been an illusion meant only to delude him into a false sense of security? If it had been a true promise given by God, then where was God now when Carleton most needed him?

Since turning his life over to God again after so many years of wandering, he had faced one disaster after another: caught in the midst of battle on the wrong side; arrested, beaten, and sentenced to hang for treason by the British; now captured and abused, either to face death by torture at the hands of the Seneca or delivery to the British and execution.

He had no one to blame but himself, of course. He had not been forced to go on this mission. In the end, despite the pressure Washington had exerted, Carleton had made the choice freely. Could it be that he had once more stepped outside of God's will and was facing the just consequences of disobedience? Was he even *capable* of knowing God's will?

Or was he being justly punished for the years he had spent sunk in a life so sinful he cringed at the memory? Was there no forgiveness after all? Certainly he did not deserve pardon.

In the unrelenting blackness of the night, another thought gradually sank in. Was this instead the attack of the Adversary? Did not the Evil One turn his severest onslaught against those most earnestly committed to serving God?

The question returned, with more urgency this time: Where was God when his children suffered extremity? Was it God's purpose to simply abandon them to fight their battles alone as best they could?

Why have you forsaken me? he cried out. *I have turned my life back to you. I am striving to be obedient. Cannot I expect your protection?*

By degrees, through his panic, he became aware of a familiar, unearthly presence surrounding and upholding him in the midst of that hostile camp—a presence that brooded over him like a barely perceptible breeze wafting from the depths of the forest.

In his desperation, he clung to that presence as a man clings by his fingertips to the rocky edge of a precipice above a vast abyss. And yet he felt more forsaken than he had even as a small child, torn away from his family and home and sent to an unknown relative in a far country.

✦ ✦ ✦

THE LINE STRETCHED for almost a quarter of a mile from outside the town gate back to the great council house at its center. A double row of men, women, and children, all the town's inhabitants and more than likely some from outlying villages, stood facing each other, chattering and laughing in anticipation.

Most of them waved in the air clubs and tree branches, supple switches cut from willows, thorn-studded lengths of blackberry whips, buckskin straps, even tomahawks. Nearest to him, several held fistfuls of what he guessed to be either dirt or stones.

They had torn from him even his breechcloth, and he faced the jeering, mocking throng without covering of any kind. Pushing to the back of his consciousness the multiple complaints of his aching body, he focused his eyes on the distant door of the council house.

If he could reach it, then he had some hope of surviving for another day. If he fell beneath their blows, they might well club him to death on the spot.

Help me! he pleaded silently.

Half Moon and Great Owl stood to each side and slightly behind him, waiting for the drumbeat from inside the council house to signal the beginning of Carleton's ordeal. In his hand, Half Moon held a particularly savage-looking club cut of pine, with sharp splinters, rough knobs, and jagged knots protruding from its surface.

His teeth gritted, Carleton poised on the balls of his feet. At the first beat of the drum, he sprang immediately forward.

Taken off guard, Half Moon swung his club a half-second too late. It whistled across Carleton's shoulder blade, tearing skin in a ragged welt, but failing in its goal of sending him sprawling.

Head down, shoulders hunched, Carleton streaked past the beginning of the line before his tormentors could strike. Their howls of frustration spurred him to even greater speed.

Within a few strides, however, the first blows began to rain across his back and buttocks. Stinging switches ripped at his arms, legs, and face, while thick clubs and the blunt end of tomahawks wielded by enraged participants all but knocked him off his feet. Several times he stumbled but regained his footing by sheer desperation and fought his way forward.

Before he had gotten halfway down the line, every heaving, panting breath seared his lungs. Sweat, tears, and blood mixed with the dust and small rocks flung into his face to blind him. Every muscle in his body shrieked in agony, but by a power outside himself, he blocked out the awareness of physical torment and forced himself to run on.

At first he managed to avoid blows to his head. But when he slipped on the dusty path and sprawled onto hands and knees as the result of a particularly malicious blow across his legs, a tall warrior brought his club down across the back of Carleton's neck, dropping him to the ground.

The world contorted into a mist-shrouded jumble of unintelligible images. Disoriented, dizzy, and nauseated, he scrambled back onto his feet, arms crossed over his head to ward off a punishing hail of blows.

By now he was bleeding profusely and every inch of his skin was afire. Through a haze of pain and flailing weapons, he focused on the fat, middle-aged matron who stepped into his path, club uplifted, face contorted with demonic glee.

From some unsuspected depth of resolve, he found a last reserve of strength. Springing forward with a piercing scream, he ripped the weapon out of her hands and shoved his astonished adversary out of his path. As she tumbled to the ground, wailing, he saw with grim satisfaction that those in front of him scrambled back with shrieks of alarm. Swinging the club viciously to right and left, he cleared the path forward.

Shouting until he was hoarse, he clawed to within ten paces of the council house door. By then the line had collapsed back on him from behind. To every side swelled the deafening bestial roar of vengeance.

Without warning, a brutal blow caught his head at the same point Great Owl had struck him three days earlier. With a strength outside his own power, he blindly staggered the last few steps, until his hand found the rough bark of the council house wall. Like a stone he collapsed across its threshold.

A thick, inky wave of blackness pierced by bolts of lightning rolled over him, obscuring his vision. Inside his skull throbbed a red-hot pulsebeat that threatened to burst the very bone. He rolled over, gasping for air, then a last savage blow put an abrupt end to all sensation.

⊕ ⊕ ⊕

PAINFULLY CARLETON pushed aside the wool blanket that covered him and levered himself upright. Grimacing, he drew his legs under him until he was seated cross-legged on the sleeping platform.

As nearly as he could make out, almost two weeks had passed since he had been forced to run the gauntlet. Every muscle still protested against movement, but this morning the throbbing soreness of his body had diminished to an endurable level. To his encouragement, he had regained a large measure of mobility.

Under the expert ministrations of the two matrons delegated to care for him, his wounds had made much progress toward closing up, and the bruises that darkened his skin had faded to a yellowish tinge. The excruciating headache and disorienting dizziness that had plagued him for days had finally eased as well.

Faint light filtered into the longhouse through the smoke hole above the fire circle outside his compartment. It was shortly after dawn, and the families living in the longhouse had already gone outside to begin the day's tasks in the morning's relative coolness. For some moments he listened to the song of the awakening robins, the murmur of distant voices and chatter of children playing, the barking of a dog near at hand.

Moving gingerly, he rose and put on the breechcloth, leggings, and moccasins that had been left for him. Although the garments were worn and dirty, he was not disposed to complain. The ability to cover his nakedness left him feeling somewhat less vulnerable, though he smiled grimly at the illusion.

Regardless of his captors' intent, the final decision regarding his fate would have to be made by a vote of the town's full council. In that lay some measure of hope. And now that his condition was improving, it could not be long before they met.

Again weakness overcame him, and he sat back down on the sleeping platform. Shortly, footfalls padded down the central passageway of the longhouse, then in the doorway appeared Laughing Waters, the younger of the two women who had spent much of the interval since his ordeal massaging a salve of stewed comfrey leaves mixed with bear grease into his wounds.

She was slender, about his own age, though the hardships of the native way of life already etched her pleasant face. Giving him a keenly appraising glance, she beckoned him to follow her. When he hesitated, she frowned and made a peremptory gesture.

There was no choice but to obey unless he wanted her to summon aid to force his compliance. That was a less than appealing prospect, so he clambered to his feet, wondering what new torments the day might hold in store.

His movements stiff and cautious, he followed her down the passageway and outside. Since they had brought him there he had only been allowed outside to relieve himself. Now he drew in deep lungfuls of the fresh air, savoring the breeze-borne scents of wood smoke, dew-damp grass, boiling maize, and the clean, cool fragrance of the forest beyond the palisade. The yellow sun hung behind the eastern treetops, casting long bars of misty golden light and dark shadow across the ground.

For that brief moment he felt glad just to be alive. He avoided any thought of the future.

A few yards away, several women varying from teenaged girls to middle-aged matrons gathered around an open fire. They looked in his direction, their stares neither hostile nor welcoming. Clad in calf-length doeskin skirts, leggings, and moccasins adorned with beads and colorfully dyed quills, they had already discarded their shirts in the rising heat of the day. Sweat glistened on the copper skin of bare shoulders and breasts.

Chattering companionably, they clustered around the large iron kettles hung over the fire on tripods, the source of the scent of cooked maize and meat that made Carleton's mouth water. His stomach growled, and he realized that for the first time in days he was hungry.

Beside him, Laughing Waters motioned for him to step behind the longhouse, and he went around the side to the pit in the back and relieved himself. As he returned to Laughing Waters, he threw a hopeful glance at the open gates of the palisade a hundred yards away at the end of the nearest row of longhouses. Outside the wall, he remembered, a stream curved along the edge of the town, widening beyond the gates into a placid pool perfect for swimming and bathing.

Laughing Waters and her companion had washed his wounds several times each day, then massaged them with bear grease mixed with pungent herbs. The mixture had speeded healing, but at the moment, and in spite of his hunger, he wanted nothing more than to dive into the refreshing water and scrub the odor of rancid fat from his skin.

Laughing Waters followed the direction of his glance, but scowled and shook her head. She led him to the fire and issued a sharp command, this time motioning him to sit.

Disappointed, he sat down, cross-legged, and ran his fingers through his tangled hair in an effort to tame it. Giving up the attempt, he tentatively investigated the two weeks' growth of beard that covered his jaw.

He wished he had some way of shaving. As a youth, once his beard had begun to grow, he had taken care to keep himself clean shaven whenever he spent time among the Shawnee. The Indians did not tolerate bearded men among them, and to appear unshaven before their council now would put him at an even greater disadvantage.

Absently he watched a matron grinding corn with a heavy pole, which she pounded rhythmically into a mortar hollowed from a large log. After a moment, his attention was drawn to the girl who stirred the contents of one of the cooking pots. She glanced toward him, then filled a pottery bowl with the pulverized, boiled maize and stewed venison. This she brought to him along with a piece of bread baked in the nearby earthen oven and a small clay pot filled with fresh water.

Carleton estimated her to be sixteen or seventeen years old. Slender as a nymph and shapely, she moved with the unconscious grace of a doe. Gleaming, blue-black hair tamed in long plaits framed her delicately formed face and trailed down her back to the sensuous swell of her buttocks.

Standing over him, she scrutinized him with an expression akin to amazement—because of his blond hair and blue eyes, he guessed. Without speaking he nodded his gratitude for her kindness and accepted the simple meal.

As he mopped the bowl clean with the last fragment of bread, he became aware of a commotion behind him. Hastily he swallowed the morsel and looked around in time to see the men of the town filing into the council house. At the same time, Laughing Waters grabbed the empty bowl from his hand and said something that he interpreted as an order to get up. He complied with deliberate slowness.

As he did so, Half Moon strode toward them from the council house door. Carleton noted that his gaze rested first on the young woman who had fed him, and that she returned the look with a toss of her head.

Half Moon's face clouded with a frown, and he turned his attention to Carleton, his dark eyes glittering with unconcealed malice. He carried a thick leather thong, and when he grabbed Carleton's arm, Carleton instinctively jerked away, took a step backward.

By now a couple of the younger warriors had joined them. They immediately took rough hold of Carleton, one on each side. Knowing that further resistance would gain him only more grief, Carleton stood motionless while they bound his hands behind his back so tightly he winced as the leather bit into the bruised flesh.

So the time had come for the council to decide his fate. Anxiety formed a hard knot in his stomach.

As he had before running the gauntlet, he lifted his anxious gaze to the brightening sky. *Help me!* he pleaded once again. *Stay beside me!*

This time, painfully, he added, *Whatever your will is, Lord, I give myself to you.*

Immediately, a quiet assurance stole through his veins. The fear and uncertainty that had threatened to capsize him like storm waves overturn a foundering ship subsided and gave way to steady calm. Offering no resistance, he allowed the three men to lead him to the council house.

Inside the dim interior the men were seated on bearskins around a clearing in the center of the large room. Most of them were smoking pipes, and the scent of tobacco mixed with dried sumac leaves hung heavy on the air. The older matrons had taken seats along the building's far side, and the younger women were rapidly swelling their ranks.

As Carleton was brought in, all eyes turned to him in appraisal. Some faces were intent and sober, probing him for signs of fear, while others reflected eagerness for the council's proceedings to begin.

Half Moon went to sit beside Great Owl directly opposite the doorway. As Carleton's eyes met theirs, again he read an intense hatred that seared through him.

He did not drop his gaze, however. Deliberately he threw back his head and returned a level, challenging stare.

Without ceremony, he was thrust into the circle's center and shoved to the floor. Off balance, he managed to keep his legs under him, to sit clumsily on the beaten earth. His shoulders and arms already ached from being bound in their unnatural position.

When the last of the men had entered and found seats, one of the elders, whom Carleton took to be the principal sachem of the town, rose with great dignity. He called on Half Moon, who stood up and began to speak.

Carleton struggled to follow the debate that followed as speeches by elders, chiefs, and subchiefs were interspersed with comments and questions from the audience. At intervals, as if to punctuate his point, one or another of the speakers gestured toward Carleton or cast him a dark or a calculating look. But his knowledge of the Seneca language was too limited for him to grasp more than the general gist of what was said.

More than once Half Moon's responses included the name Detroit and reference to the British. The members of the party that had captured Carleton supported him, along with a substantial number of the younger men. One in particular, a young warrior named Cackling Crow, argued their case with arrogant vehemence.

His suspicions had been correct, Carleton concluded. From the expressions of the speakers and many of those who took little or no part in the discussion, it was obvious that the size of Gage's reward was a highly attractive inducement to sell Carleton back to the British. The opportunity to curry favor with the side they judged to be the stronger in the coming war had to be an equally powerful argument.

While the debate continued, hotly contested on several sides, Carleton scrutinized the face of the sachem. His name was Lone Wolf, from what Carleton could make out, and his demeanor gave no hint as to which side he supported. Several of the elders and middle-aged men clearly disagreed with Half Moon and Great Owl's arguments. Gradually it became apparent that some argued for enslaving him, some for torturing him to death. He could not determine that there was any discussion at all of adopting him into the tribe, and he cherished no hope that anyone advocated setting him free.

Listening without being able to understand much of what was said, to protest, or to present a defense was supremely frustrating. He was confident that many of the council members understood either English or French, but no one spoke to him or offered to translate.

He made no objection, however, knowing that to speak without permission would earn him a beating.

After the discussion had ranged for almost two hours, one of the older matrons rose. A small, sprightly woman of perhaps sixty years of age, with skin weathered to the color of aged leather, she spoke at some length while Lone Wolf and the others listened with deference.

The oldest matrons, who were the heads of the clans, Carleton knew, would already have formed an opinion and lobbied their husbands and sons to support their side. As owners of the tribe's fields, longhouses, and children, the women were listened to more often than not by the men, who well knew what was in their best interests.

This woman's arguments appeared to carry special weight, and Carleton noted that Half Moon's face fell, as did Great Owl's. Increasingly a frown darkened their faces.

At last the woman, Basket Weaver, came over to scrutinize Carleton at closer range. At her approach, the two men who had dragged Carleton into the longhouse jerked him to his feet. He clenched his teeth at the pain that shot through his shoulders and arms, but refused to allow any sound to escape his lips.

He could not, however, erase smoldering anger and defiance from his gaze when he met Basket Weaver's hawk-like eyes. Far from appearing displeased, she bared broken teeth in a wide grin and reached out bony fingers to probe the muscles of his arms, chest, and thighs.

Involuntarily he flinched back from her touch. The onlookers erupted in snickers and contemptuous jeers accompanied their derisive laughter.

Once more cold dread clenched Carleton's stomach. Did she appraise his use as a slave or seek to determine how long he might be able to endure torture?

The prospect of enslavement was little improvement over that of torture. That misery, at least, would last hardly more than a day, and then he would be released to the mercies of God. It would be proof, at least, that they considered him a warrior worthy of respect.

In contrast, the lot of a slave among the tribes was characterized by the unabated rigors of labor and abuse, degradation, insult, and humiliation. A slave was not considered a human being.

Like his own slaves.

The thought shocked him. He had never attended a slave auction, had, in fact, always intentionally avoided that obscene transaction. Now he felt as though he was on the auction block.

Lord God, save me from this! he pleaded silently. But he could discern no reassuring response.

His face set like stone, he forced himself to keep his eyes fixed on a point straight ahead, to endure the prodding touch that repelled him. Through his mind echoed Isaiah's words describing his own revulsion at being so used, and horror overcame him.

At last the matron withdrew to her seat, and Carleton's guards forced him back to the floor. The debate resumed, but now it was clear that Half Moon's position had lost favor.

Which left the choice of slavery or torture.

At length Lone Wolf held up his hand to halt the discussion and signal that the time had come for a decision. In turn, each speaker rose to briefly state his final opinion. As each one spoke, Lone Wolf kept track of the vote by marking in the dirt with a sharp stick, dividing the tally into three separate groups.

When the last vote had been cast, two columns showed nearly the same number of marks. Quickly Lone Wolf assessed them, then announced the decision. Basket Weaver's smile broadened, and she nodded in satisfaction. Half Moon's side had lost. Carleton now belonged to Basket Weaver for whatever use she meant to make of him.

His face contorted with anger, Great Owl rose. Snarling a threat Carleton could not understand, he gathered his bearskin around his shoulders and swept outside like a black cloud.

Half Moon and his supporters were on their feet as well. Approaching Carleton on his way to the door, Half Moon gave Carleton a vicious kick in the side. As Carleton sucked in a sharp breath, agony radiating through his aching ribs, Half Moon bent over him, his face contorted with hate.

"Je vous aurai encore!" he hissed.

I will yet have you.

Carleton watched him stalk through the door of the longhouse, dread washing over him. What Half Moon intended he did not know, but at the moment his immediate future was his most pressing concern.

With black humor he reflected that it had been scant weeks since his rescue from a British scaffold. This was becoming a bad habit.

At the thought, he grimaced, then rage rose in him. God had used Elizabeth to save him—for what? For this? To be captured and tortured to death like an animal? Or to live the degraded life of a slave?

He found himself berating God for his indifferent cruelty. Why could he not have been allowed to die like a man and be spared this? How could this be God's will?

It was not, of course. Carleton knew it with sudden clarity, and as quickly as rage had possessed him, it dissipated, and shame seared through him.

He could not argue convincingly that it was God who was responsible for his capture or for the ill treatment he suffered. The situation he found himself in was due to the actions of Half Moon and Great Owl. And Carleton's own decisions.

He had no time to wonder what they meant to do with him or even to pray. Jerked once more to his feet, he was taken outside to the wide grassy area in front of the council house.

The sun beat down from high overhead, and sweat began to trickle down his face and body. Several anxious moments passed before one of the elders, a wizened, stooped old man with grey hair, jutting nose, and deeply furrowed face, made his way through the crowd, carrying a curved piece of bark piled with ashes.

Comprehension dawned. They were going to pluck his beard. It was unlikely they would bother if they meant to torture him to death, Carleton decided, but there was no way to be certain.

His two guards took him by the arms and forced him to squat on the ground between them. He made no attempt to fight them, hoping by cooperation to gain some measure of favor with his captors. Resistance would have been futile in any case, as more than a dozen of the men stood by to watch the proceedings with amused anticipation.

The elder sat down in front of Carleton. Dipping his fingers into the ashes, he took hold of several strands of Carleton's beard and with a deft jerk, pulled them out by the roots. Involuntarily Carleton winced. Setting his teeth, he stared into the air, praying that this would be the worst ordeal he would have to face for the rest of the day.

By the time the old man finally finished, Carleton felt as though his face was afire. The fish oil the old man rubbed into Carleton's inflamed cheeks soothed the itching and burning of his skin, though the noxious smell turned his stomach. To his relief, no attempt was made to pluck the hair of his head. Instead, one of the matrons braided his hair into two plaits.

Carleton became aware that Basket Weaver and Lone Wolf had joined the onlookers. They were somehow related, he guessed. They were similar in build and appearance, and Lone Wolf treated her with deference. Possibly his sister, she was the elder by at least a decade.

Her plans for Carleton were quickly revealed. At her command, his guards pulled him roughly to his feet and untied his hands.

Basket Weaver looked him up and down with satisfaction, then motioned him peremptorily to follow her. *"Venez, esclave."*

Relief and dismay washed over him with equal force. His mouth went dry, and his knees felt weak.

He was to be her slave.

Chapter Fifteen

THERE COULD NO LONGER be any doubt that disaster had befallen Carleton's expedition. Why else would Stern have taken the risk of summoning her in a terse letter to come to his headquarters as quickly as possible?

Levi was waiting to pick her up in an old hay wagon just outside Winisimmit. Uncharacteristically silent, he ventured no answer as to what his father wanted. Most of the way to Roxbury, they rode in strained silence.

When they reached Tess's mansion, Elizabeth jumped down from the wagon without waiting for assistance and hurried into the house. Stern met her at the door of the parlor, which served as his office. His face grave, he drew her into the room without speaking.

She came to a halt just inside the threshold, taken aback, staring across the room at Washington, whose face reflected a gravity equal to her uncle's. At sight of him, fear closed over her throat.

A movement to her left caught her eye. She turned toward it, then, with a cry of relief and delight, tore off her woolen fisherman's cap and ran to Andrews's arms.

"Charles! Oh, I'm so glad you're safely back! It's surely been years since I've seen you. Where is Jonathan? Is he at Cambridge—?"

She stopped abruptly. If his commander and aide were here, then it made no sense for Carleton not to be.

Stepping back out of Andrews's embrace to scrutinize his face, she noted several details she had at first missed. A ragged scar angled across his cheek. His face was haggard, and his eyes were dark with exhaustion and an emotion that brought the terror flooding back.

"Where is Jonathan?" she repeated, glancing fearfully at Stern and Washington, then back to Andrews. "Didn't he come back with you?"

"Please sit down, Miss Howard," Washington said.

Stern brought forward a chair. She stared blankly at it, feeling as though it were an object with which she had no acquaintance. Rounding on Andrews, she grabbed him by the arms, all but shaking him.

"What happened? Tell me!"

In a voice that shook, Andrews gave a terse account of the events at Buck Tooth, disbelief and horror etching his features at the memory. "They were on Jon so quickly he didn't have a chance," he concluded. "The rest of us were forced back into the council house. Aupaumut and Konkapot said the Seneca were debating whether they should sell us to the British, torture us to death, or make us slaves.

"Finally the sachem of the town came in with some of the elders. He insisted that since we were his guests, we must be allowed to leave. We demanded they free Jon too, but they wouldn't even acknowledge they had him or answer any of our questions. We were taken immediately to our horses and escorted a good distance south, out of Seneca lands."

She heard him out in stunned silence, unable to comprehend his words. Clearing his throat, Andrews went on.

"Trying to circle back would have been foolhardy without a large armed force. So we followed the Allegheny River down to Fort Pitt to see if we could enlist a detachment of the militia that have taken it over. But there were barely enough men at the fort to guard it against the raids the Indians have been making in the area, much less any to spare for a wild goose chase."

"Jonathan?" Elizabeth whispered through stiff lips, her face ashen.

For a long moment Andrews struggled to find words, at length rasped, "They clubbed him down. The last I saw, they had him on the ground. One of the warriors was standing over him with a scalping knife to his head, and Jon was bleeding. That's when they drove us into the council house. We didn't see any more."

"He's . . . dead?"

Andrews shook his head. "At Fort Pitt we met a party of trappers who encountered a large, well-armed band of Seneca warriors a good distance west of Buck Tooth the day after we were driven out of the town. They had a prisoner with them. From their description, it had to be Jon, but at that point there was no way we could possibly have caught up with them. The Seneca mentioned Detroit several times, so they may have intended to take him there and sell him to the British."

"It happened a month ago, you said?"

"We came back here as quickly as we could."

Washington stood up, moved restlessly across the room and back again. "The British are offering a king's ransom to anyone who will bring Jon in alive. They have many ties with the Indians, and it is even possible they deliberately set up this meeting to capture him. I should have realized that he would be in danger even among the tribes."

"We've been discussing the possibility of sending a detachment from here to try to intercept Jon's captors before they reach Detroit," Stern broke in. "But if that's where they were going, they've surely reached the fort by now."

Elizabeth's knees gave way, and she sank into the chair beside her. "It's possible he might have escaped?"

The men exchanged glances. Finally Stern said, "The Indians drive their captives without mercy. If he survives the journey, he'll be too broken and exhausted to even think of escaping, much less to succeed. And if he attempts it, they will kill him."

She buried her face in her hands and gave way to convulsive sobs. When the tide of grief lessened, she became aware that Washington had pulled his chair beside her. His arm gently encircled her shoulders.

Stern stood on her other side, holding out a handkerchief. She fumbled for it, dabbed at her tears, too distraught to speak.

When her eyes cleared enough for her to see, Andrews was squatting in front of her, watching her with an expression that reflected her anguish. "I failed Jon—and you. I should have tried harder to save him."

"What could you have done that you have not? You mustn't blame yourself."

"She is right," Washington put in. "If anyone is at fault, it is I for sending him on this mission in the first place."

"Before we left here, Jon gave me legal authority to draw on his accounts in case something should happen to him," Andrews told them. "Stowe and Briggs met up with us in New York, and I sent them back up the Hudson along with Isaiah, Sammy, and the Mahicans, bearing letters to the tribes doubling Gage's reward for Jon's safe return. If by God's grace they intercept Jon's captors before they reach Detroit, the Seneca will find it considerably to their advantage to turn him over to us. And if he's already in British hands, they may be able to rescue him."

Blinking back tears, Elizabeth forced a wavering smile, trying to persuade herself that a ray of hope still existed. But no matter how positive a face she sought to put on the prospect for Carleton's rescue, her heart would not be deceived.

THE DRIVE TO WINISIMMIT that evening to catch the *Prudence* before she sailed passed by in a haze of misery. His face set in lines of distress, Levi reached several times to squeeze her hand, murmuring reassurances that Carleton would be found alive and well. For his sake, she struggled to pretend a hope that stubbornly evaded her.

Purple twilight blanketed the surrounding hills by the time they reached the village. Aboard the sloop, preparations to put to sea were all but complete. She took leave of her cousin and boarded the small vessel, praying no one would read the devastation in her eyes.

When she brushed past on her way to join the men preparing the nets and fishing poles, Dalton swung to regard her with a meaningful smile. "Ye had a good visit with yer uncle and cousin, I hope."

The breath left her lungs as though he had struck her a vicious blow. "I have no idea what you're talkin' about," she returned, amazed that her voice sounded level and cold.

"Oh, I think ye do, Miss Howard," he purred, his voice caressing. "But never fear, me dear. Your secret be safe with me."

For an instant she stood frozen to the deck. "You obviously have me confused with someone else."

Her movements jerky, she swung away and went to join the rest of the crew. But a gale of questions stormed though her mind.

He knows my name. Will he betray me? What price will he demand for his silence?

For certainly he would. Perhaps not now, but in time.

Was it Gage's reward for her capture he wanted? Or something else? The way he looked at her made her flesh crawl.

She felt sick to her stomach. Coming on the heels of the past hour's revelations, it was all she could do to keep from retching.

During the long hours that followed, terror worried her every step like slavering hounds. Although she threw herself into the tasks of the night, fighting against the contrary winds and tossing waves that buffeted the small vessel, two anguished questions were her constant companions.

Could Jonathan be already dead?

What will Dalton do now that he knows who I am?

Relief flooded over her when the first light of dawn revealed the outlines of Boston's wharves and warehouses. While Dalton was occupied with a customer, she slipped from the boat and escaped into the city's tangled maze of alleys and lanes. Once out of sight of the docks, she ran for home as though demons clamored at her heels. Yet when she crept through the shadows to the back door of the town house, her lungs bursting, she halted on the threshold, paralyzed by a horrifying realization.

Now that Dalton knew her name, he knew also where to find her. And since his sister-in-law was their housekeeper, he possessed access to their house.

She could hear muted footfalls descending the front staircase. Mrs. Dalton and the cook were not due to arrive for another half hour, and as she expected, it was Tess who met her in the hallway.

One look at Elizabeth's face brought alarm to the older woman's. Hastily Tess drew her into the library and locked the door.

In short, harsh words, Elizabeth poured out all that had happened. Her aunt's horrified expression loosened the tears Elizabeth had held in check all through that tortured night, and clinging to each other, the two women wept.

When they regained a measure of calm, they spent some time praying for wisdom and for protection for both Elizabeth and Carleton. At length, realizing that Elizabeth was on the verge of collapse, Tess insisted she go to bed, assuring her that she would continue in prayer for guidance and help.

Yet Elizabeth could not sleep. Appalling images of the horrors Carleton must surely be undergoing danced through her mind without ceasing.

Before, she had been able to breach even a British gaol to rescue him from the hangman. This time she had no way of helping him. Far away in the wilderness beyond the limits of her knowledge and access, he faced an unimaginable fate all alone.

Was she also to meet a terrible end? Would Dalton betray her—or use his knowledge to wrest her into his power for evil purposes?

She came at last to the stark conclusion that there was nothing she could do. The only recourse left was prayer.

That was much, she kept reminding herself, though it did not feel like enough at all. It felt as though her pleas fell into an impenetrable, unresponsive void.

Yet there was no one else to turn to, no one else who held the balance scales of life and death. And all alone in her room, she cried out to the Redeemer with an anguish too deep for words.

Chapter Sixteen

JONATHAN!

Shocked out of the profound insensibility of exhaustion, he wrenched upright, his heart thudding wildly like an imprisoned bird against his ribcage, the breath searing in labored gasps in and out of his lungs.

Her scream echoed in his ears. The vision of her was so vivid that it took agonizing moments to claw his way back to unwelcoming reality.

In spite of the night's chill, he was wet with sweat. A stinging trickle wound from his brow onto his cheeks and dripped onto his chest. The windowless compartment's stifling confines pressed suffocatingly close.

Every night without fail the vivid dreams of Elizabeth captured his mind, so real that it took minutes upon awakening for the piercing realization of his captivity to return.

Until recently, the dreams had been of her lying in his arms or of the two of them laughing, walking hand-in-hand, riding together in a race. But always carefree, safe, at peace. Then yesterday the nightly vision had carried him back to Tess's house on the day Elizabeth had left to return to Boston. The reproach in her eyes had burned into his soul, and guilt threatened to overpower him, deny him strength for the trials of the day.

Tonight, for the first time, he had seen her weeping, in great distress, had heard her cry out to him. And he thought he must tear down the walls of the imprisoning longhouse, scale the palisades of the town, and run until either he escaped from his captors and found his way back to her or died.

In unreasoning rage he fought against the leather thongs that bound him hand and foot, his choked breath rasping harsh in his ears. All he accomplished was to chafe wrists and ankles raw, and at last he gave up in renewed despair.

His limbs still trembling, he focused on the faint light of the quarter moon that slanted through the smoke hole from above the longhouse. By degrees his breathing and heartbeat steadied.

He threw a cautious glance at the opposite end of the sleeping platform. As usual, his movements had awakened Basket Weaver. In the shadows he could just make out that her hooded eyes were open, and that she stared at him.

"What do you dream, slave?" she asked in guttural French.

For a tense moment he held her gaze, careful to convey nothing by his expression. The Indians, he knew, believed that dreams were communications from the spirits and that one could gain secret knowledge or predict the future through them.

Her slave he might be, but she could not force him to share his dreams with her, nor anything else guarded in the depths of his soul. He had no intention of ever doing so no matter what the penalty. To make the point, he lay down and turned his back to her.

She grunted in annoyance and rustled around under her blanket. Would she retaliate in the morning for his defiance, he wondered, steeling himself.

He had learned that she was a widow whose husband and children had been killed many years ago by the Whites, for whom she consequently harbored no love. With no descendants and no relatives except Lone Wolf, she lived in the longhouse that belonged to the clan of his wife, Red Wing. Only Basket Weaver's need for a strong back to fetch and carry and the fact that she was Lone Wolf's elder sister had spared Carleton's life. He suspected she could as easily unspare it.

But after a few minutes all was silent, and her snoring told him she had returned to sleep. Cautiously he shifted in the attempt to find a position that his bonds did not make intensely uncomfortable, at length achieved modest success.

He was not given a blanket, so he had to sleep as best he could without covering, even though the nights were steadily cooling. And now that he lay still, the early autumn chill crept into his muscles and bones.

Despite the unremitting weariness of his physical body, the shadow of the dream kept his mind from quieting. Again he fought back the waves of desperation that threatened to sweep away his fragile control, at last cried out silently to the unyielding silence and darkness for rescue, for deliverance from the hell he found himself in.

Gradually, into his mind drifted the words of a cherished hymn learned while in England but for some years forgotten. He clung to them as to a lifeline in a storm, recited them again and again silently, breathed them as a prayer while a transcendent peace quieted his trembling and eased the tension from his limbs.

Thou hidden source of calm repose,
Thou all-sufficient love divine,
My help and refuge from my foes,
Secure I am, if Thou art mine:
And lo! from sin, and grief, and shame
I hide me, Jesus, in Thy name.

Thy mighty name salvation is,
And keeps my happy soul above;

Comfort it brings, and power, and peace,
And joy, and everlasting love:
To me, with Thy dear name, are given
Pardon, and holiness, and heaven.

Jesus, my all in all Thou art;
My rest in toil, my ease in pain,
The medicine of my broken heart,
In war my peace, in loss my gain,
My smile beneath the tyrant's frown,
In shame my glory and my crown:

In want my plentiful supply,
In weakness my almighty power,
In bonds my perfect liberty,
My light in Satan's darkest hour,
In grief my joy unspeakable,
My life in death, my Heaven in hell.

He clung to that assurance and after an indeterminate period became aware that a robin poured out his liquid trill. Along the passageway he could hear the first muted sounds of the clan's awakening: a baby's cry, a woman's soft voice and a man's guttural answer, the babble of children, finally the rustling sounds of movement.

When Basket Weaver rose to shake out her blanket, he rolled over and sat up. She took her time before coming to untie his feet, then his hands, leaving the ends of the leather thongs tied to one of the poles that framed the building.

With an effort, he clothed himself again, as at each bleak morning, in the mantle of the day's necessity for survival. Without a word, he pulled on the scuffed, stained leggings and moccasins that, in addition to his breechcloth, constituted his entire wardrobe. At least the breechcloth was in reasonable condition. The leggings and moccasins, however, had worn through in several places and gave little protection to his feet and legs.

Except for the lack of protection against the attacks of mosquitoes, fleas, and other insects that had been constant torture until his skin had toughened so that he hardly noticed the discomfort, his only concern about the garments' condition was that they were dirty and stank of stale sweat and other indeterminate, repulsive odors. At least they covered his nakedness, and until recently the weather had remained hot and humid, which made it more comfortable to wear a minimum of clothing.

But with the cooling weather, for want of any other covering he would soon have to sleep in the worn garments for what little good they would do. He did not allow himself to think about what he faced if no one saw fit to give him at least a bearskin once cold weather set in.

Stretching the stiffness out of his muscles, he grabbed the moth-eaten rabbitskin pouch that hung from a peg on the wall before heading down the passage to the outer door. Several of the men of the clan were ahead of him, but none of them took any more notice of him than they did of the lean dogs that pressed around the entry to the longhouse, whipping their tails ingratiatingly back and forth.

At pains to invite no undue notice, he waited until the men had gone outside before following into the sharp coolness of the predawn hour. The sky above the eastern wall of the palisade was brightening. Heavy dew twinkled on the grass and dripped from the domed elm-bark roof of the longhouse, making a rhythmic, sodden, plopping sound where it struck the earth below.

After relieving himself in the pit at the edge of the palisade behind the longhouse, he strode to the clustered tripods where the women did their cooking in warm, dry weather. Carefully raking the coals in the fire circles from the ashes that banked them, he took thin strips of kindling from the wood piled nearby and laid them across the cherry-red embers, fanning them until dancing tongues of flame and streamers of white smoke began to rise. Discovering that the fire in the last circle had died out, he laid kindling, then with the flint, punk, and piece of steel from his pouch, deftly relighted it. When he had nurtured a steady blaze beneath each tripod, he hung the blackened iron kettles from the hooks.

On the other side of the mortars for grinding grain lay a thick wooden yoke, smooth from years of use, with a deep notch on each end. Beside it sat two capacious wooden buckets constructed of tightly fitted elm staves. He picked up the buckets and the yoke.

Just then Basket Weaver appeared in the door of the longhouse. Motioning to one of the children playing on the grass outside, she cackled, "Go with the slave and make sure he doesn't run away."

The child, a boy of about six years of age called Walks-With-A-Limp because he had been born with a clubfoot, hobbled obediently after Carleton as he strode toward the town gate. The rest of the children, boys and girls ranging from toddlers to perhaps ten years of age, raced after them, quickly outpacing Walks-With-A-Limp. He shouted a protest, but they danced ahead of him, laughing and calling insults at Carleton. Several of them threw handfuls of pebbles or struck at Carleton with a stick as they had watched their elders do.

At first Carleton did not slow his stride. Since his arrival in the town, the children had gleefully added every misery to his life they could conceive of, and he had to fight down the urge to swing the heavy buckets violently around to drive them off.

When Walks-With-A-Limp suddenly began to wail, however, Carleton came to a halt. Ignoring his childish tormentors, he hesitated, finally turned and motioned for the crippled child to come along.

A wavering smile replaced Walks-With-A-Limp's tears, and he hurried to Carleton's side. Carleton smiled down at him, and when the child returned his smile a thread of pleasure stole through him.

Deliberately he slowed his gait to allow Walks-With-A-Limp to keep up. Following them, the other children quieted, seeming to lose interest in continuing their torments. A sturdy girl lifted Walks-With-A-Limp onto her hip and took the procession's lead.

Always before, they had delighted in darting into Carleton's path, trying to trip him and finding ways to make it difficult for him to unbar the gates. This time, two of the older boys hurried to lift the heavy bar and push the gates wide.

When they had passed outside the palisade, the children raced ahead to wade in the stream. In moments, most of them had moved off several yards downriver, looking for crayfish and other creatures, and drawing Walks-With-A-Limp along with them in their play. Several of the youngest drifted a short distance away to the edge of the cornfields to toddle after the sooty crows that hopped, cawing, among the drying stalks loaded with ripening ears.

Thankful for respite from the children's persecution, Carleton set the buckets on the bank and waded a short distance into the stream to wash his face and arms. He took a long drink of the cool water before returning to the bank to fetch the buckets and fill them.

Hooking their handles into the notches on the yoke, he knelt and heaved the burden across his shoulders. He set his teeth and pushed himself to his feet with a grunt while holding the full buckets steady with his hands. The yoke bowed under the weight and dug painfully into his shoulders and the back of his neck.

Careful to avoid spilling his load, he turned, then paused to stare off into the distance, past the orchards and the fields of beans and sprawling squash vines, past the tidy rows of corn, to the dusky line of the deep forest beyond. Like white smoke, feathery ribbons of fog hung between the folds of the misty blue ridges.

To the east, still invisible behind the undulating line of hills, but already softening the transparent veil of the sky overhead to opal, the rising sun had flung its thin, fiery edge over the far horizon. In spite of himself, the sweet song of meadowlarks and soft coo of mourning doves kindled a tentative hope in Carleton's breast.

In those first days as Basket Weaver's slave, he had fought back in senseless fury against each insult and blow. Several vicious beatings had taught him the wisdom of compliance, however, and he soon learned to swallow his pride as best he could. Death, after all, was not the escape he had in mind.

Forced to take on the heaviest of the women's labor, he at first had no energy left to lay coherent plans. For the first couple of weeks he had doubted his ability to endure, questioned whether he even wanted to.

Initially no one would give him food, and he had been forced to scavenge whatever was thrown out to appease the pangs of hunger. He had become so gaunt his ribs were clearly visible beneath the skin. One day of misery blurred into another with no hope of release or even the relief of physical suffering.

With the passage of time, however, as the women had found him useful, one or two had begun to leave food out for him, a kindness for which he was humbly grateful. As a result of constant hard work, the muscles of his arms, chest, and shoulders soon began to bulge in steely bands of muscle and sinew beneath skin burned to a deep tan by the summer sun. And with the return of strength and stamina, thoughts of escape increasingly obsessed him.

As best he could calculate, it was by now late September. An involuntary spasm of pain crossed his face at the thought. Somewhere in the weeks of his ordeal, his birthday had passed. Thirty-two years of his life had come and gone, only to find him once more lost, far from home and those he loved.

And now reduced to the degraded status of a slave—as he had been in other ways for so many years before the sweet hope of freedom had been restored to him. Only, inexplicably, to be snatched away once more.

With hardening resolve he pushed away all thoughts that would sap the determination to act. The weather was steadily cooling, and daily the canopy of trees displayed increasingly vibrant hues of scarlet and gold. Once snow blanketed the land, there would be little possibility of surviving the long journey back to civilization alone and afoot. If he was to escape before winter, he could not delay the attempt long.

His eyes were drawn to the elm-bark canoes pulled up on the riverbank, temptingly close. For a moment he stared at them, weighing the odds, finally concluded reluctantly that with the town now awake and the children nearby, he would not get far before someone sounded an alarm.

Head bent, he trudged doggedly up the bank. He could not afford to lose sight of his goal: to survive, to get away from this place, to find his way back to Elizabeth. If he was to have any hope of success, he must exercise strict discipline, patience, and resolve.

As soon as he stepped back inside the palisade, he breathed in the savory scents of maize, venison, and beans. His stomach complained at its emptiness, but he needed more than food. The most basic longing for fellowship and simple human kindness was a greater need than any other, one he felt most acutely now, when it was so completely denied him.

In walking through the town, he passed several other Whites and gazed at them with a longing he found difficult to disguise. One bent, skinny older man was also a slave but appeared to move freely around the town without interference. On Carleton's approach, the old man cast him a quick, fearful look, then shrank out of his path and hurried away.

An attractive young girl in her late teens whose belly bulged with her unborn child also detoured hastily away from him and took refuge in the longhouse of her husband, a middle-aged warrior with whose viciousness Carleton had become more familiar than he wished. A boy several years younger scrutinized Carleton from behind his adoptive father, who kept his narrowed eyes on Carleton until he moved out of his sight.

Carleton's efforts to speak to them or even to come near them in the first days of his captivity had met with brutal clubbings, and he had learned to give them a wide berth. It was obvious they were also forbidden any contact with him, though they conversed freely with each other. Daily it was made clear that he was considered an outcast, a pariah with no rights or privileges.

At the cooking area where the women gathered around their iron kettles, he knelt to set down his burden, then got to his feet with relief. Grateful for the fire's warmth, he rubbed his aching shoulders before hefting the buckets one at a time to fill the large, clay water pots.

As usual, the teenage girls tittered behind their hands—at the sight of a man doing women's work, he assumed. In the morning coolness, in addition to their doeskin skirts, all the women wore either cape-like leather shirts or colorful calico blouses made of trade goods.

Sitting on a log near the fire, a cluster of young maidens laughed and chattered while they combed and braided one another's glistening hair. Two mothers nursed their infants, and nearby Basket Weaver sat cross-legged on a blanket, deftly weaving supple white oak strips in and out of the splints of the basket she had just started.

Dressed in a bright red shirt open to a little below her round, firm breasts, Little Grey Dove stirred the contents of one of the kettles. Seeing him glance toward her, she bared her perfect white teeth in an impudent smile that told him she was used to receiving admiring glances. When she had filled a bowl, she brought it to him along with a flat oval of bread.

He accepted the food, as usual nodding his gratitude, but not speaking. He did not trust the expression in her eyes whenever she looked at him, and he gave no indication that he understood what it implied. Had it not been for her and a couple of the older women, he would have starved by now, and the last thing he wanted to do was to offend any of them.

"Eat, slave," she ordered him in her own language, her tone cheerful. "We've much work today, and we'll need all your strength."

That too he pretended not to understand, and his only answer was a noncommittal grunt. He did not merit even a name, but to his encouragement, he understood what she said.

Over the past month he had accumulated enough knowledge of the Seneca language to decipher much of the conversations he overheard. He carefully guarded the extent of his comprehension from his captors, however, to the point of making himself appear dim witted. It was not likely to do him any good if they found out how much he knew.

Little Grey Dove, who had taken an interest in him from that first day by the fire, had turned out to be Lone Wolf's youngest child. In the past weeks it had become clear to Carleton that in her parents' eyes she could do no wrong. A flirt and a tease, she had indulged in relations with several of the men of the village, as was customary and even expected among the tribes, but so far had refused to settle on a husband from among several eager suitors.

Carleton's old nemesis, Half Moon, made no secret that he considered her to be his own. The trouble was that Cackling Crow, younger and less experienced, but equally hot-tempered, acted as though he held first rights. And Little Grey Dove appeared to take great delight in pitting them against each other, all the while flirting with the other eligible men—and with a few who were not so eligible.

And now her glance wandered increasingly often to Carleton. Since they lived in the same longhouse, there was nothing he could do to avoid her. And it seemed to him that she went out of her way to tempt him.

He had to admit that she was quite alluring. He had even considered the possibility that by giving in to her he might better his situation since her favor held much weight with Lone Wolf. But that was a course that could equally result in disaster for him, and for her as well since it was unlikely that even for her a liaison with a slave would be accepted.

The greatest argument against taking the risk, of course, was that it would require him to renounce all hope of ever returning to Elizabeth. That he was not willing to do. And so he prayed fervently that Little Grey Dove would quickly lose her fascination with him and turn to other, fairer game.

Another discovery troubled him equally and spurred the urgency of his making an escape: The women's fields were almost spent because of overcultivation. Game was also becoming scarce in the area due to the white hunters who ranged in growing numbers through Seneca lands. Consequently, the townspeople were planning to move after the completion of the harvest. A party had already located a suitable site two days' travel to the southwest and were beginning to clear the land and cut poles and elm bark to construct longhouses.

That day turned out to be particularly exhausting and full of more than the usual humiliations. The weather remained oppressively warm and humid, and the air throbbed with the dry, brittle whirr of grasshoppers and the lazy hum of bees plying their last foraging runs before a hard freeze felled them. From first light until early afternoon, he toiled with the women, picking squash, beans, corn, and the first apples. He carried endless elm bark boxes and large baskets laden with produce back into the town.

All day Little Grey Dove found an excuse to work nearby, if not next to him. Later in the afternoon, as he sat shucking corn, his hands raw and bleeding from the coarse husks, he heard someone approach. Guessing who it was, he kept his eyes on his work.

The footfalls stopped beside him. Without turning his head, he noted that the moccasins of his visitor belonged to Little Grey Dove.

He clenched his teeth, wondering what she wanted and wishing she would go away. But she sat down beside him, hugging her knees to her chest.

When he continued to rip the husks from the ears of corn without acknowledging her presence, she gathered several strands of his hair that had fallen loose from his braids and began to rub them sensuously between her fingers.

"Like sunshine," she murmured.

He sat paralyzed, uncertain what to do. He didn't need this. He fought back the urge to wave her away, knowing he dared make no objection that could be interpreted as disrespect.

Brushing back his hair, she dropped her hand to his shoulder, trailed her fingers across the hardened curve of muscle and sinew. Fire followed her touch.

"Get away from her, slave."

The words hissed like the warning of a rattlesnake. Both Carleton and Little Grey Dove started to their feet, turning at the same time. But even before he faced him, Carleton recognized that vindictive voice.

It was Cackling Crow. He stood twenty yards away, his eyes boring into Carleton's, his face contorted with resentment.

Carleton saw that for the first time fear flashed in Little Grey Dove's eyes. Tipping her nose upward in defiance, she flounced away and disappeared into her mother's longhouse, leaving the two men standing alone opposite each other.

Before Cackling Crow could move, Basket Weaver strode out of the longhouse and came toward them. Looking from one to the other, she commanded, "I need the slave to bring clay for my pots."

Relieved at the interruption, Carleton turned to do her bidding, but he stopped himself in time and stared at her with pretended confusion. Cackling Crow directed a calculating look at Carleton that he felt certain boded no good, then strode off.

"Clay," she repeated in French, wasting no words on him. "Two boxes."

He followed her out of the palisade, knowing she would watch his every movement with eagle's eyes, but grateful for rescue, though it was undoubtedly only temporary. He calculated that Cackling Crow would find a way to make him pay dearly for Little Grey Dove's attentions.

The clay pit was on the other side of the stream and a short distance farther along its bank. Digging the sticky red mud was his least favorite task. It weighted the already back-breaking elm-bark boxes like rocks, then they had to be carried one at a time across the slippery ford and into the town. No matter how much care he took, he invariably ended up liberally bedaubed with the clinging clay.

It was just before sunset when he brought the second box into the village. Hurriedly he made his way back down to the river to wash, knowing that he risked a beating for being outside the gates at nightfall. Wading out a short distance from the bank, he began to scrub away the grime and sweat of the day with handfuls of sand and small stones, shivering in the evening chill, but determined to get clean. After scrubbing as much of the mud from his leggings, breechcloth, and moccasins as possible, he unbraided his hair and rinsed it in the stream.

When he returned to the bank to dress, the possibility of escape again crossed his mind. For the moment no one was in sight either outside the palisade or through the gates.

Sitting down, he absently combed the tangles out of his matted hair with his fingers and tried to come up with a plan that held some hope of success. Every muscle in his body ached, and he was so weary it was all but impossible to force his mind to any semblance of logical thought.

As he threw a wary glance back toward the town, Cackling Crow appeared at the open gates. Catching sight of Carleton, he marched down the slope toward him, shouting an unintelligible rapid-fire of words. At the commotion, a cluster of townspeople soon gathered to watch the proceedings, laughing in anticipation.

Carleton got to his feet and for a moment sized up his tormentor with cold calculation. The man was shorter and younger than he, and Carleton weighed the possibility of overcoming him, wresting the Indian's knife out of its sheath, and making a dash for freedom.

As quickly he discarded the thought. Even if he was not dead on his feet, reinforcements were too close at hand to make the contest winnable. If all else failed, they would simply shoot him down before he reached the cover of the forest.

Gritting his teeth, he started up the slope, keeping his head bent and his posture a submissive one. This only served to further infuriate his adversary.

Uttering a stream of invective, Cackling Crow motioned for Carleton to precede him back to the village. Keeping his expression carefully neutral, Carleton obeyed.

As he stepped cautiously past him, Cackling Crow directed a powerful kick at Carleton that caused him to lose his balance. He slipped and slid sideways down the muddy bank, unable to stifle a curse at the pain that shot through his thigh where the blow had landed.

Rage at this fresh indignity seared through him. He struggled to his feet, smeared with greasy earth and rotted leaves, and with a power he knew to be entirely beyond him, fought down the impulse to tear his tormenter limb from limb. The laughter of the townspeople ringing in his ears, he turned and walked silently back into the village, refusing to limp in spite of the throbbing pain in his leg.

Without warning, Isaiah's words reverberated in his mind: *No man owned by another be treated well. But how would you know?*

Now he did know. And he was confronted with the vivid memory of the black men, women, and children he owned as property, inherited, though unwillingly, at his uncle's death.

Especially did he remember Moses, the powerfully built, middle-aged black man who had been the unofficial leader of the slaves, and their pastor. How often as a child he had gathered with them to hear Moses preach at their Sunday afternoon worship services and to join in the intensely moving songs they chanted in compelling rhythms. It was from Moses as much as from Sir Harry and the priest of the Anglican chapel that Carleton had learned to desire to follow God and to live a life of purity and righteousness.

At last he was forced to confront the moral dilemma that until now he had tried his best to avoid, even despite Isaiah's accusations. Although the institution was personally repugnant to him, he had accepted the rationales of the slaveholding society he had grown up in.

As a child he had thought little about the morality of owning human beings. The slaves Sir Harry owned had simply been a part of the landscape of his life from his earliest memories. It had not been until his years at Harvard, and then later on his return to England, that he began to question the right of one person to own another, and to be convicted of the evil of it.

While still in England he had heard many conversations in which the colonists were dismissed contemptuously for advocating a freedom for themselves that included the right to enslave other human beings. Carleton had tried unsuccessfully to comfort himself with the argument that Sir Harry had not owned many slaves, that he had never sold any that belonged to him. The ones he owned had been well treated, as far as Carleton had observed. Several of the house slaves had even been treated like members of the family.

Almost. For they were slaves. No matter how kindly they were treated, they were still not free to go where they would, when they would, or to choose what they would or would not do. They belonged body and soul to another human being, and there was much that daily reminded them of that fact.

That was the realization that impressed itself on Carleton as he crouched on the edge of the firelight that night, watching the dancers who circled, chanting, to the beat of hand drums and rattles. Now he himself was the chattel of another human, and the bitter resentment that ate into his soul at being considered mere property left him with an intense sense of shame.

Ironically he had been given the opportunity to learn how it felt to be treated as a thing less than human. Yet reason and emotion insisted that he was in every way the equal, and in some ways the superior, of those who had placed him in bondage. How, then, could he believe himself superior to those at Thornlea, who society told him were his inferiors, even less than human? Might they not in some ways also be superior to him?

Later as he stretched his aching body on the sleeping platform, his wrists painfully chafed by the leather thongs that bound him, the condemning thoughts would not give him peace. He saw clearly that there could be no benign form of slavery. And finally he pledged that if God saw fit to release him from this bondage, to bring him back to his own people and to Elizabeth again, he would waste no time in setting free every human being enslaved to him.

He came to another decision as well. He would trust God, even in his own slavery.

Thinking of the story of Joseph, cherished from his childhood, Carleton reminded himself that Joseph also had been carried away into bondage, unjustly accused, imprisoned, and abused. And yet, God had not forgotten him, but in God's own perfect time had raised him to a place of honor.

As it had been for Joseph, everything had been stripped from Carleton as well—home, love, even the most basic needs of life. Nothing remained.

Except God.

In the unrelieved darkness of that night, he knew that God *did* remain. When all else was gone, still over him brooded that sheltering, loving presence.

There was purpose in his suffering, though he could not fathom it. There *was* an answer, though it still eluded him.

At the thought, he felt suddenly as though the faintest sliver of silver light fell upon him. Into his mind crept Job's unyielding response to his wife, who, when disaster befell them, urged him to curse God and die: "Shall we receive good at the hand of God, and shall we not receive evil?"

Perhaps it would please God to raise Carleton again to freedom and honor. But if not, then he resolved to bear with patience and hope whatever trials his Master allowed him to endure.

"Your will, not mine," he whispered into the darkness. "Your will, not mine."

And with that cry of his heart, an unearthly peace settled over him as tangible as a physical covering.

Chapter Seventeen

AUGUST 23, 1775
London

Dearest Daughter,

I can't begin to describe the grief we feel at the news not only of the terrible battle on Breed's Hill, but also that Stony Hill has been destroyed. So many things we held dear—all gone. And worst, dear Major Pitcairn dead, along with so many of the officers. We are inconsolable.

By now we are settled in the new house and feeling ourselves as much at home as possible in a strange city. Your father's practice prospers, and Abby is adapting as well as may be expected, though she daily asks when you and Tess will come.

I must admit there is much here that repels us. I am not so sorry now, Daughter, that you chose to stay behind. I would not have you exposed to the indolence, obsession with gossip, and casual indifference to godly standards that we encounter too often here. I confess, I dearly long for my own country, and, if truth be told, so does your father. I do not think now our stay will extend for many years, and I pray that this conflict will be quickly mended so we can be on our way back home again.

It was wise of you to send word of Major—or rather, General—Carleton's defection to the rebel army. Not long after we received your letter, the news was repeated to us from other sources and in much harsher terms. In spite of the justifications you supplied for General Carleton's actions, the depth of his betrayal at first appalled us. Your father was more angry than I have ever seen him. Yet I could not *find it in my heart to hold General Carleton entirely at fault. The shocking attack upon his uncle, resulting in Sir Harry's death when he was wholly innocent of any wrongdoing, would force any honorable man to hold accountable those who committed such grievous injustice.*

Several times since then I have found your father rereading your letter when he did not think I noticed. In time, perhaps, he may find it in his heart to forgive. Though you did not say so in your letter, I believe you do love General Carleton, and I account him an honorable man despite the course he chose under such provocation . . .

"Your mother was wise to send this through Joshua to prevent its being intercepted." Tess glanced up at Elizabeth, who leaned on the back of the loveseat, scanning the letter over her shoulder. "Well, this is hopeful in every respect. If I know my brother, his heart will soften before long."

"Not so much that he will ever accept that I am Oriole, I fear. But if Papa can find it in his heart to forgive Jonathan, then he need never know the rest."

At Elizabeth's wistful tone, Tess shot her a keen look. "Still no news of Jon's whereabouts?"

Moving around the loveseat, Elizabeth sat down beside her aunt. "Isaiah and the others returned a couple of days ago. The only thing they know for certain is that Jonathan never reached Detroit."

Tess considered the news with a thoughtful expression. "If he had fallen into the hands of the British, they would have made a cause célèbre of him."

"Lord Percy admitted to me yesterday that they've also been frustrated in their attempts to find him. When he never showed up in Virginia, as I led them to believe he would, Gage sent out agents to all the colonies. He went so far as to send a message to Governor Carleton in Canada, in hopes that since they are distant cousins he might have gotten some word of Jonathan's whereabouts. But that was fruitless as well. It's as though Jonathan has vanished from the face of the earth."

"Then the odds are good that he is still alive, though undoubtedly still being held by the Seneca. They must be aware of the reward for his arrest, so I'd think it unlikely they would kill him."

"Then why haven't they turned him over?" Elizabeth's shoulders drooped. "Hope is a false friend, Aunt Tess."

Tess rose and went to the fireplace to add another log to the burning coals. "Did Joshua have no good news for you at all?"

"Dr. Church was finally exposed, and in a way that eliminates any question of his treachery. In spite of every possible protest and excuse, he now languishes in Cambridge gaol."

Tess brightened. "Although we've lost a convenient conduit for spreading false intelligence, I can't bemoan seeing his true character revealed at last."

"He did no more than Jonathan and I have done."

Tess's lips twisted into an ironic smile. "The difference lies in our point of view—and the justice of our cause. Church betrayed us merely for money, not on principle. How was he discovered?"

"By means of a coded letter meant for an officer on Gage's staff. A woman from Cambridge delivered it to a former lover in Newport, with instructions to give it to the commander of a certain British frigate. Being no more a lover of the British than he is any longer of the lady, the man neglected to deliver it, eventually grew suspicious, and brought it to General Greene at Cambridge."

"Oho!" Tess exclaimed.

"Of course, General Washington had the lady brought in, and under pressure, she confessed that the letter had been given her by Dr. Church. With the news out in the open, the General had no choice but to arrest the culprit. He could be no further use to us now."

Tess wagged her head. "Could the letter be deciphered?"

"Indeed, though it took several days. The extent of the political and military intelligence it contained was quite shocking." Elizabeth hesitated before adding, "The letter also claimed that Washington has planted a spy very near Gage—possibly a woman."

Tess sucked in her breath sharply. "Oh, if it had reached its destination!"

"God was watching over us, to be sure." Elizabeth frowned down at her clenched hands, finally looked up. "If I had been identified, you also would have been implicated. I am taking this risk of my own will, and I know you joined me freely. But if I were ever to be the cause of harm to you—"

Tess returned to her seat and covered Elizabeth's hands with her own. "I seem to remember saying the same to you once."

Elizabeth could not suppress a giggle. Impulsively they embraced, but after a moment, Tess raised Elizabeth's chin with her hand, forcing the younger woman to meet her sober gaze.

"We don't know if Church suspected you, but there may be others who do. And Dalton knows. We must take extra care not to test the Lord's protection by running beyond what he calls us to do."

"I am learning little by little, though the lesson is a hard one. I thought it would grow easier once I fully submitted to God's will for my life. But my wayward nature stubbornly keeps cropping back up."

Tess hugged her, laughing. "The sinful flesh still remains. My experience is that once we commit ourselves to a life of obedience, the Adversary's attacks become sharper." She sobered. "Now that Gage is being called home by the Ministry, we must be even more cautious. Howe is reputed to be a more decisive commander, and one who brooks no opposition."

"Oh, very decisive, indeed," Elizabeth scoffed, "judging from his skill at the faro table and his speed in seducing other men's wives." When Tess shook her head sadly, she rushed on, "I feel sorry for Betsey Loring. I wish we could get close enough to her to offer her our friendship, perhaps encourage her to follow a more virtuous path."

Her expression grieved, Tess said, "Betsey seems entirely oblivious to her ruin. And her husband acts as though he has the best of the bargain. Of course, his fortunes have been greatly elevated because his wife caught the eye of a powerful man, but what will their future be when this is over and Howe is gone?"

"We cannot know the hurts of their hearts. All we can do is pray for them."

Tess agreed, then said abruptly, "Captain Dalton made no further advances last night?"

"I made sure he found no opportunity. The way he looks at me—" Breaking off, Elizabeth shuddered.

Throwing a wary glance toward the drawing room's open door, Tess leaned closer to Elizabeth and lowered her voice. "I made a point of drawing Mrs. Dalton out yesterday. After we'd discussed our families at length, she let fall that the captain has been a widower for five years. He had one son, who died on Breed's Hill, and evidently it has changed him. He is angry about his son's loss, and some comments he made in her hearing caused her to think he blames the patriots. Then too, he has much to gain by supplying the British, and much to lose if they are forced out of Boston."

"What am I to do?" Elizabeth demanded urgently.

"Have no more dealings with him! Find another passage to the mainland."

"Even if that were possible, what might Dalton do if I tried to avoid him now?"

Frowning, Tess sat back, resting her chin on her hand. "Ask Joshua what can be done. Ask the General for help."

Elizabeth sprang to her feet and moved closer to the heat of the fire crackling on the hearth. Crossing her arms, she rubbed them against the chill.

"We have calls to make this afternoon, and we'd better hurry or we'll be late for our own dinner party tonight."

Tess regarded her silently for a moment before nodding toward the windows, where fine spearpoints of rain tapped against the windows. "Be sure to wear your heavy cloak. October has brought with it weather as dreary as I've been feeling of late."

While her aunt went upstairs to fetch her cloak and hat, Elizabeth stopped in front of the mirror in the foyer to smooth her tightly fitted bodice over the full curves of her bosom and at her slender waist. Turning this way and that, she noted with indifference that the warm ruby color of the fine woolen cloth and the gown's stylish cut were more than flattering.

Outside, rain continued to gust against the house unabated, and for a moment she considered suggesting they postpone their social calls for another day. Deciding they might as well fulfill their obligations as spend a dull afternoon at home with their anxious thoughts, she settled her beribboned hat on top of her upswept curls and pinned it in place.

She pulled on her gloves, turned to reach for her cloak. And stopped, movement and breath arrested as though she had been slapped across the face.

At the end of the passageway, just outside the rear door that led into the kitchen, stood Dalton.

She reached blindly to steady herself against the edge of the hall table, unable to remove her eyes from his, fascinated with horror as though she stared into the unblinking orbs of a python.

While she stood thus paralyzed, unable to think or even to breathe, small, sparrow-like Mrs. Dalton stepped through the kitchen doorway. Taking the captain's arm, she led him toward Elizabeth.

"Look who's stopped by to call on me, my dear," the housekeeper exclaimed. "This is my husband's brother, Zebulun Dalton.

He's captain of the fishing sloop *Prudence*," she added, unnecessarily. "Zeb, this is my young mistress, Miss Elizabeth Howard."

Elizabeth could feel Dalton's gaze slide across her like violating hands, baring her body and soul to his lustful scrutiny. Involuntarily she drew back, feeling tainted with barnyard muck.

The rising blood scorched her cheeks, then drained away. It was all she could do to return his bow with a stiff nod.

Before either could speak, Mrs. Dalton exclaimed in sudden alarm, "Here now, I'm forgetting the cakes I have in the oven for tonight. If you'll excuse me for just a moment." Releasing Dalton's arm, she hurried back to the kitchen.

Elizabeth wrenched her gaze to the captain, found his hungry gaze licking over her like a cougar slavering over its prey. Sickened, she turned abruptly away.

"If you'll excuse me—"

He was beside her in a step. A soft outcry escaped her lips as he jerked her around, his fingers digging painfully into the tender flesh of her upper arm.

"That I won't. Ye set me on fire, girl, and I mean to take ye. Ye see I know where to find ye now, and I ain't lettin' ye get away. If ye'd not stretch a noose with that lovely neck o' yours, then ye'd better come to me when I say."

She tore out of his grasp. "You lost a son to the British," she spat, "and is this how you'd repay them—by betraying one of your own into their hands?"

His laugh raised the hair on the back of her neck. "Oh, the lobsters shot 'im, all right, but he'd not been on that cursed hill were it not for the Sons o' Liberty. First my wife dies at the hand of a worthless butcher of a doctor like yer own pa, then my son be taken from me for a fool's cause. No, girl, it be time for me to be gettin' some back. I ain't had a woman in mor'n five years, and a daring wench like ye be just what I'm hungerin' for."

Again he took her in from head to foot with a look that caused her stomach to roil. "I never seen nothing like ye, so pretty and fine, so ye better make up yer mind quick 'cause I won't be waitin' long."

Giving her a meaningful smile, he retreated down the passage and through the door out of her sight. She collapsed against the wall, shaking, eyes closed, breath coming in short sobs.

What shall I do? Is there is no escape from this? Lord God—!

But there was no discernible response. It felt as though the Almighty had withdrawn to the far reaches of the universe with no intention of ever being found.

"GOOD EVENING, General Burgoyne." Elizabeth made a deep curtsy. "We're honored to have you and your guest join us."

Burgoyne straightened from his bow, his gaze flickering from Elizabeth to Tess, who stood close to one side, fixing him in a cold gaze that her smile did nothing to soften. Judging from the general's sardonic expression, it was becoming increasingly clear to him that whenever he was in Elizabeth's vicinity, her aunt would be attached to her like a guardian dragon.

After Dalton's unexpected visit, the two women had cancelled their round of social calls. Instead, they had spent the afternoon trying to come up with a solution to Elizabeth's dilemma and seeking guidance from the Lord.

It had not been possible to cancel their dinner party, however. By now Gage, Howe, Joshua and Betsey Loring, Clinton, Lord Percy, Smith, and a couple of the other generals were gathered in the parlor.

As usual, Burgoyne was the last to arrive—in order to make a suitably theatrical entrance, Elizabeth suspected. He drew in an expansive breath of the rich scents coming from the direction of the dining room. And allowed his deliberate gaze to travel to the swelling regions of Elizabeth's bosom, where her gown's supple sea-green damask revealed more than she now wished it did, before rising to her lips. Against her will, the color deepened in her cheeks.

"I would never deny myself the pleasure of *your* company under any circumstances, my dear child," he purred. Drawing forward his companion, he added, "I beg your indulgence for taking the liberty of bringing along an old friend who is only today arrived from England. Allow me to present Lady Caroline Randolph."

Lady Randolph waved a languid hand and drawled, "I do hope my joining you won't cause a problem. John wouldn't hear of leaving me behind."

Elizabeth and Tess quickly assured her of their delight at her presence. As they exchanged curtsies, Elizabeth regarded Lady Randolph with interest.

Perhaps in her early forties, she was slightly shorter than Elizabeth and still strikingly beautiful, with large, violet eyes, glossy brown hair, and a pale, flawless complexion. Her rose-colored gown of the newest style exposed to greatest effect the maximum of bare shoulder, neck, and bosom.

She took Elizabeth's hands and stepped back to look her up and down. "Why, how lovely you are—and as kind as you are beautiful. John has not ceased to sing your praises, and as usual, his taste in the feminine gender is impeccable."

Glancing in Burgoyne's direction, Elizabeth caught the briefest shade of malice in his eyes. It was gone so quickly, however, that she dismissed the impression and led the way into the parlor. Several of their guests were acquainted with Lady Randolph, and they spent the interval until dinner gossiping about the latest news from England.

All of them lauded the king's refusal even to receive the Continental Congress's Olive Branch Petition, an offer to negotiate a resolution of the colonies' grievances that they considered the height of presumption. A discussion of the merits of the Proclamation for Suppressing Rebellion, issued by George III in August, followed.

Clinton noted that the effect of the edict was to end all hope of reconciliation, and the others agreed that the Americans would find themselves properly chastened as a result.

Only Howe took little part in the lively conversation. As usual, his attention was centered on blonde, blue-eyed Betsey Loring, while her husband, a short, brutish man, studiously directed his elsewhere.

Elizabeth and Tess had wrestled with the decision to invite the Lorings, but by now wherever Howe went, the Lorings were expected to follow. Since the evening's purpose was to honor Gage before he sailed for England on October 11, a couple of days hence, they had decided to invite them rather than to spoil the party by Howe's absence.

At dinner Lady Randolph insisted on being seated between Elizabeth and Tess. Throughout the meal, she regaled them with entertaining stories of her life in London.

In spite of her languid manner, as the evening progressed, it became clear that she was perceptive and intelligent, possessed of an excellent grasp of the political issues that had led to armed conflict between England and her colonies. But although the woman's charming manner and wit drew Elizabeth to her, she found herself at the same time repulsed by a subtle jaded and cynical edge to Lady Randolph's conversation.

Learning that Elizabeth's parents were residing in London, she cried, "By all means, I must call on them the moment I return! Judging by my hostesses, they will be the most delightful company."

She turned her wide, violet eyes fully on Elizabeth. "I simply can't imagine why you chose to remain buried in this undistinguished backwater when you could have gone with your parents. They must have been heartbroken to leave you behind, especially when London can offer all the advantages of the best society. How I wish you would agree to let me take you back to England! My love, with my sponsorship added to your beauty, accomplishments, and disposition, you would simply sweep all the eligible men off their feet."

Elizabeth laughed, flattered against her will, but at the same time put off by Lady Randolph's patronizing manner. "According to Mama she has found no men of our station in London who are as admirable as those of our acquaintance here."

Lady Randolph gave a teasing laugh. "Now, do you mean to tell me that any of these colonial rustics is a match for a nobleman at the highest rank of London society? If that is so, why have you not married one of them by now?"

"It has not been for want of offers from legions of the young men of the area, to say nothing of the officers of this garrison," Gage interjected, smiling.

"All of them are quite charming, to be sure," Elizabeth parried, "but I've yet to meet any man for whom I would give up my independence—whether a colonial rustic, as you deem them, or an officer of His Majesty the King."

"And yet," Burgoyne drawled, "your name was linked quite closely with that infamous traitor, Jonathan Carleton. I overheard considerable speculation that you would wed—before he was exposed, of course."

A sudden hush fell over the room. Feeling Tess's alarmed gaze on her, Elizabeth covered her discomfort with a light laugh.

"Dear sir, I believe we have mined that unproductive territory to an ample depth."

"There are some who hold a different opinion of its productiveness," Burgoyne countered.

"Jonathan Carleton? He was your suitor?"

Elizabeth directed a quick glance at Lady Randolph, startled by the catch in her guest's voice.

"Did you know, Miss Howard, that Jonny boy and Lady Randolph were at one time most intimately acquainted?" Burgoyne asked.

A painful tightness closed over Elizabeth's heart. Burgoyne was watching her intently, his heavy-lidded eyes narrowed. This time she could not discount the malice that flashed in them.

The older woman waved his words away. "Oh, it was no secret that we were lovers, my dear, certainly not after my late husband so rashly challenged Jon to a duel. Alas, Jon is much the better swordsman, and even though he gave Bertie every advantage, my poor husband did not survive the contest."

Elizabeth did not trust herself to make a response, prayed that her horror and dismay did not show in her face. She could not stop her gaze from wandering to Lady Randolph's wrists, but any scars that remained from the attempt to end her life were well covered beneath her long sleeves.

It was obvious to Elizabeth as well that, for all the lady's attempts to pretend amused unconcern, it *was* pretense. Did she still love Carleton? Had she, in fact, come to Boston to find him?

Why else would she have come?

On Lady Randolph's other side, Tess sat stiffly upright, disapproval and repulsion contorting her features. "Perhaps such matters are viewed differently in London society, but you must pardon me if I cannot find them laughable."

"You'll find complete agreement in this quarter, Miss Howard. I find Jonny's actions despicable in every regard."

Elizabeth hazarded another glance at Burgoyne. His eyes still probed her, and girding on a self-possession wholly alien to her true emotions, she forced her expression to register nothing more than disgust.

Ignoring the others at table, who were by now entirely engrossed in the exchange, Lady Randolph leaned back in her chair, observing Burgoyne with lazy amusement. "Oh, you're too hard on him, John. He did attempt to do the honorable thing and begged me to marry him. But he was so young and so . . . callow. Looking back now, I hardly know why I allowed him to seduce me in the first place when there were so many more experienced and well-connected prospects vying for my attentions."

She pressed one hand to her bosom, a sensuous smile curving her full lips. "Though with a little tutelage Jon did turn into a most excellent lover. I admit, even though I tired of him in the end, I did so regret dismissing him—for a little while, at least." She laughed.

By now Elizabeth was trembling. Even though, as a doctor and a spy, she had been exposed to scenes and conversations from which young women of her station were carefully shielded, she had encountered nothing like the coarseness of Lady Randolph's discourse. Every nerve cried out to slap the woman. At the same time it was all she could do not to weep.

It had been hard enough to hear Carleton's side of the story, sordid as it was. But to face his former mistress now, to see the physical beauty that had drawn him into her clutches, coupled with an apparently total absence of morality, to listen to her vulgar disparagement of Carleton's most intimate actions was worse than if she had run Elizabeth through with a sword.

Burgoyne gave a soft, calculating laugh. "Well, he has turned to far more dangerous games in the meantime."

"So I understand, though I could hardly have credited his imagination as being capable of carrying off such a dangerous pose." Lady Randolph turned expectantly to Elizabeth. "Is it really true he brazenly passed intelligence to the rebels through that spy and smuggler Oriole that John has told me so much about?"

"General Burgoyne knows far more about the matter than I do." Elizabeth lifted her wine glass in his direction, her hand feeling as icy as the crystal. "I'm afraid you'll have to ask him."

"General Carleton's actions were as much a shock to us as I'm sure they were to all of you," Tess put in coldly. "He is most certainly a master of deceit."

"Can you tell me that, as close as you once were, you caught no hint of his treachery, Miss Howard?" Burgoyne purred.

Lady Randolph clapped her hand over her mouth in affected alarm. "Don't tell me you were lovers!"

Elizabeth stiffened. "Most certainly not, Madam. General Burgoyne seems determined to believe what I keep denying—a determination unworthy of a gentleman. Whatever else he may have done, General Carleton always behaved honorably in my presence."

Lady Randolph arched an eyebrow and tilted her head to scrutinize Elizabeth. "Why, then . . . the charming devil must have lost his touch. But you are a mere child, after all—so perhaps he lacked the interest." She gave a regretful sigh.

"On the other hand, it may be that he respected me too much to ruin my reputation and honor." Elizabeth smiled kindly at her tormentor. "And in any case, I would not have given in to him."

Touche. With satisfaction she saw that her words had struck home.

They had all but finished the last course, and Pete was quietly circling the table, refilling the wine glasses. Distracted by the guilty knowledge that she *had* been willing to give in to Carleton, Elizabeth waved her hand in a dismissive gesture just as Pete reached past her to refill Lady Randolph's glass. Elizabeth's hand collided with his arm, sending the wine spurting over Lady Randolph's bare shoulder, across her fashionable gown, down her bosom, and into her lap.

"*You stupid buffoon!*" cried the lady, springing to her feet.

Elizabeth jumped up at the same instant, overturning her chair. "Oh, I'm so sorry!" she gasped. "It's all my fault. Please forgive me."

Grabbing her napkin she attempted vainly to sop up the stain that spread in a lush, dark shadow all down the soft rose brocade of Lady Randolph's fashionable gown, while Tess and Betsey Loring clustered around to offer help. An equally deep stain spread across Pete's dusky cheeks. He hastily set down the wine bottle and reached to sponge the spilled liquid with the napkin he carried over his arm.

"Excuse me, Madam. I didn't mean to—"

She jerked away from him. "Oh, shut up, you vile creature! Don't you dare touch me!"

He stepped back, his expression stricken. The faces of the others around the table reflected variously sympathy or convulsed amusement.

Elizabeth bit her lip hard to suppress a giggle, wavering between horror at what she had inadvertently done to a guest in her home and a wicked glee. A large part of her felt that the unlucky lady deserved her impromptu baptism, if only to cut off her scandalous and hurtful comments. This, the accident had decisively accomplished.

"It isn't your fault," she murmured hastily to Pete. "Go back to the kitchen, and ask Mrs. Dalton to come see if she can help. If we need anything else, I'll call for you."

He wasted no time retreating, while the three women dabbed at Lady Randolph's gown with napkins dampened in their water goblets. As the case clock in the parlor tolled the hour, Mrs. Dalton quietly joined them to survey the damage.

"It's growing late," Tess noted. "I'm sure by now you gentlemen are longing to smoke your pipes and drink your scotch in peace. The library is at your disposal, and I'll have Pete wait on you while we take care of this little accident."

"It's hardly a little accident," Lady Randolph wailed. "This gown cost a pretty penny, and now it's ruined!"

The men had been finding considerable entertainment in the proceedings, and they adjourned to the library with perceptible reluctance. Mrs. Dalton bustled off upstairs with Lady Randolph and Betsey Loring to remove the sodden gown and see what could be done about the stain.

As soon as they disappeared up the stairs, Tess drew Elizabeth aside. "Did you know?"

Elizabeth nodded, tears welling into her eyes. "He told me, though not the lady's name. I never thought I'd meet her."

The words choked in her throat, and she broke off.

"Was what she said true—that he seduced her, then wanted to marry her?"

"It's not as Jonathan described it. He was young and quite naïve. From what he told me, it seemed very evident that she seduced him. He said she . . . she slashed her wrists because he attempted to break off their affair. It caused a great scandal, of course, and the duel. After . . . after her husband died . . . he could not bear the thought of marrying her."

"I'd believe Jon before her."

"I know he told the truth. And he blamed no one but himself."

Tess engulfed her in an embrace. "It's almost as if Burgoyne brought her here tonight deliberately intending to do this."

"I'm certain he did," Elizabeth admitted tremulously. "Since he can't get at Jonathan by seducing me, perhaps he's determined to destroy our relationship by whatever means he can."

Tess's arms tightened around Elizabeth's shoulders, and she whispered fiercely, "Nothing that happened before you and Jon met matters one whit. It's in the past. He's been forgiven for it, and he's changed. It's you he loves—none other."

Elizabeth nodded, her eyes downcast. "Yes. And yet it still hurts."

"Tell Mrs. Gage how much we miss her. I hope and pray all will go well with you both."

Gage met Elizabeth's sympathetic gaze with a veiled one. For a moment he hesitated, began to speak, finally said gruffly, "Thank you for your good wishes. I'm afraid we shall need them."

It was early Wednesday afternoon. Buffeted by the wind gusting off the ocean, their parasols raised against the intermittent drizzle, Elizabeth and Tess stood beside the disgraced commander halfway down Long Wharf, awaiting the signal for the departure of the ship that would take him back to England and an uncertain future.

Two months earlier, from that same dock, Margaret Gage and her children had set sail aboard a ship loaded with the most desperately injured of the soldiers who had survived the carnage on Breed's Hill. That day the wharf had teemed with well wishers and those who wept to see loved ones in such sad state being borne away. Today she and Tess had found Gage hauntingly alone, except for his former aide and a couple of the officers who had been the closest to him. No one else had come to bid farewell to the man who had ruled the colony for more than a year as its first military governor.

They lingered only until the ship's passengers boarded before they hurried back to Tess's chariot waiting at the end of King Street. It was a relief to climb inside, out of the piercing east wind and the penetrating damp.

Leaning back against the padded seat, Elizabeth reflected that in seeking to steer a moderate course, Gage had pleased neither patriot nor loyalist. He had been the wrong man in the wrong job in the wrong place at the wrong time. And now he had been superseded by a man whose private conduct made it impossible for Elizabeth to respect him.

Her thoughts drifted to Washington. She had seen evidence of his temper, but also of his compassion and kindness, his stern determination to do what was right and good. If ever a man had been placed in high position by God, surely this man had been.

As so often in the past weeks, her thoughts made the same anxious circuit, and unconsciously she clenched her hands. What was she to do about Dalton? She could not put him off much longer. She had been foolish to hesitate so long because her pride insisted that she could find a solution to her dilemma without seeking aid. There was now no longer any choice but to appeal to Stern, and if necessary, to Washington for rescue.

But what was she to do if even they could not stop Dalton before he betrayed her—or worse?

Chapter Eighteen

"AIEEEE! Shining Star — no!"

Swinging around, Carleton sucked in his breath. At the edge of the fire circle several feet away, the toddler teetered, one foot tangled in scattered kindling, her tiny arms windmilling as she tipped perilously close to the cherry-red coals.

There was no time to think. Laughing Waters was too far away to reach her daughter in time. Taking two swift steps, he bent and scooped her out of danger.

Burning pain seared all along his lower arm where the bare flesh had come into contact with the shimmering coals. The child screamed and thrashed against him as he straightened, more frightened now of him than of the fire. He cradled her close, biting his lip hard against the white-hot agony that radiated along the burn.

By now the women and children had run to where he stood. Fearful that touching one of their children would earn him a beating, he hastily surrendered the screaming child to her mother and turned to retreat to the mortar where he had been grinding corn.

Before he could step away, Red Wing caught him by the arm. Tensing, he stopped at once, but kept his head bent, not meeting their stares. Careful not to touch the burn, she lifted his arm for the others to see.

"Look, he burned his arm. It's bad too."

Laughing Waters held her baby against her shoulder, patting her back. The child clung to her with one arm, hiccupping as she rubbed the tears from her eyes with her small fist.

"He saved Shining Star. He didn't have to do it."

Basket Weaver came to Carleton's side, brought her face close to his arm to scrutinize the wound. Glancing down, Carleton winced at what he saw.

A wide, raw welt oozing blood and clear fluid stretched along the outside of his arm from wrist to elbow. It was not as bad as he had feared, but left untreated it would certainly become infected. The wound could well cripple him. Or kill him.

Little Grey Dove hurried to join them. "I'll bandage it. Here's the poultice."

She held a strip of cloth and a small pottery jar filled with a mixture of herbs and bear grease. Grunting, Basket Weaver motioned to Carleton to sit down on the log next to the fire.

He obeyed, sat unflinching as the two women washed the wound, then covered it with the poultice and wrapped it loosely. They took obvious care not to hurt him more than necessary, and involuntarily he began to tremble, tears rising near the surface.

It was the first kind touch he had felt in two months. The women who had cared for his wounds after he ran the gauntlet had shown no feeling for him as an individual. He might as well have been a piece of leather they kneaded for all the concern they demonstrated in their care of him. The emotion that swept over him now astonished him at its strength.

Within moments, the intense burning sensation diminished to a dull ache. To his surprise, Red Wing ordered one of the younger women to finish grinding the corn. When he began to get up, Basket Weaver motioned to him to stay where he was. One by one the other women drifted back to their work, all except Little Grey Dove, who as usual found an excuse to linger nearby.

Appearing to take notice that he shivered in the cold wind, Basket Weaver and Red Wing disappeared into the longhouse. After a short interval, Basket Weaver returned carrying a buckskin hunting shirt. He recognized it as an old one that had belonged to her long-dead husband.

"Put this on, Fire Builder," she ordered.

He obeyed hesitantly, careful not to chafe his bandaged arm. The shirt showed wear in places, but at least it was in better condition than his leggings. And though it was tight across the shoulders and the sleeves were too short, it provided welcome warmth.

Evidently he was not to freeze after all, he concluded, a thin thread of hope rising in him. And now he had a name. From his struggle to remain obedient to God had come this small step forward. Perhaps in time he would win favor with his captors after all.

For all hope of escape was certainly gone until the spring. It was mid October, and in spite of the sun that shone brightly high overhead in the cloud-dotted sky, the wind held an icy edge. The brilliantly colored leaves were almost all gone from the trees.

Three more weeks had passed, with never a time when at least some of the men of the village were not in the vicinity. Basket Weaver constantly watched over his work, and always there was another task to keep him busy. And in sight.

The previous week, the villagers had completed their move to the new site on the bank of a turbulent river in what he guessed to be northwestern Pennsylvania. Two additional days and considerably more unfamiliar territory had been added to the already long and perilous journey home. With his arm injured, it was unlikely he could withstand the rigors of the forest or defend himself if he was attacked. And if the wound became infected, he would have no way of treating it.

At thought of the cruel winter that lay ahead, despair swept over him. Would he ever see home again? For that matter, *where* was home?

The only answer that made sense was that it was wherever Elizabeth was.

Which raised the question of whether the British still held Boston. Had they broken the siege, or had Washington driven them out? Was Elizabeth still safe?

He might never know. The only thing he could do was to pray.

Another improvement in his situation provided additional encouragement, however. After the incident with Walks-With-A-Limp, the child had gravitated to Carleton. His father had died of smallpox before his birth, and because he was hindered in keeping up with their play, the other children often neglected him.

Against his will, Carleton began to take an interest in the child. Later that week he found Walks-With-A-Limp struggling to shoot a small bow. Again and again he drew the bow and aimed for the target the older boys had set up. But each time his arrow went astray or fell short.

Finished splitting wood and building a fire in the outdoor oven for Laughing Waters to bake bread, Carleton made sure the women were all occupied at their tasks before he went over to the boy. He squatted down beside him as once more the child drew back on the bowstring.

The weapon was too large for him, and he could hardly bend it. When he let the arrow fly, it twirled away to fall several feet short of the target. The boy's face crumpled, and he threw a sidelong glance at Carleton from downcast eyes, clearly humiliated at his failure.

"You work hard," Carleton said, struggling to find the words in the Seneca tongue. "A little help, and you hit target. Show you?"

Walks-With-A-Limp's face brightened, and he nodded eagerly. Carleton motioned to him to fetch the arrow. Patiently he waited until the child limped over to pick up the fallen arrow, then returned.

Kneeling behind the boy, Carleton put his arms around his slender shoulders and helped him nock the arrow into the bowstring.

With both their hands on the bow, Carleton's large ones over the child's small fingers, they drew the bow together until the slender piece of wood bent almost double.

With his cheek next to Walks-With-A-Limp's thin one, Carleton showed him how to aim for the center of the target, then raise the bow slightly to allow for distance. Together they let the arrow fly.

This time the slender shaft arced through the air and struck the target with a solid thunk well in from the outer edge. Walks-With-A-Limp clapped his hands and hopped up and down in delight on his good leg.

Laughing, Carleton sent him to retrieve the arrow. Several more tries, and the arrow found the target's center.

This time Carleton was rewarded with a hug. He knelt in the dust, eyes closed, gathering the child to him at the fervent pressure of the thin arms tightening around his neck, the smooth cheek lovingly pressed against his.

Abruptly he became aware that someone stood over them. Looking up, he steeled himself for a blow but met the eyes of Spotted Fawn, Walks-With-A-Limp's mother.

Far from appearing displeased, she met his wary gaze with a warm one. As Walks-With-A-Limp turned to her, she took his hand, smiling. Giving Carleton a respectful nod, she led the boy back to her longhouse.

IT SOON BECAME EVIDENT that the stories of Carleton's kindness to Walks-With-A-Limp and of his saving Shining Star from the fire had gained him favor among the women and children. From that day, the women not only took an interest in the healing of his arm, but also found excuse to share the best of their food with him. They often beckoned him to join them around the fire as they worked and talked.

Basket Weaver's treatment of him also softened. He found an old bearskin on the platform where he slept, which made the cold nights endurable. Though she still slept between him and the door, she stopped binding him at night, and she made new moccasins for him. Faithfulness in his tasks and going beyond what was expected in order to help her, which he had not thought she noticed, made a difference after all.

As the days passed, he was also increasingly trusted alone with the children, where before one or more of the women had kept an eye on the young ones when he was nearby. More and more the children followed Carleton as he worked and even included him in their games.

Often when the adolescent boys shot at targets with bows and arrows early in the morning or in the evening before sunset, they called him to join them. As his burn crusted over and closed up, he began to practice casually with their child-sized bows when his tasks were completed, pretending to take part in their play. Deliberately he honed his skill until he was satisfied that he could once again shoot as accurately as any of the young warriors. At the same time, he took care not to draw the attention of any of the adults to his accomplishments.

The children proved to be a storehouse of language. They delighted in teaching him new words and giggled when he mispronounced a word or phrased something awkwardly. Day by day he deciphered more of their conversation, but though he spoke freely to the children, he remained guarded around their parents, answering only in grunts or gestures and deliberately pretending to understand little of what they said.

It helped that the men of the village excluded him from their company. He had learned early on that to approach any of them was to hazard insult, even physical abuse, so he gladly kept his distance.

To be included as part of the circle of women and children, however, made his life more tolerable. Their acceptance provided an encouraging, though small, measure of freedom. If only he could endure until the spring, their favor might become an open door.

To escape. To return to Elizabeth.

Daily the thought obsessed him more. He had to fight to keep the memory of her at bay so he could focus on enduring whatever each day might bring. But in the dark nights the longing for her gave him no rest.

The greatest distraction took the form of Little Grey Dove. As he went about his work he often felt her gaze resting on him. Whenever he involuntarily met her glance, hers softened and she made no attempt to conceal the heat and the invitation there. After the incidents with Shining Star and Walks-With-A-Limp, she made even more excuses to put herself in Carleton's way.

Every interaction with her filled him with anxiety. All he needed was to run afoul of Half Moon or Cackling Crow, both of whom already took it upon themselves to make Carleton's life as miserable as possible anytime they took notice of him. Neither appeared to have yet marked Little Grey Dove's growing attraction to him, but it was surely only a matter of time. Yet for all Carleton's worrying, he was unable to come up with any idea of how to tactfully discourage her attentions.

Late in the month Half Moon and a large party of the men left the village before daybreak to hunt. Mid-afternoon, while Carleton built up the fires for the women to cook the evening meal, Little Grey Dove came to squat beside him at the fire circle.

She was so close to him that her skirt brushed against his leg. Looking up, he read unmistakable desire in her eyes. In spite of the chill, she carried her leather cape rather than wearing it, and when she leaned toward him, her full, round breast pressed against his arm.

He drew quickly away. "Slave," he said, pointing to himself and hoping mightily that she would take the hint and leave him alone.

The blood rose into her cheeks and a look of stubborn resolve hardened her jaw. "If I want you, my father will give you to me."

The words hit him like a blow to the pit of his stomach. Abruptly he stood up, put the fire between them.

"No," he said, measuring every word, trying to speak ingratiatingly but firmly. "Half Moon and Cackling Crow want you. They good warriors, strong and brave. I am slave. Not right—you and me."

She laughed and slowly got to her feet, her large, dark eyes drinking in the length of his lean form and the tautness of the buckskin shirt across his arms and shoulders. "We dance tonight."

Stunned, he prayed that he had not understood her correctly. If she had said what he thought she had, her willfulness could only result in disaster.

That night the unmarried men and women of the village would dance around the fire. During the dance some would choose a marriage partner. If Little Grey Dove were to offer her attentions to him, everyone in the village would be witness to it. They would believe he had encouraged her, even seduced her, and the reprisals would certainly be severe.

As if in echo of his thoughts, just then the hunting party returned, bringing the game they had taken. Half Moon hurried toward them, with Cackling Crow, Lone Wolf, and several of the others following.

Seeing Carleton and Little Grey Dove standing across the fire from each other, Half Moon came to a halt, his eyes narrowing as he looked from one to the other. This time Little Grey Dove made no attempt to veil her desire. She kept her gaze boldly on Carleton for an interval that lasted far too long before she conceded Half Moon and the others a deliberately challenging glance.

Comprehension came into Half Moon's eyes, then his face contorted with anger. For a moment he appeared beyond speech, but finally he spat out, "You want our women, slave, so we will show them what you are made of."

Striding over to Carleton, he grabbed him by the arm. At his touch, a bolt of rage surged through Carleton, and he tore out of his tormentor's grasp.

Before Half Moon could react, Carleton strode over to Lone Wolf and Cackling Crow. A crowd was gathering, and he faced them all with unflinching defiance, head high, teeth clenched, resolved that if he was to suffer a beating anyway, he might as well give them sufficient provocation.

"I hear from the children's chatter that he is good with the bow. Have him show us," Cackling Crow sneered.

The men circled around Carleton. Shoving him into their midst, they drew him outside the palisade to where the older youths had marked targets for their practice on the trunks of several trees edging the nearest field. Cackling Crow brought along a quiver of arrows and a couple of bows, one of which he thrust into Carleton's hands.

Nocking an arrow to his bowstring, Cackling Crow took aim and let the arrow fly. It struck dead center the mark on a tree one hundred yards away.

Thoughtfully Carleton tested his bow, pleased to feel its quality and tension. A typical Seneca hunting bow, it was about four feet long and skillfully crafted of both cedar and hickory, with the wood backed by rawhide. It had a good weight in his hands and a nicely resilient draw.

Choosing an arrow, he took aim, estimating the arc the arrow would need to reach the target, and then let go. The arrow sizzled through the air and impaled itself into the tree less than an inch below the mark.

The onlookers roared with derisive laughter. Conceding a faint smile, Carleton chose another arrow and this time aimed a fraction higher. Hissing through the air in a true arc, it struck the mark with a solid *thunk,* burying its head tightly against Cackling Crow's.

No one laughed this time. His gaze deadly, Half Moon disappeared back inside the palisade and quickly returned, carrying a rifle. As he approached Carleton, he tossed the weapon in his direction. His movements instinctive, Carleton caught the weapon in midair with his free hand.

Half Moon gestured toward the branch of a tree on the far side of the field. Intent on finding a hiding place for the acorn he carried in his mouth, a squirrel leaped from branch to branch.

"You are good with the bow." Half Moon motioned toward the squirrel as though firing at it. "We will see what you can hit with a rifle."

Fairly choking on frustration and resentment, Carleton dropped his bow to the ground. In rapid sequence he snapped the rifle to his shoulder, sighted it, and pulled off the shot. A puff of smoke rose from the rifle's barrel as the reverberation echoed among the trees. Nearly three hundred yards away, the squirrel plummeted to the ground.

For a long moment, Half Moon stared in the direction of the shot, his hands clenching and unclenching. Then he raised both fists and let out a shriek.

"You see that this slave is skillful with a bow and can shoot a rifle as accurately as the best of us! Who knows what he might do with tomahawk or knife. He is one of their most renowned warriors and a grave danger to us."

"What I do?" Carleton demanded, fury boiling up. "You tell me shoot squirrel, and I do. Now you—" He stopped, silently cursing his stupidity.

They were all enraged now. "See, he understands our words," Cackling Crow accused. "Half Moon is right. The slave only waits for an unguarded moment to attack us or to escape. I have watched him try to win Little Grey Dove, who is too young and innocent to guard herself against him. Our women even leave the children with him. He cannot be trusted. Better that we take him to Detroit and sell him to the British rather than waiting for him to seduce our women and kill our children."

The men surged around Carleton and dragged him to the council house. The entire village was quickly called together. Her face sober, Red Wing escorted her defiant daughter inside and sat protectively beside her.

Forced to his haunches in the middle of the room, Carleton saw the stern glance that passed from Lone Wolf to Little Grey Dove, and a painful tightness constricted his breast. It was as he had feared. Her willful insistence on pursuing him had done nothing but harm.

Half Moon was the first to speak. "The slave pretends to be a half-wit, but in truth he understands everything we say. Clearly he has been plotting to escape so he may return to the Long Knives and bring them to war against us. He is an officer in their army and expert with weapons. As if that were not enough, he has bewitched the heart of Little Grey Dove to desire him even though he is a slave and a white man."

He paused, then added with malice, "The only explanation is that he is possessed by one of the False Faces."

A gasp of dismay rose from the elders. Carleton managed to keep his expression impassive, but horror flooded over him at the mention of the Iroquoian belief that disembodied, evil faces appeared in the forests to bewitch the unwary, causing them to fall into dangerous illnesses. There was no way to combat such an accusation against the highly superstitious Seneca.

Lone Wolf held up a hand to silence the angry murmurs that rippled through the council room. "You bring serious charges that we must weigh carefully. What is your counsel for dealing with the slave?"

"The British will pay richly for him," Half Moon answered. "He was one of their own officers, but he betrayed our Father Gage to the Long Knives, so great is his treachery. We took him to carry him to Detroit and sell him for the ransom offered for his capture. Instead we lost our resolve and have kept him here all these months, which gained us nothing. If our friends the British find out that we have kept him from them, or if he escapes to return to the Long Knives and fight against the British, they will justly withdraw their protection from us."

He turned to face the council. "Before he can do us any more harm, let us take him to Detroit as we planned. The reward will purchase many goods—food, clothing, rifles, ammunition, and much more with which to feed and clothe our people through this winter and to protect ourselves against the Long Knives."

Murmurs and nods of agreement met his words. Lone Wolf turned to Carleton.

"What answer do you make to these charges, slave?"

Ignoring the edge of contempt in the old man's tone, Carleton got to his feet and straightened to his full height. Speaking in French, he said, "I have not touched your women or plotted against anyone. I was sent by the great General Washington to counsel with your sachems and conclude a treaty for your protection so that when the Long Knives defeat the British, trade may continue between us. I was promised safety while I treated with you. Instead, I was beaten and brought here for no reason, my friends were taken away, perhaps killed, and I was made a slave.

"If I wished to hurt the Seneca, would I have saved Shining Star from the fire or befriended your children? Basket Weaver can tell you this is true."

He looked at Basket Weaver in mute appeal. As she hesitated, he sent up a desperate prayer that God would give him favor with her and with the elders.

Basket Weaver nodded. "It is true that this slave prevented the daughter of Spotted Fawn from falling into the fire. He acted when he could have done nothing, and he even burned his arm saving the child. As for the charges that he bewitches our young women—" She stopped, then said dryly, "They can see that he is a notable warrior, well formed of body and strong for siring sons. It takes no False Face for our daughters to see that he is desirable as a husband."

Several of the young maidens covered their mouths to stifle their giggles. Frowning, the elders appraised Carleton and traded glances among themselves.

As Half Moon again rose to speak, Lone Wolf motioned him to silence, his glance challenging. Finally he said, "What is your council, Basket Weaver? He is your slave. What are we to do with him?"

Basket Weaver looked Carleton up and down. "We have three choices. He has proven himself, and I am willing to adopt him as my son. But we gain little advantage from this."

Carleton held his breath. Little Grey Dove obviously hoped for this alternative, but she dared not speak in the council. Biting her lip and frowning, she lowered her eyes, suppressed rebellion in every angle of her body.

"The second choice is to sacrifice him to torture," Basket Weaver continued. "He is strong and brave and will acquit himself with honor, undoubtedly for well more than a day. Then when he dies, we can eat his flesh and partake of his bravery."

Nausea swept over Carleton. He stared into the air, willing himself to appear unmoved.

"Or we can do as Half Moon counsels and sell him to the British," Basket Weaver concluded. "By doing so, we strengthen our ties with them and gain great advantage in trade. One thing we must consider well before we decide on this course, however, is that by turning one of the Long Knives' renowned warriors over to their enemy for execution, we make ourselves odious to them. If the Long

Knives succeed in their war against the British, then they will make war on us."

"They will make war on us regardless of what we do," Half Moon cried out. "We must either fight them or surrender like cowards and let them drive us far away across the Great River."

Intense discussion followed, with Half Moon pressing for the last alternative. The possibility of adopting Carleton into the clan was quickly dismissed. Half Moon's charges that he could not be trusted and that he was a danger to them bore too much weight. Even Carleton's reminder that he had been promised protection while treating with them, only to be betrayed, accomplished nothing but to add fuel to the fire.

Carleton could never be loyal to them, Half Moon insisted. With this, the elders were in unanimous agreement. Even Basket Weaver and Red Wing deserted Carleton. All the women, whose respect and sympathy he had won through painstaking effort, turned against him now, and the decision was made to take him to Detroit.

Somewhere in the back of his mind Carleton knew that resistance was the worst response he could make. But the long months of injustice and degradation were finally too much. When they surrounded him to drag him outside, he gave in to unreasoning fear and rage.

Maddened beyond enduring, he fought them with every vestige of his considerable strength, clawed his way to the edge of the enraged mob, and very nearly won through to make a desperate run for freedom. But in the end their numbers were too great, and at last they bore him, bleeding and unconscious, to the ground.

Chapter Nineteen

"I<small>T'S TO BE A FARCE</small> entitled *The Blockade of Boston,*" Lady Randolph confided over the crowd's enthusiastic applause and whistles as the curtain began once more to rise. "I believe John is to play General Washington. It's going to be just too delicious!"

Elizabeth cocked her head. "Did you hear that?"

Tess listened for a moment, straining to make out another sound below the excited rustle of the audience that filled Faneuil Hall's expansive second-floor meeting hall. "It's only thunder. Will this infernal rain never stop?"

As if in response to her words, the curtain froze slightly above halfway on its ascent. At the same moment an actor clad in the rustic attire of a Yankee sergeant appeared at center stage. Visibly agitated, he motioned vehemently to the audience for silence.

"The alarm guns are firing! The rebels have attacked Charlestown! All soldiers are ordered to report to their stations at once!"

Laughter and jeering catcalls greeted his words. Elizabeth and her aunt exchanged puzzled glances.

Tess leaned toward Elizabeth, her hand cupped around her mouth. "I don't think this is part of the play."

"That cannon fire sounds entirely too real," Elizabeth agreed. "And it does seem to be coming from the direction of Charlestown."

Even over the boisterous crowd, they could hear repeated booming reverberations, and below it, the sharp crack of what sounded disturbingly like muskets.

"I'm not acting!" the counterfeit rebel shouted, his face turning purple. "This is real! We're under attack!"

Whistles and boos greeted his words, but when he repeated his protests, adding vehement curses to them, apprehension, then alarm, gripped playgoers and actors alike. In moments chaos reigned, with officers and soldiers together shoving through the crush, while here and there women slumped, swooning, in their chairs.

Elizabeth could hear the steady, late October drizzle drumming against the building, and through it, the repeated boom of cannon. She and Tess lingered until most of the audience had vacated the hall. By then Lady Randolph and the rest of their party had disappeared. When they came downstairs, however, Elizabeth and her aunt found the others huddled at the outer doors, waiting for their carriages to be brought around.

With them was Burgoyne. As though nothing unusual had happened, he grandly beckoned the two women to join them.

"Not to worry," he boasted loudly enough for everyone in the vicinity to hear. "We'll drive the ruffians off shortly and give them a sound drubbing in the process."

Elizabeth suppressed a smile at the general's appearance. He still wore a costume meant to portray the uniform of a general of the Continental Army, and his makeup lent a particularly villainous cast to his countenance.

"Once they see you coming, sir," Tess agreed drolly, "I've no doubt they'll flee to the hills with their tails between their legs."

In spite of herself, Elizabeth giggled. Far from appearing offended, Burgoyne laughed and made a sweeping bow.

"I vow they shall indeed, Madam."

Deliberately he transferred his gaze to Elizabeth. "Before I run off to give those devils the spanking they have due, I must share the wickedly delightful news we received just today. General Carleton has been found at long last. The reason we've heard nothing of him is that he was captured by the Seneca months ago. Now here's the best part: They've made him their slave."

Elizabeth felt as though Burgoyne had struck her a hard blow across the face. How she kept from staggering backward, she had no idea.

She became aware that Tess's fingers dug into her upper arm and heard her challenging laugh. "Oh, you don't say! How perfectly amusing."

Elizabeth's sickened gaze skimmed the others in the party. They were all laughing, obviously in high good humor at the fate they envisioned for the one who had deceived them so spectacularly. For that instant she could not force herself to meet Burgoyne's stare and read the smug satisfaction there.

To her dismay, he took possession of her hand. "You may console yourself, Miss Howard, with the knowledge that he would undoubtedly have been better off if we'd merely hanged him. I hear to be made a slave by the natives is a fate worse than death."

She forced a light laugh. "I've heard shocking stories of what the Indians do to their captives, though it's no more than he deserves. You are certain it's him?"

Burgoyne's steady stare bored into her eyes. "Positive. The report came from a chieftain of the Mohawks named Great Owl who was actually involved in his capture. Jonny boy and this Andrews fellow were trying to persuade the Iroquois to turn against us and support the rebels. Great Owl wanted to drag him off to Detroit and sell him back to us, but it seems the Seneca decided he'd be of more use to them as a slave.

"According to Great Owl, he was taken to one of their towns in southwestern New York near the Pennsylvania border. Great Owl told our contact that the last time he saw Jonny he was half dead from being forced to run the gauntlet."

His voice sounded curiously muted. Elizabeth could hardly feel his hand tightly imprisoning hers.

"I presume you will go after him and bring him back to face justice."

Burgoyne's smile held anticipation and malice. "Oh, most assuredly, though I do regret that we'll be forced to cut short his misery. But if we've gotten a line on him, the rebels will also learn his whereabouts sooner or later. And I mean to make absolutely certain that we get to him first."

Washington will know what to do.

Elizabeth stared across the harbor toward Winisimmit, willing the *Prudence* to cut through the bay more quickly. It seemed the town drew nearer at the same agonizingly interminable speed that had characterized the night.

Long after the rebels' bombardment finally ceased, she still tossed restlessly on her bed in sleepless torment. The first, faint light of coming dawn had found her already at the docks awaiting the sloop's arrival.

Her fingernails dug into the weather rail's smoothly worn wood. *If he's in a meeting, I'll break in. I'll persuade him to send Charles and Isaiah right away.*

She gasped as a hand jerked her around. Her fearful eyes met Dalton's malevolent glare.

" 'Tis about time ye came to me," he ground out. "I've been right patient, but no more. Ye've had all the chances I'm givin'."

Elizabeth threw an apprehensive glance toward the fishermen

who brushed past them as they hurried to complete their tasks. The cramped expanse of deck was crowded, and they were becoming the object of curious looks.

Dalton noted the direction of her gaze. "Don't ye worry none about that. No one'll know. Tonight when ye get back from takin' care o' yer business, I'll tell Jabez somethin' come up and send him and the boys on out."

Her thoughts scrambled, trying to focus on what he was saying, trying to put Burgoyne's malicious words aside so she could deal with this new problem. Tess had begged her not to go, not to put herself once more into Dalton's power. But with Boston's perimeter tightly sealed, there had been no other choice.

Again I've made a mess of things! she cried out silently. *Father, show me what to do!*

"But Jabez will question why you're not going with them," she protested, saying the first thing that came into her mind. "They'll wonder about my not returning as I've always done. I'll be exposed, and—"

"All right," he growled, to her relief giving in without objection. "I can't afford anythin' going wrong with my boat anyways or bein' out the money if they fail to catch a full load."

He thought a moment. "We'll go out tonight as usual, but 'stead o' stoppin' off at Boston ye'll come back with me like we got some business to take care of. With ye dressed like a boy, nobody'll guess what that business be. I ain't got nobody at home no more, so we'll be alone."

Bringing his face close to hers, he whispered, "I like ye, girl, and I'll take care o' ye. Ye ain't got nothin' to fear from that standpoint. I intend to make this right pleasant for ye."

She tried not to shrink away or show her revulsion. "Yes," she agreed, forcing a smile she hoped was inviting. Trembling, she pressed her arm against the loaded pistol concealed beneath her short fisherman's jacket, grimly determined that if he tried to force himself on her and she could find no alternative, she would use it. At least she had bought a little time.

Nervously she glanced toward the Winisimmit dock, now swiftly drawing nearer off their starboard bow. The fishermen were hauling down the sails, and the *Prudence* slowed as the pilot feathered the tiller to ease her against the pilings.

Watching her closely, Dalton narrowed his eyes. "And don't ye be thinkin' o' trying to slip away. I been talking to one o' Admiral Graves's captains. If I tell him anything, he'll talk to Graves, and Graves'll talk to Howe. If ye don't come back tonight, then I'll tell him about how ye and yer aunt's been spyin' fer Washington. They'll hang her and come lookin' fer ye too."

Elizabeth tried to swallow, but her mouth was too dry. "Of course, I'll—"

"Hey, Cap'n, it's gettin' late, and we got this load to finish up."

Dalton turned to Jabez, who stood only a couple of feet away, looking from his captain to Elizabeth with an uncertain expression. Already the Winisimmit and Cambridge merchants waited in expectant clusters along the dock to scrutinize the last of the sloop's load of fish.

"Keep yer shirt on," Dalton growled. "Me and Tom is done with our business. Get the men busy clearing the hold."

Directing Elizabeth a meaningful look, Dalton stalked off to the gangplank to meet with his buyers. Elizabeth willed her trembling to still and quickly slipped off the boat, praying that none of the fishermen had taken especial note of her confrontation with Dalton.

In moments she left the town behind. Making sure no one was in the vicinity to observe her, she detoured to a small farm a short distance from the causeway down to Penny Ferry at the Mystic River. When the weather had turned cold, Stern had begun stabling her black mare there, and the farmer's teenage son wasted no time in saddling the animal. Like his father a staunch Son of Liberty, he asked no questions and took care not to observe her too closely.

She encountered neither wagon, carriage, nor rider until she reached the outskirts of Cambridge, cold through from the swift ride through the bracing wind. The aide who guarded Washington's headquarters like the mythical griffin looked her up and down with a barely concealed sneer.

"His Excellency is not to be disturbed. If you'll tell me what your business is, I'll convey it to the General when he has time to consider it."

Clearly he regarded a youth clad in the short blue jacket and tarred trousers of a fisherman as of less than no importance. Gambling that Washington was behind the closed doors of his office, she darted around the aide and, before he could stop her, threw open the door.

Washington looked up from the maps spread in front of him, his brow furrowed with annoyance. Seated in front of the desk, old Colonel Gridley of the artillery sprang to his feet to intercept her.

"Your Excellency," she began, her voice shaking.

He had already risen, his frown softening. Abruptly he motioned to Gridley and his aide to leave her alone and go out. With dubious looks and considerable reluctance, the two officers obeyed.

Nodding to the seat Gridley had vacated, Washington strode to the door to make sure it was securely latched. Elizabeth sank into the chair, her face buried in her hands, the strain of the past hours washing over her.

In two swift steps Washington was at her side. Gently he pulled her hands away from her face to see the tears that coursed down her cheeks.

"You have had news of Jon?"

"At a play last night . . . Burgoyne . . . they've gotten news that . . . " She stopped, unable to go on.

Drawing a chair to her side, Washington sat down, held her hand tightly between his large ones. "He is not dead?"

She shook her head. "Burgoyne told me they've just learned that . . . that Jonathan has been enslaved by the Seneca. He said it's a fate worse than death, that Jonathan deserves it, that—"

"Do they know where he is?"

She drew in a deep breath, by sheer willpower steadied herself enough to speak coherently. "All he could tell me was that the village is in southwestern New York near the Pennsylvania border."

She looked up, desperate appeal in her eyes. "Howe is sending a detachment to try to take him, bring him back here for execution. We must find him first!"

Washington stood up, drew her to her feet. "We must also exercise extreme caution if the British are not to catch wind of this. Are you able to ride to Roxbury to bring my orders to Colonel Stern?"

"Yes—of course." Relief coursed through her veins, so powerful it left her weak. "I'll go right away."

He returned to his desk, quickly wrote on a piece of paper. "Major Andrews and Sergeant Moghrab shall go, of course, since they have some familiarity with the area. And anyone else your uncle thinks will be needed."

"Let me go too!"

"You will only slow them down." When she opened her mouth to protest, he cut her off. "A swift journey so far through the wilderness is not an assignment for a woman, no matter how strong or skilled she is. If anything were to happen to you, their mission would be compromised. And I have too great a need of you here."

The guilty memory of Dalton's threats rose up to accuse her. For a moment she considered confiding their confrontation, quickly dismissed the thought. Her first priority was to make sure every possible action was taken to save Carleton. She would have to trust God for the rest. Swallowing hard, she finally gave way.

Washington summoned Andrews, and after giving him a quick summary of what Elizabeth had learned, sent them to Roxbury with a warning not to attract any notice. Together they covered the road to Tess's house at a leisurely trot, though every foot of the way was agony.

It was shortly past noon when they arrived. They found Stern mounting his horse, on the way to review the units posted along the army's outer lines.

He wasted no time sending for Isaiah. The next several hours were spent in consulting maps, laying plans for the journey, deciding who would accompany Andrews and Isaiah. Stowe would refuse to be left behind, they knew, and with him would go Briggs. In addition they would bring the two Mahicans, along with Isaiah's platoon of Blacks, a detachment strong enough for protection, but small enough to travel rapidly and stealthily.

In hope of obtaining Carleton's freedom without a fight, Andrews would bring with him the large sum of money he had withdrawn from Carleton's accounts. As the sun sank toward the western horizon, they all scattered to prepare for their departure in the morning.

With reluctance and dread Elizabeth turned her mare onto Cambridge Road, wondering bleakly how she could endure the weeks that stretched out before her until Carleton's safe return. If he was still alive. If they were able to bring him home.

For they had yet to find him before the British did. And that was the easiest part of their task.

SHE WAS ONLY DISTANTLY AWARE that in the past hour the freshening wind had made an abrupt shift to the north northeast and that, sweeping up from the horizon, an intense blackness had begun to swallow the stars. Turning her face into the icy spray from the waves that slapped over the bow, she clung to the weather rail to steady herself as the *Prudence* plunged through the surging sea.

"Storm's risin', Cap'n." Jabez's voice held an uncharacteristic note of shrillness.

Shivering, she threw a sidelong glance at Dalton, who leaned on the railing little more than a yard away, faint lantern light slashing across his gaunt cheekbones and windblown hair. He had shadowed her ever since they had left Winisimmit, never letting her out of his sight.

An hour earlier, when the rest of the crew had been occupied with the nets and out of earshot, he had deliberately brushed his body against hers, making it seem like an accident. But his harsh whisper had made his intent clear.

"Yer stirrin' my blood, girl. I be wantin' ye bad."

Involuntarily Elizabeth shuddered at memory of his heavy-lidded look that had scorched her like fire. Her stomach churned, but not from the heaving sea or the reek of fish that rose from the slimy decks and open hatch.

Dalton stared into the black void that obscured the northern horizon, then jerked his head toward Simon, who strained against the tiller. "I seen it. A bit of a blow, that's all. We'll get by."

Jabez's bulk loomed black in the fitful light of the dim lantern. "If ye ask me, we're in for a squall. I vote for headin' back now."

"We ain't turnin' back 'thout a full load. Simon, steady 'er into the wind."

His expression reflecting his unease, Simon braced his body against the tiller. A thick curtain blacker than the surrounding night had by now spread broad tentacles across the bowl of the heavens directly above the swaying masts. The freezing wind worried the bellying sails and shivered the creaking shrouds, its moan rising to the shrill keening of a banshee.

Elizabeth could faintly make out a grey line of foam galloping toward them like surreal stallions across the rearing waves. Without warning, a powerful shudder ran through the sloop's timbers as she collided head-on with the racing squall line. Tossed on the brow of the rapidly steepening waves, she pitched at a sharp angle into the trough on the other side.

"Reef the sails, boys!" Dalton shouted. *"Haste!"*

Taking advantage of his distraction, Elizabeth edged around the binnacle to the ship's starboard side, barely able to keep her feet against the slippery deck's wild rise and fall. She scrambled forward toward a clutch of fishermen who had abandoned their nets in a desperate race to shorten the sails before the wind could capsize the vessel or snap her masts.

Dalton jerked her roughly around, brought his contorted face close to hers. "Ye ain't getting' away from me that easy," he hissed through clenched teeth, shoving her toward the blacker rectangle of the open hatch. "Into the cabin with ye till this blow is over, lest ye be washed overboard."

Just then a bolt of lightning split the darkness off the port bow, tracing an incandescent zigzag line between the shrouded sky and the sea below. A deafening crack of thunder followed before its glow had time to fade.

At the same instant, cold rain sluiced over them as though an unseen hand unleashed a biblical deluge. A huge wave towered up over the bow, for terrifying seconds hung suspended before crashing down on the deck to wash men and gear the sloop's length.

The flood extinguished the lanterns at once, and they were plunged into inky darkness, unrelieved except for the rapidly diminishing illumination from the few stars still visible low on the southern horizon and the lightning that at intervals sizzled across the sky. Clutching her arm with one hand and the weather rail with the other,

Dalton somehow kept them both from being thrown into the tangled mass of men and nets and fishing poles at the sloop's stern.

With a strength she hadn't known she possessed, she ripped free the pistol concealed beneath her jacket. "Let me be, or I'll report you to General Washington!"

His harsh laugh curdled her blood. "The Gen'l has more important concerns than the likes 'o a wench like ye. Ye'd best be thinkin' o' pleasin' me, else I'll toss ye to the fish."

The slimy deck heaved violently as another massive wave poured across the ship from bow to stern. Losing her footing, she slipped and fell to her knees. Only Dalton's renewed grasp on her arm kept her from being washed away.

He towered over her, and she shoved the pistol into his side. Snarling a curse, he struck her unsteady hand hard. The pistol spun from her paralyzed fingers and dropped to the deck, where the foaming tide sweeping across the boards immediately swallowed it.

Oblivious to their struggle, all around them men scrambled to clear the deck of the fishing gear that with each motion of the ship slid from bow to stern and back again, threatening to knock everything in its path overboard. Grasping for a handhold, Elizabeth clawed to her feet.

"Don't ye fight me, girl!" Dalton raged.

Before she could regain her balance, he shoved her back against the railing so violently that she bent far outward over the boiling cauldron bare inches below. She screamed, clutched the neck of his shirt in terror.

As he reared back to break her hold, her eye caught movement behind him, a long, indistinct, black bar that swung through space at menacing speed. With a shock she could both feel and hear above the storm, the mainsail boom connected with the back of Dalton's skull at the same instant wave and wind raked the sloop to starboard.

She felt the sharp intake of Dalton's breath, then he slumped on top of her, a dead weight bearing her down into the freezing flood. Panicking, she fought to twist free, losing her grip on the rail, coughing and retching on the burning water that bore her into its seething depths.

✻ ✻ ✻

SHE HUDDLED on the deck against the weather rail, soaked to the skin, shivering with cold and shock. By some miracle, with the churning waves on the verge of sucking her into oblivion, she had bobbed to the surface to bang against the rail and found strength to clutch it. As the *Prudence* righted with a mighty shudder, an unseen hand had grasped the collar of her jacket from behind and heaved her over the side. All but unconscious, she had collapsed onto the deck.

There to lie for the past hour while the storm blew itself out and the waves moderated into short, choppy swells. Now, near at hand, Elizabeth could make out the intermittent flash of the lighthouse lantern on Little Brewster Island at the entrance to Boston Harbor.

All the fishermen's energy and attention had been focused on keeping the *Prudence* afloat and riding out the squall, thus it had been some time before any of them noted Dalton's absence. Hardly able to move or even to speak, Elizabeth could only nod when Jabez bent over her to see if she was all right.

"He's gone," he muttered.

She levered herself upright, wrapped her arms around her bent legs. "Yes." Looking up, she met his piercing gaze.

"He won't be botherin' ye no more."

She studied him with wonderment, her mouth falling open. His answering smile was grim.

"I been watchin' over ye. Ye be safe now. None o' these men'll ever hurt ye. We be right grateful for all ye done and will do."

He clasped her hand, and she found strength to squeeze his in gratitude. But after he left her, she pressed her forehead to her knees, overcome. Hugging her trembling legs, she wept.

Chapter Twenty

THE DAYS BLURRED INTO ONE ANOTHER. Each night of the punishing ourney Carleton's captors staked him spread-eagled to the ground so that the long, black hours held misery greater even than that of the daylight, when they dragged him along on foot behind Half Moon's horse.

Numbing exhaustion and burning hunger, the agonizing discomfort of his bonds and his unnatural posture, even the sapping cold that seeped relentlessly into his bones were all more endurable than the thoughts that tormented him. With exhausting monotony, fearful speculations about what his fate was to be revolved through his mind. The moment he was relieved of the necessity to keep up with his captors' unsparing pace, the agonizing fears swarmed over him like a horde of stinging flies.

He tried to pray, came back time and again to cling to one thought: *You also were stripped naked, beaten. You were tortured even to death. You took the worst they could do. For me. And you promised you would not leave me.*

In the short periods when he slipped into oblivion, he dreamed again of Elizabeth. But now she came to him as hardly more than a wraith who moved steadily away from him, not looking back.

Each time he awakened, a sense of deep hopelessness and fearful aloneness oppressed him. By the fourth day of their journey, despair grew so intense he began to pray earnestly to die, to be spared the suffering that still lay before him.

Still he lived.

They must by now be deep in Ohio territory, he calculated. The day before, they had turned northwest, undoubtedly to curve around the southwestern tip of Lake Erie. To head toward Detroit.

Low overhead, a thick layer of grey clouds scudded before the stiffening wind, and all day the temperature dropped steadily. By late afternoon, fine, stinging snow pelted them, searing his naked flesh. He was soon shaking so uncontrollably that time and again he slipped on the greasy earth and fell, only to be dragged to his feet and urged forward with a vicious blow from the knotted stick Cackling Crow carried.

At first he had paid scant heed to his captors' terse conversation. Now it sank into his consciousness that they were crossing through Shawnee territory, a fact that made the Seneca increasingly uneasy. They moved even faster now, stopping to rest only when full night fell.

Several times that day they came across the tracks of Shawnee hunting parties, and at last a couple of the men began to demand that they stop at the nearest town and seek formal permission to cross their rivals' lands. Half Moon countered that since bad blood existed between the two tribes, they were likely to be killed outright. The safest course was to remain as invisible as possible and try to avoid any contact.

As Carleton listened to their debate, a flicker of hope kindled in him. At his last contact with the Shawnee before returning to England ten years earlier, the largest concentration of the tribe had been in western Virginia and southwestern Pennsylvania. With substantial numbers of colonists already trickling into the area, however, there had been much discussion in the council houses of either moving south among the Creeks or returning to the Shawnee's ancient ancestral lands in Ohio Territory. According to Washington, many of them had taken the latter course, a fact his captors' conversation confirmed.

On his return to Virginia at Sir Harry's death, Carleton had attempted to contact Black Hawk's clan, only to discover that they had disappeared from the area they had occupied during his youth. Could they also have moved into Ohio Territory?

All that day he concentrated on the possibilities that might open up if his captors were intercepted by a Shawnee party. He tried to rehearse their language, which as a youth he had spoken with considerable fluency. And he began to pray with renewed intensity.

MISTY TWILIGHT EASED over the forest, softened by the muted glow of the pale snow that lay thinly on the ground. A short time earlier Half Moon had called a halt for the night, and now beneath a tall oak tree crackled a small, smokeless fire screened from the surrounding forest by piled brush.

Slumped against the seamed trunk of a huge poplar, Carleton stared into the flames, longing to creep nearer and warm his freezing flesh in its warmth, but not daring to move. When Cackling Crow and three of the others approached to drag him to the ground and tie him to the rough stakes for the night, he watched them with stoic indifference.

The barely perceptible rustle of dry leaves brought the Seneca whirling round in alarm to search the shadowy aisles of the forest all around them. A shock went through Carleton as to every side the members of a strongly armed Shawnee raiding party emerged from the shadows. With the warriors' movements, firelight glinted across silver armlets and ear and nose rings.

Half Moon broke the silence first, speaking too rapidly for Carleton to understand much of what he said. But he felt the tension rise as one of the Shawnee answered, his tone thick with anger.

A few years older than Carleton, the warrior was tall and gaunt, with a pockmarked face that featured a prominent nose and cheekbones streaked with red, white, and yellow paint. The hair of his head had been plucked, except for a long scalp lock ornamented with the tip of a wolf's tail at the crown. Strung from a leather thong and interspersed with silver beads, the claws and fangs of wolves hung around his neck.

Carleton stared at him in dismayed recognition.

Wolfslayer. They had been rivals as youths. From the first Wolfslayer had been jealous of the favor Black Hawk and his son Pathfinder showed Carleton. Over time that jealousy had turned into resentment, then open enmity.

Swiftly Carleton looked away, praying under his breath that Wolfslayer had not also recognized him. At the same time, the realization overtook his fogged brain that if the man was indeed Wolfslayer, then this party must be from Black Hawk's clan.

He returned to an intent scrutiny of the faces of the men who surrounded them, sharply drew in his breath. One warrior, the band's leader, whom he estimated to be a year or two younger than he, carried a spear decorated with feathers and a string of scalps. He was handsome and well-formed of body, and although his face was streaked with paint, there was no mistaking his identity.

With every passing second, it was becoming increasingly evident that the Shawnee did not welcome the intrusion of a Seneca band onto their lands. Carleton was able to understand enough of the Shawnee leader's angry words to realize he was insisting that the Seneca leave. But his captors stood their ground, stubbornly refusing to back down.

Searching for some means of drawing attention, Carleton managed to squirm around until he could reach a sturdy stick on the ground beside him with his bound hands. He pressed one end against the ground and leaned all his weight on the other until it bent to the breaking point. The loud crack as it snapped startled everyone in the clearing, and they swung to glare at him.

There was an instant of suspended silence, then the leader of the Shawnee warriors strode over to Carleton, arrogantly pushing aside Half Moon and Cackling Crow, who tried to block his path. Squatting down, he laid his hand on Carleton's shoulder.

Hoarsely, in what he could remember of the Shawnee tongue, Carleton said, "Help me, my brother. They take me to my death."

Astonishment came into the Shawnee warrior's eyes. "Is it you, Golden Hawk?"

"Are we not brothers, Pathfinder?"

Abruptly Pathfinder turned to the Seneca chief. "This is Golden Hawk, my blood brother. Where do you take him, and why?"

"He is a traitor to our friends the English," Half Moon responded, his tone sullen. "He was an officer in their armies, but he betrayed them and escaped from their justice. He tried to treat with us for the Long Knives, who war against the redcoats, and we made him our slave. But he is cunning and too great a danger to us, so we return him to the English to claim the reward they offer for his capture."

Pathfinder directed a questioning look at Carleton. In French he said, "Can this be true, my brother? Were you not born of the French? How can you be an officer in the armies of the English king?"

"My white mother was French, my white father English, though his ancestors were French as well," Carleton returned, also in French.

Pathfinder considered this. "Then you turned your back on the French and gave your soul to the English. But now you have left them for the Long Knives," he concluded, his tone dry.

Carleton gritted his teeth. "I never gave away my soul to the English king. He would steal the freedom of both the Long Knives and of our people. I have seen too well that the hand of friendship he offers holds a knife to stab us in the back. Do not be deceived by the lies of the British."

"So the English king lies and the Long Knives steal our lands. It would seem we can trust none of the white men."

"Are we not brothers, Pathfinder? Has our blood not mingled? Have we not eaten the same bread, slept in the same wigewa, hunted in the same forests, defended each other against danger? Will you turn your back now and let our enemies sell me to the English so they may kill me?"

Bitterness and desperation edged Carleton's voice, and for a tense moment, Pathfinder gazed with deep earnestness into his eyes. At last his fingers tightened on Carleton's shoulder. He straightened and faced the Seneca warriors.

In his own language, he said, "You must leave our lands by the shortest route and quickly. Golden Hawk will return with us to our people."

Half Moon's face hardened. "He plotted to corrupt our women and kill our children. He is our captive, and we will take him to Detroit and return him to the English."

Struggling to find the words in a language he had not spoken for more than ten years, Carleton answered haltingly, "You have known me since we were boys together at your mother's fire circle. Did I ever act dishonorably? No, my brother, it is English gold they hunger for."

At this, Wolfslayer strode over to them. "Golden Hawk left us many years ago. We have heard nothing from him in all this time. Your father's heart sickens because he loved him, yet Golden Hawk abandoned us to return to the Whites. Is it not justice for us to take him and claim the reward for ourselves?"

By now they had been joined by Red Fox and Spotted Pony, the sons of Black Hawk's sister, who as youths had been Carleton's close friends as well. "He lived among us as a brother," Spotted Pony said to Pathfinder. "Your father would have adopted him as his own son had he only returned once more."

"Surely to sell our brother to the English would dishonor us and make our names odious in our own clan," Red Fox agreed.

Wolfslayer's eyes narrowed. "We will have to fight these dogs to take him from them. I say his life is not worth one drop of our blood."

Pathfinder swung away, anger darkening his face. Again he faced the Seneca, but now Half Moon and Cackling Crow moved toward them, brandishing their rifles menacingly as they reached to grasp Carleton by the arm and drag him away.

Without warning, a shot rang out from the surrounding forest. Half Moon spun around, a crimson fountain spurting from his chest. His eyes widened, then he went limp and crumpled facedown onto the cold ground. Blood-chilling cries and shrieks filled the forest. Everyone except Carleton was suddenly in motion, and gunfire reverberated between the trees.

With no time to even raise their weapons, the Seneca were instantly overcome. In less than a minute, all six of them lay dead, scattered across the small clearing.

It took bare moments longer for the Shawnee warriors to claim their scalps. Without speaking, Pathfinder cut the leather thong that bound Carleton's hands and supported him as he struggled to his feet.

It was quickly apparent that Carleton had not the strength to go far even on horseback. They rode only long enough to put a couple of miles between themselves and the scene of the massacre. On the bank of a fast-flowing stream, they made camp.

He was too exhausted to eat much of the bread and dried venison he was offered, though his stomach burned with hunger. The Shawnee party's unexpected emergence from the dark, mist-shrouded forest, followed by the abrupt death of his tormentors, seemed so unreal he questioned whether his rescue might be only an illusion induced by physical suffering and despair. Yet, warmly clothed and wrapped in the blanket Pathfinder provided, that night Carleton slept by the fire, his mind for the first time in months free of the dreams that had tortured him for so long.

They remained there the next day as well, though Wolfslayer and two of those closest to him made vehement objection. The day was sunny and warmer than the previous one, and Pathfinder steadfastly insisted that until Carleton had regained at least some strength, they would delay the long ride south to Black Hawk's town.

While the others went off briefly to hunt and later lounged around the fire, roasting the game they had killed and trading leisurely, often humorous stories, Pathfinder and his two cousins questioned Carleton about the years of his absence. After explaining that it had been necessary for him to leave abruptly for England on learning of the final illness of his birth father, Lord Carleton, and that he had not been able to return to the colonies until after Sir Harry's death a little more than a year earlier, Carleton eagerly asked about Black Hawk and the rest of his clan.

As Washington had told him, increasing pressure from white settlers had caused the Shawnee to move back into Ohio Territory not long after Carleton's return to England. Recently Black Hawk's health had suffered because of grief over the death of his wife, Owl Woman, two years earlier and Carleton's extended absence.

It was clear that Pathfinder, Red Fox, and Spotted Pony viewed Carleton's return with joy, and the closeness they had known as youths returned as though it had never been broken. For Carleton, delight at being once more in the company of these men who had been a great part of his growing up and anticipation of seeing Black Hawk again overshadowed even relief at rescue from the Seneca. Nor could the awareness of Wolfslayer's sullen scrutiny dim his genuine happiness, its intensity greater because of the suffering of the past months.

With food and rest, his strength began rapidly to return. The second morning, however, when the horses were saddled, Wolfslayer confronted Pathfinder, his face set in hardened lines, his rifle clenched in his hand.

"To take this Long Knife back with us is folly," he snarled. "He is like all the Whites. They lie to us and pretend to be our friends, but their intent is to destroy our towns and kill us all so they may take our lands."

Pathfinder cut him off. "Golden Hawk is my blood brother—"

"He betrayed our allies the British as he has already betrayed us. Did he come back to us of his own will? No! He would not be here if the Seneca had not captured him. He will leave us again, this time to bring the Long Knives to war against us for he is now one of their warriors."

By now the rest of the warriors had gathered around them. Their faces sober, they looked from Wolfslayer to Pathfinder and his cousins, weighing their arguments.

"Why do you hate me, Wolfslayer?" Carleton demanded, fumbling for the words in the Shawnee tongue. "I have done nothing to you."

Wolfslayer ignored him. "The Seneca were right, and now that he has fallen into our hands, we should make good use of him. The British will pay a handsome price to get this traitor back."

Without warning he raised his rifle to his shoulder and sighted down its barrel at Carleton. "I will take him to Detroit myself—if not alive, then dead."

"*Stop!*"

In a single, swift step, Pathfinder moved in front of Carleton and reached to strike the rifle from Wolfslayer's hand. Instinctively Carleton grabbed his friend to drag him out of the line of fire, but at that instant Wolfslayer's rifle discharged at point-blank range.

Pathfinder gave a violent jerk, then staggered backward, the breath expelling from his lungs with a grunt. The force of the blast drove him into Carleton, and both together lost their balance.

Carleton hit the ground hard, Pathfinder's weight and the momentum of their fall ramming him back across the gnarled roots of the tree beneath which they had been standing. As he sprawled onto the ground, his head struck a rock with a sharp, glancing blow.

Instantly dizzy and sick to his stomach, he tried to writhe to one side, lever himself upright. Through a fog he realized that he was splattered with Pathfinder's blood, heard dimly the appalled shouts of the others.

Then the rushing beat of powerful wings above his head blocked out all other sound. To his vague astonishment, he seemed to be engulfed in feathers.

Strong snowy wings beat against his face and chest. Ripping talons clawed at his buckskin shirt, and piercing red eyes bored into his through the mists that filmed his vision.

A wave of nausea surged over him, and he collapsed back against the earth. Like the sudden extinguishing of a lamp, consciousness left him.

⊛ ⊛ ⊛

He could not have been insensible for long. When he opened his eyes, although the Shawnee still surrounded him, they cowered at a short distance, watching him with expressions he could only identify as fear and awe.

Pathfinder sprawled across his legs, facedown in the rotting leaves. The pool of blood in which he lay left no doubt that he was dead.

Teeth gritted, Carleton managed to drag himself free and into a sitting position, torn between the shock of what had happened; anguish at the loss of his brother, so lately regained; and fear of what Wolfslayer might do now. His head throbbed from the blow against the rock, though surely that could not account for the inexplicable weakness that sapped every muscle of his body.

His shirt and leggings were splattered with the crimson gore of Pathfinder's blood, he noted with a sick feeling. Then his eyes caught the flash of something white.

Nestled against the sodden leaves beside the hand with which he propped himself upright lay three white feathers. The feathers of an eagle.

So the great bird had not been a figment of his disordered mind after all, but flesh and blood. Or had it?

Tentatively he reached out to touch the feathers. Although they lay between him and Pathfinder, they were flawlessly white and light as gossamer, unspotted by the crimson blood that had dropped onto the leaves all around them.

They felt strangely warm when he lifted them in his hand, and he had the strange sensation that the spirit of the mysterious eagle still resided in them.

His movements apparently made some progress toward alleviating the Shawnee's fears. Wolfslayer and Red Fox edged toward him cautiously, as though fearful of what he might do.

"Did my bullet strike him as well?" Wolfslayer demanded.

Red Fox shook his head. "No. Yet I saw Pathfinder's spirit rise as he fell and enter Golden Hawk," he muttered in a hushed voice.

"The white eagle would not let us touch them," Spotted Pony said from behind him.

"It could only have come from Moneto," Red Fox returned.

Carleton staggered to his feet. Steadying himself with one hand against the tree's trunk, he measured his words, cold rage in the glance he leveled at Wolfslayer.

"I have done nothing to earn your hatred, but you have done much to earn mine. Your hands are now stained with the blood of my brother—your own kin—and it is my right to take vengeance for Pathfinder's murder when and where I will. From this day, your life belongs to me."

All of the Indians stared at Carleton in wonder. Before, his attempts to speak their tongue had been clumsy. He had needed Pathfinder to translate words he could not remember from his youth.

But now, abruptly, thought flowed to word and word to thought without effort. He heard himself speaking with authority, yet it was as though the words were those of a stranger.

"Only Moneto can decide your punishment for murdering one of the leaders of our people," Red Fox broke in. "See, Moneto has sent the white eagle to Golden Hawk, and he has given the white feathers to him as an *opa-wa-ka*."

Again Carleton became aware of the strange warmth of the feathers he held. He knew that Red Fox referred to a token by which the Shawnee believed an individual could receive power from Moneto, the Supreme Being of the universe, and Wishemehetoo, the Great Spirit.

Wolfslayer's gaze flickered to Pathfinder's body, quickly away. For a brief instant, anguish contorted his features, then he bowed his head, his expression hardening.

"Take my life then—if you have the courage." Defiance edged his voice.

By sheer effort of will Carleton fought off an increasingly potent desire to lie down, to sleep. Reaching out his hand, he demanded, "Bring me Pathfinder's spear."

Red Fox brought the feathered lance to Carleton. "You will be our war chief, White Eagle. We will follow you."

"Only one born of us can be a war chief!" Wolfslayer objected.

"You, as well as the rest of us, saw how Pathfinder's spirit rose and went into Golden Hawk," Red Fox returned. "It is Moneto who has chosen him to lead us, not any man."

The others exchanged glances, then repeated fervently, "We follow White Eagle."

His jaw tensing, Wolfslayer kept silence.

Taking the lance from Red Fox, Carleton extended the weapon until the cruel tip pressed hard into the hollow of his adversary's throat. Meeting his steely gaze with an unyielding one, Wolfslayer did not flinch even when a crimson drop trickled from beneath the razor-sharp point.

"You live at my pleasure," Carleton said, the words soft, but menacing. "You die when I choose. Take heed to your steps."

Chapter Twenty-one

WHITHER SHALL I GO FROM THY SPIRIT? *or whither shall I flee from thy presence? If I ascend up into heaven, thou art there: if I make my bed in hell, behold, thou art there. If I take the wings of the morning, and dwell in the uttermost parts of the sea; even there shall thy hand lead me, and thy right hand shall hold me. If I say, surely the darkness shall cover me; even the night shall be light about me. Yea, the darkness hideth not from thee; but the night shineth as the day: the darkness and the light are both alike to thee.*

The words of the psalm formed in White Eagle's mind as he stared down the path they followed through the dense forest. With them, a measure of comfort eased the deep grief that ate into his soul.

The events of the past days blurred together in his mind. To find Pathfinder again after so many years, only to have him snatched away forever, had affected him more than he could express in words. How he was going to explain to Black Hawk what had happened was unimaginable.

He rode at the head of the Shawnee party, Pathfinder's blanket-wrapped body hanging limp across the back of his horse. Beside him, Red Fox from time to time pointed out the way they must travel to reach Black Hawk's town along the bank of the Scioto River.

Since Pathfinder's death and the incident with the ghostly eagle, Red Fox and the others in the party had demonstrated a marked respect, even awe. Only Wolfslayer's hostility remained unabated.

The three white eagle feathers he wore now tied into the crown of his hair so the tips trailed down to his shoulder. He also carried Pathfinder's lance and tomahawk, and from the way his companions deferred to him, it was clear they believed that the spirit of Pathfinder, and even more, of Moneto himself, had taken possession of him.

In truth, that seemed to him the only explanation for his sudden ability to speak the Shawnee language with his former fluency, to anticipate his companions' thoughts, what they would say and do, and the strange and complete alienation he now felt from his former life.

They had told him that the great eagle with fiery red eyes and feathers of pure, unspotted white had appeared out of the sun-streaked mists of the treetops as if it were an unearthly spirit. It had settled on his breast as he lay unconscious, and at every attempt they made to approach either him or the body of Pathfinder, it had hissed fiercely and beat its wings. For some minutes it had remained there, warning them back.

At last, as though summoned by an unseen signal, the eagle had risen majestically into the air, for a moment hovering above him and Pathfinder's lifeless body. Then, circling upward in the draft of their campfire's smoke and heat, it had drifted into the misty sunlight and disappeared back into the sky.

He had listened to the story with detachment, as though they spoke of someone else, someone who was dead. He could not fathom whether the eagle had been an apparition—a spirit—or a creature of the earth. It had saved him, that was certain, and had mysteriously bestowed on him a new name.

But he had to wonder whether it been a demon—or the hand of God.

They traveled steadily southward, and with each passing hour, he was increasingly oppressed by a deepening sense that he no longer knew who he was, that miles away in the shadows of the forest, beneath the wings of that ghostly white eagle, he had lost the man he thought he was and become . . . whom?

✦ ✦ ✦

"MY FATHER, I have come home." His voice husky with emotion, White Eagle gently embraced the stooped old man.

Black Hawk grasped White Eagle's arm, his claw-like fingers digging into the flesh with surprising strength. "I have longed to see you all these years, and I have wondered—why did you leave us? Why have you not returned until now?"

A spasm of pain passed over White Eagle's countenance. "Soon after I left you that last time, I was summoned to England, to the deathbed of my white father. Though he gave me away when I was a child, Sir Harry urged me to go to him. So I sailed across the great waters—only to find that he was already buried. Once there, however, I was hindered from returning to this land until after Sir Harry's death, and by then you had moved away. I did not know where you had gone."

Black Hawk's gaze became piercing. "This uncle who adopted you felt you came to us too often, and so he sent you away to keep you from us."

Troubled, White Eagle considered the old man's words for some moments. "He did not understand," he said at last, "yet he loved me. He feared for my safety."

Black Hawk regarded him thoughtfully. "Now he too has gone to his ancestors, as Pathfinder has."

"Yes."

"Both of us mourn those we loved. They tell me Wolfslayer killed Pathfinder by accident. They say his spirit went into you."

Struggling to mask his grief, White Eagle looked around the bare walls of the spacious, square wigewa constructed of sturdy saplings covered with long strips of birch bark. With a pang of sadness, he reflected how different Black Hawk's abode had looked while Owl Woman still lived. It seemed now barren and bereft of life. The old man had suffered many losses in his long life, but the unnecessary death of his firstborn son had to be the most painful.

"So they say," he said gruffly. "Wolfslayer meant to kill me, for after all these years his hatred has not diminished. Pathfinder stepped between us, and I could not save him. He gave his life for mine."

The old sachem bent his head, grief deepening the lines of his face. "Wolfslayer is a powerful shaman. His medicine is very strong. Had not Moneto himself intervened, he would easily have killed you."

After a moment, he loosened his hold on White Eagle's arm and stroked his fingers across the feathers entwined in his hair. "But Moneto bestowed this *opa-wa-ka* on you. Your medicine is now stronger than Wolfslayer's, stronger even than Pathfinder's was."

White Eagle looked away, frowning. If Black Hawk was right, then it would only cause Wolfslayer to hate—and oppose him—the more.

Sighing, Black Hawk sat down on his bearskin close to the warmth of the fire crackling in the fire circle. He motioned White Eagle to sit beside him, pain and pleasure mingling in his features.

"You are indeed favored by Moneto. I knew it would be so when you first told me of Moneto's son coming down to the earth to live among his children. None of our people had heard this story in a way we could understand before you came to us." He frowned. "Speak his name once more. The years have erased it from my memory."

White Eagle sat down cross-legged beside him. "The white men call him Jesus."

Black Hawk nodded. "I am an old man, and I have borne many sorrows. But I have hungered to hear more of this Jesus and to be reminded of all you taught us."

"We will speak more of these things after we bury Pathfinder, my father. I pray you will choose to be baptized before you die."

"Your words have burned in my heart since your leaving. I trust no white man to tell me of these things, for I know not who seeks his own advantage and who speaks the truth. But you were always as faithful to me as the sons born to me of Owl Woman's body, the last of whom has now journeyed to the wigewas of Moneto. Since you return to me again, I know that your love for me is no pretense."

White Eagle laid his hand over the older man's wizened one. "I love you with all my heart, as my own father. I have always told you only what is true, and that truth will lead you to life that is unending."

"Soon I will die and go to Pathfinder and to our ancestors."

"If you receive Jesus into your spirit, then you will go where he is, with Moneto, there to live forever. Jesus died and rose again so that your spirit will never die. Do you believe?"

"Yes." Black Hawk nodded gravely. "I receive this Jesus."

For a moment Black Hawk closed his eyes, his face settling into weary lines. White Eagle held his hand, joy rising in him at the old sachem's affirmation. When Black Hawk opened his eyes again, his gaze became piercing.

"You will leave our people again."

"I will not leave you!"

Startled by Black Hawk's unexpected words, White Eagle spoke without thinking. Yet even at the wrenching thought of Elizabeth, of the promise and the duty of that former life that had been torn from him, he was struck by the realization of how difficult it would be to leave the old sachem again, especially now, after Pathfinder's death. Because of him.

As he had when Washington first asked him to return to the wilderness to negotiate with the tribes, he felt poised against his will between two opposing worlds, between two dear loves, with no possible way to reconcile them.

Black Hawk shook his head with sad resignation. "When I die, then you will go away."

With each word, the old sachem's voice became stronger and more prophetic. "You will wander many days and become a great warrior among the Long Knives. You will help them to overcome the British and drive them from this land. After you go, our people will be forced to journey many marches west, yet they will never find rest for the soles of their feet or a place to lay their heads in peace. And you also will wander all the moons of your life, for among the Long Knives you will never find a home."

White Eagle could feel the hairs prickle on the back of his neck. He averted his eyes to prevent the old man from reading the turmoil his words had stirred in his breast. For deep inside he knew that Black Hawk also spoke truth.

THE FOURTH DAY OF NOVEMBER dawned with sunny skies and warmer temperatures. White Eagle awakened early, his spirit still heavy from the days of mourning for Pathfinder. The important sachems of the tribe, along with people from many of the towns in the area, had gathered the previous day to show their respect for Black Hawk's son, the clan's war chief, and to participate in the somber burial rite. Yet that night, after the mourners left for their homes, White Eagle had slept little.

For hours he wrestled with his dilemma. Now that he had been miraculously freed from captivity, his greatest concern was to send a message to Elizabeth assuring her that he was alive. But there was no way to do that. More than 600 miles of rugged terrain, most of it occupied by hostile tribes or controlled by the British, separated them. And with severe winter weather rapidly coming on, the probability of finding a messenger who was not only trustworthy, but also willing and able to undertake such a journey was nonexistent.

For him to travel back alone was even less of an option. The rigors of the journey would require at least two companions, and not even Red Fox and Spotted Pony would likely agree to leave their families to accompany him. Even worse, added to White Eagle's concern over leaving Black Hawk, with every passing day Wolfslayer's unabated hostility made it increasingly clear that he only waited for White Eagle to hand him the opportunity to finally settle the score between them.

If there was a solution, White Eagle was unable to uncover it. At last he rose to dress warmly in buckskins, wrapped himself in a buffalo-hide robe, and went outside.

He found Blue Sky already tending the fire. Barely twenty years old, she had married Pathfinder a year after the pox had claimed his first wife, their son, and two daughters. According to Black Hawk, Pathfinder had cherished Blue Sky, but even after three years of marriage, she remained barren.

Tall and willowy, with regular features and even, white teeth, she possessed a striking beauty made even more appealing by the deep sadness that haunted her face and movements. In the few days of their acquaintance, White Eagle had been impressed by the sweetness of her nature, tempered now by the pain of loss.

To his growing discomfort, however, she watched over him possessively, even jealously. His attempts to brush off her ministrations met with gentle, but stubborn, persistence. The sudden, tragic death of her husband and the talk of Pathfinder's spirit entering him obviously made him, in her eyes, his brother's natural successor in more ways than as war chief.

Black Hawk's insistence that he make Pathfinder's wigewa his own and allow Blue Sky to manage the tasks that were a woman's responsibility had not made his situation any less awkward. Neither had ensuring that she slept nearest the fire while he made his bed on the opposite side of the wigewa by the door. The subtle tension between them was daily becoming harder to ignore.

He was relieved when Black Hawk emerged from his wigewa and joined them by the fire to break his fast as he had each morning since White Eagle's arrival. "Today will be a solemn day," he told them, his expression grave.

To White Eagle's questioning gaze he returned a sad smile. "Of all my children there is left to me but one daughter and Blue Sky. But Moneto has brought you back to me again and put within you Pathfinder's spirit so you may comfort me in my old age. Now that the days of mourning are done, I will take you as my son, as I intended to do before you journeyed far away across the great ocean. Today we will wash away your white blood so there will no longer be any distinction between us. You will finally be one of us in body, as you are in spirit."

White Eagle bowed his head, overwhelmed. He had wondered whether Black Hawk would do this, but the reality of it moved him even more than he had expected. A sudden, deep sense of homecoming swept over him, erasing the night's turmoil.

The old sachem nodded to Blue Sky, who hurried to his wigewa and quickly returned carrying a bundle wrapped in a cougar's pelt. At Black Hawk's direction, White Eagle removed his clothing except for his breechcloth. From the bundle Black Hawk removed several pots of paint, a belt of wampum, and a silver armlet. Solemnly he proceeded to paint White Eagle's face, shoulders, chest, and arms in bright colors.

After placing the wampum around his neck and the armlet on his upper right arm, Black Hawk took him by the hand and led him along the main pathway between the wigewas. As they walked, Black Hawk called out in a loud voice until all the townspeople gathered around them, jostling to see what was going on.

Speaking loudly enough for all the bystanders to hear, the old sachem reminded the people of their ancient custom of adopting as members of their tribe those who were deemed worthy. None of his sons were now left in the land of the living. But this man, whom Moneto himself had brought to them and named White Eagle, had been sent to carry Pathfinder's spirit, to assume his place of leadership within the tribe, to comfort Black Hawk in his old age, and to perform the duties of a son at his death. Today he would adopt White Eagle formally as his own son in acknowledgment of the bonds of respect and love that had existed between them for many years, bonds that henceforth could never be broken and that all members of the tribe were obligated to recognize and uphold.

For his part, by adoption White Eagle also would be bound by obligations of love, loyalty, and responsibility to Black Hawk and to his clan, to the townspeople, to the Kispokotha division of the Shawnee, and to the Shawnee nation as a whole.

The solemnity of Black Hawk's words struck White Eagle with great force. He felt the seriousness of the charge and the honor it carried. What was being offered to him was a great privilege, one he eagerly embraced.

When the old sachem motioned to him to go with three of the young women, White Eagle followed them willingly out of the palisade and past the fallow cornfields and orchards. Although the leafless fruit trees and dry, broken cornstalks shivered in the cool breeze, the sunshine felt warm on his bare skin, and he welcomed both the coolness and the warmth.

The townspeople trailed behind them, laughing and calling to each other in anticipation of what was to come. At the riverbank, the young women dipped their toes gingerly into the water. White Eagle followed their example and sucked in his breath.

The water was icy. Although they grimaced, shrieked, and shivered, that did not deter the maidens, however. With no more hesitation, they plunged into the river, pulling at his arms to drag him with them until all four stood waist deep in the cold stream.

While the townspeople gave every evidence of thoroughly enjoying the spectacle, the young women proceeded to plunge him repeatedly below the surface of the water, rubbing his entire body briskly with handfuls of small, smooth stones and sand until he wondered whether he was in greater danger of drowning or freezing. Laughing along with the onlookers, he gave himself over to the ordeal. When they finally drew him out of the river, his teeth were chattering and his skin felt raw.

Black Hawk, along with Grey Cloud, the eldest of the town's subchiefs, Red Fox, and Spotted Pony, received him as he waded, shivering and sputtering, to the bank. They threw a bearskin around his shoulders, then everyone followed the maidens, who were wrapped in blankets and apparently none the worse for their soaking, back into the town. The procession ended at the council house, a long log structure with a gabled roof.

While the others dispersed to their wigewas to prepare for the ceremony to follow, Red Fox and Spotted Pony dressed White Eagle in a ruffled linen shirt and ribboned and beaded leggings and moccasins. Once more Black Hawk painted his face in bands of various colors and secured the white eagle feathers to his hair. After seating him on a bearskin in the center of the council house, they presented him a tomahawk, a pipe, and a leather pouch that contained killegenico, punk, flint, and steel.

When they had finished, the men of the town filed into the council house. All of them had put on their most ornate clothing and painted their faces in brilliant hues. Silver armlets encircled their arms, their glitter reflected in the rings that hung from their noses. Many of the men had their head shaven except for a long scalp lock in which were wound silver trinkets, feathers, or other adornments, while others wore their hair plaited or wrapped in a colorful silk kerchief.

After taking seats on their bearskins, for a long period the assembly sat in unbroken silence, the smoke of their pipes gathering among the log beams that supported the roof. At length Black Hawk rose majestically and began to speak to White Eagle in solemn tones.

"My son, you are now flesh of our flesh and bone of our bone. By this solemn ceremony, performed this day, every drop of white blood has been washed from your veins. You are taken into the Shawnee nation, adopted into this great clan, and received as my own son with the utmost seriousness and by our ancient laws and unbreakable customs. My son, you have nothing to fear, for from this day we hold the same obligation to love, support, and defend you as we hold to all those born among us by natural birth. Therefore you are to consider yourself as one of our people and no longer as a white man."

The words of the man who was now his father sank deep into White Eagle's soul. The family into which he had been born had been ripped from him as a child. The man who had adopted him and loved him like a father had been killed by British soldiers. Even Elizabeth, and the promise of the family he might have had with her, seemed now far away and beyond reach.

But God had granted him a new family, and more—a new identity—that bought with it strong bonds of love and loyalty. In that moment, he felt that his past had indeed been washed away and that he was newborn.

All members of the tribe were bound now to consider him no different from them. That injunction included even Wolfslayer, he realized with sudden hope. Perhaps at last his adversary would choose to set aside the unreasoning enmity he had harbored for so many years.

Looking up, he sought Wolfslayer. And as their eyes met, White Eagle read the flicker of deep resentment and opposition in the shaman's gaze that even the Shawnee's most solemn ceremony had not erased.

Stiffening, White Eagle returned Wolfslayer's gaze with a hard one. *So be it,* he thought grimly.

Wolfslayer had chosen the path he would follow. And although White Eagle determined to yet make every effort at reconciliation, he no longer doubted that one day the warning he had given Wolfslayer on that tragic morning in the forest would surely be fulfilled.

Chapter Twenty-two

IN THE DAYS THAT FOLLOWED, the lowering grey skies, heavy frosts, and piercing wind of approaching winter kept the townspeople, for the most part, close to the warmth of wigewa and council house. With winter's progression, as he joined in the rhythms of the town's life, participating in games, rituals, and councils and traveling to outlying camps to hunt and back again, White Eagle felt his spirit and body grow stronger. He awoke each morning refreshed and eager to see what the new day would bring.

The transition was eased even more by the other Whites who lived in the village: a French trader with his Mingo wife and their children as well as several children and adults who had been captured and adopted into the tribe. White Eagle noted no difference between them and his other Shawnee kin, and as though he had never left it, he quickly entered without restraint into the easy freedom of a way of life he had grown to love as a boy.

Even though the memory of Elizabeth never left him completely, nor the ache in his heart to hold her once more, how he could ever return to her and to the white way of life remained a puzzle to him. It was more than the sheer distance with its physical obstacles or that such a journey would be fraught with danger. The past months had changed him irrevocably. They must have changed her as well.

Would they even know one another now? Was there any way to reconcile the people they had become?

Another concern nagged at him in quiet moments as well. What about his responsibility to Washington and to the army? Had the British finally been driven out of Boston, or did the stalemate continue? Did the army even still exist?

He asked himself if he could he ever break the strong ties that now bound him to the Shawnee. It seemed less possible with each passing day, as impossible as asking Elizabeth to leave everything behind to travel hundreds of miles to a people and a way of life entirely foreign to her.

There seemed to be no answer to White Eagle's dilemma. Determining to embrace the new life that had been given him, he pushed the troubling reflections as much as possible out of his consciousness.

Long, thoughtful discussions with Black Hawk about the Shawnee traditions and spiritual beliefs and how they related to Jesus helped to clarify his thinking. He discovered many points of connection between the truths revealed in the Bible and the tribe's ancient stories. To see his adoptive father quickly grasp, then embrace, these spiritual truths deepened his assurance that there was meaning and purpose for his life among the Shawnee, and even for the months of struggle among the Seneca.

When Black Hawk asked him to share this teaching at the next meeting of the council, White Eagle welcomed the opportunity even though he knew that any such discussion was likely to arouse much opposition. Yet he felt a deep eagerness that he knew could only come from the Great Spirit.

That morning he stepped out from behind the wigewa's leather door flap to find Blue Sky already tending pots of stewing beans and strips of turkey meat that sizzled over the hot coals. As usual, she welcomed him with an eager smile. Studiously ignoring her, he directed a hopeful glance in the direction of Black Hawk's wigewa next door, but there was no sign of the old sachem. Disappointed, he turned to look in the opposite direction.

Wolfslayer's wigewa was a short distance away, past several others on the opposite side of the broad pathway. Bundled against the cold, the gaunt warrior sat at his own fire circle, talking lazily with his wife and older sons and daughters while he cuddled his two-year-old son in his lap. They laughed together, then Wolfslayer looked around, and his glance met White Eagle's. Instantly his eyes narrowed, and his face darkened with undisguised malice.

For a deliberate moment, White Eagle held his gaze, keeping his expression neutral, then he turned back to Blue Sky and settled himself within the circle of the fire's heat.

She set the food before him, and he began to eat, too aware that she watched every movement with an almost desperate longing. When she made no move to take any of the food, he placed a portion of the seasoned meat and beans into a clay bowl and offered it to her.

"Eat. Strengthen yourself."

"Pathfinder, I—"

"I am not Pathfinder," he said steadily.

"They say his spirit went into you—"

He cut her off with a quick, dismissive gesture. "Whatever happened, I am not your husband. Pathfinder is dead."

Guilt twisted in his breast as tears came into her large, expressive eyes. Blinking them back, she looked down, back up again.

"The council meets today." Her tone was flat, without emotion. When he nodded, she said, "You will tell them about this man you call Jesus?"

"Black Hawk asked me to."

She frowned, studied him for some moments without speaking. At length she ventured, "Pathfinder told me that he is Moneto, that he came to earth as a man to live among his people. He told me other things, too, that I did not understand."

He smiled at her, a slow, quiet confidence filling him. "Perhaps what I tell the council today will help you to understand."

Early that afternoon, after the people of the village had gathered in the council house, Black Hawk motioned for silence. "When White Eagle lived among us many years ago, he told us about the man Jesus, who came down from Moneto. I have asked him to tell us more."

A look of contempt came over Wolfslayer's face. "This is white man's religion. It has nothing to do with our people."

White Eagle stood up and looked from one expectant, doubtful, questioning, or hostile face to the next all around the crowded room. "Jesus was not a white man. He came for all people, whether red or white, black or yellow."

"Moneto himself taught our earliest ancestors his ways," Spotted Pony broke in, his expression puzzled. "These truths have been passed down to each generation from their time to ours. Why should we now change our beliefs?"

"We must return to the true beliefs of our ancestors," Wolfslayer ground out. "If we turn away from their teachings, then Moneto will desert us, and we will be overcome by our enemies."

White Eagle held up his hand for silence. Speaking with quiet humility, he answered, "To accept Jesus is not to turn away from Moneto, but to turn toward him. What our people have always believed is true, but incomplete, nor have we understood everything that our ancestors taught us.

"Do not our people believe in Moneto, the Supreme Being of the universe, and also in the Great Spirit, the grandmother who eternally weaves a great net? Do we not believe that one day, when her net is completed, she will drop it over the world to gather up those who prove themselves worthy and take them with her to a better life? All these beliefs were given to us so that after Jesus came into the world we would understand and believe in him."

He stopped and regarded them earnestly. "My brothers, my sisters, have we not seen how each morning after the darkness of the night, the sun arises, bringing us new life? We can do nothing either to cause the sun to rise or to prevent it. It is so because it is Moneto's will to care for all his children, whether their hearts are good or bad.

"So also the rising of the son of Moneto from death was to bring new life to his children. Moneto freely gave us his love by coming down from his heavens in the form of the man Jesus to live in the wigewas of man and to speak to us in human language so that we could fully understand his truth. He healed many who were sick and even raised the dead to life. He taught that no one should injure his neighbor but do good to them because Moneto loves all people."

"Is this not what our people already believe?"

White Eagle turned to Red Fox. "Yes, but Jesus also told us that all human beings are our neighbors, not only those of our own kindred. Moneto made all people, and in his eyes we are all his tribe. He calls us to do good to everyone, even as he does."

"The Long Knives say they believe in this Jesus," challenged Wolfslayer. "Yet they steal our lands, break the treaties we make with them, and kill even our women and children."

"Even among our own people, not all live according to what they claim to believe," White Eagle reminded him. "But those who would be caught up in Jesus' net at the end of all time must not only say they believe, they must also walk in Moneto's ways."

"Why should we believe you?" Wolfslayer demanded.

"Because Jesus proved it is true. His enemies were jealous of his strong medicine, and they killed him. His body lay in the grave, even as Pathfinder and all our ancestors lie dead and buried. But unlike them, death held no power over him.

"The power of Moneto's enemies is as nothing in his eyes. After three days, he brought Jesus back again to life. Not even the strongest warrior or the wisest elder or the most powerful shaman can do this. Only Moneto has power to overcome death."

He saw that Grey Cloud was shaking his head, his brow furrowed with doubt. "Indeed, only Moneto can overcome death, but how can we know this Jesus was raised to life as you say?"

"Many people saw him after he had risen from the dead. Before he went back into the sky to Moneto, he promised that one day he would come to earth again and in his great net gather up those who choose to be his people."

Wolfslayer sneered. "And you know this Jesus personally though he is nowhere to be found on the earth."

"He is to be found on this earth in the spirits of those who seek to follow his way," White Eagle countered. "He lives, and I know him. Each one of you can also."

A low murmur rose across the wide space, and heads bent together as the townspeople debated his words. Finally Red Fox asked, "What would Moneto have us to do?"

"We can seek to hide ourselves in the darkness," White Eagle shot back, "or we can choose to come into the light of this new life Moneto offers us."

He hesitated before continuing passionately. "All of us have felt the favorable winds that Moneto sends from the south to bring healing to the land and to all people. Even so, Moneto calls back to him those whose hearts are sick, who have lost their way, who do not follow the true path but wander in the darkness of death.

"On this earth the different tribes fight with each other because they have forgotten who they are and they do not walk in Moneto's ways. Our elders teach us that as the sun travels from the east to the west, it leads us to the wigewas of Moneto. Those who remember who they are and choose to follow Moneto's path will reclaim the root of their being. Only then can there be peace among all people."

Wolfslayer shook his head and looked around at the others, his expression sullen. "This is a fool's talk. The day we stop fighting the Long Knives is the day they will finally overcome us."

For White Eagle it was as if a window opened deep into Wolfslayer's soul. The shaman truly believed his opposition was necessary and right. To him, White Eagle threatened his tribe, his family, and their way of life. He was jealous of the power White Eagle wielded, of his physical prowess, and of the favor he had been given in the tribe and even by Moneto. And if White Eagle won converts to this new faith, Wolfslayer would consider it a sacred duty to destroy him.

"Moneto's path is a difficult one," White Eagle said slowly. "It demands great wisdom and great self-restraint. Even the strongest warrior cannot follow it in his own strength. But just as Moneto sends the mighty north wind to sweep across the land so that no tree or animal or man can stand against it, so also he breathes into his children the mighty power of his Spirit, who gives wisdom, guidance, and strength to follow the true path. All those who stand against this Spirit will be swept away."

By now the light was rapidly fading, and the shadows of twilight deepened at the corners of the council house farthest from the dying fire. Grey Cloud, next in authority to Black Hawk, rose, gathering his bearskin around him.

"Your words hold wisdom, White Eagle. We will hear more of this another day."

White Eagle inclined his head. Waiting while the men filed out of the council house, he noted that some appeared indifferent and others thoughtful or even intrigued by what he had told them. Several waited to talk further with him.

A small group clustered around Wolfslayer as well. And the dark looks they directed toward White Eagle warned him that the shaman meant to oppose him with deeds as well as with words.

⊕ ⊕ ⊕

Lifting the buffalo robe, she lay down close beside him on the bearskin, tentatively laid her arm across his bare chest. When he did not move, she trailed her fingers with wanton sensuality across the taut muscles of his chest onto his thigh. He caught his breath, instantly aroused, the aching need for physical release igniting a fire in his loins.

For a moment longer he lay paralyzed, unable to will himself to move, either to respond or to draw away. Yet why should he not respond? It had been years since he had lain with a woman. Why not take an Indian wife and sire children?

The bitter questions resounded in his mind. Should he not satisfy her? Was not Elizabeth forever lost to him?

It was the vision of Elizabeth, materializing in vivid detail before his eyes for the first time in many weeks, that shocked him to action. Catching Blue Sky's arm, he tore it from his flesh, with rough force ripped back the buffalo robe that sheltered them, pushed her away, and rose to move across the wigewa.

"Leave me!" He made the words deliberately harsh, icy.

He heard her jagged intake of breath. Rolling over, she sat up, wrapped her arms around her bent knees. In the faint light of the fire's dying embers, he could make out the tense outline of her body.

"A war chief needs a wife and children," she flung back at him, her words shaking, but defiant. "I have no husband or children, and the children of Pathfinder are dead. Take me to wife. Give me sons of Pathfinder—warriors of White Eagle!"

Taken aback by the intensity of her plea, he searched for the words to counter it, at length answered, "I cannot. Moneto forbids it."

For a long moment she sat silent, motionless. Finally she whispered, "You are promised to another."

It was not a question.

"Yes."

"She is not here. I am."

He waited. Still she did not move, and finally he said into the darkness, "She is here. She is wherever I am. Though I never see her again, I will wait for her until death."

The words came unexpectedly, without forethought. And with them, peace fell over him, and certainty.

She gave a soft sob and bowed her head upon her bent knees. "Must I die without husband or children? What have I done that Moneto leaves me to live without love?"

Returning, he knelt beside her, groped in the darkness for her hand, and closed his fingers over hers. "It is not Moneto's will for you to live alone. He will comfort your heart and provide you a husband and children in his time. Do not doubt him."

Wrenching her hand from his grasp, she struggled to her feet. Weeping, her face buried in her hands, she fled out into the night.

Chapter Twenty-three

THEY HAD NOT FOUND HIM.

After weeks of anxious waiting that dragged Elizabeth's emotions to and fro like the ebb and flow of the tide, Andrews and his party finally returned to Cambridge at the winter solstice, empty-handed.

News of their fruitless return reached Elizabeth along with the report that Colonel Knox had secured the artillery at Ticonderoga and loaded the guns on sledges pulled by eighty yoke of oxen for the arduous journey south across the deepening snow. She felt no joy at this welcome news. In bleak misery, she answered her uncle's summons to Roxbury, where she found Andrews with him.

His face gaunt with fatigue and disappointment, Andrews explained, "We found what appeared to be the town, but it had been abandoned for some time. After spending a couple of weeks scouring the area with no success, we finally concluded it was too dangerous to push farther. No one in the surrounding villages would tell us anything about where the townspeople had gone or even admit that they held a white captive."

Elizabeth sprang to her feet and paced closer to the fire. "Howe's detachment returned yesterday. They had no more success than you, thank God."

Andrews forced a smile that did nothing to persuade her of his mirth. "I suppose that's good news. But considering that Jon's fate remains a mystery, it feels like cold comfort."

"Shall we never learn what happened to him?" she said, her voice breaking. "My only comfort is in thinking he could not be dead and I not know it."

Overcome by bitter disappointment, she did not delay her return to Boston. The one bright note was that Burgoyne had returned to England to press his ambition for advancement before the Ministry. And, to Elizabeth's relief, along with him went Lady Randolph.

As the old year unraveled toward the new, the weather turned even more piercingly cold, beset by storms that followed one another in dismal succession. Everything necessary for survival was carefully rationed now, and all of Boston's inhabitants, including Elizabeth, Tess, and their servants, were forced into a severely spartan way of life that mocked the forced gaiety of balls and concerts meant to provide some diversion.

Every window and door of the Howards' town house was swathed in blankets in an effort to keep out the drafts, but even so, they all wore cloaks and gloves inside as well as out to maintain some degree of comfort. Stocks of firewood had grown so dangerously low and so many trees had been cut down that soldiers and townspeople alike began to tear apart fences, abandoned buildings, and even wharves to salvage the wood.

Carleton and Andrews's former troop, the Seventeenth Light Dragoons, went so far as to commandeer Old South Meeting House for a riding school, spreading the floorboards with tanbark to accommodate their horses, while pulpit and pews furnished tinder for their warmth. At last Howe was forced to threaten punishment to stop the destruction.

After the incident with Dalton and his shocking death, it seemed to Elizabeth that she had fallen into a deep, black well. She told Tess little other than that Dalton had been swept overboard and lost at sea. And Tess did not pry. Although offering a sympathetic ear to their housekeeper, who mourned her brother-in-law, she also made it clear that she was available whenever Elizabeth needed to talk.

But Elizabeth could not speak to anyone of what had happened. She went through the motions of living, but could discern no meaning in any of it.

Jabez proved faithful to his promise of protection, however, and her stealthy trips to the mainland became more frequent. Over time, increased contact with Stern, Levi, and Andrews eased her despair. Finally concluding that she would never understand completely what had happened or why, she simply left the incident at God's feet and plodded on.

Missing Carleton was another matter altogether. Nothing—not prayer, not confiding in those closest to her, not stern admonitions to herself—could ease the agony that lay in her breast day by day like a heavy, jagged stone.

All hope that he might yet be found and rescued seemed completely wanting now. And through the weary hours when she lay abed, sleep resolutely deserting her eyes, unreasoning fear for him tormented her mind.

At last one night in desperation she slipped out of bed and groped across the unlighted room to the dresser, where Carleton's violin lay. Clutching the instrument to her breast, she returned to the bed and sank clumsily to her knees beside it, her forehead pressed against the mattress.

How long she knelt there, she did not know. But after a time she laid the instrument beside her, prostrated herself on the cold, draughty floor, and implored the Almighty to preserve and protect Carleton, to make a way for her to find him or at least to learn his fate.

Gradually she became aware of birdsong. Hearing it, she began to shake uncontrollably. The blood pounding so hard in her ears that she could not make out the sound clearly, she scrambled to her feet.

The faintest melting grey light illuminated the edges of the shuttered window. Downstairs, she could hear the tall case clock chime the half hour after five. As she ran to tear open the shutters, again the melodious trill sounded from outside, and now she covered her face with her hands, tears seeping through her trembling fingers, her mind denying what her eyes revealed.

Among the leafless, ice-crusted limbs of the maple tree that brushed against her window, totally unexpected to her sight and incongruous in the winter's chill, flashed the well-known and loved black and orange of an oriole. Swinging on a slender branch, tail atilt and black eye cocked to where she stood, dumbfounded, on the other side of the frosty panes, he poured out liquid praise into the hazy light of early dawn.

As the new year dawned and Elizabeth continued to ply the dangerous circuit between Boston and the mainland, she concluded that the stalemate could not endure much longer. Increasingly, Howe and his officers debated evacuating the town.

Already Howe had begun to assemble a fleet to sail to North Carolina under Clinton's command, there to meet up with a force under Lord Cornwallis. The British were confident that on their arrival all Tories in the Carolinas would grasp power, allowing the British to take over the southern colonies with ease.

There was no debate on either side that the logical base for any war against the colonies was New York City, with its deep, broad harbor. The news that Montgomery and Arnold's attack against Quebec had failed, with General Montgomery dying outside the city's walls while the wounded Arnold was forced to retreat, made such a move even more sound. If Howe succeeded in gaining control of the

Hudson, without a substantial American force standing in their way, the British could gain control of the entire waterway to Canada, splitting the colonies in half and providing unlimited access to reinforcements from the north.

Against this threat, Washington faced the continuing dilemma of keeping a force on the field at all. For the moment he had staved off the problem of replacing the troops whose enlistments had run out at the end of the year by persuading militia units to stay temporarily. While new enlistments trickled slowly in, anxiety grew in the American camp that Howe would discover their vulnerability and mount an attack. Far from moving to break the siege, however, Howe gave increasing evidence that he intended to withdraw.

If the British tried to take New York, Washington made clear, then he would need Elizabeth and her aunt there. Before her departure from Boston the previous summer, Margaret Gage had provided them with a letter of introduction to a wealthy friend in the city, and the two women reluctantly began preparations to move.

Often confined to the town house by blizzards and bitter cold, they spent much time studying and debating a pamphlet entitled *Common Sense.* Written by Thomas Paine, a British immigrant, and widely circulated throughout the colonies, the essay was beginning to turn increasing numbers of the colonists against Britain. Paine argued passionately that an immediate declaration of America's independence would gain the support of France and Spain. He emphasized America's role as a moral force in the world, and advocated a republican form of government.

Parliament, for its part, blithely cast dry tinder on the conflagration. At the end of January news arrived of the passage of the Prohibitory Acts, which declared that a state of war existed between England and her American colonies and placed an embargo on trade.

The unintended effect was to give the colonial governments the status of independent nations. And since the king now denied them the benefit of his protection, many Americans reasoned, they no longer owed him any allegiance at all.

Newspaper reports and letters exchanged between committees of correspondence across the colonies, Andrews told Elizabeth with glee, made it clear that talk of independence had begun to receive an eager hearing.

On the twenty-first of January, Elizabeth hurried to Cambridge to report that five British transports loaded with troops had set sail from Boston Harbor. She had as yet been unable to learn if or when others would follow, but Washington decided to dispatch General Lee to New York without delay to take charge of the city's defenses.

Better news was at hand, however. Washington's council had agreed to attack Boston as soon as they had sufficient men and gunpowder, and Knox had at last come within twenty miles of Cambridge with the long-awaited train of artillery.

Even February's nor'easters could not dampen the army's jubilation now. The only obstacle that remained was to determine how to build fortifications on Dorchester Heights in one night on ground solidly frozen to at least a foot deep. And a solution was busily being readied.

THE NIGHT OF MONDAY, March 4, was filled with the rattle of musket fire and the repeated deep-throated roar of cannon and mortars, followed by flashes and ribbons of light as impressive as any fireworks show. Already Tess, Elizabeth, and the servants, had endured two previous nights of bombardment that raised fears for their safety and robbed them of sleep. For hours the Continental Army's cannonade continued unabated, answered by all the batteries in Boston and by several ships in the harbor.

When a particularly noisy round plowed into the Common right across the street, Tess said dryly, "I assume Howe no longer considers our new flag to be a flag of surrender—regardless that the canton bears the British colors."

Still shaking from the impact, Elizabeth giggled, thinking of the flag with thirteen red and white stripes that had flown over the American camp since early January and caused a stir in the British garrison.

The bombardment, they knew, was meant to distract the British from the Americans' real objective of erecting fortifications on Dorchester Heights before dawn. Under cover of the unseasonably mild night, fascines and chandeliers, specially designed for constructing earthworks on top of the ground, were being hauled onto the heights, assembled, filled with bundles of hay, and covered with earth to make the parapets on which Ticonderoga's guns would be mounted. For this purpose militia from miles around had been called in, and every wagon that could be found had been commandeered—three hundred teams and three thousand men.

By dawn, when the bombardment finally slackened, they were all exhausted and heavy-eyed. Elizabeth could not rest, however. Donning her disguise, she crept out of the house and hurried through the deserted streets to Windmill Point. Finding a secluded vantage in the lee of an old brewery, she studied the four hills on Dorchester Neck, faintly visible in the hazy light.

She quickly noted that overnight the peninsula's extensive orchards had been cut down to provide an unobstructed view. At the top of two hills steeper and higher than the rest, she could make out what appeared to be fortresses. Large bodies of soldiers clustered inside each. As the light strengthened, it glimmered across great metal cylinders that studded the imposing walls: the menacing mouths of the long-range guns from Ticonderoga. From the heights they commanded every square foot of Boston, the ships of His Majesty's navy anchored in the bay, the sea roads, and Castle William, the fort that guarded access to Boston's harbor.

When these batteries roared to life, there would be few areas on Boston peninsula or on the expanse of water surrounding it that would be out of their reach. And with the guns, she knew, Knox had brought a substantial supply of gunpowder. This time the rebel army would not run out.

Elizabeth stifled an exuberant outcry, but the effort was unnecessary. For she was not the only one who noted the changes one night had wrought.

From a nearby wharf a detachment of sentries saw it, too, and raised the alarm with angry shouts that brought their mates running. The dismayed warning quickly echoed from the ships in the harbor.

Unlike the immediate reaction at discovery of the rebels' redoubt on Breed's Hill, this time the ships did not open fire. Within moments, however, manned longboats swept across the water to the nearest wharves. As the alarm raced throughout the town, soldiers and civilians, some still in their nightshirts, began to gather on the wharves along Boston's South End.

Taking advantage of the spreading confusion, Elizabeth hurried back to the town house. She and Tess spent the rest of the day making social calls on their circle of friends to commiserate with their panic and see what they could learn as well as to keep an eye on the action unfolding all along the waterfront.

The British garrison's complete disarray became quickly apparent. While the Continentals labored feverishly to strengthen their hastily constructed forts, Howe and his officers drove forward preparations to dislodge them. By mid-afternoon, as thunderclouds gathered in the east, strongly armed units began to embark on every available ship. Nightfall found Admiral Graves's transports anchored in a tidy line side by side facing the expanse of Dorchester peninsula.

Seated in her phaeton, staring across the water, Elizabeth watched the scene with dread. She could not help remembering that other day almost nine months earlier when from the heights of Breed's Hill she had stared down at the men-of-war in the harbor revolving on their anchor ropes as they brought their cannon to bear on the hastily constructed rebel redoubt. Again the stage of war was set, and morning would determine which side would prevail.

Gradually the evening mist gave way to a slow drizzle that glistened on the cobblestones and dripped from the phaeton's raised top. Hours after returning to the town house, she awakened from a fitful sleep to the roar and boom of what she at first took to be cannon fire. The entire house shook under the assault, and brilliant flashes of light repeatedly shattered the intense darkness. Terrified that Washington had lost patience and opened the bombardment, she ran to the window, shaking with cold and fear.

As she tore open the shutters Tess rushed into the room. They clung to each other while outside a violent gale buffeted the house, driving torrents of rain horizontally against its walls and shattering the limbs of the trees. Not until the black sky lightened with sullen dawn did rain and wind at last abate. And in the harbor, the new day revealed what the storm had wrought.

Like a mighty, avenging hand reaching from the heavens, the gale had driven the transports afoul of each other. Torn from their anchors, many of the ships listed sluggishly in the dirty, debris-laden water, their sides staved in by collision, jagged spars angled across their decks, sails and rigging ripped to tatters. Even the vessels suffering lesser damage had been rendered useless for the planned assault.

Before Elizabeth's jubilant eyes, the British navy's vaunted fleet bobbed helplessly on the choppy swells, its haughty splendor reduced to ruin.

"I CAN'T BELIEVE General Howe is abandoning us to the mercy of those brutes!" wailed the elderly woman. Pressing her lace handkerchief to her lips, she stared, distraught, through the open door of her chariot at the scene of chaos unfolding along the eastside wharves.

"There, there, Mrs. Reeve," Tess comforted, patting her hand reassuringly. "I can't believe it will be as bad as everyone seems to fear. They are our countrymen, after all."

The older woman fixed her in an indignant gaze. "Have you forgotten that their infernal Congress has given them the power to arrest anyone they perceive to be a threat? And what about all the reports of the poor souls who've been tarred and feathered, ridden around town on rails, and of the mobs attacking anyone who dares voice an opinion favorable to the crown." She waved her handkerchief in a passionate gesture. "They will stop at nothing, I tell you! I will not put it beyond them to execute us all!"

Standing outside the carriage, Elizabeth shot Tess a concerned glance. By now feelings on both sides ran so high that, in spite of the older woman's exaggeration, further violence against the loyalists was a very real possibility. In spite of her and her aunt's opposition to British policies, neither of them relished seeing innocent civilians caught in the crossfire between the opposing sides.

Moodily Elizabeth returned her attention to the fantastic scene that surrounded them. A week earlier Howe had sent a message to Washington through Boston's selectmen stating that if the rebel commander allowed Howe to evacuate without hindrance, he would abstain from burning the town to the ground. Washington's serene reply had been that Howe was under no obligation—implying that neither was Washington.

The result had been panic, and something other than an orderly withdrawal. Every day more ships were being hastily loaded and withdrawn toward the mouth of the harbor. Elizabeth watched the proceedings in a fever of impatience to reach Washington. By Howe's orders, however, all vessels except those belonging to the navy were barred from the harbor, thus closing her only route to the mainland.

Now on Sunday morning, March seventeenth, a roiling sea of soldiers shoved their way onto the wharves. Sweating and swearing, they pressed through the crowd to reach one of the last ships that remained at dock. Baggage and plunder from the ravaged town were carted aboard with no concern for order or the safety of man or goods.

Elizabeth started as a familiar coach drew up a short distance ahead of them. Betsey Loring descended its step on her husband's arm, dressed in her best gown and cloaked against the keen wind blowing off the sea. For a moment she paused and glanced around her with an expression of distaste, then her eyes lighted on Mrs. Reeve's chariot, and she marched toward them with her husband scuttling to keep up.

Tess leaned out of the carriage. "You're off to New York with the general, I take it."

Mrs. Loring gave her blonde head a toss, setting the plumes on her hat bobbing. "According to His Excellency, we're bound for Halifax. And from there . . . who knows."

"I suspect a visit to New York is in your future," Elizabeth returned. "Aunt Tess and I have found the shopping marvelous in the city. There's not a thing in all the world you can't purchase."

Mrs. Loring directed a resentful glance around her. "Then I can't wait till we get there. I'm afraid Halifax is destined to be deadly dull—though, knowing the general, we'll soon get up some games to pass the time." She brightened. "Did you hear how much I won at faro last night?"

Elizabeth smiled politely and turned her attention to Joshua Loring. "Undoubtedly Admiral Howe is on his way by now—or soon will be," she said, referring to Admiral Richard Howe, the general's brother, who had been ordered to join his fleet to the conflict.

"Once the fleet gets here, we'll set these ruffians back on their heels," Loring responded with a sneer.

He broke off as a tall, spare figure strode up and paused beside the chariot. Bowing, Lord Percy bent over each of the ladies' hands in turn, ending with Elizabeth.

"I couldn't leave without first bidding you adieu. I wish our farewell were under happier circumstances," he added, raising his voice to be heard over the jostling crowd's din.

"What are those of us loyal to the crown expected to do?" Mrs. Reeve demanded. "We'll not be able to stay here in Boston once the garrison and the navy are gone, but since you're taking all the ships, we're left no means of escape."

"I wish there was something I could do," Percy said forcefully. "If it hadn't been for that infernal storm, we'd have had a chance to take the Heights. Unfortunately, that gave the rebels just enough time to make their position impregnable."

A cruel smile twisted Loring's lips, and his eyes narrowed. "Ah, but we're going to have the final word. Didn't you hear? Burgoyne is being dispatched to Quebec as Governor Carleton's second in command. He'll take control of the Hudson in no time and split the colonies asunder. Then we'll see how long they all hang together."

Around noon the laden transports began to move sluggishly down the main sea road to where the rest of the fleet rode at anchor below Castle William. As soon as the last ship cleared the wharves, Elizabeth donned masculine dress, and taking Pete with her, roamed Boston's deserted streets.

Her most urgent concern was to scout out the fortifications the British had left behind. To her relief, the defensive works Gage and Howe had built on the peninsula had been left intact. Much of the heaviest artillery remained in position, though all had either been spiked or had a trunnion broken off—damage that could be repaired.

The rest of the town presented the ugly aftermath of war. The homes and buildings occupied by the garrison had almost all been ransacked. Shattered furniture and other debris lay strewn across trampled yards, and in the streets numerous fires sent gouts of smoke into the air. Broken windows stared blankly from houses where doors had been ripped from their hinges and holes chopped through the walls. Everything that could be carried off had been taken, and what could not be loaded aboard ship had been consigned to the flames.

Elizabeth found something that disturbed her even more. All along Orange Street from the Neck into the town, on many of the main streets, and along the wharves, the British had thickly scattered four-pointed iron devices called crow's feet. Designed to always fall with one of their sharp points facing upward, they effectively hindered the advance of a pursuing force.

She and Pete reached Barton's Point just as a small flotilla of boats emerged from the mouth of the Charles River off to their left and hesitantly made its way between the mud flats of the Back Bay. Suddenly Pete caught her arm and motioned toward the heights of Charlestown peninsula. While they watched, a detachment appeared at the top of Bunker's Hill and began to edge cautiously down the steep slope toward the redoubt on Breed's Hill.

Meanwhile, the boats were nearing Sewall's Point. With Pete leading the way, they ran to intercept them and found General Putnam in command. After hearing their report, the short, rotund general wasted no time in sending a detachment to secure the town, while the rest of his command hastened back to Cambridge to alert Washington.

By the time Elizabeth and Pete returned to the town house, a large contingent of troops was flooding through the town gates, proudly carrying their standard and only pausing long enough to sweep the scattered crow's feet out of their path. With their arrival, all the inhabitants of the town sympathetic to the rebellion emerged from their shuttered houses, laughing and dancing in the streets for joy at the siege's end. Only the loyalists continued to cower inside in fearful seclusion.

Although the British had at long last surrendered the town, it quickly became evident that they were reluctant to end their reprisals against its inhabitants. Two nights later, after a long day of packing for their move to New York, Elizabeth and Tess were startled by a series of thunderous explosions from the direction of the bay that shook the entire house. They hurried outside and climbed to the top of Beacon Hill to investigate.

To the southeast, the buildings of Castle William just off Dorchester Point glowed against the black sky like a monstrous, incandescent funeral pyre. And while they watched the wanton destruction of the fort in anger and dismay, a British ship stood off from Castle Island to rejoin the rest of the fleet still gathered a short distance below it.

"CONGRATULATIONS ON YOUR PROMOTION, Colonel Andrews."

Smiling, Andrews turned from the drawing room window. "It came as a surprise, I assure you."

"Not to me. You more than deserve it."

It was late afternoon on Wednesday, the twenty-seventh of March. That morning the British fleet had finally left the harbor and disappeared off the New England coast.

Regarding her friend with mingled pleasure and melancholy, Elizabeth realized how true her words rang. Andrews had changed in subtle ways during the past months. He had become more serious, more confident in his actions, steadier and more purposeful. Sadly she reflected that Carleton's absence had in many ways been good for

Andrews. No longer in his friend's shadow, he had grown into an independence and maturity that became him more than she wanted to admit.

Andrews cleared his throat. "I apologize for missing your birthday party yesterday. I couldn't get away in time to come."

"I understand. You were missed, though."

"Twenty-one," he teased. "Where has the year flown? And in a couple of months, I'll be a positively ancient twenty-seven."

She blinked back tears at the memory of how Carleton had often teased her about the difference in their ages.

"Forgive me," he apologized, his voice muffled. "I didn't think—" He broke off.

"Aunt Tess and I are leaving tomorrow," she said with an effort. "Sarah and her boys will stay a few more days to finish packing the things we're shipping to New York." Raggedly she added, "It feels as if we're abandoning him. How will he find us if he . . . " She stopped.

Biting his lip, Andrews turned back to the window. "I'll be gone by the end of the week myself," he said, his voice gruff. "The General is sending me to Virginia to finish raising the regiment of Rangers Jon was to command."

Involuntarily Elizabeth clasped her hands. For some moments she could only stare bleakly at him.

"I was hoping you'd be posted to New York. It will be very hard to have my dear friend so far away."

Pain shadowed his eyes as he crossed the room to enfold her hands in his. "I'll return as quickly as I can. You have only to send for me if you need me. You know there's not a thing in all the world I'd not do for you, Beth."

She fought vainly to keep back the tears. "I know."

Throwing her arms around his neck, she clung to him. He held her tightly, and she felt him draw a shaky breath. At length he pulled back to look earnestly into her eyes.

"If we never . . . if Jon doesn't come back—"

She pressed her fingers against his lips. "I can't bear to think of it. Not now. You know I shall always love you as my dear brother."

He covered her hand with his, kissed her fingertips, finally released her, and swung away. "If you ever have need of me, send for me. Fare thee well, sweet friend."

Shoulders bowed in resignation, he strode from the room.

Chapter Twenty-four

WHITE EAGLE STARED at the still, blanket-wrapped form that lay on the low platform at the center of the council house. A pungent fog of tobacco smoke drifted to the rafters and clogged the air, but he took no notice of it. It was now the fourth day of mourning, and since the hour he had learned of Black Hawk's death, his heart had lain like a stone in his breast.

Beside Black Hawk's body lay the old sachem's hunting knife, his tomahawk, his rifle, and his pipe. All around the platform were piled calico and linen fabrics, blankets, and other offerings of trade goods presented by the members of the clan in respect and love for their fallen leader.

Black Hawk. Dead at the hands of white settlers. Shot down like a dog while traveling to a distant village on the Ohio River to visit kinsmen.

There had been no reason for his slaying, and Black Hawk's companions had made sure those responsible paid with their lives. Vowing terrible retribution on all Long Knives who invaded Shawnee lands, they had carried his body home for burial.

The council house was filled with the men of the town, their faces painted, their clothing and hair hanging loose in mourning. The chiefs and townspeople of all the villages in the region had also gathered for the last rites of the old sachem they held in deep respect. At their head was Cornstalk, the principal sachem of the Maquachake, one of the five subnations of the Shawnee; his son Elinipscico; Black Snake, the Kispokotha division's primary sachem; Black Fish of the Chillicothe division; and other important sachems of the tribe. No one spoke, and all eyes glittered with unshed tears.

Renewed grief stabbed through White Eagle at the conviction that he should have accompanied Black Hawk that day instead of going with a hunting party. If he had been at the old sachem's side, perhaps Black Hawk would yet live. Or he would have died with him.

The shadows deepened toward nightfall, and finally four of the warriors surrounded Black Hawk and lifted his body from the platform with wide leather straps to carry it to the freshly dug grave. White Eagle got stiffly to his feet, followed by the others, and they left the council house.

It was the last week of March, and the weather was cold. Here and there patches of wet snow still clung to the sodden ground. A penetrating drizzle seeped through the trees as, in slow procession behind the body, they walked through the barren cornfields and the orchard to the graveyard a mile from the town.

Behind White Eagle, their faces drawn in anguish, walked Flying Swan, Black Hawk's only daughter, her husband and their three children, and Blue Sky. The sachems of the tribe followed them in silence, then the men, from oldest to youngest, with the women and older children bringing up the rear.

The grave was already prepared and lined with wide strips of bark. After Black Hawk's body was carefully lowered into it, the last clothing he had worn was laid across his body along with his moccasins, which had been cut into pieces. Finally more strips of bark closed the top of the makeshift coffin.

Standing at the head of the grave, while the mourners raised their voices in the haunting, undulating notes of the death chant, White Eagle took a small leather bag from his belt. From it he took sacred tobacco, which he sprinkled into the grave while walking slowly around it. Returning to the head, he sifted the last of the tobacco through his fingers onto the bark below, tears streaming unchecked down his cheeks, then dropped the empty bag after it.

Without a word or a glance toward those gathered around him, he turned and walked back to the village. The rest of the mourners followed, continuing their mournful dirge and leaving behind the men who would cover the grave with earth and construct a log grave house over the site.

All that night, gathered in the council house, the men continued to share memories of their fallen leader while the women roasted and served the abundant game that had been provided. Feeling as though he was sleepwalking, White Eagle spoke and ate little. It was a relief when the first light of dawn greyed the eastern horizon and most of the guests from the outlying villages returned to their homes. Cornstalk, along with the sachems and many of the warriors from the area stayed behind, however.

White Eagle knew a confrontation was coming and dreaded it. Rage and anguish consumed him. Every fiber thirsted to exact vengeance against the Whites who invaded Shawnee territory and killed both game and men with casual disregard. Equally, he wrestled with compelling reasons to stay his hand.

During the interminable storms that had confined the townspeople to wigewa and council house for much of the winter months, there had been considerable discussion of the gospel he had brought to them. For the most part, they had listened to him with respect, and he had answered their probing questions with careful thought and much prayer.

The fact that Black Hawk, his daughter and her family, and Blue Sky chose to be baptized held much weight. And over time, several men, including Red Fox, Spotted Pony, and Grey Cloud, with their families, had also accepted this new faith, as had several others. By late winter, White Eagle had gathered a small, steadfast congregation that was growing in grace.

Most of the rest of the clan members so far viewed his teachings with tolerant indifference, but as he had expected, a core of hostility gathered around Wolfslayer. The shaman was actively recruiting a band of supporters who advocated a return to the old ways and the uprooting from their people of anything perceived as coming from the Whites.

There lay White Eagle's greatest dilemma. After carefully outlining God's justice and mercy for his Shawnee kindred, could he now in good conscience seek vengeance against those who violated their right to live in freedom and safety on their own lands? What could he say to his kinsmen—and to himself—when deep anger burned in him at what had been done to Black Hawk?

Could he be an instrument of God's justice? Or would he only end up being a tool of man's unrighteous wrath and in the end bring destruction on them all?

Late that afternoon, the people gathered once more in the council house, every face drained and grim. Wolfslayer rose to speak first, spitting out his words in suppressed fury.

"The Long Knives swarm into our lands like hornets. They are *wannine*—crazy! They have no respect for the earth and sky and water. Instead, these *motchitteheckie*, these evil-minded people, cut down and burn all the trees to build their forts and houses and clear fields for planting. Their cattle devour the food the deer and other animals of the forest need to survive. The Whites ravage our sacred hunting grounds in Can-tuc-kee and kill any of our people they find there. Black Hawk is not the first to be killed for no reason.

"It is not enough that the Whites have made us dependent on them for food and clothing and other goods, but they also give us their firewater to make us as crazy as they are," he continued, his voice rising. "They build their forts on our lands to keep us as their slaves. The Long Knives insult us, our families, and our ancient ways. From the time of our ancestors, have we not always repaid our enemies for the injuries they did to us? After the outrage that was done to Black Hawk, if we continue to sit idly by like old women, then we will have no respect left—nor will we deserve any."

Slowly Kishkalwa, the sachem of the Thawekila division, pushed himself to his feet and looked from one face to another, his expression grim. "They will wipe us from the earth no matter what we do. To fight them will bring destruction on our heads all the sooner. A few years ago I led many from our division south to live with our brothers the Creeks. Recently we returned, believing we could now live here in peace, but it is not so. If the Shawnee strike the tomahawk into the war post again, the Thawekila will sever our connection to the nation and withdraw across the Great River, never to return."

An audible intake of breath passed through the council house. Black Snake turned to Cornstalk, his seamed face grave.

"What is your counsel, Cornstalk? Shall we go to war against the Long Knives once more or seek to keep the peace?"

Moving with easy grace, Cornstalk rose to speak. In his mid fifties, he was tall and lithe, still majestic in stature despite the slight stoop of his shoulders. His reputation as a powerful speaker and an implacable warrior had been well earned.

"Two years ago, after the war with Lord Dunmore, I pledged to keep the peace between the Shawnee and the Long Knives. Yes, we have kept the treaties the white man forced upon us while one after another they have broken every one. Their people continue to flood into our country and take our homes and our lands, take even the lives of our old people and our young children. And it will only grow worse.

"But how are we to fight them, my brothers? Have we not learned that it is futile to resist them with arms? They have guns and

ammunition, which we must buy from them if we are to defend ourselves against them. If they refuse to sell to us—as they surely will if
we fight them—then we are helpless. Bows and tomahawks are no
match for rifles."

Raging Bear, a husky young warrior allied with Wolfslayer, broke
in, his tone steely. "The counsel of Cornstalk is the counsel of old
men whose blood runs thin. For those of us who are yet young and
full of strength, to bear these insults is intolerable, and to leave our
ancestral home is unthinkable. I say we have no choice but to fight
for our homes and families, for our hunting grounds, for our very
lives! Who will stand with us?"

Murmurs of angry assent followed his words, and the voices that
called out their support were from the Chillicothe, Piqua, and
Kispokotha divisions. At last Red Fox raised his hand for silence.

"You are our brother and the war chief of Black Hawk's clan of
the Kispokothas, White Eagle. You have lived among the Long
Knives. You know them better than we do. What do you say?"

White Eagle rose with reluctance, for some moments remained
silent, praying for wisdom as he studied the hard faces of the men
illuminated by the flickering light of the fire. When he spoke, his
voice trembled with emotion.

"My heart thirsts for revenge against the Whites for the murder
of my father as much as yours do—and even more. If it were left to
me alone, I would fight them to the death. But Kishkalwa speaks
wisely.

"I have lived among the white men. I have seen their weapons
and how numerous a people they are, like the waves of the sea breaking without end against the shore. Already they outnumber us, and
every day more arrive from far across the great waters. Nor will they
cease to come. The Long Knives will attack us time and again in ever
greater force until not one of us is left. Our wives, our children, our
old people will suffer greater hardship than any we have yet known,

and in the end not one of us will remain to sing the songs of our ancestors or to bury our dead.

"What choice have we but to make peace as best we can, to find some way to live with the white man—or if that is impossible, to leave our ancestral lands and withdraw far to the West where they may leave us in peace?"

He stopped and earnestly searched the faces upturned to him. "Whatever we decide, we must choose by sober reason—not hot emotion. And we must act with wisdom and restraint."

"Moneto is with us," Wolfslayer ground out. "He has caused the Whites to fight among themselves, the Long Knives against the British. Now is our opportunity while they are in confusion, and I say we must take it or we are fools! The Whites cannot defeat us, for the Great Spirit fights on our side."

White Eagle swung on him. "How can we know that? Do you know the mind of Moneto and of the Great Spirit?"

"The Great Spirit came upon you, White Eagle," Spotted Pony pointed out. "You know the ways of Moneto, and we will follow your counsel."

A murmur filled the council house as a number of warriors from the other divisions eagerly echoed Spotted Pony. White Eagle lifted his hand for silence.

"I am a man, as you are. No human being can know the ways of Moneto perfectly. But one thing I do know: All peoples are the children of Moneto. He created them all. His ways and his purposes are his own, not ours. He is no respecter of persons—not of the Shawnee nor of the white man. Why should he favor us above his other children?"

"It was Moneto who gave us these lands," Spotted Pony protested.

"Can he not take them back again or give them to another if he so chooses?"

For a long moment no one spoke as the men looked from one to the other. At last Cornstalk said, "My heart cannot tell you it is wrong to fight. The young men are in the right, and I will not stand against them. But heed White Eagle's counsel and choose your course carefully. No matter which side we fight on, the Long Knives and the British will be like two great stones. Between them they will grind us to dust."

Black Fish sprang to his feet, his stocky frame tense and trembling with suppressed anger. "The white man has proven time and again he cannot be trusted. If we do not keep our self-respect, then we have nothing. I am for war. What is the council's decision?"

One by one, some eagerly, some hesitantly, the majority of the tribe voted to make war upon any who encroached on their lands. When the last voice had been heard, Kishkalwa clambered to his feet, and with a nod to the subchiefs of the Thawekila who accompanied him, led them out of the council house without a word or a backward glance. Sorrow hardened with determination etched the faces of those who watched them leave.

Wolfslayer waited until all of the Thawekila clan had gone before rounding on White Eagle, his face contorted with triumph and malice. "You have taken Pathfinder's place as our war chief," he said, contempt dripping from his tongue. "Do you have the courage to lead us against the Long Knives, or must we choose another?"

Spotted Pony frowned. "We have no war chief but White Eagle. He has proven himself among us and earned the respect of our people. He gives generously to everyone in need and welcomes all to his fire. He counsels wisely and holds nothing back from anyone, whether elder, woman, or child."

"White Eagle was trained in warfare by the Whites," Red Fox broke in, his hawk-like face taut. "He knows their ways. Who better to lead us against them?"

Without warning, in White Eagle's mind reverberated his casual comment to Washington months earlier as they talked about General Braddock's ill-fated expedition during the French and Indian War: *I didn't relish joining in on the annihilation of my countrymen.*

But he had been led—no, brought—by God to this country and to these people. They were now his own. In truth, he could never join in the annihilation of his former countrymen, but at his adoption had he not accepted the responsibility to help the Shawnee defend themselves against all who would destroy them?

He met Cornstalk's steady gaze. "How can I do this?" he said in an undertone, despairing.

Cornstalk grasped his shoulder, his dark, compelling eyes boring into White Eagle's. "You must follow the counsel of your heart."

Overwhelmed by dread, White Eagle turned and for a tense moment held Wolfslayer's malicious stare with sad resignation. Dismayed at what he read there, he transferred his gaze from one face to another, each eye fixed on him, waiting for his decision.

What am I to do? he questioned bitterly. *Am I to turn my back on them when they most need a wise leader? Or am I to lead them to their destruction?*

There was no solution to the riddle, no quiet voice that whispered an answer. There was only a growing, dread certainty in his gut that drew him inevitably forward.

At last he pulled his tomahawk from his belt and strode to the war post that stood in the center of the council house. Raising the weapon over his head, he swung it in a powerful arc that sank its sharp blade deep into the stone-hard wood.

Rounding to face the assembly once more, he said hoarsely, "I will lead you. We will burn their buildings and drive them out of our territory. But we will fight only when attacked, kill only when there is no other choice.

"If Moneto gives us success, so be it. But if we do not prevail, then we will withdraw beyond the Great River and never again return to this place."

⊕ ⊕ ⊕

Silent as a shadow, White Eagle appraised the fort's mist-shrouded outline. To each side, well within the cover of the forest, ranged his warriors, their naked bodies, like his, heavily streaked with black paint. They stood motionless with bows at the ready, awaiting his signal. At short intervals between them and well hidden from view of the fort, small fires smoldered, the pale streamers of smoke quickly melting into the mist that wrapped the base of the trees.

It was an hour before dawn, and only a few guards were visible behind the top of the fort's palisade walls. His movements fluid, White Eagle took from his quiver an arrow whose head was wrapped in a short length of cloth thickly daubed with pine resin. He held the saturated fabric into the fire, and when it hissed into flame, nocked the arrow to the bowstring, raised the bow high, and drew it until it bent almost double before letting fly.

In a high, true arc, the burning arrow seared through the hazy light, soaring above the palisade wall to thud into the shingled roof of the largest building inside. It was followed instantly by a sizzling flight of dozens of flaming arrows.

A second and a third flight found their marks while cries of alarm rose from inside the fort. Before the soldiers could reach their posts, the fort's walls and buildings blazed at numerous points.

Discarding his bow, White Eagle slung his loaded rifle over his shoulder and, careful to keep under cover of the trees, swiftly led a large, strongly armed party around the fort while the rest of his warriors continued their attack. As he expected, all the fort's defenders now battled the fires that raged across the front, and the rear wall lay unguarded.

Four of the warriors carried ropes, which they looped into nooses and twirled overhead to drop, one after another, over the pointed end of one of the palisade's logs. In moments the war party had stealthily scaled the wall and dropped unnoticed inside.

By the time they rounded the barracks and gained the parade ground, much of the fort was engulfed in flames. Using his rifle butt to knock aside anyone who tried to block his path, White Eagle raced through the dancing firelight and smoke and the chaos of shouting, swearing militia and screaming women.

He ignored the sharp explosions of rifle and musket fire that rent the dawn. Most of the warriors with him spread out to each side, but a small party followed on his heels as he fought his way toward the cluster of soldiers guarding the gates, whose attention was on the attack from outside. Before the wails from behind them could alert the gate's defenders to danger, White Eagle and his men were on them. Overwhelmed, the soldiers were quickly struck down by Shawnee tomahawks.

Tearing the bar out of its brackets while his warriors wrestled back the men who clawed to stop them, White Eagle heaved the heavy gates open.

"Get everyone outside before this place burns to the ground!" he shouted to his warriors. "All of them! Hurry!"

The fort's inhabitants needed little urging to abandon the blazing fort. They stumbled through a curtain of fire into the clearing outside, prodded roughly forward at the point of rifle, lance, and tomahawk. The Shawnee war party quickly engulfed them.

Coils of black smoke studded with brilliant sparks swirled into the sky's brightening expanse from cherry tongues of flame that danced along charred walls and collapsing roofs. Coughing and choking, skin, hair, and clothing fouled with gunpowder and ashes, soldiers and settlers alike stared fearfully at their captors.

Unnoticed, White Eagle slipped away into the forest. From a hidden vantage point he watched as Red Fox took charge of the prisoners.

Only when the captives had been herded away under guard to be driven out of Ohio Territory did White Eagle emerge to rejoin the rest of his party. Jubilant at their triumph, the warriors danced around the blaze until the last of the walls collapsed. White Eagle alone took no pleasure in the sight.

In the weeks that followed, under White Eagle's canny leadership, a series of lightning raids burned many of the white settlements to the ground and forcibly pushed their inhabitants back out of Shawnee lands. Yet as he had foreseen, retaliation was not long in coming.

By late April the frontier was aflame. And the name of White Eagle had begun to spread beyond the borders of Ohio Territory.

Chapter Twenty-five

"I TRUST YOU'RE COMPLETELY SETTLED at Montcoeur by now."
Elizabeth returned the smile of the sprightly widow
ensconced on the garden bench across from her. "We are indeed,
Mrs. Van Cortland. Thank you for your very kind assistance in
securing such a pleasant establishment for us. We'd despaired of
finding a suitable place in the city, and we much prefer being just
outside of it."

It was mid-April, and the weather that embraced New York City
could not have been more glorious. Although they were in the middle
of the city, the vine-shaded veranda where they sat afforded a gar-
denlike prospect. Linden and locust trees, stately elms, chestnuts,
oaks, and beech, interspersed by pines and firs, cloaked the low hills
of York Island, the islands in the harbor, and the New Jersey shore
across the Hudson River in every hue of fresh, delicate green. The
rooftops of expansive mansions were visible at intervals through this
canopy, punctuated here and there by soaring church spires that towered into the serene azure sky.

Tess turned her face into the breeze that stirred the interlaced
honeysuckle vines overhead. "Montcoeur is convenient, yet removed
from all the hustle and bustle," she concurred. "We were quite concerned about the move here, but to remain in Boston after it was
taken over by the rebels was intolerable. I don't know what we would

have done had you not come to our aid. I do hope you'll call on us often now that we're established."

Mrs. Van Cortland beamed at them, the color rising into her withered cheeks. Despite her advanced age, her face retained the fire of the beautiful woman she had obviously been in her youth.

"It will be my pleasure. I'm delighted that Margaret directed you to us. I can't remember when we've been blessed with such charming company. One does become quite dull with only the usual circle for entertainment. You have brought us to life again."

"I can't imagine you've ever been dull here," Elizabeth teased. "Everyone we meet remarks on how you manage to keep things in a lively state."

Mrs. Van Cortland rose to refill her cup with steaming tea. "I do everything I can, my dear, but it isn't always so easy to rouse these Philistines out of their niggling routines. You'll find we're quite an obstinate and conventional lot."

Elizabeth became aware that the butler, a lean, hunch-shouldered black servant, hovered in the open doorway. "Dr. Vander Groot, Madam."

Mrs. Van Cortland dismissed him with a ring-encrusted hand, her eyes sparkling with pleasure. "Show him outside, Joshua." She turned back to Elizabeth. "How wonderful! I've been hoping for an opportunity to introduce you to my grandnephew."

Before Elizabeth could question their hostess, Joshua ushered the visitor outside. Dr. Pieter Vander Groot stepped into the dappled sunshine, his smiling gaze sobering as it traveled from his great aunt to her companions. For a moment his eyes lingered on Elizabeth, then he made a graceful bow, which Elizabeth and Tess returned with curtsies.

When they resumed their seats, he came to kiss the hand Mrs. Van Cortland extended to him. "I see you're much improved, Aunt Euphemia. I should have known better than to worry. Agreeable company is all the tonic you ever need."

Mrs. Van Cortland chuckled. "Let me introduce you to my charming new friends, Pieter."

When she had done so, Dr. Vander Groot waved away her offer of tea and turned to Tess. "You've taken over the Montcoeur estate, I understand."

While the others conversed, Elizabeth discreetly scrutinized the young doctor. He appeared to be in his late twenties, of medium height, slender and blond, with handsome, regular features and clear blue eyes.

"I'm afraid your plan to escape this unhappy conflict has mis-fired," he observed with a sympathetic shake of his head. "General Washington arrived in the city last Saturday at the head of a substantial detachment."

"So we heard," Elizabeth acknowledged.

"It seems to me our authorities ought to arrest him," Mrs. Van Cortland said acidly.

"You forget, dear aunt, that the militia consists entirely of Liberty Boys, and what is left of the British garrison is safely holed up aboard ship in the harbor."

Mrs. Van Cortland's expression registered her disapproval. "How inconvenient. But when our old friend, General Howe, finally arrives, I suspect they'll soon discover the courage they're wanting."

Elizabeth shot a veiled look at Tess and saw she was thinking the same thing. They could not have made a more fortunate connection. Mrs. Van Cortland and her family had become acquainted with Howe a couple of decades earlier during the French and Indian War and had maintained a regular correspondence with him after his return to England at the war's end.

"I can't say I'm entirely opposed to someone challenging the British," their hostess continued. "They've had everything their way in the century since they conquered us. Though we old ones still cling to our traditions and mother tongue, the younger generation has deserted their heritage and become more English than Dutch."

"Dutch is still spoken at all the markets," Vander Groot pointed out with a smile.

Mrs. Van Cortland tossed her head. "Need I remind you, Pieter, that every other Sunday the sermon at church is delivered in English?"

"Considering that after a hundred years sermons are still being preached in Dutch at least half the time, I wouldn't call that an excessively speedy desertion."

Suspecting that the comfortable banter between the two reflected their usual mode of communication, Elizabeth exchanged an amused glance with Tess.

"What concerns me more is that if the rebels succeed in their aims, the likely result will be that we exchange the tyranny of the British king for that of the mobs," he continued. "None of those who oppose the rebellion will be safe, including us. Just last night several more loyalists were tarred and feathered. It's all very well to talk of liberty, but shouldn't that include freedom of conscience even for those whose opinions are out of favor?"

Elizabeth agreed wholeheartedly. At the same time she had to bite her tongue to keep from pointing out that since the British steadfastly refused to address the colonies' grievances, they should not be surprised at reaping an unpleasant harvest.

The sun was lowering, and with it a chill had crept into the spring breeze. Mrs. Van Cortland drew her shawl around her shoulders.

"I confess I never believed the rebels would take their discontent this far. Truthfully, we have prospered under English rule. In my opinion, a few minor disagreements are not sufficient grounds for taking up arms."

"Apparently the rebels don't believe their grievances are so minor," Tess noted with a shrug.

"Whatever the rebels' justifications, my interest is in healing, not politics," Vander Groot returned. "In the final analysis, it doesn't much matter whether we're governed by the British or by the Continental Congress as long as we're governed fairly and honestly. But I don't look forward to the carnage we'll face if New York becomes the center of the war, as it likely will."

For several minutes they discussed the steady decline in the city's population. Since the previous summer, hundreds of families had moved away in fear of the coming conflict. Each month more houses along the tree-shaded streets were left shuttered and empty. Already many of them furnished quarters for the Continental Army and the militia regiments that were arriving daily from neighboring colonies.

At length Vander Groot turned his attention to Elizabeth, and a pang cut through her. His eyes were a paler, softer blue than Carleton's and his hair a darker blond, but the young doctor's easy charm and unaffected manner reminded her uncomfortably of him.

"My aunt told me you served as your father's assistant and that you are a trained doctor, Miss Howard. That's an unusual profession for a lady, though a most admirable one. I've always thought women possess a superior temperament for the healing arts, but knowing my colleagues, I suspect you have encountered opposition to your ministrations."

She looked down to keep him from reading her troubled thoughts. "I respect any objection to my presence, though I've quite often discovered that people find occasion to change their minds when they are in need. Papa maintains that God has given me a healing touch and that not to use it would be a sin."

"When one's calling is from God, the Almighty will provide means and opportunity for obedience. I would be honored if one of these afternoons you would allow me to show you my surgery."

She readily accepted his invitation. He and his great aunt, as well as his parents and youngest sister, were members of the nearby New Dutch congregation, and before they took their leave, Elizabeth and Tess agreed to join them for worship the following Sunday.

After they left Mrs. Van Cortland's home on Lower Broad Way, Tess's chariot rolled at a leisurely pace north. The scene could not have provided a more striking contrast to the narrow, winding lanes and overhanging, half-timbered houses that gave Boston the look of a medieval town.

As on their previous visits to the city, both women admired the wide thoroughfares that extended to each side, where old Dutch and newer English brick residences, tidy office buildings, merchants' establishments, butcher shops, and manufactories crowded together willy nilly. Along the wharves, shouldering up against the usual complement of ropewalks, sailmakers, distilleries, grog shops, and prostitutes' dens, clustered expansive warehouses that stored every imaginable type of goods, from lumber to grain to furs harvested in the continent's interior to exotic cargoes imported, whether legally or illegally, from England, Europe, Africa, and the Orient.

New Amsterdam, renamed New York by the conquering British the previous century, covered less than a square mile at the southern tip of York Island. But although during the past months more than a third of the inhabitants had fled in fear of the coming war, it was still the second largest city in the colonies after Philadelphia, with close to fifteen thousand residents.

Repeatedly the portents of imminent battle jarred Tess and Elizabeth from their admiration and reminded them of their purpose in coming there. William Alexander, commonly known as Lord Stirling—a title he claimed in spite of Parliament's denial of the Scottish earldom he claimed—had taken charge of fortifying the city. To all sides the raw earthen walls of newly constructed forts and ditches scarred the landscape. Time and again Pete was forced to guide the chariot around barricades erected to block the passage of enemy troops along the streets.

Turning onto Murray Street, they passed the graceful buildings of King's College and finally reached the bank of the Hudson River, where they turned north onto Greenwich Road. Along the promontory that overlooked the river's turbulent waters, just beyond the Harrison manor, they came to a wrought-iron fence supported by solid limestone columns that enclosed a broad sweep of lawn.

Of all the properties she and Tess had considered, they had found only one that offered the secluded access both to bay and mainland necessary for Elizabeth's nighttime forays. The owners had left the sprawling, Italianate limestone mansion four months earlier to return to France for the duration of hostilities with England. Their factor had been more than pleased to lease the home to Tess and Elizabeth for a reasonable fee, undoubtedly to avoid its being commandeered and ransacked by either Continental or British troops.

Montcoeur's grounds extended to the steep cliffs of the Hudson, where a tangled growth of trees and underbrush shaded a broad stairway carved into the bluff. On the narrow, rocky beach far below, a tidy boathouse sheltered a small sailboat named appropriately, if incongruously, *Implacable.* The vessel would provide access either to New Jersey on the opposite shore, where a number of militia regiments already made camp, or to the islands in the bay.

An estuary of the Atlantic, the Hudson was wide and fast-moving at this point, treacherous at the turning of the tides. Pete was experienced at sailing on Boston's bay, however, and by now was becoming a master at maneuvering the nimble craft through the river's deceptive tidal currents.

The owners had left behind most of the gracious furnishings of the expansive rooms, and Sarah had overseen a rapid and smooth transfer to their new home at the beginning of the previous week. With Mrs. Van Cortland's help a suitable cook and scullery maid had quickly been engaged.

In addition to Jemma and Mariah, Caleb Stern, Colonel Stern's twenty-nine-year-old nephew, had also joined them, ostensibly to serve as their butler. A staunch Son of Liberty from the beginning, in reality his most important role was to assist Elizabeth, along with Pete, in planning and carrying out her clandestine activities. In this she had already found the taciturn, muscular man to be steady and level-headed.

Not only were they by now comfortably settled, but with Mrs. Van Cortland's unwitting assistance, they were beginning to cultivate the network of contacts they hoped would prove invaluable in the weeks to come. With the introduction to the elderly woman's nephew and soon his parents as well, Elizabeth was fully confident their efforts in that regard were destined to bear much fruit.

"When I invited you to visit my surgery, I had no intention of pressing you to service."

Elizabeth looked up from the tiny girl whimpering on her lap to meet Vander Groot's concerned gaze. "You mean you're not in the habit of arranging horrendous carriage accidents so you can impress your guests with your medical prowess?"

He gave a rueful chuckle. "I assure you, I am not."

Elizabeth gently adjusted the splint that bound the child's thin leg before lifting her against her shoulder. "I'm glad I was here to help."

"I couldn't have managed without you, Elizabeth."

She returned his smile, then carried the child to a slender woman who leaned her head against the back of the wing chair where she sat. Her bandaged arm rested in a sling, and her face was abnormally pale except for the bruised, swollen knot that distorted the right side of her forehead.

When Elizabeth approached, she forced her eyes open. "Patsy!" she cried, reaching her good arm for her daughter.

Elizabeth settled the drowsy child in her lap. "I've given her opiate for the pain, Mrs. De Lancey. She's almost asleep, which is the best medicine for her right now. Fortunately the fracture was not displaced, and I was able to set the bone without causing too much pain. There don't seem to be any internal injuries."

Mrs. De Lancey shifted her gaze to Dr. Vander Groot. "I trust you've examined her, Doctor."

He said stiffly, "Dr. Howard gave Patsy a thorough examination and did an excellent job of setting the fracture and stitching her cuts. I couldn't have done better myself."

Mrs. De Lancey's expression still reflected some doubt. Indicating the man slumped in a chair across the room, his head in his hands, she demanded, "How is my husband?"

"I'm quite all right, Jane," snapped Mr. De Lancey without lifting his head or glancing toward his wife.

"There are no broken bones, but he's pretty badly bruised, with several deep cuts," Dr. Vander Groot explained. "At the moment, I'm sure his headache is as severe as yours."

"What happened?" Elizabeth prodded.

De Lancey lifted his head with a groan. "We came to one of the rebel's cursed barricades and had just begun to pass a wagon stopped in the middle of the street when a large keg rolled off the back and shattered right at our horses' feet."

"I'll wager it was deliberately thrown down by one of those miserable Liberty Boys!" his wife wailed.

De Lancey grimaced. "Of course, the horses reared, then plunged ahead at breakneck speed."

He was interrupted by a knock on the door. It swung slowly open to reveal Tess, who peered cautiously inside, averting her gaze from the injured family. When Dr. Vander Groot beckoned her to enter, she gave her head a weak shake.

Elizabeth giggled at his puzzled expression. "Aunt Tess can't bear the sight of blood. She's useless in a sickroom or surgery."

He grinned and led the way across the room. Edging over the threshold, Tess stopped just inside the door.

"One of the horses had to be put down," she informed them. "The other is being taken back to the De Lanceys' estate. I'm afraid the carriage is a complete loss."

"I think we can safely send the De Lanceys home in my carriage," Dr. Vander Groot decided. "Please join me for dinner. It's the least I can do to thank you for your aid, and I can't think of company I'd enjoy more."

Elizabeth and Tess needed little persuasion to accept his invitation. The De Lanceys were soon on their way home with the promise that Vander Groot and Elizabeth would call on them after Sunday worship the next day. Following his employer's instructions, the carriage driver returned with Mrs. Van Cortland while the lamplighter was finishing his nightly rounds to light the gas lanterns hung at intervals along the streets.

By then the young doctor had escorted Elizabeth and Tess on a tour of the lush gardens that surrounded the hundred-year-old Dutch-style brick mansion situated, as were its neighbors, so that its stepped gable end faced Pearl Street. The one-story addition at its rear that housed the surgery extended almost to the back of the property and was surrounded by a profusion of flowers, bushes, and espaliered fruit trees. The melodious peal of birdsong added to the pleasant illusion of isolation from the surrounding houses.

On Mrs. Van Cortland's arrival, the elderly woman insisted they take in the view from the third-floor balcony. This vantage presented a breathtaking vista of the darkening bay and the Hudson, with the verdant New Jersey shore directly to the west and Staten Island to the south. The flickering glow cast by the streetlights and the lighted windows of houses studded the shadowed hills that surrounded them like candle flame against velvet.

From the balcony they could also make out the rapidly expanding camps of the Continental Army north of the city. Glowering in their direction, Mrs. Van Cortland jerked her shawl around her shoulders and led the way back into the house and downstairs, where Dr. Vander Groot's parents and sister shortly joined them.

They spent a pleasant hour before dinner conversing around the hearth in the parlor, where a crackling fire dispersed the spring evening's chill. During their brief acquaintance, Elizabeth and her aunt had found the Vander Groots to be delightful company. Andreas was an older version of his son, while his wife, Verbena, exhibited the same elegance and liveliness Mrs. Van Cortland and Tess shared.

It was the doctor's eighteen-year-old sister Isobel who attracted Elizabeth the most, however. As they laughed and chatted about the newest styles, the latest parties, and Isobel's numerous suitors, Elizabeth reveled in the temporary release from talk of politics and war.

Once seated at the dining room table, however, Mrs. Van Cortland merely tasted her soup before putting down her spoon with a sigh. "I can hardly eat anymore for worry. We used to talk of nothing more serious than our inbred local politics—or which wine to serve at dinner. Now our main topic of conversation is war, our main activity is preparing for battle, and our main fear is being caught in the crossfire between the British and the rebels. It makes me long so for the old days when there was always a concert or ball to look forward to and we feared nothing so much as being out of fashion."

Andreas Vander Groot fingered the stem of his wine glass, moodily assessing its pale contents. "I'm afraid we have lived luxuriously far too long. The realities of life were bound to catch up with us."

His son nodded. "We New Yorkers have become rampant materialists. Our indulgence and excess have weakened, if not destroyed altogether, any moral fiber we used to have."

"With the Liberty Boys strictly enforcing the Continental Congress's non-importation and non-exportation agreement, perhaps our moral fiber will undergo a revival," observed Mrs. Vander Groot dryly.

Elizabeth could not suppress a giggle. "I confess I was so looking forward to the merchant fleet arriving this month with the latest goods from London and visiting all the shops in Hanover Square. What a disappointment to discover that the rebels refuse to allow ships carrying English merchandise to land! I'm in dire need of new gowns for the summer, but what am I to do?"

"If things continue as they have, I fear you won't need them," Isobel put in, her voice plaintive. "I'm beginning to think the summer is going to be as dull as the winter."

"According to the latest rumors, things are likely to become even more exciting than we could wish," Tess interjected. "Have you heard that the king is going to hire German mercenaries—Hessians—to fight his battles for him?"

Dr. Vander Groot pushed aside his plate. "On every side, even among those who still hope for a reconciliation with Britain, I hear bitter talk of the king unleashing on us a horde of barbarians who've been promised their choice of our homes and property. While I don't believe it true, I'm afraid George III will make a very grave mistake indeed if he sends German troops over here."

Despite her disavowal of hunger, Mrs. Van Cortland had returned her attention to her soup. Pausing with her spoon in midair, she said, "If you ask me, Governor Tryon would do much to bolster confidence in British rule if he returned to the city instead of cowering aboard ship for fear of the Liberty Boys."

Mrs. Vander Groot dismissed her words with a wave of her hand. "It's prudence, not cowardice, Euphemia. In fact, the governor continues to communicate freely with our leaders despite General Washington's efforts to cut off their contact. Nor, for all the rebels' threats, has our merchants' and farmers' commerce with the British suffered any decline."

"When there's profit to be made, politics inevitably takes a backseat to trade," her husband observed.

While the next courses were served and cleared, they discussed every aspect of the political and economic situation. At last, noting that it was growing late, Tess insisted it was time she and Elizabeth returned home.

As Dr. Vander Groot escorted them out to their waiting chariot, Elizabeth reflected that he reminded her increasingly of her father, whose advice and counsel she missed more and more each day. The young doctor's kindness and intelligence drew her to him. After the long months of grief, to be in the company of one so serene and confident of his life's course steadied her, stirred emotions she thought had died with last autumn's frost—emotions that warmed her, yet filled her with sadness and uncertainty.

Feeling his gaze as he turned to her from handing Tess into the chariot, she lifted her eyes with trepidation to meet his.

"I've thought for some time of hiring an associate to assist me in surgery two or three days a week. After today, I'm confident we could work well together, and a woman's touch would contribute much to my practice. Would you consider such a position?"

Surprised, she hesitated. "I would love to work with you, Pieter, but . . . my father was widely known and respected in Boston and so could open doors for me that might not so easily be unlocked elsewhere."

He smiled down at her, his clear blue eyes registering an emotion that caused her heartbeat to quicken. "I am known and, I believe, respected in the city, as is my family. I would not propose this if I did not believe that I could open doors for you here as well."

She could not resist his smile, and a long-unaccustomed lightness flooded through her. "Then I accept most heartily."

"And what is it you are accepting?"

Both of them started and looked up to find Tess surveying them, head tilted in question. Elizabeth felt the heat climbing to her cheeks. Tess's apprehension was unmistakable, and Elizabeth hastened to explain.

Tess relaxed visibly. "Then if Pieter believes he could smooth the way for you, I wholeheartedly encourage your association. God has given you a gift, Elizabeth, and I cannot believe he would have you hide it under a bushel."

Vander Groot captured Elizabeth's hand and bent to kiss it. "I'll see you at church tomorrow morning, then. We'll work out the details later."

"Until tomorrow," she agreed, noting with both pleasure and dismay that he released her hand with reluctance.

As May melted into June with no sight of the British fleet, Elizabeth and her aunt began increasingly to wonder whether there had been any reason for them to come to New York at all. Social obligations claimed their lives, and the better part of Elizabeth's free time was taken up with mandatory calls on acquaintances and the endless teas and dinners they hosted at Montcoeur. In spite of Isobel's fears, every week also brought at least one invitation to a ball or a play, a concert or a dinner.

Yet no one in their circle knew anything more about Howe's intentions than they did, and in the absence of any intelligence, the number of Elizabeth's visits to Washington's and Stern's headquarters dwindled. Nonetheless, she regularly sent young Pete under cover of night to maneuver the *Implacable* up and down the Hudson and across the bay until he became confident enough of his knowledge of the tides to land on the New Jersey shore and on any of the islands in the harbor.

The highlight of the long weeks was the mail that arrived from England once a month. The moment the small packet was sighted entering the bay, all else was quickly forgotten as the townspeople hurried to the East River docks to receive letters, packages, and the latest London newspapers. Reflecting the tastes of their readers, local newspapers reprinted much of the news received from abroad and little of events and politics in the other colonies. For all Elizabeth and Tess's anxiety to learn about conditions in Boston, the town might as well have resided on another planet.

Though much of their communication was by necessity veiled, Elizabeth's greatest comfort was the warm and loving correspondence that had developed over the winter with her mother in London. Separated by a vast ocean, they once more had grown as close as they had been during Elizabeth's childhood. Abby's letters were also exceedingly precious to her, and her father wrote regularly as well, often detailing the latest medical advances in long missives that completely absorbed her.

Shortly after their arrival in the city, Elizabeth had written her parents about their move to New York, citing as their reason the rebels' reprisals against loyalists who remained after the siege was broken. It was a suspect argument, she knew. Not only had Dr. Howard guessed his daughter and sister's sympathy with the patriots shortly before sailing to England, but he would most assuredly know of Howe's intention to take New York. But while her letter and her parents' reply were in transit, she hoped to come up with a stronger rationale that didn't involve an admission that she was serving as a spy for Washington. For the time being, she simply dismissed any concern about her father's likely response until she received it.

In spite of these diversions, Elizabeth was soon consumed with boredom, certain that if she was required to attend one more party at which she had to listen to the same unchanging dissection of the military and political situation, with the attendant ridicule of Washington and his army, she would scream. By heroic effort, she managed to maintain her composure, to listen with apparent interest, and to smile and nod her head in pretended agreement. The only relief she found was during the absorbing hours she spent assisting in Dr. Vander Groot's surgery.

It would, of course, have been unthinkable not to invite Mrs. Van Cortland and the Vander Groots regularly to Montcoeur, invitations they eagerly accepted as well as reciprocating with their own. And with regular attendance at the New Dutch church, Elizabeth was thrown into Dr. Vander Groot's company each day of the week. To her dismay it became increasingly obvious that his feelings for her were growing into something deeper than mere friendship or professional courtesy.

What she felt for him in return she had difficulty fathoming. Certainly, the more time she spent in his company, the more she liked and admired him. He was highly intelligent, handsome and charming, thoughtful and kind, with an easygoing temperament and a quick wit that often surprised her into delighted laughter.

And he was a devoted believer, unvarying in his attendance at his church, where services were marked by the same passionate evangelical preaching that had characterized the Great Awakening of the previous decades and inspired the widening belief in personal liberty that was the foundation of the rebellion. All Vander Groot said and did assured Elizabeth that his testimony was no pretense. That, added to the fact that he was a skilled and compassionate doctor, greatly attracted her in spite of the defenses behind which she struggled to barricade her emotions.

Toward the end of June, Elizabeth received from her father a recently published medical text, *Practical Remarks on the Treatment of Wounds and Fractures*. She brought it to Vander Groot's surgery, where they pored over its diagrams and discussions of new procedures.

"I'm exceedingly glad Dr. Jones places such emphasis on hygiene and sanitation," Vander Groot said as he paged through the text. "In my experience such precautions are the surest defense against contagion, yet they are all too often neglected."

Elizabeth nodded. "One of the first things my father taught me was the benefit of proper cleanliness and ventilation in a surgery and sickroom. Our patients suffered considerably less infection and healed all the more rapidly as a result."

They were standing quite close to each other, their shoulders brushing as they bent over the table where they had laid the text. When Elizabeth glanced up, she found Vander Groot looking down, and the warmth that sprang into his eyes caused her heart to constrict.

She tried to tear her gaze from his, to step away from him. But it felt as though she was rooted to the floor.

Catching his breath, he murmured, "Elizabeth, I know it is too soon to make a declaration. We've known each other for such a short time, yet already you've become so dear to my heart that I—"

She pressed her fingers lightly to his lips to stop the words. "We must not—"

His face growing pale, he captured her hand, fervently kissed her fingertips, then the palm of her hand. "Why? Is there another?"

"I . . . no!" Her thoughts racing, she blurted out the first explanation that came into her head. "It's just that . . . you see . . . I was betrothed two years ago. He . . . he became quite abusive. When Papa discovered what was happening, he broke off our relationship."

Sympathy and understanding came into Vander Groot's eyes. He was bending so closely over her that he could easily have kissed her. Trembling, she bent her head, heat flooding into her cheeks at the memory of her painful relationship with Hutchins.

"How difficult that must have been for you—and how deeply it must have hurt. I well understand your hesitation to trust any man. But I promise you, I will earn your confidence. I am willing to wait until you can give your heart without reservation."

Misery washed over her and shame at the necessity of telling him only a part of the truth. "You must not hold out hope for me, Pieter. I can promise you nothing—especially not now, while our situation is so uncertain."

Before she could stop him, he bent to kiss her lightly on the cheek. "I ask nothing of you. I want only what is God's best for you, what will bring you joy and true happiness, whether that is to be with me or with someone else. I will accept your decision, whatever it may be. In either case, I pray that we may remain colleagues and dear friends."

She stared down at their interlocked hands, tears welling into her eyes. Taking a shaky breath, she nodded.

"Thank you," she whispered. "You are most kind."

Wrenching her hand from his tender grasp, she turned and fled from the room. But whether she was running from his love, or because there was much in him that drew her, she could not tell.

Chapter Twenty-six

TILTING HER PARASOL to block the sun while hanging onto her wide-brimmed straw hat with the other hand, Elizabeth squinted across the bay's sparkling whitecaps. It was early afternoon, Tuesday, June 30th, and the hot wind blew steadily into her face, skimming through the long grass beneath her feet and ruffling her ivory gauze gown with its peacock-blue ribbons.

They stood at the edge of the Battery, an ancient stone battlement that curved around the island's tip from the Hudson all the way to the mouth of the East River. Below them, the outgoing tide slipped imperceptibly farther from the shore with each receding wave.

Staring out across the harbor, she felt as though the wind and the waves swept her breath away as well.

An hour earlier she, Tess, and Dr. Vander Groot had joined the throng on the Battery for a closer view of the British fleet, expected by Whig and Tory alike for so many tense weeks. And in one fell swoop, her concern that the move to New York had not been necessary was decisively proven false.

Never had she seen a sight like this. The fleet gathered in Boston Harbor had been intimidating. This went far beyond that.

The ships had begun arriving the previous day, announced by the firing of alarm guns that quickly aroused a general panic among civilians and Continental soldiers alike. During the afternoon, close to fifty vessels had anchored near Sandy Hook.

With this morning's favorable wind and tide, more than eighty troop transports, supply ships, and warships had bolstered their numbers, and they had begun to tack cautiously through the Narrows into the bay. By now, with new arrivals steadily joining them, the British armada formed a line that extended along Staten Island for more than a mile. They lay anchored so closely together that one could not see open water between their hulls.

All along the wharves and at every window and rooftop visible to her, onlookers jostled to look at this unprecedented invasion force. Glancing around, Elizabeth noted with surprise how many of the town's inhabitants still remained after the wholesale exodus from the island over the past months. Every vantage point was clogged with representatives of New York's polyglot population.

The clamor of a multitude of languages assaulted her ears. Dutch and English residents rubbed shoulders with Indians, black slaves, and freemen. Germans jostled Irish, French, Spanish, and the members of a multitude of ethnic groups and religious persuasions.

She threw an apprehensive glance behind and to her right at the moldering bulk of Fort George, which occupied the island's extreme southern tip. Until Governor Tryon had fled aboard the *Duchess of Gordon* for fear of the rebel mobs, every royal governor had lived in the house inside its open rectangle. Although most of the ancient guns once mounted along the Battery's perimeter had been removed by the militia the previous summer, and in spite of the deterioration that more than 160 years had wrought, the fortress still provided a highly visible reminder of Britain's authority over her colonies.

If any further emphasis was needed, the statue on the nearby Bowling Green provided it. Mounted on a prancing horse behind a high, wrought iron fence, the figure of George III wore the garb of a Roman emperor.

Elizabeth returned her sober gaze to the bay. Through her mind passed scenes of the Continental troops mustering in their camps north of the city, parading before their officers, fumbling through unfamiliar maneuvers.

To make matters worse, in April the Continental Congress had ordered Washington to send ten of his seasoned regiments to bolster Arnold's force in Canada—an effort that turned out to be doomed when Burgoyne arrived with reinforcements in early May and helped to drive the American force from Quebec in chaotic disorder. Washington had gone personally to Philadelphia to appeal to Congress for reinforcements to replace those he had lost. New levies totaling almost twenty-four thousand troops were promised, but of the small contingent who actually appeared for duty, most were raw, untrained militia recruits whose lack of discipline inspired no confidence in their ability to stand firm under enemy fire.

Making the best of a bad situation, Washington stationed the brigade of his most trusted general, Nathanael Greene, on Long Island around Brooklyn Heights. The rest of his force extended in a thin line across York Island and was busily at work fortifying every defensible rise of ground from the city all the way north to where King's Bridge connected the island to the mainland.

For whatever it was worth, Elizabeth reflected unhappily. The army did not have enough artillery to supply all the forts under construction.

"Did they bring the whole o' London with 'em?" demanded a bent, white-haired man who leaned on his cane next to her.

"It doesn't appear they could have left any troops or ships behind to defend England," Vander Groot conceded dryly.

"The Continentals should feel greatly honored that Howe respects them enough to mount such an armada to oppose them." Despite her light words, Elizabeth felt as though her heart had sunk to the soles of her slippers.

"They'll not feel so honored when hot lead buzzes about their ears."

Although Tess made as brave a show as Elizabeth, she read the dismay in her aunt's eyes and prayed that her own betraying emotions did not give her away.

"Curse 'em all!" whined a stout, middle-aged housewife a short distance behind them. "These rebels'll never be able to stop the British from sailing up and down the rivers and blowin' apart every house on this island with their guns!"

A low murmur passed from mouth to mouth. In rising panic parents began to gather their children. Within moments the crowd surged toward the nearby houses and the carriages that lined the streets. One arm around her shoulders, his other hand on Tess's elbow, Vander Groot gently, but insistently, shepherded the two women out of the crush until only a few onlookers remained in their vicinity, still staring at the ships as though transfixed.

"Trust you to clear the entire Battery with a word," Elizabeth teased her aunt. "Did you have to bring up the subject of hot lead?"

Tess assumed a pained expression. "It was becoming far too crowded. You have to admit, we've a much better view now."

Vander Groot threw back his head, laughing. "You and my irrepressible aunt—what a pair you make!"

Elizabeth smiled up at him, grateful that in the week since their tender confrontation, the doctor had not pressed any further attentions upon her. It was impossible for either of them to pretend that nothing had happened, but although subtle undercurrents flowed between them now, Vander Groot's steady manner had allowed them to return to their former easy comradeship, at least on the surface.

Elizabeth's emotions were in too great a tangle for her to even begin to sort them out, and for the time being she was content simply to drift along as they had been during the past two months. Yet all the while she prayed that Carleton would at last be found and that the necessity to think about what her future might hold apart from him would be erased by his return to her arms.

She allowed no hint of her thoughts to show, however. "Aunt Tess always manages to display a high sense of the absurd in the face of disaster," she said lightly.

The doctor sobered. "Once the fighting begins everyone will be in equal danger in this unhappy city. My parents and sister are making arrangements for an extended visit with my younger brother and his wife in Philadelphia. Perhaps it would be wise for the two of you to consider removing from here as well."

"Will you leave?"

He gave Elizabeth a brooding look. "My practice is steadily dwindling with the flight of so many of my patients to safer regions. Aunt Euphemia will resist leaving her home, however, and as long as I have strength and skill to care for the ill or wounded, I also prefer to stay. But at some point, that may well become impossible."

"We face the same decision," Elizabeth said. "Our choice will depend upon the success of Howe's arms—or of Washington's."

"THE GENERAL SENT ANOTHER DETACHMENT to Long Island to strengthen Greene's force. Uncle Josh's regiment has gone too." Standing at the edge of the terrace late Sunday afternoon, July 7, Elizabeth stared out across Montcoeur's lawns and gardens, her back to her aunt.

"Washington thinks Howe will attack there first?"

Sighing, Elizabeth came to join her aunt. "At this point, there's no way of knowing. There are as many theories as generals."

Tess gave her a sharp look. "According to the lookouts, Howe has landed all his troops on Staten Island and is setting up a very tidy camp. He doesn't appear to be in a hurry to make a move."

Elizabeth sank onto a stone bench. "According to Pieter's father,

Howe is waiting for his brother to arrive with an even larger fleet and more troops. Washington is understandably concerned. Tonight I'm going to have Pete drop me off on the island. Perhaps I can find out what's really going on."

Before Tess could respond, she buried her face in her hands and began to weep. "Oh, what does it matter? I'm sick of talking about it! It has been a year now since Jonathan left us. I can hardly visualize his face anymore. Even if he still lives, he may well be lost to me. Perhaps his situation has grown tolerable, and he will choose to stay with the Seneca forever."

Tess sat beside her. "Or perhaps he is trying to find his way home even now."

Elizabeth pressed her fingers against her temples. "I can't keep hoping forever! I might as well give up."

"How do you do that? Even if Jon never returns, your life will go on, and you have to live it. Believe me, the pain will lessen in time. It has to, or no one could survive loss."

Elizabeth rounded on her. "How would you know what I feel? Have you ever loved someone so deeply you felt you could not live apart from him, only to have him torn from you—not because he ceased to love you, but because of events neither of you could antic-ipate or reverse?"

For a long moment Tess stared into space. "I do know what you feel," she said at length. "I wasn't always this old spinster you see now. Once I was as beautiful as you, and I also gave away my whole heart, only to lose the one I loved."

Elizabeth caught her breath, her anger melting away. "Oh, Aunt Tess—I'm so sorry! Please forgive me."

"You had no way of knowing. Even your father knows little of what happened back then. There is a great difference in our ages, and at the time he was a young boy away at school. After I moved to Boston, we had almost no contact at all. In fact, we hardly knew each other until I persuaded him to establish his medical practice there."

Elizabeth took her aunt's hand and rubbed it gently between hers. "Who was the man you loved? What happened to him?"

Tess's face softened into a smile at the memory. "Daniel Scott was the captain of a merchantman named *Dolphin*. I met him when I was about your age, and although I cannot say he was handsome, he had something better—a lively, intelligent face and a quick wit. What attracted me the most, however, was that he was fair and kind, even with his crew. Everyone who knew him respected and liked him . . . except my parents."

Giving a muffled sigh, Tess stared down at her folded hands. "Daniel had little money or prospect of advancement, and my mother's choice for me was a nobleman who had extensive lands, a fine estate, and important political connections. He was also vain, arrogant, and churlish, and I adamantly refused to marry him."

"What did you do?" Elizabeth prompted when Tess fell silent.

With some hesitation, Tess explained that when it became obvious that her parents would never consent to their marriage, Captain Scott had found investors in a voyage to the Orient. The *Dolphin* would carry goods to China with which to trade for cargo to sell in the American colonies. With his share of the profits he planned to purchase an estate outside Boston, where, after their marriage, they would make their home far from her parents' interference.

If all went well, he promised, he would return within two years. But he did not return. More than three years passed with no word until Tess came to believe that all had been a lie and he had abandoned her.

Then one day she had received a letter from a lawyer in Boston. The *Dolphin* had been lost in a storm off Newfoundland a little more than a year earlier. No one survived the wreck.

Days later the captain's body had washed onto the beach. He was buried on the island.

"I felt my heart was also buried that day." Tess's voice faded into silence.

Tears welling into her eyes, Elizabeth gently touched her arm, but Tess did not acknowledge her. She stared down at her hands as though she did not see them.

"Before leaving Boston, Daniel purchased an estate in Roxbury. He was on his way back to England to take me home with him when he sailed into that storm. The lawyer informed me that he had made a will, leaving the estate and a substantial living to me in case anything should happen to him. By then, my father had died, and over my mother's protests, I sailed for Boston.

"The hardest thing I have ever done was to walk into that house alone. Daniel had completely furnished it as he thought I would like it to be. His touch was everywhere. But he was not."

Elizabeth brushed the tears from her cheeks. "How could you bear it?"

"It took a long time, but when the shock and grief at length lessened, I came to realize I truly had no choice but to accept my losses. They are an inalterable part of me. And I have become content with my life as it is. Because God knows me better than anyone, I am assured this is his best for me. He has given me tender memories to comfort my heart. I know I will see Daniel again, and then our love will be made perfect."

Elizabeth bit her lip and looked away. "Should I also wait, then— and if Jonathan never returns, learn to be content with memories, as you have?"

"How can I advise you? What was right for me may not be so for you."

Elizabeth frowned at the lush barrier of bushes and trees that separated Montcoeur from the neighboring property. "After Papa broke off my betrothal to David, I told myself I didn't need or want any romantic involvement ever again. Flirtations were for the sole purpose of gathering intelligence, nothing more. Until Jonathan. But it's different now. Perhaps having opened my heart to love, I realize now how empty my life was without it. I long for a home, for children, for a husband to cherish me."

"That is natural."

"But what if God has taken Jonathan away and sent someone else to be my life's companion? Pieter has been a great comfort to me these past months. He's a believer. We talk about our faith and about medicine just as Papa and I used to. In spite of the fact that he's a Tory, I like and respect him. He's thoughtful and reasonable in all his opinions. I think I could learn to love him, though I shall never love anyone as I love Jonathan. Yet when we're together, I feel at peace."

"And what of your commitment to our cause and your pledge to work for Washington?"

"You've seen what lies out there." Elizabeth gestured in the direction of the bay. "We are so few and so ill-equipped. How are we ever to prevail against all that England can throw against us?"

Tess gave her a reproachful look. "Are you ready to give up the fight for our liberty because we face opposition?"

"No!" The word was out of her mouth so quickly both of them laughed.

"You're just discouraged right now—we all are because we don't see a way. But God is in the business of making a way where there is none. Is anything impossible with God?"

"I know." Looking down, Elizabeth twisted the sash of her gown between her fingers. "I could never in conscience turn my back on our cause, not for any man. But someday this war will end, whether it is God's will for us to defeat England or not, and then . . ."

With an impatient gesture, she hurried on, "And there's Charles, who's like a brother to me. How I wish he were here! He is all I have of Jonathan now. He knew and loved him before I did. I care a great deal for him, and I know he loves me."

At thought of Andrews, a deep sense of hopelessness swept over Elizabeth. She had received only two letters from him, included with reports to Washington. These she had reread until she knew them by heart, but all they accomplished was to make her miss him even more.

During the bleak winter in Boston he had become her anchor. He was her last connection to Carleton, and his continuing absence felt increasingly as though a door had been finally closed and locked against any remaining hope that Carleton would ever be found.

Tess's voice interrupted her reverie. "You must decide whether to choose what is good or to wait for the very best that God has for you."

"What *is* God's best? How do I know it is not Charles or Pieter— or someone else?"

Tess shook her head. "I cannot decide that for you. You must follow God's leading. And trust your heart."

Feeling as though she was suffocating, Elizabeth sprang to her feet and paced across the terrace, then back again, her movements jerky with frustration. "But I can't seem to fathom what God would have me to do. The questions go round and round in my mind, and—"

"You're hurting too much right now to be able to hear his voice. Do nothing for the time. There is no urgency to make a decision. In any case, you must wait until this conflict is decided."

"Pieter made it clear he intends to wait for my decision," Elizabeth said raggedly. "How I hate deceiving him like this!"

"You haven't deceived him. You simply didn't tell him everything."

"Isn't that the same as lying? Perhaps if I told him all the truth, then—"

"Even if you don't mention Jon's name, he might learn something that would allow him to guess it," Tess protested in alarm. "All you can do is continue to put him off."

"And what of Charles? His letters are tender and sweet. Every time we're together, I feel as if I'm leading him on. He mourns Jonathan's loss as deeply as I do. I don't want to hurt him more."

"He knows your situation. You need explain nothing to him. Seek God's face. He will bring healing to your heart and make everything clear in his good time."

Elizabeth nodded, tears slipping down her cheeks. "I'm getting better, truly. I'm learning a little at a time to curb my impatient nature. It's just that I . . . I miss Jonathan so. I miss the love we shared. I want him to be well—to be alive. I want him to come home. I want a man's strong arms around me. I want *his* arms."

Tess rose and came to enfold her. Fighting back sobs, Elizabeth laid her head on her aunt's shoulder.

"Oh, Beth, he *will* come home—I feel it. I haven't said anything because I don't want to raise any more false hopes, but this certainty grows stronger every day. Jon *is* alive and he has not forgotten you. *God has not forgotten you.* He sees your pain and how you are struggling to be faithful, and he will bring to pass every promise he has made to you."

Drawing strength from the sorrow and hope mingled in Tess's brimming eyes, Elizabeth dabbed away her tears. Her sobs stilled, and she gazed beyond the cliffs of the Hudson, her thoughts carrying her far to the west, where the sun's golden orb pursued its gradual decline over forests that stretched for hundreds of miles across valley and plain and mountain ridge.

Tess was right. Despite the fear and anguish that so often flooded over her with the force of a spring torrent, her heart stubbornly clung to the certainty that Carleton was yet alive. Perhaps even at that moment he also was looking toward the east, thinking of her, yearning for her, praying for her, as she did for him.

And with that thought, a measure of peace settled like a soothing balm upon her wounded spirit.

Chapter Twenty-seven

FROM A ROCKY BLUFF above the Scioto, White Eagle stared bleakly down at what remained of the once prosperous town of Chillicothe. Stretching along the riverbank as far as the eye could see, twisted pillars of dirty smoke, punctuated here and there by the flicker of scarlet flame, rose over the charred debris of wigewa and council house. Expansive fields that only a day earlier had overflowed with an abundance of crops lay hacked to pieces, the summer's bounty plundered or smashed.

All that remained was a wasteland.

Among the ruins, sprawled in unnatural postures and already smelling sickeningly of decay in the humid July heat, lay heaped the bodies of women and children, elders, youths, and warriors, brutally slaughtered and mutilated. Here and there clusters of the survivors, many of them wounded, hobbled through the carnage in the effort to identify the dead and drive off the wild dogs and wolves that crept, snarling, along the outer edges of the destruction.

His shoulders sagging, White Eagle leaned on his lance and covered his face with his hand, wanting to erase the scene of devastation from his mind. But he could not block out the wails of the mourners.

He became aware of approaching footfalls and looked up as Red Fox came to stand beside him. The warrior's face was contorted with the same emotions that filled White Eagle's breast, and as he laid one hand on White Eagle's shoulder, both men brushed the tears from their eyes.

Bitter rage and despair churned in White Eagle's heart. Retaliation for Black Hawk's murder had initially succeeded far beyond his hopes, and during the spring and early summer his war party had pushed hunters and settlers alike back out of Ohio Territory. He had followed these attacks with raids against the scattered British outposts throughout the area, burning several forts to the ground and forcing their garrisons to withdraw to the larger forts along the region's borders. But as he and Cornstalk had warned, mounting reprisals were beginning to take a horrifying toll.

Cornstalk, along with the other leaders of the Maquachake division, continued to press for making any concessions necessary to maintain the peace. The majority of the Kispokothas, Chillicothes, and Piquas, however, argued for meeting bloodshed with even greater bloodshed. With every counterattack by the settlers or the British, the ranks of White Eagle's warriors swelled dramatically, until the conflict had expanded into all-out war.

The smoking ruins of Chillicothe testified to the harsh price the tribe would pay for continuing to fight the overwhelming forces they had unleashed. But the vindication of his counsel burned like bile in White Eagle's mouth.

"How many survivors?" he demanded, his voice hoarse.

"Two hundred at most—those who managed to get away into the forest once the attack began." Red Fox indicated a group of warriors who were helping to gather the dead for burial. "Black Fish has brought a large party. He counsels moving the town northwest to a location on the Little Miami that can more easily be defended."

White Eagle shook his head. "The next time may leave us nothing to defend and no one to defend it. Each time we throw them back, they come against us with a larger force. We cannot prevail much longer—though some among us refuse to listen to reason."

While they were speaking, Grey Cloud and Spotted Pony joined them. "As soon as the dead are buried," the old sachem said, his reedy voice quavering, "then we must haste to move our town to a safer location as well. We have lost many warriors already, but if we lose our children, our nation will cease to exist, and even memory of our greatest warriors will be blotted out."

Spotted Pony turned to White Eagle. "Wolfslayer's followers insist they will fight to the death rather than surrender. They are planning the war dance for tonight, and they say that if you lose your courage, then they will make Wolfslayer their war chief and follow him."

White Eagle thrust the point of his lance into the ground with suppressed anger. "It is what he has wanted all along. But though he refuses to see it, the path he walks will lead our people to annihilation. I will not stand aside and see my brothers and sisters destroyed to feed his ambition—and his pride."

"What will you do?" Red Fox asked.

White Eagle spat on the ground. "First we will answer this butchery. But we will fight their men only. By Moneto, I swear we will not do this." He jerked his hand in the direction of the scene of misery and suffering spread out below them.

Turning to Grey Cloud, he continued, "While we go to punish those responsible, remove our town to the Little Miami. I will counsel with Black Snake to see if the rest of the Kispokotha division will not withdraw with us to a more remote location where the Whites will have a harder time finding us and less chance of succeeding if they attack. Then after I return, our council—not Wolfslayer—will decide our future course."

Grey Cloud met White Eagle's hard gaze with a sober one. "I fear the time will soon be upon us when we have no choice but to follow the Thawekila division beyond the Great River."

The reality of their situation struck White Eagle like a hard blow to the gut. Turning his back to the others, for some moments he stared off to the west, the muscles of his jaw hardening. When he rounded to face them once more, grim determination shadowed his face.

"They will drive us from here in the end. But to do it, they will water this ground well with their blood."

White Eagle squinted down the arrow's length. It was perfectly straight, well balanced, and the sharp flint point was securely attached. Twirling the shaft between thumb and forefinger, he admired its fletching before returning it to the boy who leaned affectionately against his shoulder.

"Excellent work, Little Deer. I couldn't have done better myself."

The boy shifted from one foot to the other, a pleased smile illuminating his handsome features. "Yours are the best of all our warriors." He bent to pull an arrow from the beaded, fringed quiver at White Eagle's feet and ran his finger along the delicate line of white paint that coiled along the shaft's length from its razor-sharp point to the precisely trimmed white eagle feathers at the opposite end. "Someday I'll be a great warrior too, and I'll fletch my arrows with eagle feathers," he boasted.

Then his face fell. "My father says I am still too young to go with you to fight our enemies."

White Eagle accepted his arrow back from the boy's hand. "Right now it is more important for you to help your mother and sisters move to the new town. If there is an attack while we are gone, the women and children will need you to defend them."

Little Deer brightened and puffed out his chest. "I will watch over them and make sure they are safe."

"I know you will."

Although White Eagle returned the boy's smile, the realization that even the children were preparing for war deeply troubled him.

He had not wanted this, but now that war had begun, he could not see any acceptable means to end it.

He did not hate his former countrymen, nor did he wish to fight them. He only wanted them to leave his people in peace. Did the Shawnee not, after all, have the right to defend their families, their homes, their lands—even as the Americans were doing against England? Yet violence resulted only in more violence in a never-ending cycle of destruction and death.

On their return home the previous day, Grey Cloud had lost no time in marshalling the townspeople for an immediate move. Now in the soft light of early dawn, White Eagle and his warriors, along with a small group of the younger women who would accompany them, finished their own grim preparations, while the rest of the women hurried to gather all the crops that were ripe enough to harvest. At each wigewa, elders and children occupied themselves in bundling up all the possessions they could carry with them.

After Red Fox had led his son away to his own wigewa, White Eagle pulled his tomahawk from his belt and studied its handle, frowning. Notches carved into the wood recorded the battles he had led, how many of his warriors had been killed or wounded, the number of prisoners captured and driven from the Ohio.

At length he rose from beside his fire circle, his thoughts preoccupied with the coming raid. Each foray confirmed a long-held conviction that an irregular band moving with swiftness, secrecy, and surprise held a distinct advantage over a conventionally trained enemy superior in numbers.

With every raid during the past months, he had refined his tactics. Quickly he had forged what had begun as the traditional, loosely organized war party into a disciplined, cohesive fighting force, with Red Fox and Spotted Pony becoming his most trusted lieutenants. Carrying a minimum of supplies and living off the land, they could travel swiftly over long distances without being detected, lie in wait for the opportune moment, then strike hard and fast and melt back into the wilderness before the enemy could mount a counterattack.

It was a strategy calculated to unnerve the enemy, and one he had intended to try with the brigade of Rangers Washington had commissioned him to raise.

Abruptly he wrenched his thoughts away from that treacherous territory. He would not allow himself to wonder how that other war was faring. It was no longer any concern of his.

Shaking off his disturbing thoughts, he became aware that Blue Sky knelt in front of her wigewa a short distance away, packing dried venison into a large basket. As though attuned to his every move, she immediately looked up to meet his gaze with an inviting smile.

After Black Hawk's death, he had taken over the old sachem's wigewa, hoping to relieve the tension between him and Pathfinder's widow. Imposing a separation, however, had seemed to increase her desire rather than to cool it.

She continued stubbornly to cook for him and to attend to other necessary tasks as though she hoped by persistence yet to win him. And whenever any of the unmarried women looked at him—which they did too often as far as he was concerned—she made it clear he was off limits.

It was becoming maddeningly obvious that he could say what he would, show the young maidens no attention at all, and even brush them rudely aside. But as far as they, and notably Blue Sky, were concerned, his growing reputation as a warrior and the fact that he had so far not taken a wife only increased his attraction.

He gave an unconscious sigh and turned away. For long moments he stared off toward the east, where the shadow of night rushed toward him on the breath of the rising wind. Although the air held the warmth of summer, it chilled him to the core.

Unbidden, images long buried tumbled through his mind with sudden, piercing vividness. Muted now like the haunting notes of a violin in a darkened room far away, the memory of Elizabeth still lay cherished in his breast. And at thought of her, sorrow constricted his breath and dimmed his sight.

Between the two of them stretched hundreds of miles of daunting terrain and mortal danger. For the British still sought him—of that he could be certain. And as the Shawnee's war chief, he had aroused the implacable hatred of the Americans as well. The settlers would be more than happy to arrest and execute him anytime he traveled outside the tribe's protection.

Added to that, Wolfslayer's enmity complicated his situation even more. Although the shaman and his followers joined in the raids, they remained aloof from White Eagle's leadership and openly critical of his strategy and tactics. It was certain Wolfslayer would not only protest, but also take violent action to stop him if White Eagle so much as hinted at returning to the Long Knives.

Yet there was even more that stood between him and Elizabeth now. Physical distance and danger might be overcome in some way, but the man she had known seemed entirely alien to him now. How much more so would the man he had become seem to her? Could she ever understand or accept who he now was, all that he had done, and his reasons for acting as he had?

Nor could he even guess at all she must have suffered in the year of his absence. Perhaps by now she believed him dead. Perhaps she had given her heart to another—possibly even to Andrews. She would have had no choice but to pick up the threads of her life and go on without him, and his return would only undo any healing time had wrought.

For a moment longer he stared into the gathering night, pain stabbing through him with the sharpness of a lance thrust. She was beyond his reach forever, and he beyond hers. He also had no choice but to pick up his life and go on.

Hearing someone approach, he turned to face Spotted Pony. The warrior came to a halt beside him and studied him intently, without speaking.

"It grows late and we have a long ride," White Eagle said, his voice husky.

"The horses are ready and so are the men."

Giving his friend a curt nod, White Eagle caught up his weapons and the rawhide packs that held his gear and led the way to where his warriors waited. But as he mounted his horse, he could not hold back an earnest plea that the Almighty would protect Elizabeth in the midst of her own battles and bring solace to the heart that his heart told him was aching.

If you enjoyed this story and would like to offer feedback, we invite you to email the editor, Joan Shoup, at jmshoup@gmail.com. We'd love to receive your comments.

We always appreciate positive reviews posted on the book's detail page on Amazon, Barnes and Noble, Christianbook.com, and other online sites. Thank you for telling other readers about this series!

Appendix

COMMON NAMES AND TERMS OF THE REVOLUTIONARY PERIOD

cartouche box: the case in which soldiers carried a supply of cartridges.

camp follower: women who attached themselves to an army, including wives, mistresses, prostitutes, laundrywomen, and cooks, and their children.

canister: cylindrical cases full of pistol balls shot from a cannon at close range to kill people.

gaol: jail.

grapeshot: iron balls the size of a tennis ball, bound together in a canvas bag to be shot from a cannon.

match coat: a coarse wool blanket worn wrapped around the body as a coat by Native Americans and frontiersmen and held closed with one hand; generally one color, decorated with colored ribbons sewn along one side.

man of war: 18th century warship.

stroud: a coarse woolen trade cloth or blanket.

sutler: a merchant who supplies provisions to the army.

York Island: original name of Manhattan Island.

vault: latrine.

NATIVE AMERICAN CHARACTERS, TRIBES, AND TERMS

Seneca

Cornplanter: the principal sachem of the Seneca, who favored close ties with the British.

Red Jacket: an important Seneca sachem who also favored the British.

The Six Nations of the Iroquois League

Onondaga: the central tribe of the League and keepers of the League's Council Fire, located in upstate New York near Onondaga Lake.

Mohawk: the League's Keepers of the Eastern Door, located along the Mohawk River.

Cayuga: located near Cayuga Lake in New York.

Oneida: located between Oneida Lake and the Mohawk River.

Tuscarora: migrated to New York from North Carolina in the early 1700s and joined the League in 1722.

Seneca: the League's Keepers of the Western Door, located in western New York state.

Shawnee

Cornstalk: the principal sachem of the Maquachake, one of the five subnations of the Shawnee, and of the Shawnee tribe as a whole. After defeat in Lord Dunmore's War in 1774, he refused to fight the Whites and counseled the tribe to honor the peace treaty.

Elinipscico: son of Cornstalk.

Black Snake: the primary sachem of the Kispokotha division, who favored war with the Whites.

Black Fish: the Chillicothe division's primary sachem, who favored war with the Whites.

Kishkalwa: sachem of the Thawekila division, which left Ohio Territory rather than be drawn into another disastrous war with the Whites.

The Five Subnations (Septs) of the Shawnee

The *Chillicothe* and *Thawekila* septs controlled political matters as well as relationships between the Shawnee and other native tribes. The Shawnee's principal leaders and tribal historians were always chosen from among these two septs. Although there was substantial inter-marriage between them, the Thawegila were considered to be the southern Shawnee, and the Chillicothe the Northern Shawnee.

The *Maquachake* sept controlled matters pertaining to health and medicine.

The *Piqua* sept was in charge of the worship of Moneto, the Great Spirit, and lesser deities and spirits.

The *Kispokotha* was the warrior sept of the Shawnee. They provided the tribe's warriors and war chiefs. Although their chief leader was ineligible to become the Shawnee's principal chief, in power and prestige he stood second to the tribe's chief.

Each sept's chief leader was autonomous in matters that pertained to his own sept. In matters concerning the whole tribe, however, the leaders of each sept were subordinate to the nation's principal chief.

Native American Terms

False Faces: an Iroquoian superstition that disembodied, evil faces appeared in the forests to bewitch the unwary, causing them to fall into dangerous illnesses.

killegenico: tobacco mixed with dried sumac leaves.

longhouse: a long, bark-covered dwelling that usually housed several families of a clan.

Long Knives: the Americans, who carried swords.

Matchemenetoo: the Bad Spirit, the devil.

Moneto: the Supreme Being of the universe.

motchitteheckie: evil-minded people.

opa-wa-ka: a token the Shawnee believed was given by Moneto to transmit power to an individual.

wampum: strings, belts, or sashes made of shell beads used either as ornaments, tribal records, a medium of exchange for goods, or to transmit messages of peace or war.

wannine: crazy, insane.

wigewa: a domed round or rectangular dwelling for one family framed with poles and overlaid with bark, woven mats, or animal hides.

Wishemehetoo, the Great Spirit, not as powerful as Moneto, often visualized as a grandmother who weaves a great net in which she will catch up the world at the end of all time. Those who have proven themselves to be worthy will be taken up to the heavens, while those who are not worthy will drop through the net to an unspeakable fate.

Discussion Guide

1. How did Elizabeth and Carleton individually react to Washington's unexpected opposition to their marriage?

2. Have you ever been faced with the indefinite delay of a dream that was dear to you? How did you react? What was the outcome of your response?

3. Knowing they might never have another opportunity to fulfill their love, both Elizabeth and Carleton were deeply tempted to seek temporary comfort in physical intimacy. Why did Carleton refuse to give in to it? How did he demonstrate his deepest love for Elizabeth and honor her by refusing to succumb to momentary desire?

4. When everything important to Carleton, even his very identity, was stripped away, what was his response?

5. Have you ever faced extreme suffering—whether it was physical or emotional, or both—similar to what Carleton faced during his enslavement by the Seneca? What carried you through your time of testing?

6. What do you think God's purpose is in allowing the kind of suffering Carleton experienced? Do you think it is ever God's will for his children to suffer? Would that be the action of a loving parent?

7. Does suffering only result when we are disobedient to God's laws and will? Does God ever make someone do what is wrong? When other people treat us unfairly, even persecute us, is it ever God's fault?

8. Do you think God sometimes allows us to suffer even when we are fully submitted to him and obeying his leading in our lives? If yes, why do you think he permits our pain when we are being obedient?

9. Explain what free will means. Should God keep someone from choosing to do what is wrong and hurting others? Should God have made us so that we have no choice but to obey him? Find scripture passages that support or contradict your opinions.

10. How did his own enslavement change his attitude toward the black slaves he held in bondage, though unwillingly? What did he resolve to do?

11. When months passed after Carleton's disappearance, and Elizabeth began to give up hope that he was still alive, she found herself being drawn to another man. Why was she attracted to him? In what painful dilemma did this attraction place her?

12. Tess counseled Elizabeth to wait for God's perfect will for her life. Have you ever gone through a painful time of doubt and of questioning what the Lord's will was for your life, when there seemed to be no answer? What did you choose to do? What was the result of your decision? What would you resolve to do today?